PRAISE FOR
THE SEVE

GW00986025

'With sly touches of romance and Shakesp... criminous menu, Hammer keeps on getting better and better. A winner.'
Maxime Jakubowski, *Crime Time*

'Hammer has been recognised as a leading proponent of Outback Noir, and his latest epic is simply superb.'
Jon Coates, *Sunday Express*, **UK**

'Count me in the "I applaud it" camp. I read it twice.'
Robyn Walton, *The Australian*

'Hammer is at his best in this tale that successfully builds the sense of menace created by a small-town clique when there's a threat to their entrenched sense of entitlement born of their wealth and privilege.'
Alison Walsh, *Herald Sun*

'Chris Hammer knits a three-ply narrative . . . to create a hefty thriller that is Shakespearean in its depth and range.'
***The Times* Crime Book of the Month**

'A detailed, highly researched murder mystery that unfolds over three different decades, and the combination of thriller and historical works extremely well . . . Hammer fans, new and old, this is a must-add to your TBR pile.'
Better Reading

'A gripping tale of political intrigue and corruption.'
Nicole Abadee, *The Age*

'A masterful, stunning thriller. A twisting mystery epic in scale yet intricate in detail. Irresistible.'
Chris Whitaker, author of *We Begin at the End*

PRAISE FOR
THE TILT

'Richly layered . . . the characters are drawn robustly and definitively. Hammer has confirmed and underlined his reputation as numbering among the very best novelists in detective fiction.'

Sydney Morning Herald

'Chris Hammer has surpassed himself . . . It is constantly intriguing, shocking and moving . . . I doubt I'll read a better novel this year.'

The Times

'It would be unfair to say Chris Hammer is at the top of the crime writing game. Chris Hammer IS the game. *Full Tilt* may be a better title, given the speed with which readers will devour Chris Hammer's exceptional novel.'

Benjamin Stevenson, author of
Everyone in My Family Has Killed Someone

'Ominous, pacy and intricately plotted, *The Tilt* hits the ground running and never lets up. Hammer's best yet!'

Emma Viskic, author of *Those Who Perish*

'Chris has another absolute cracker on his hands here . . . A new book from him is always an unmissable event . . . The way Chris weaves three different timelines without ever losing focus, and creates such a broad cast of compelling and emotionally complex characters is truly impressive.'

Shelley Burr, author of *Wake*

'Chris Hammer at the height of his powers . . . absolutely not to be missed!'

Hayley Scrivenor, author of *Dirt Town*

'A darkly simmering mystery, gorgeously told . . . Utterly brilliant.'

Dervla McTiernan, author of
The Rúin and *The Murder Rule*

'Hammer has written a compelling novel, exercising all his strengths as a master of outback crime fiction . . . *Treasure & Dirt* is platinum class detective fiction. [Hammer] is an undeniable master of the carefully layered novel, which unfolds remorselessly to reveal the perpetrators of murder on the arid frontier.'

Weekend Australian

'Chris Hammer's detailed descriptions and layers of outback crime drama will have readers gulping up every page of this unforgettable tale . . . Reading *Treasure & Dirt* was like finding a rare black opal—an unforgettable experience.'

Glam Adelaide

'Whether you're already a fan or you're about to experience the greatness of Chris Hammer for the first time, *Treasure & Dirt* is worthy of a place on your bookshelf.'

Booktopia

'If you haven't read Hammer before, this is the perfect time to experience one of the best writers Australia has to offer. Rife with intrigue, murder, and small-town secrets, *Treasure & Dirt* is a spectacular thriller that delivers some unforgettable characters with twists and turns you won't see coming. Hammer has raised the bar for Australian crime, and this is a must-read.'

Better Reading

'Classic Hammer, with the heat and the small town obsession with secrecy and past grievances. A crime novel that will stay with me for a long time.'

Ann Cleeves

'The novel—tighter, tougher, tenser—is Hammer best work yet.'

The Times

PRAISE FOR
TRUST

'A tightly constructed and well-paced crime thriller that smoothly moves to a suitably surprising and bloody finale . . . The descriptions of Sydney are vivid and evocative and there are also sharp-eyed comments on politics, corruption and the modern media . . . a terrific read.'

Jeff Popple, *Canberra Weekly*

'Chris Hammer has excelled himself with *Trust* . . . a thriller strong on character development, social insights, ethical issues and dramatic action.'

Robyn Walton, *Weekend Australian*

'A dark and gritty Sydney, superb character work and a fast-paced mystery to keep you on your toes . . . This thrill ride of a story is everything we have come to expect and more. Perfect for those looking for a fright this October!'

Better Reading

'Immersive, pacy . . . one of Australia's best new crime authors.'

Irish Independent

'With Corris and Temple departed, Chris Hammer almost makes up for the hole they left in Australian crime fiction. Wickedly well-written, a phrase turner that powers a page turner, trust me: *Trust* is a rip-roaring read.'

Richard Cotter, *Sydney Arts Guide*

'Another twisting and turning thriller from the author of *Scrublands* and *Silver*. Australian crime writing at its best.'

Village Observer

'This is Hammer's most elegant plot thus far.'

Sydney Morning Herald/The Age

PRAISE FOR
SILVER

'Chris Hammer is a great writer—a leader in Australian noir.'

Michael Connelly

'A terrific story . . . an excellent sequel; the best Australian crime novel since Peter Temple's *The Broken Shore*.'

The Times

'Elegantly executed on all fronts, *Silver* has a beautifully realised sense of place . . . There's a lot going on in Port Silver, but it's well worth a visit.'

Sydney Morning Herald/The Age

'The immediacy of the writing makes for heightened tension, and the book is as heavy on the detail as it is on conveying Scarsden's emotional state. *Silver* is a dramatic blood-pumper of a book for lovers of Sarah Bailey and Dave Warner.'

Books + Publishing

'Hammer has shown in *Silver* that *Scrublands* was no fluke. He has taken what he learnt in that novel and built on it to create a deeper, richer experience. He has delivered a real sense of place and uses the crime genre to explore some very real current social issues and character types.'

PS News

'A taut and relentless thriller—just jump into the rapids and hold on.'

Readings Monthly

'The action unfolds at the same breathless pace as it did in *Scrublands* . . . Hammer's prose brings the coastal setting vividly to life. An engrossing read, perfect for the summer holidays.'

The Advertiser

'An enthralling, atmospheric thriller that fans of Aussie crime won't be able to put down.'

New Idea

PRAISE FOR
SCRUBLANDS

'One of the finest novels of the year.'

Peter Pierce, *The Australian*

'Vivid and mesmerising . . . Stunning . . . *Scrublands* is that rare combination, a page-turner that stays long in the memory.'

Sunday Times **Crime Book of the Month**

'So does *Scrublands* earn its Thriller of the Year tag? Absolutely . . . It's relentless, it's compulsive, it's a book you simply can't put down.'

Written by Sime

'A superbly drawn, utterly compelling evocation of a small town riven by a shocking crime.'

Mark Brandi, author of *Wimmera*

'An almost perfect crime novel . . . I loved it.'

Ann Cleeves

'A heatwave of a novel, scorching and powerful . . . Extraordinary.'

A.J. Finn, author *The Woman in the Window*

'Stellar . . . Richly descriptive writing coupled with deeply developed characters, relentless pacing, and a bombshell-laden plot make this whodunit virtually impossible to put down.'

Publishers Weekly **(USA), starred review**

'*Scrublands* kidnapped me for 48 hours . . . This book is a force of nature. A must-read for all crime fiction fans.'

Sarah Bailey, author of *The Housemate*

'Immersive and convincing . . . This will be the novel that all crime fiction fans will want . . . a terrific read that has "bestseller" written all over it.'

Australian Crime Fiction

'Debut thriller of the month (and maybe of 2019) . . . Beautifully written.'
Washington Post

'Incendiary . . . A rattling good read, ambitious in scale and scope and delivering right up to the last, powerfully moving page.'
Irish Times

'Desolate, dangerous, and combustible. A complex novel powered by a cast of characters with motives and loyalties as ever-shifting as the dry riverbed beneath them, Hammer's story catches fire from the first page.'
J. Todd Scott, author of *High White Sun*

'Impressive prose and brilliant plotting . . . It is hard to imagine *Scrublands* not being loved by all crime/mystery fans. FIVE STARS.'
Scott Whitmont, *Books + Publishing*

'There is a very good reason people are calling *Scrublands* the "thriller of the year". This impressive debut is a powerful and compulsively readable Australian crime novel.'
Booktopia

'As one bookseller commented, *Scrublands* is another sign we are in a Golden Age of Australian crime. Reading it is a pulsating, intense experience, not to be missed.'
Better Reading

'Much like the bushfire that flares up in the mulga, *Scrublands* quickly builds in intensity, until it's charging along with multiple storylines, unanswered questions and uncovered truths. It is a truly epic read.'
Good Reading

'Shimmers with heat from the sun and from the passions that drive a tortured tale of blood and loss.'
Val McDermid, author of *How the Dead Speak*

'*Scrublands* is the read of the year. Unforgettable.'
Tony Wright, *Sydney Morning Herald/The Age*

Chris Hammer is a leading Australian crime fiction author. His first book, *Scrublands*, was an instant #1 bestseller upon publication in 2018. It won the prestigious UK Crime Writers' Association John Creasey New Blood Dagger and was shortlisted for awards in Australia and the United States.

Scrublands has been sold into translation in several foreign languages. Chris's follow-up books—*Silver* (2019), *Trust* (2020), *Treasure & Dirt* (2021), *The Tilt* (2022) and *The Seven* (2023)—are also bestsellers and all have been shortlisted for major literary prizes. *The Valley* is his seventh novel.

The Tilt (published as *Dead Man's Creek* in the UK) was named *The Sunday Times* Crime Book of the Year for 2023.

Scrublands has been adapted for television, screening globally, and production is underway for a second series based on *Silver*.

Before turning to fiction, Chris was a journalist for more than thirty years. He has written two non-fiction books, *The River* (2010) and *The Coast* (2012).

He has a bachelor's degree in journalism from Charles Sturt University and a master's degree in international relations from the Australian National University.

THE
VALLEY

CHRIS HAMMER

ALLEN&UNWIN
SYDNEY · MELBOURNE · AUCKLAND · LONDON

First published in 2024

Allen & Unwin
Cammeraygal Country
83 Alexander Street
Crows Nest NSW 2065
Australia
Phone: (61 2) 8425 0100
Email: info@allenandunwin.com
Web: www.allenandunwin.com

Allen & Unwin acknowledges the Traditional Owners of the Country on which we live and work. We pay our respects to all Aboriginal and Torres Strait Islander Elders, past and present.

 A catalogue record for this book is available from the National Library of Australia

ISBN 978 1 76147 088 2

Map by Aleksander J. Potočnik
Set in 13/18 pt Granjon by Bookhouse, Sydney
Printed and bound in Australia by the Opus Group

10 9 8 7 6 5 4 3 2 1

TO JACK & ALEX & FELICITY & CAITLIN—THOSE MIGHTY BRITS!

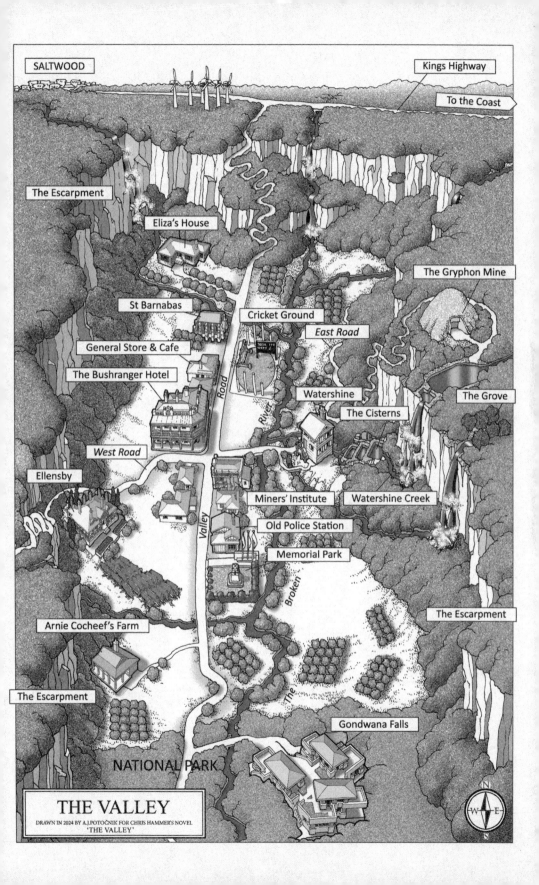

prologue

1988

GUY AND RAZ ARE THE LAST TO ARRIVE; STOLEN CAR, STOLEN LICENCE PLATES, driving at night, taking the back roads. The radio is talking of them and nothing else: the gold, the daring, the dead. Raz drives, smoking relentlessly, chewing gum incessantly, laughing intermittently. And every ten or fifteen minutes, a statement to the night. 'We did it. We fucking did it.'

Guy feels electric, as if wired to a generator, like lying in a hyperbaric chamber filled with happy gas. His heart is beating so hard it's almost dancing; he can feel it fluttering under his ribs like the wings of a caged bird. Everything seems hyperreal: his pulse, the red tail-lights ahead, the sound of his companion chewing gum, the smell of the cigarette smoke. He thinks it strange, this elation, this surge of energy, coming now when they are free and safe, almost home dry, whereas at the time, back at the warehouse, bullets flying, the gun kicking in his hand, the screams of the dying echoing, he had felt calm, focused, almost relaxed.

'We did it,' Raz informs the world once more. 'We fucking did it.'

They'd done it all right, but not the way it had been planned. There'd been no intention to use their guns, no agreement to shoot anyone. In and out, with the whole night to make their getaway before the heist would be discovered. That was the plan. But they'd all been carrying, they'd all fired. He'd hesitated in those first frantic seconds, but he'd fired as well. Thought he'd hit someone. One of the cops, or one of the security guards. His heart beat a little harder. He'd put a bullet into someone. Another human being. Back when they were planning he'd said the words, 'I'm all in,' and he'd meant them. But now it's a fact, they are all of them 'all in'. Those who have survived, and those who haven't. Bert Glossop is dead, one of the ringleaders, cut down by a copper not two metres from where Guy had taken cover behind a pallet of red wine, bottles exploding into scarlet shards with the impact of bullets. Glossop, bleeding out with a soft groan, blood mixed with wine. You can't get any more 'all in' than that.

The car in front turns off onto a farm track and they have the road to themselves, alone in the night, moving across the plain. An image comes to Guy, a bird's-eye view from up in the cloudless sky, looking down on the pool of light created by the headlights, a small and tenuous thing crawling across a world of darkness.

He flicks Raz's disposable lighter; reads the map by its stuttering flame. 'Slow down a little,' he tells the driver. 'Should be a railway crossing, then a bridge.'

Raz slows. He's been doing a good job, disciplined, resisting the temptation to speed, keeping the car trundling along steadily.

It's a good car. A suitable car. A Holden Commodore, white, a few years old, the most popular car in Australia. The most common. The most nondescript.

They come to the level crossing. No boom gate. No lights. Just a series of signs, riddled with bullet holes. Raz takes it gently, being extra cautious with the suspension, not wanting to tempt fate: they've pushed their envelope of good fortune, they know that. No use asking for more when they don't need it. Guy feels a moment of pride in his comrade, this stranger, for staying cool; the cigarettes and chewing gum the only outward indication of nerves. They almost crawl across the railway lines, Raz conscious of the load in the boot.

They approach the bridge. There's a sign: DEEP WATER CREEK. They're where they should be.

Guy peers at the map. 'Turn-off coming up to the left. Three red reflectors on the gate.'

'There,' says Raz, changing down to second gear, flipping the indicator on, following the road rules to the letter, pulling onto gravel, stopping. 'We did it. We fucking did it.'

'Sure, we did it,' says Guy, climbing out, opening the gate, waiting while Raz guides the car through, then closing it again. There are no other vehicles on the road. The night is windless. Expectant. The sky is a black dome, moonless, pierced by stars— the only witnesses.

Raz steers along the drive, just a track through a paddock, a fence to one side, nothing more. They reach the woolshed. Corrugated iron. Lights inside, creeping out through gaps in the windows. Three cars parked around the back, out of sight. The others are already here.

3

They stop. Raz unlocks the boot while Guy holds up the lighter. They take a bag each, calico, bearing the branding of the bank. The one Guy carries is smeared with blood, deep brown, almost black, in the half-light. And then they lift the metal carry case, not so big but heavy for its size, lug it between them into the shearing shed.

Inside, the others are sitting in a circle around a large open space: six men on crates and chairs and a sawhorse, anything they can find, staring silently at the centre of the room, where bags are piled—the same calico bags, stuffed with cash. And five more of the aluminium carry cases, reinforced, with rubber-lined steel handles on each side. No one is moving, no one is laughing. They seem shell-shocked. Guy and Raz walk to the centre of the room, drop their bags with the rest and lower the metal case laden with gold. They walk to the periphery, join the circle of men staring at the accumulated millions like they're gazing into a camp fire, warming themselves in its glow, hoping it's been worth it.

Curtains stands, tilts his head, silently acknowledging Guy and Raz. The big man is the leader, real name Hec Curtin, universally known as 'Curtains', his nickname well earned. 'That's it then. That's all of us.' The men are all looking at him, saying nothing as he continues. 'You've heard the reports. Glossop is dead. Not good. At least he won't be talking.'

'We need to take care of his missus—see she gets her share,' says a large man with a neck tattoo, one of the bikies.

'We'll look after her,' says Curtains. 'Priestly and Barker are in custody. Priestly shot up bad, Barker more walking wounded.'

'How do you know?' asks a hard-faced man. Morelli: another of the bikies.

Curtains doesn't answer, but Guy understands. Their leader is connected. Has someone on the inside. Not just in the security firm, in the cops.

Curtains holds his hands aloft, like a preacher, then gestures at the pile of loot. 'Look at it, gentlemen: behold what we've achieved.'

And all of them turn to admire the treasure; how could they not? Which is when Curtains takes two steps back, three, then reaches behind his back and pulls a handgun, taking another step back. Boyd Murrow backs up to join him, now brandishing a small machine gun, the promise of death, indiscriminate, with plenty to go around.

'Stay calm!' says Curtains, voice firm but not yelling. In command. 'No one moves, no one gets hurt. Pull a weapon and we'll fucking drill you.'

Someone swears, Guy isn't sure who. He thinks of his own gun, nestled in the small of his back, tucked into the waistband of his jeans. Useless. If he reaches for it, he'll be dead before he hits the floor. He lifts his hands, signalling his surrender, his compliance. Around him others are doing the same.

'Excellent. Thank you,' says Curtains to the group as a whole. Then he addresses Guy. 'Mate. You can go first. You carrying?'

Guy nods. 'Yeah. Handgun.' He turns, back to them, lifting his polo shirt so they can see the handle.

'Don't move,' says Curtains.

Guy stays perfectly still, feels the weapon reefed from his trousers.

'Good man,' says Curtains. 'Now very slowly, remove your shirt.'

Guy turns around, so he can look Curtains in the eye. His heart is no longer a caged bird, it's a pneumatic drill, and his vision has closed in, like peering through a tunnel. He makes his movements slow, deliberate, lifting off his shirt, dropping it on the ground by his feet.

'What the fuck is this?' says a voice behind him.

'All will be revealed,' says Curtains.

If he's making a joke, no one is laughing.

'Pants,' he says to Guy. 'Leave your shoes on, just drop your trousers to your ankles.'

Guy signals his comprehension, does what he's told. He understands what's going on now, suspects the others must as well. Wonders why he's first; maybe because he and Raz were last to arrive, maybe because he's the youngest, the last to be recruited, the least well known. He breathes a sigh of relief, knowing he's clean. Turns a slow circle so Curtains can be sure.

'Good man,' says Curtains again. 'Pants up. Come and stand by us. Away from the others, but where we can see you.'

Guy leaves the circle, walks across to where Curtains and Murrow have the others covered. He stands off to one side of them, putting as much distance between himself and the two gunmen as possible, careful to stay just in front of them so they can see him. He no longer holds his hands above his head, but more at chest height, still clearly visible.

The air is so volatile it smells like avgas.

'Raz, you're next up,' says Curtains softly.

'I ain't wearing no fuckin' wire,' Raz spits indignantly.

'Someone is,' says Curtains.

And that's when the shooting starts. Guy doesn't see who fires first; it doesn't matter as the machine gun coughs death in reply. Guy hits the ground; can see the bullets tearing through men even as they claw for their own weapons; hears the rattle as bullets pierce the steel walls, like hail on a tin roof; sees the shattering of a fibro partition as if in slow motion, like the wine bottles at the warehouse.

And then nothing. A silence. A whimper. A low moaning.

He feels no elation, no horror. He rises to his feet, surveys the carnage.

— —

It takes him an hour, maybe more, maybe less, to do what needs to be done. Time has become tenuous, not flowing smoothly but coming in lumps, like clotted blood. Eventually he is back in the Commodore, behind the wheel, no longer excited, no longer thrilled. Not calm, just frayed, his nerves burnt out. Moving mechanically, trying to be methodical, attempting not to rush, to do it right. Raz is in the passenger seat, breath shallow, blood oozing. Still chewing gum. Guy takes it slowly, feeling the weight in the boot, the suspension sagging, the car threatening to bottom out. The six boxes of bullion, the calico bags. He leaves the engine running while he opens the gate. Takes the rag, wipes the metal clean. The moon is rising, a half-moon. Looking back across the paddock, he can see the aura, the woolshed on fire, a lanolin-fuelled pyre, arcing into the sky like a nebula, the other cars burning. They need to be far away before the dawn.

PART ONE

chapter one

2024

DETECTIVE SENIOR CONSTABLE NELL BUCHANAN AND DETECTIVE SERGEANT IVAN Lucic come from the north, leaving Dubbo behind and moving from the haze of late summer into the clarity of autumn, traversing the rolling hills of the Central West, edging east through the uplands of the Dividing Range, green tinge defying the lateness of the season, pushing past ridge lines crested with windfarms, edging onto the bleached periphery of the Monaro. She and Ivan mostly travel in silence, sharing the driving, breaking out into sporadic bursts of conversation, the easy patterns of friendship and collegiality, a partnership now three years old.

The country has weathered the summer well. Nell can see water in the landscape: farm dams full, ducks floating, cattle lounging. The road verges are freshly mown—council budgets, like the weather, buoyed to temporary equilibrium. A good year, and not just for the farmers: she's been promoted and Ivan has mellowed. She believes the death of his father has lifted a weight from him, released the tension within. Before he'd always seemed wound tight, on the defensive, as if constantly expecting something to catch him off guard.

She glances across at him from behind the steering wheel. He's dozing, head lolling on the headrest. That never would have happened when she first met him. The intensity is still there when necessary, but nowadays she senses that he's controlling it, and not the other way around. He's bought a house in Dubbo and has a new girlfriend: Carly, a quietly charming librarian. She'd come as a surprise to Nell, after the brassy blondes he'd first dated when he started on the apps. She's still not sure how she feels about it. A little jealous perhaps—not of Carly, but of Ivan. She'd always been the one out there playing the dating game, everyone from blue-collar muscles and mullets to white-collar Coke-bottle glasses with pockets full of pens. She'd thought herself wise in the ways of the world, and now Ivan has not only matched her but surpassed her, getting into a steady relationship while she still finds herself floundering away with the 'not quite rights' and 'at a different times' and 'outright creeps'. She knows it sounds a little silly, and a lot selfish, but she can't help resenting that she no longer has him to herself.

It's not a difficult drive, this one. Just six hours, the roads long and easy, the traffic light so far from Sydney, distant from the congested highways of the coast. Being based in Dubbo, at the centre of the state, looks good on paper and resonates in the baritone of the police minister: a dedicated flying squad out in the heartland, connected to the community, close to hand when violence strikes. The reality is different. They are close to hand only if a killer is considerate enough to commit murder near Dubbo, but not if the homicide is at some far-flung corner of New South Wales. Then it means flying, and flying invariably means transiting through Sydney and flying back out again, defeating the purpose. But six hours is driveable, The Valley not so very far. The call had come through late morning, and two hours later they were on the road, the police four-wheel drive packed with equipment and clothing, the list refined again and again through the experience of the past three years.

A roo, then another, bound onto the road ahead, and Nell taps the brakes, judging the distance, sounding the horn. The kangaroos bounce away nonchalantly, this way and that, before disappearing into the bush.

The manoeuvre has woken Ivan. He asks their whereabouts.

'Another hour. We're not far from Saltwood.'

'Right,' says Ivan, sitting up straight, yawning. He turns to the brief, reading it aloud from his phone. 'Wolfgang Burnside. Aged thirty-three. Body found in the village's Memorial Park at dawn this morning, partially submerged in the Broken River. Suspected drowning.'

Nell concentrates on the road. There's no traffic, but she's wary of animals and potholes, summer rain causing an exponential increase in both. 'Why assume murder?'

Ivan gives a small grunt. 'You mean why us?'

'Yes.' Most regional homicides were handled in the first instance by local area detectives and only assigned to Ivan's flying squad if they proved difficult. Or complex. Or political. The body of Wolfgang Burnside had only been found this morning. 'What did Plodder say?' asks Nell, referring to Detective Superintendent Dereck 'Plodder' Packenham, head of Homicide, their boss.

'Burnside was a local mover and shaker. Entrepreneur. Rich. Connected. But divisive. Or so Plodder reckons.'

Nell steals a glance at Ivan before returning her eyes to the road. Ivan is staring out the side window. 'Divisive?'

'Pro-development in a valley full of tree changers.'

'Still doesn't explain the urgency to get us involved.' She steals another look at Ivan; he's frowning.

'You're right,' he says. 'Must be more to it.'

'You didn't ask?'

Ivan laughs. 'I did. Plodder told me he didn't want to prejudice the investigation.'

'Jesus.' Nell returns the laugh, can't help it, responding with grudging affection. 'Considerate of him. Machiavellian bastard.'

'Yeah. Never acts without reason.'

Nell grows serious. 'You think he's protecting us from something?'

Ivan looks across at her. 'Well, I don't think he's setting us up, if that's what you mean.'

——

They reach Saltwood late in the afternoon, passing billboards for the Billabong Cafe (best coffee between Canberra and the Coast), the Timberland Motel (free wi-fi, hot tubs) and state MP Hannibal Earl (getting the job done), and entering the town through an honour guard of poplars, yellow leaves turned gold by the descending sun. The shopfronts, once old, have been made new again, tricked up to attract tourists. Nell continues past a bakery, eliciting a sigh from Ivan, but she doesn't want to stop: they are almost there.

Leaving the town, passing signs to Majors Creek and Araluen, they travel out through fields of harvest-ready wheat along the Kings Highway, the coastal range ahead, foothills enveloped by the khaki spread of eucalypts, the growth effusive, the trees taller, the undergrowth thicker. Somewhere on the other side is the sea. Nell cracks the window, breathes in the air, feels the moisture on her lips, an easterly wind carrying a hint of the ocean. She's missed such a landscape, where the trees don't come in clumps but lather the hills in forests, filling valleys and climbing hills, the fulsome olive of massed eucalypts.

The sat nav vocalises an instruction just as she sees the roadside sign pointing to the right: THE VALLEY. She slows, turning south off the highway, the secondary road winding over and around the low hills rather than cutting through them. They pass a battle-rank of windmills then drop over the lip of the plateau with unexpected abruptness, signs insisting that trucks and buses use low gear, the way narrow and twisting, descending down and down into the greenery of The Valley through switchbacks and hairpin turns, down four hundred metres, down into the shadows. Above them, the sky is bright, the sun flaring the clouds orange and white, but in the depths of The Valley it is already dusk, only the eastern cliffs remaining bright with the rays of the dying sun, golden sandstone like ramparts. Nell's ears pop, then pop again. The air at the bottom seems richer, more moist, more fragrant. Warmer.

The Valley is not a town. It's a village at best, a hamlet, buildings strung out along the Valley Road as it runs southwards from the pass, surrounded by dairy pastures, stone fruit orchards and vineyards. There's a cricket ground, football goalposts already erected at either end. A church. A smattering of houses, a dozen at most, another church. A street library. Then a general store boasting a solitary petrol bowser, and a crossroad, Miners' Institute on one corner, a pub diagonally opposite. A few more houses, a park, and the road continuing south. Nell pulls over, turns back towards the pub. She feels she recognises The Valley: the sort of place where everyone knows everyone else; the sort of place where people leave their doors open at night, the keys in the ignition of their cars, toys unattended in the front yard. Except now there's been a murder. It looks peaceful, but Nell wonders at the conversations behind closed doors, the speculation and the fear; understanding it's their job to quell those fears, to catch the perpetrator or perpetrators, to return The Valley to its slumber.

She pulls into their accommodation, the Bushranger Hotel. The two-storey pub is well into its second century, settled into the landscape like a grande dame, secure and entitled, the iron lace on the wraparound verandah a statement of gentility. It overlooks the crossroad, sitting on the north-west corner. To the south, the road continues into the darkening distance; to the east and west, a thinner ribbon of asphalt runs towards the encompassing escarpment. The hotel doesn't quite make sense to Nell; it seems too substantial, the only two-storey building in a one-storey town. A sign above the door notes it was established in 1868. There must have been a lot of optimism a hundred and sixty-odd years ago.

— —

There is no police station in The Valley, so they meet in the hotel's beer garden, Nell and Ivan and the sergeant from Saltwood, the detective from Queanbeyan. It's a quiet evening; the four police officers have the outdoor space to themselves. The sergeant, Vicary

Hearst, overweight and red-of-face, is jovial enough, happy to help, but Nell can sense a wariness in the detective, perhaps a lingering resentment. She can understand why. The body was found at first light, and Detective Sergeant Ed McMahon rushed down with a three-person team and started investigating, only to have the case lifted from him by lunchtime. And then he was required to cool his heels, waiting another six hours for Ivan and Nell to arrive.

'I'll walk you across to the scene,' says Sergeant Hearst. 'Take two minutes.'

'Useful place to start,' says Ivan.

Nell knows the respect her partner feels for the victims, his need to connect, to bear witness. She knows he will jog the local roads in the morning, pace them in the evening, size the place up, get a feel for it. Part of his method. As if the crime has embossed itself onto the landscape, leaving a lasting impression.

'We needed to remove the body, you understand,' says Sergeant McMahon as they leave the pub. 'It was partly submerged in the river, lying in the sun.' His voice trails off momentarily as they move south through the crossroad. Night is almost complete, two streetlights distinguishing the intersection from the descending dark, insects clouding the lights. A couple watering their garden in the evening cool wave a wary greeting, knowing what the four of them represent. Ivan offers them a distracted, 'Good evening.'

The police officers come to the park on the east side of the main road, opposite the last of the houses.

The Queanbeyan detective speaks again. 'We had what we needed. I authorised the removal of the body not long before we were informed you were taking over. But we photographed the shit out of it, including video. Collected samples. And the crime scene is preserved, taped off.'

'Where's the body now?' asks Ivan.

'Saltwood morgue. The forensic pathologist came down from Sydney this afternoon. Blake Ness. Said he knows you.'

Nell glances at Ivan. He'll be thinking the same thing: Plodder is prioritising this investigation. 'He's the best,' Nell says aloud.

The Saltwood sergeant laughs. 'He said the same about you two.'

The Queanbeyan detective isn't laughing. 'A crime scene investigator came with him. Dr Nguyen. She's already been here, inspected the scene.'

The park stretches between the road and a willow-lined river. A single floodlight illuminates a couple of public barbecues, a few tables with benches. In the shadows, there's a war memorial and a flagpole. There's a playground, equipment motionless, a toilet block, a phone booth next to the road. Sergeant Hearst leads them to the riverbank, police tape denoting the location. The detective lifts the tape and they enter the crime scene, using their phones to light the way.

There is a silence here, emphasised by the call of a solitary frog and a chorus of crickets. There is no wind, not even the slightest breeze. The Broken River flows soundlessly. This is where time ended for Wolfgang Burnside, where all his possibilities terminated. They stand without speaking for a moment. Maybe Ivan is right, thinks Nell; maybe violence does leave its mark.

The Queanbeyan detective, McMahon, speaks. 'Some locals gather at the park three times a week for tai chi. One of them walked over here, says she's not entirely sure why. Maybe attracted by the river; it can be changeable. Saw Burnside in the water, face down, raised the alarm. Didn't touch the body.'

'Didn't check for signs of life?' asks Nell.

'No. You'll see from the photos. Obvious he was dead.'

They stare a moment more, a spontaneous vigil, Nell's imagination firing. Next to her, Ivan is looking around, squinting into the darkness. They're down a bank, quite steep, the river capable of more power and more flow than its current passivity would suggest, flanked by willows, out of sight of anyone in the park. 'Any signs of a struggle?'

Sergeant McMahon shakes his head. 'Dr Ness can tell you about the body, whether there are defensive wounds, that sort of thing, but the physical environment, this place, nothing.' He sweeps his arm around, an encompassing gesture. 'I haven't spoken to Dr Nguyen, but we conducted a thorough search. I doubt she's found anything we didn't.'

'You think he was killed here, or dumped after the fact?' asks Ivan.

'Hard to say. There's nothing that would confirm he died here. No obvious scuff marks. Again, Dr Ness and Dr Nguyen may have more insight than me.'

'What was he wearing?' asks Nell. 'Could he have been out jogging?'

'Doubt it,' says McMahon. 'Jeans, a shirt. Expensive boots, a very expensive watch. Wallet still in his pocket. Phone missing. Casual wear, work wear—it can be hard to tell the difference. It's all listed, all photographed.' There's a hint of disapproval in his voice, the suggestion Nell should already know this.

'Car?'

'No. We're not sure how he got here. One of our lines of inquiry.'

'He doesn't live within walking distance?' asks Ivan. 'Pretty small community.'

It's Vicary who answers. 'Lives about five kilometres south, on the edge of the national park. He's developing a resort down there. Ecotourism. Cabins in the woods. Very upmarket. Calls the place Gondwana Falls. Worked from there as well.'

Ivan is inspecting their surrounds, swinging the torch beam from his phone across the grass. 'For argument's sake, say he died elsewhere, then was dumped here. The killer or killers would need to carry him from the road, correct? What's that, about sixty metres?'

The Queanbeyan detective is nodding. 'Yes. We've been over the park surface. There are no signs of a vehicle crossing the lawn. So either Burnside walked here and was killed, or he was carried.'

'Does that seem likely?' Nell directs her question to the Saltwood sergeant rather than the detective. 'Seems risky, lugging a body across this open space.'

Vicary Hearst shrugs. 'Not necessarily. If it was the middle of the night, the early hours, chances are there'd be no one about.'

'We doorknocked nearby houses, all eight of them,' says the detective, reinserting himself into the conversation. 'No one saw or heard anything. The pub has CCTV extending out across the front car park to the road, so it should have picked up any overnight traffic. Same with the general store. We've requested the files; they'll be uploaded into the system.'

Nell thinks of the road she and Ivan have just traversed. 'Most traffic coming into The Valley would come from the north, right? Down the pass from Saltwood?'

'Yes,' says the sergeant.

'Is that the only way in and out? What's to the south?'

'Not a lot. A few farms, some orchards.' It's Sergeant Hearst who replies, the local. 'The Valley Road turns to dirt when it hits the national park. Follows this river into the forest. Bit of a goat track, but it will take you through to the coast—eventually. And the West Road, it runs up the escarpment. Not much up there, but it's possible to get through to Araluen and Majors Creek, on to Captains Flat and Queanbeyan. The East Road is a dead end.'

'You've done an excellent job, both of you,' says Ivan, and Nell suppresses a smile. He's learning.

But the Queanbeyan detective isn't mollified. 'We've ticked all the boxes, everything you'd expect. I'm pretty confident of that.' And then, 'Good luck with it.'

And again Nell thinks she senses an underlying resentment.

chapter two

NELL WAKES IN HER KING-SIZE BED AND FOR A MOMENT RELISHES THE experience, looking up at the antique light fitting descending from an ornate plaster ceiling rose. The Bushranger Hotel feels more like a luxury B & B than a pub, done up in an attempt to lure tourists from the Kings Highway between Canberra and the coast. There are high ceilings, sash windows, a skilfully added ensuite with a claw-foot bath. She wonders what the pub's original name was; there can't have been much sympathy for bushrangers when it was built. It's certainly a change up from the places where she and Ivan typically stay: dogbox motels and business hotels. She has the corner suite, overlooking the verandah and the crossroad beyond. She yawns, stretches and catches herself—a man is dead; she should not be congratulating herself on the comfort of the accommodation. She gets out of bed, gets moving, donning her detective persona even as she changes into her exercise gear.

She leaves for her pre-breakfast martial arts workout. Recently, her routine has become more meditative, less explosive, as she's found herself revelling in the immersion instead of wanting to hit something. The natural place to practise the drills would be in the Memorial Park, but she eschews that. Too close to the crime scene: she wants to clear her head, not clog it. Instead she walks north and finds the cricket field, paint peeling from its boundary fence, an isolated pavilion, a toilet block. No one around, just a few curious cows grazing out near the wicket to keep her company. They gather to watch her, deferential and polite. She wonders where Ivan might be: jogging the back roads, summing up the place.

— —

They meet Carole and Blake for breakfast in the cafe attached to the general store. Whereas the pub has been completely renovated, full of clean timber and tasteful art, the cafe remains largely untouched, a hotchpotch of tables and chairs scattered before a glass-fronted counter at least fifty years old. There are fans in the ceiling and lino on the floor. But it's clean and the old-fashioned menu looks enticing: no avocado or haloumi or wheatgrass juice; just bacon and eggs and white-bread toast, help yourself to tomato sauce.

The forensic experts have overnighted in Saltwood, close to the hospital and its morgue, but have driven down early. It's just the four of them for the moment; Detective McMahon returned to Queanbeyan the previous evening, but Sergeant Hearst has overnighted with friends in The Valley and is planning to join them. Nell likes him, suspects he wants to make himself useful, give them the benefit of his local knowledge.

Blake has already ordered the English breakfast and is clearly pleased with his choice, plate piled high. He compliments the bacon even as he devours it.

'Take us through what you know,' Ivan says to the pathologist.

'Drowned. But probably more to it.'

'Such as?'

'Blow to the back of the head. Probably not enough to kill him outright, but maybe enough to daze him or render him unconscious. Contemporaneous with the drowning.'

'Detective didn't mention that,' says Nell.

'Easy to miss,' says Blake. He hesitates, knife and fork hovering above his meal, as though he's spied something untoward on his plate. Something healthy, perhaps. 'Also, there are suggestions of poisoning.'

'Suggestions?'

'I've taken the samples, had them driven to Canberra for toxicology. Hopefully we'll know more later today or tomorrow.'

'Not drugs? Not an overdose?'

Blake sounds dismissive. 'Doubt it. None of the typical signs.'

'What sort of poison?' asks Ivan.

'Let me get back to you on that.'

'Working theory?'

'Murder,' says Blake. 'The blow to the head. If it was the front or side, an accident would be more plausible. But who falls over, hits the back of their head, then goes face first into a river? Hard to imagine, even if the poisoning comes to nothing.'

Ivan looks to Carole, who agrees. 'That's consistent with the crime scene.'

'But he was still alive when he went into the river?' asks Nell.

'Yes,' says Blake. 'Water in his lungs. That's what killed him.'

'Time of death?'

'Late Tuesday, or early yesterday morning. An hour either side of midnight. That Queanbeyan detective knew what he was about. Measured the body's temperature soon as he got here.'

Ivan is staring hard at Blake, that unnerving blue stare of concentration that Nell has come to know so well, as if he's working through it, imagining the last moments of Wolfgang Burnside's life. 'Would he have died anyway, if he hadn't drowned?'

Blake is shaking his head. 'Too much speculation. I still haven't fully established the damage wrought by the blow to the head or confirmed there was poison in his system.'

Sergeant Hearst comes bustling in, greets them, spies the remains of Blake's breakfast and licks his lips. 'I'll grab something.' He goes to the counter, orders, then returns, pulling up a chair. 'You got everything you need?'

'Tell us about the victim,' says Ivan. 'We hear he was quite prominent.'

Vicary raises his eyebrows. 'That's one way of putting it.'

'Go on,' says Ivan.

Vicary looks around, surveying the room as though seeing beyond its walls and out into the surrounding valley, perhaps trying to summarise it in his own mind before responding. 'This place feels like Sleepy Hollow, but that doesn't mean everyone's a happy camper. There are the established farming families, conservative for the most part. Then there are the old hippies, who came in the seventies, bought cheap bush blocks. Just lately, there's been an influx of cashed-up tree changers. A few young families looking for a better lifestyle, but mainly wealthy retirees coming out of Sydney and Canberra. Former lawyers and doctors and company directors, setting up vineyards and wineries. You follow?'

'Not really,' says Ivan bluntly. 'What's that got to do with Wolfgang Burnside?'

Vicary Hearst appears momentarily surprised, perhaps thinking his exposition should have been self-explanatory. 'No one really wants development. Not the farmers, not the hippies, not the tree changers. They like it the way it is.'

'And Wolfgang?' Ivan persists.

'No one called him Wolfgang. I didn't even know that was his proper name. Everyone called him Wolf or Wolfie. And he was all in favour of progress. A self-declared champion of it.'

'What did that entail?' asks Nell.

'Started in real estate. Got rich selling it. No formal education, but a millionaire by the time he was in his early twenties. And that was just the beginning. He restarted an annual harvest festival, a one-day writers' festival, established a monthly farmers' market. He brought bands and musos and comedians here to play the cricket ground like in the old days. Put an ATM in the general store. Owns a share in the pub and helped fund its upgrade, and like I told you, he's developing an eco-resort next to the national park. He got elected to council up at Saltwood, lobbied hard to set up a community internet in The Valley, but when council didn't back him, he resigned and built his own. Then people complained when he charged them to use it.' Vicary holds his hands wide, palms up, like he's balancing competing ideas. 'So depending on who you ask, he was either some kind of saint, advancing the community, or he was in it for himself, only interested in making money.'

'Quite the entrepreneur,' observes Ivan.

'I see how he could have put people offside,' says Nell, 'but none of that sounds like a motive to murder him.'

'True,' says Vicary. 'But he was also into property development. He graduated from merely acting as an agent and started buying out a few of the old hippies. A bunch of them are getting on, getting sick of living hand-to-mouth, subsistence. On paper they're wealthy because their land has appreciated so much. Asset rich, cash poor. Wolfie helped sell a few blocks to tree changers. Then he went further, started buying the blocks himself, subdivided, put housing on some. Made millions. People resented that.' Vicary grimaces. 'And then there's the power company.'

'In The Valley?' asks Nell.

'His latest scheme. He was proposing to take the entire community off-grid, make the place self-sufficient, do with electricity what he did with the internet. He built windmills up on the plateau; you probably saw them on your way in from Saltwood. He put in a solar farm and was planning more, owned a company that installs rooftop solar. He reckoned we can be net generators, putting electricity into the grid and taking money out. Wanted to build a battery, even proposed developing pumped hydro using the lake up by the Gryphon Mine.'

'Gryphon Mine?' asks Ivan.

'Abandoned goldmine up on the escarpment, overlooking the eastern side of the valley. Lake up the top, settling ponds at the bottom.'

'Pumped hydro,' says Blake, finishing his breakfast, plate wiped clean. 'That's ambitious.'

'Like a huge battery,' says Vicary. 'Pump excess power generated by wind and solar during the day up to the lake, then feed it down through turbines at night when the power is needed. There's four hundred metres of fall. Some people think it's wonderful:

self-contained, sustainable energy; no more coal. But others worry that he would control it, accrue too much influence.'

'So big money, and big sway,' says Ivan: an observation, not a question.

'But is that enough motive?' Nell asks.

'There's a rumour he was thinking of making a run for state parliament,' says Vicary. 'I can ask around at Saltwood, but you'd probably need to speak to people in Queanbeyan about that.'

Nell looks at Ivan. Politics. Their eyes meet, and Ivan raises his eyebrows. She knows what he's contemplating: Plodder's motivation for assigning them the case so early.

'Personal life?' Ivan directs the question to Vicary.

'Married young. High school sweetheart, Janine. Divorced a couple of years ago. She still lives in The Valley. He remarried last year. Sydney girl. Tyffany.'

'She lives here?'

'Yes. At their eco-resort.'

They finish their breakfast, and Nell leaves a tip. Always useful to befriend the locals. Outside, Carole and Blake say their goodbyes. They're heading back to Saltwood and Queanbeyan and, most likely, to Sydney, their work largely done.

'Speak soon,' says Blake. 'Let you know what I find.'

Vicary Hearst leads Ivan and Nell to the Miners' Institute, explaining that they can use it as their base, that The Valley's one-man police station closed back in the 1970s and was later sold off altogether. The Institute sits diagonally opposite the pub, on the far side of the crossroad, a solid, compact brick building— scaffolding erected, perhaps anticipating repair work that is yet to eventuate. But serviceable. Lockable.

'Lot of miners then?' asks Nell.

'There was once, when The Valley was first opened up, when the future looked bright,' says Vicary. Then, flicking his head towards the building: 'Heritage-listed, can't be demolished. Good to put it to use. Should have everything you need. Power, water, toilets and a kitchen. Downside: no aircon, wood heating. This time of year you should be sweet. Upside: Wolf Burnside's fibre-to-the-premises internet. Rocket-fast. Better than Sydney or Canberra.'

'Holding cells?'

Vicary shakes his head. 'Nah. If it comes to that, give me a bell and we'll deal with them at Saltwood.'

Once the sergeant has left, returning up the escarpment, Ivan and Nell set up their laptops and screens, power boards and a printer/ scanner, a process practised and refined over the past three years. They find the internet connection is every bit as fast as promised, but Ivan tells Nell he doesn't want to waste time online. He says he's already been through the material collected by Detective McMahon, seen the photos of the crime scene. He wants to get out, talk to people, glean new evidence, not revisit second-hand information.

— —

Tyffany Burnside meets them at Gondwana Falls, the eco-resort that was being developed by her late husband. It's at the southern end of the valley, in among the rainforest, bordering the national park. It's green and lush and dark, with tree ferns and a towering canopy, spotted gums and staghorns. They drive through stone gates, across a small bridge, and pull up outside the lodge entrance framed by a couple of ancient cedars.

She's young and blonde and no-nonsense, wearing a loose linen top, the sort you need to pull over your head, capri pants, Birkenstocks. Beach chic, adapted for the forest. And yet Nell notices the watch: understated but expensive, the sort that warrants full-page ads in in-flight magazines. The sort that Nell will never be able to afford. And the nails: perfect. Burnside was thirty-three, but Tyffany looks younger, maybe mid-twenties. Nell supresses her judgement; that's not why she's here.

There are no tears. The widow's demeanour is professional, her greeting smile brief and functional. She guides them into a modern lounge, rich leather armchairs around a coffee table, its top a single slab of rough-hewn wood. Looking out through floor-to-ceiling windows, Nell sees an infinity pool, beyond it, surrounding it, the forest.

'Our condolences, Mrs Burnside,' Ivan begins. 'Thank you for agreeing to see us so promptly.'

'Whatever I can do to help.' Her voice is husky, half an octave lower than Nell would have expected. 'I still can't quite believe it. Still processing.'

'You identified the body?' asks Ivan.

'No. I just arrived back this morning.'

'You've been away?'

'Sydney. Wolf was coming to join me for the weekend. We were heading to New Caledonia for a few days' downtime. Swimming, scuba, some sailing. It's divine this time of year.'

Nell frowns. 'Just lead me through that, please. Today is Thursday, your husband's body was found first thing yesterday morning, he died around midnight on Tuesday. You were in Sydney the whole time?'

'Since last weekend.'

Ivan leans forward, voice conciliatory. 'Mrs Burnside, we will need to confirm that. A formality, routine, but necessary.'

She blinks, doesn't appear to take offence. 'I understand. The spouse is always a suspect.'

'Correct,' says Ivan, and Nell winces at his directness.

Tyffany Burnside appears unfazed. 'There are witnesses. The hotel staff, CCTV. Credit cards. Receipts. I am sure you can access it.'

'We have your permission?'

'Of course.'

'Including your phone records?'

She frowns. 'Why would you need those?'

Nell interjects. 'Not text messages or voicemail, just locations. Where the phone has been, where it was when you made and received calls.'

'The metadata?' says Tyffany.

'Precisely.'

'No. If you really need it, come back to me. But you should have more than enough already.'

Ivan sighs, seemingly reluctant to get bogged down on such a detail. 'Is there any particular reason for your reluctance?'

'Some numbers, some contacts, are confidential. Business deals. If you need them, you can get a warrant, but I can't just surrender them. Wolf gave assurances of confidentiality to some of his associates. But if you want to check the phone's location, I'm sure you can do that through the telco. It's Telstra.' She finds her phone. 'I'll give you my number. It will make it easier.' She reads it out; Nell writes it down.

'Thank you,' says Ivan, tone steadfastly neutral. 'You keep the numbers of your husband's business associates on your phone?'

'You sound surprised,' says Tyffany, arching an eyebrow.

Ivan doesn't answer, deftly changes tack. 'As you know, your husband's body was found in the Memorial Park, by the banks of the Broken River, but we're not sure how he got there. His car wasn't nearby. What vehicles do you own, and is it possible to account for them all?'

'I'll have to check. We have two Teslas, one each, and a diesel four-wheel drive. Plus various dirt bikes, quad bikes, e-bikes, mountain bikes. And the resort has various trucks and utilities.' She pauses. 'I can run through them, see if anything is missing.'

'You drove to Sydney?'

'I took one of the Teslas down to Moruya, left it at the airport, flew to Sydney. Again, there will be plenty of records.'

'Thank you,' says Nell. 'Was your husband depressed at all? Taking medication?'

Tyffany looks her in the eye. 'No. Just the opposite. Wolfie was an inveterate optimist. Depression wasn't in his vocabulary. Nor were lethargy, despondency, or anything else along those lines. And he sure as hell didn't need artificial stimulation.' She grimaces. 'You're homicide detectives. He was murdered. Let's move on.'

Nell bristles, doesn't appreciate being told what to do. 'Very well. Did your husband have any enemies?'

Tyffany laughs, her teeth immaculate, glowing like pearls. 'Plenty. Not personally; everyone was fond of Wolfie, warmed to him, his dynamism was infectious. He was gregarious and generous. His former wife can be a bit of a bitch, but that's hardly his fault. I know you need to check her out, but I can't see her killing Wolfie. Professionally, though, there are plenty of people opposed to his vision for this valley. I guess one way to stop all that would be to kill him.' She pauses for a moment, like an actor, giving the following words greater impact. 'Of course, if they think that, they're mistaken.'

'How's that?' asks Nell.

'Because I intend to push ahead with it. All of it. To honour him, to vindicate him, to avenge him. To fuck the fuckers. Whoever did this.' She takes a deep breath, allowing herself time to judge their reactions, letting the emotion recede from her voice. And when she speaks again, it's softer, more like she's confiding in them. 'We're the same, you and me: we all want justice for Wolfie. For you, that means catching the killer or killers. For me, justice means seeing his projects through to completion, not letting the luddites win.'

'Let's assume it is murder,' says Ivan. 'You've suggested some locals are opposed to your husband's plans. Can you supply us with a list of names?'

'Anonymously?'

'If necessary.'

'Yes.'

'What about business partners or competitors or aggrieved investors, that sort of thing?' he asks.

'No. Some of Wolf's ventures are more profitable than others, but none are failures. No business partners have lost out. There are no unpaid debts.'

'How did he structure all of this, the different projects?'

'There are five companies. The largest is Burnside Holdings. That's real estate and property development. That's how he made his fortune and it's what still generates most of the cash. There is an investment company, mainly land that we might go on to develop. Then there are separate companies for the internet and the renewable energy initiative, and one for this place. We also have a family trust that holds some of our personal wealth.'

'Major business partners, investors?'

'You're looking at it.'

'You? Partner or investor?' asks Ivan, raising an eyebrow.

'Both.' She glances at Nell, then addresses Ivan. 'I know what you were thinking. Attractive young woman, second wife, maybe ten years younger than her multimillionaire husband. A gold-digger. A trophy. But I brought significant money and expertise to this marriage. Yes, inherited wealth, but I also have a doctorate in electrical engineering. And I'm older than I look. Thirty next year.'

Nell lowers her head, chastened. 'My apologies.'

Tyffany laughs, generous in her victory. 'Don't worry, my dear. You're not the first to underestimate me. You won't be the last.'

'And politics?' asks Ivan. 'We heard he was considering running for parliament.'

The humour leaves Tyffany Burnside. 'No. Not in a million years.' She looks almost offended at the suggestion. 'What is true is that we were searching for a candidate. A teal, or a country independent.'

Nell can see Ivan has come alert, is sitting erect.

'Why would you do that?' he asks.

'The incumbent. Hannibal Earl.'

Ivan says nothing, blue eyes unblinking.

Nell takes up the slack. 'He's opposed to your developments?'

A sardonic smile plays on the widow's lips as she speaks to Nell, not Ivan. 'No. More personal than that. You get your oglers, you get your gropers. Earl is both.'

Ivan finds his voice. 'Hannibal Earl. Son of Terrence Earl?'

'The same. Creep begets creep.'

The intensity has not left Ivan. 'Was your husband investigating Earl? Digging for dirt?'

Tyffany Burnside is shaking her head. 'No. That's not Wolf, not the way he operated.'

'What about you?' asks Nell.

'I've been known to hold a grudge, if that's what you're asking.' And to Nell, the widow's gaze appears just as steely and resolute as Ivan's.

chapter three

NELL WAITS UNTIL THEY ARE IN THE FOUR-WHEEL DRIVE BEFORE SHE ASKS,
'Who's Terrence Earl?'

'Former police minister, back in the bad old days, thirty years
ago. Hannibal is his son. A political dynasty.'

'You think that's why we were dispatched so quickly? Plodder's
antennas picking up potential problems?'

'Let's find out.'

Ivan rings their boss, the head of Homicide, phone on speaker.
But it's no use. *'This is Dereck Packenham,'* comes the recorded
message. *'Leave a message. I'll get back to you.'*

'Hannibal Earl,' says Ivan to the handset. 'Terrence Earl.
Anything we need to know?' And he ends the call with a sigh.

'Looks like we're on our own,' says Nell. 'What's next?'

'Let's talk to the first wife.'

——

They find Janine Burnside living in an original homestead dating
back to when The Valley was first settled by Europeans. Ellensby

is out along the West Road, past a field covered in solar panels. There's a stone gateway with a cattle grid leading to a long blue-metal drive lined with firs, the house itself sitting on a low rise, surrounded on three sides by trees: deciduous closer to the house, oaks and Japanese maples and Manchurian pears, a complete palette of autumn colours, shielded from wind and prying eyes by an outer barrier of evergreens. Climbing from their car, Nell feels the wealth accumulated over the decades, a cushioning in the air. She senses it in the luxuriant lawn, the banks of rosebushes, the crunch of the gravel drive underfoot. The air is fragrant, the light subdued. High in the sky, wafer-thin clouds are scuttling towards the coast, but here in the valley, protected by its sandstone cliffs, and particularly here at Ellensby, cosseted behind its trees, the air is almost still, only the slightest suggestion of a breeze.

The house is sandstone, the colour of the nearby cliffs, thick walls and sash windows, wide verandahs and wisteria. A high-pitched green roof made of steel, a rooster weathervane and six brick chimneys, a satellite dish.

They step onto the verandah and Nell rings the bell.

'Not too shabby,' she says to Ivan.

'Very *Homes and Gardens*,' he replies.

The door is opened by a trim-looking woman, face tanned and lacking obvious make-up, wearing jeans and a white cotton shirt. She smiles momentarily, perhaps out of politeness, but Nell can see the grief in her eyes.

'Janine Burnside?' asks Nell. She had imagined someone more middle-aged, but recalls Wolfgang was only thirty-three. The first Mrs Burnside appears no older than the second.

'Janine Macklin. I've reverted to my maiden name. Please come in.'

She leads them down a hallway, oil paintings fighting for space on the walls, depicting The Valley and Ellensby, horses and stiffly posed patriarchs, a black-and-white photographic print of hundreds of grim-faced workers posing before a mine wheel. And through to a conservatory, glowing with dappled light, plants hanging, plants in planters, plants in beds, a miniature forest of bonsai. An automated system misting small clouds at the far end.

'My favourite room,' explains Janine, gesturing for them to take a seat: wicker furniture gathered around a glass-topped table. 'Tea or coffee?' she offers. 'Water? Juice?'

'We're good for now, thanks,' says Ivan.

'It's an amazing house,' says Nell.

'Isn't it? Built in 1842. Neglected when we bought it. I've spent years restoring it to its original condition.' She looks like she's about to continue, then shakes her head. 'Sorry. You didn't come to hear about that.'

'You lived here with Wolfgang, when you were married?' asks Nell.

She nods, a sadness upon her now, her vitality ebbing, and she becomes still. 'Yes. He was the one who hankered after it, not me. I thought it was too big at first, too rundown. But I've really grown to love it.'

'You own it, then?'

'Yes. Wolf agreed I should have it in the settlement.'

'So he no longer hankered after it?' asks Ivan, using her words.

Janine Macklin smiles—rather affectionately, it seems to Nell. 'No. He wanted it so much, but once he possessed it, he was ready to move on. That was Wolf, never looking back, always wanting to move forward to the next project.' She takes a breath, then continues, as though trying to explain. 'He grew up in The Valley, his family owned the general store. Not much money. A struggle. For him, Ellensby was the pinnacle, the classiest place in The Valley, owned for generations by the local squattocracy, the Clovertons. He saw it as the ultimate symbol of success. It brought him great satisfaction to buy it. But then he realised this was someone else's legacy; he wanted to build his own. When we split, I wanted it and she didn't.'

'Tyffany?'

'Yes. Her. I don't think Wolf cared one way or another.'

Nell can see the emotions playing across her face, isn't sure how to interpret them. 'You sound quite fond of your former husband,' she observes.

'I guess. Wolf was Wolf. Full of energy, dynamism. But no off switch. Totally exhausting. Always trying to prove something. So yes, I think in some ways I still love him. Bits of him. He's been very generous.' She turns away for a moment, gathering herself before continuing. 'He was a good father, brilliant whenever he was around; totally absent when he wasn't.'

'What do you make of his new wife?' asks Ivan.

Janine seems pensive. 'I don't think she was good for him. I tried to have a calming effect; she egged him on. Maybe I'm being unfair. She didn't need the money, but she's just the same as he was, into the stimulation of achievement. Like two adrenaline junkies. Never take a day off. Even when they went on holidays, it was heli-skiing or scuba diving or big-game fishing or racing sailboats.' She pauses, maybe reconsidering. 'To her credit, she understands business, would have been a good sounding board, been willing to challenge him. Business never really interested me. I left all that to Wolf.'

'So you weren't involved in the business side of his life?' Nell inquires.

'No. I kept the home fires burning, was there for the kids. But Wolf was always talking, bubbling over with ideas, so I had a pretty good idea of what was obsessing him at any given time. He always had two or three things on the go.'

'Now that he's dead, what will happen to all these projects?' asks Ivan.

Janine stares momentarily, perhaps brought up short by Ivan's blunt reference to her ex-husband's death. 'I have a copy of his will, if you want to see it.'

'A copy?'

'Yes. The original is with his lawyers, but he gave a copy to me and one to Tyffany. He wanted it all above board, all transparent. A very Wolf thing to do.' She smiles, and Nell again sees the residual affection. 'He was an oversharer.' And she stands, walking back into the house proper, leaving them alone.

Ivan gazes at Nell, those laser blue eyes connecting. He shakes his head and she knows what he's indicating: Janine Macklin is not her former husband's killer.

She returns to the room, hands the document to Nell, talking as she does so. 'It's all quite complicated. His wealth will be split into quarters, evenly divided between Tyffany and myself, and the two kids. Tyffany has a son from a previous marriage, but he's not included. She already owns significant equity in the companies.'

'So no one is left wanting?' asks Nell.

'No. He was always good at it. Money and finances. The kids and I were well cared for, before he left and after.' Her lip quivers for a fleeting moment. 'And now.'

'So your separation. It was amicable?'

Janine looks down, a tremor running through her. 'I guess. As far as it goes. I was very upset. The kids hated it. Wolf was always cordial and considerate and polite, but it was a hard time.'

'Where are your children now?' asks Nell. 'It must be difficult for them.'

'In their rooms. Normally they'd be at school in Saltwood.'

There are more questions, more answers, but nothing that advances the investigation. Even before she talks it over with Ivan, Nell is eliminating the two wives from suspicion. And both have said none of Wolfgang Burnside's business associates would have any reason to be bitter, let alone homicidal.

Ivan and Nell are just leaving, out on the driveway, when Ivan gets a call.

'That was quick,' he says into the handpiece. 'We'll be there in five minutes.'

—▬—

Vicary Hearst is waiting at the Miners' Institute, smile on his face, moving his weight from one leg to the other, like a schoolboy in need of a pee.

'CCTV,' he says. 'In the system.'

'Let's have a squiz then,' says Ivan.

Vicary takes a seat, logs in under his own name. 'There are two exterior cameras at the pub: one overlooking the car park out the back and one covering the space in front of the entrance. Just catches the main road in the background.'

'The crossroad?' asks Ivan.

'Not quite,' Vicary responds. 'The road just to the north of the intersection.'

'And the Memorial Park is just to the south of the crossroad, right?'

'That's right. A hundred and fifty metres from here. So a car passing from left to right on the screen is heading south towards the park.' Vicary plays the video, shuttling through long periods of nothing. 'I've been through it slowly. No sign of anyone on foot, Wolf included. Only two cars going south during the three hours between eleven pm and two in the morning. I have a firm ID on this one.' He pauses the vision, then runs it through frame by frame. It shows a man with a mess of snowy white hair leaving the pub, staggering slightly; he climbs into a farm truck and heads out onto the road, travelling south. 'Arnie Cocheef,' says Vicary. 'Full-time orchardist, part-time artist, committed environmentalist. Pub regular. Has a property further down the valley.'

'Helpful,' says Ivan, but his voice is ticking a box, not lifted by excitement. 'He's travelling by himself, not unusual for him to be there, no sign of Wolfgang Burnside.' He turns to Nell. 'But we'll need to chase him up, in case he saw something.'

'And then there is this,' says Vicary. He shuttles back a little. 'Ten minutes after midnight. Ten minutes before Arnie Cocheef leaves the pub.'

The vision catches the blur of a passing van, caught in the top of the frame, heading south. It's side on, so no chance of a number plate, no impression of the driver, just a pale yellow van. Lemon-coloured.

'Not a lot to work with,' says Vicary. 'I've asked at the pub but no one recognises it. Not a local. Someone passing through.'

'Passing through to where?' asks Ivan, sounding intrigued. 'Why would someone be heading south at that time of night?'

Vicary shrugs. 'I'm checking with Saltwood. We have cameras on the main street. It's about a half-hour drive, so we know when to look; should be able to pick it up, if the van came through there. If it came up the other direction, from Batemans Bay, there are cameras at the turn-off onto the Kings Highway.'

'Excellent,' says Nell. 'But the park where Wolfgang Burnside's body was found is south of the crossroad, so the camera at the pub wouldn't have picked up any vehicles coming up from the south of the valley, either locals or cars from the coast. Right?'

'That's right.'

'Or cars coming into the crossroad from the east or west?'

'True. Not much to the east; it's a dead end. Runs to several farms below the escarpment and stops. Maybe a half-dozen properties. The road to the west goes further, runs out of the valley.'

'It passes the homestead where Janine Macklin lives,' notes Ivan.

'Ellensby?' asks Vicary, frowning. 'What are you suggesting?'

'Nothing,' says Ivan. 'Just building a picture. Understanding the geography.' He places his hand on the officer's shoulder, a reassuring gesture. 'This is good work. Helps a lot. So much of a murder investigation is doing this work, weeding out possibilities, working through the process of elimination.'

Sergeant Hearst beams, looking chuffed.

After discussing other possible lines of inquiry, Vicary heads back to Saltwood, promising to check the town's CCTV to see if he can identify the yellow van, glean a number plate. He'll also request vision from his colleagues at Batemans Bay and the roads department.

Ivan suggests Nell see if any locals recognise the vehicle while he visits Arnie Cocheef, just in case the farmer saw anything as he drove past the park. Nell prints out the blurry image of the pale yellow van and walks across towards the pub and the general store. This is the spade work, the shoe leather that can break open an investigation or at least rule out a suspect. More often, it will lead to nothing, but it has to be done.

The manager of the pub, a dour woman named Wilhelmina, says the van means nothing to her, that she doesn't ever recall seeing one like it.

The store has a bowser outside, so Nell wonders about CCTV, whether Vicary checked. She thought they were almost compulsory at petrol stations, set to catch thieves unwilling to pay for fuel.

Inside, an elderly man with a beer gut straining against a Rolling Stones t-shirt that's two sizes too small is sitting behind the counter reading a fishing magazine. He peers over his reading glasses when Nell approaches. 'G'day, love. What can I do you for?' Nell introduces herself and the man leans over the counter, shakes her hand with a fleshy mitt. 'G'day, Nell,' he says. 'Barny. You investigating Wolf's death?'

'That's right. Checking for CCTV.'

'Vicary Hearst's already been through, asked the same thing. We've got cameras, but only one outside. Looks down at the bowser, parallel to the road. Doesn't catch passing traffic. I spooled through for him, but I've got nothing. No reason for anyone to pull in here at that hour; we close at seven.'

'Pity,' says Nell and shows him the printout from the pub's video. 'You don't recognise it?'

The bloke scrutinises it, squinting through his glasses. 'Unusual colour, isn't it?' He hands it back. 'Don't know anyone in The Valley with a van that colour. You know what make that is?'

'No. Not yet.' She looks around the store. It seems pretty basic. Cans of food, toiletries, dry goods. Mossie coils and firelighters and fishing gear. Milk and bread and chocolate. Newspapers and a few magazines. A big freezer with a scattering of ice creams. 'How long you had the place, Barny?'

'Going on eight years now.'

'I was told Wolfgang Burnside grew up here. His family owned it.'

'That's right. Me and the missus bought it off his mum. Eliza. She was glad to let us have it. Didn't have to work no more. Wolf built her a kit home at the head of the valley and bought her a neat little car.'

'She still live there?'

'Sure. Drops in every now and then to get her mail and buy the papers. Have a natter.' Barny sighs. 'She'll be gutted. Adored her son.'

Nell thanks Barny then walks next door to the cafe and buys herself a pre-made wrap for a late lunch, gets a chicken salad roll for Ivan.

— —

Back at the Institute, Ivan returns with news. 'Arnie Cocheef. Says he didn't see anything. But after I showed him the image on my phone, he reckoned he might have seen a van pulled up by the park. Thought it was more of a cream colour, but that might have just been the lack of light.'

Nell blinks: it couldn't be this easy, surely? 'Right time frame. You think he's credible?'

'Doesn't really matter, does it? We need to chase it down. Could be the break we need.'

'What was Arnie doing leaving the pub after midnight? Surely it was shut by then. Tuesday night.'

'Reckons he'd exhausted himself with the harvest. Fell asleep in the beer garden and no one noticed. Let himself out.'

Nell laughs. 'Exhausted? Pissed more like it.'

Ivan laughs as well, before becoming serious once more. 'We need to find that van.'

They're discussing their next move when Ivan receives a call on his mobile.

'Blake. What news?' His voice is light, imbued with familiarity. Nell grins at that, the informality of the team, everyone pulling in the same direction. But now a frown appears on her partner's face like clouds before a change. 'Just a moment,' he says, and leaves the room, walks outside. Nell can see him through the window, out by their car, pacing up and down, talking into the phone, gesturing with one hand.

She has a bad feeling. Since when would Ivan feel the need to leave the room, to discuss something in private with Blake, not allowing her to hear his half of the conversation? Something strange is happening.

She watches as he ends the call, then looks towards the Institute, sees her watching him. He waves, a reassuring gesture. Then he's back on his handset, calling someone else. Soon he's talking again, pacing again.

'What is it?' she asks, when he eventually returns to the office.

'Blake. Blake and Carole. They've found something. They're already on the way here. Called from the car. Be here in a few minutes.'

Nell feels unsettled. 'They're coming back?' This must be important. 'What is it?'

Ivan takes a deep breath. 'Blake has the details.'

Moments later, a van pulls up and the pathologist and the crime scene investigator emerge, enter the building, trying to appear normal, but to Nell's heightened senses there is something forced in their self-control.

They take a seat around a table, she and Blake and Carole, while Ivan remains on his feet. She can feel his nervous energy.

'We're making progress,' says Blake, addressing her first, then looking up to Ivan. 'The blow to the head was probably enough to knock out Wolfgang Burnside. He was struck immediately before the drowning. Impossible to say if he was held under, or whether he was simply unconscious.'

He looks around the table, but there is no response. Carole is staring at the tabletop.

Blake continues. 'I was half right about the poisoning. He had cyanide in his system, but not enough to kill him or to impair his breathing. Just trace amounts.'

'Cyanide?' says Ivan. He sounds surprised. 'Did he ingest it?'

Nell is feeling even more uncomfortable. Why didn't the two men discuss this on their phone call? Why drive down?

'No,' says Blake, answering Ivan's question. 'Nothing in his stomach contents.'

Nell has had enough. She interjects, addressing the room. 'You guys didn't come here just to tell us that. What is it?'

Blake glances at Ivan then takes a deep breath before looking Nell in the eye. 'No easy way to say this, sorry. But we've run DNA on the dead man, on Wolfgang Burnside.' He pauses, swallows. 'He's a blood relative of yours, Nell.'

Nell stares at him. 'To me? Can't be that close: I'm adopted. As for blood relatives, I'm the only child of an only child.'

'So you are,' says Blake. 'On your mother's side.'

Nell says nothing, the implication throwing her, her stomach somersaulting. They wait her out, anticipating her reaction. 'My biological father?' she whispers at last.

'What do you know of him?' asks Ivan.

'Nothing. Nothing at all. My mother, my biological mother, died within days of giving birth to me. She was all alone. No one knows who my father was. No one has ever known.' She thinks about her mother. 'Amber lived alone the last few years of her life, in almost total solitude. Never left her shack, never left the forest. Ventured out for essential supplies, but that's about it.' She looks around, knowing what she says can't be true even as she says it. Somewhere, somehow, her mother met Nell's father.

The room suddenly feels claustrophobic, oppressive. She rises, walks out of the room, out into the fresh air. She stares off into the distance, towards the rising cliffs. She'd wondered if she would ever find out who her father was, if he was still alive, ever since she learnt two years ago that she was adopted. She'd thought she had convinced herself it didn't really matter. But for it to catch up with her here? In The Valley, hundreds of kilometres from her home town?

She returns inside, speaking from the doorway. 'You say Wolf Burnside was a close relative of mine,' she says to Blake. 'How close?'

'Your brother,' Carole says to Nell. 'Half-brother. Different mother, same father.'

And it's then that she realises. They know who it is. They must. 'Who is he?' she asks. 'Who is Wolfgang Burnside's father?'

It's Carole who answers. 'His name is Simmons Burnside.'

There's no resonance; the name means nothing to Nell.

'A former cop,' says Blake.

chapter four

1990

BY THE TIME WE ARRIVED FROM SALTWOOD AND REACHED THE FOREST AT THE far end of The Valley, we knew it was going to be bad. We'd already passed one ambulance. The Valley itself felt as peaceful as always: cows on the grass and fruit on the trees—but the forest was a different story. Leaving the pastures and running past the sign reading TOOBARRA STATE FOREST, the scene could have been something from the western front, the Valley Road becoming a quagmire churned up by logging trucks. The council couldn't see any point in grading it and the loggers didn't care. It followed the Broken River from The Valley and into the woods. Before the logging intensified, you could get all the way through to the coast, even in a two-wheel drive, provided it wasn't raining heavily. Now, I was glad we were in the big four-wheel drive as we churned through the slurry. Even then, the wheels were sliding this way and that, and I was constantly forced to correct and correct again.

'Sure this is the right way, Simmons?' asked the Sarge. He knew I'd grown up in The Valley; it was probably the reason he'd brought me with him. He wasn't long in Saltwood, a recent transfer from Sydney. His name was Cornell Obswith, but he hated it, especially his first name, so everyone just called him 'Sarge' or 'the Sarge'.

'There is no other way. Won't be much further.'

Another half a kilometre into the forest and we came across a logging truck stopped in the middle of the road, with barely enough room for us to edge up alongside. The truck had a full load on, the logs in the back splattered with orange paint. The driver was leaning against the door, smoking a rollie, the name of the local sawmill on the truck: CATHCARTS. I pulled up and we got out, stepping tentatively through the mud.

'Morning,' said the Sarge.

'They're fuckin' feral,' said the man. 'Fuckers.'

'What happened?' asked the Sarge.

The driver laughed, spat, gestured towards the logs with his thumb. 'They chucked balloons at the logs as I drove them out. Full of paint. Think it will decrease their value.'

'Will it?' I asked.

The logger squinted at me as he dragged on his smoke, like he was noticing me for the first time. 'Nah. 'Course not.'

'Why've you stopped?' asked the Sarge.

'One of the little cunts must have stabbed me tyres with a screwdriver as I passed their barricade. I've got two flats.'

'You can't fix them?' I asked.

The driver squinted at me again, like he was assessing me for impairment, then shook his head. 'Not with a full load on, son. We'll need to offload it, then we can jack it up, get at the tyres.'

'You can't drive it at all?' asked the Sarge.

The driver lifted his nostrils in the suggestion of a sneer before answering. 'Prefer not to.'

'Do us a favour,' said the Sarge. 'Just take it a little further, out into the farmland. Easier to swap your load there. Less likely to get bushwhacked by protesters.' The Sarge was the smartest cop I ever met. Maybe not the straightest, but definitely the smartest: he saw all the angles, all at once.

The driver considered this proposition before relenting. 'Yeah, fair enough.'

'Where is it, this barricade you mentioned?' the Sarge asked the driver.

'Fowlers Gap. Off to the right. Just follow the tracks.'

It wasn't hard to find, a turn-off taking us deeper into forest, the access track turned to sludge by trucks and machinery. We were moving not much faster than walking pace; I was being extra careful not to get bogged or slide off the road. Not far along it, we encountered a couple on foot, walking out, a young man with long hair, a beard and a bloodstained bandage wrapped around his head. One eye was swollen shut where he'd been hit. He was being led by an elderly woman. It reminded me of that photograph from World War II. Kokoda. The digger with the bandage around his head being helped along by a native porter. The woman might have been the young man's mother, might have been his grandmother, her hair a messy grey mop. She was wearing a green raincoat and gumboots, even though there was little chance of rain. Just part of the uniform. I pulled over and we got out again.

'What happened?' asked the Sarge.

'Bastards beat the shit out of him,' said the woman.

'So it's on,' said the Sarge, addressing no one in particular.

'I want to make a formal statement,' said the old biddy. 'I want the bastards arrested.'

The Sarge grimaced. 'All in good time. More important we get in there. See if we can stop it getting out of control.'

We reached the barricade another kilometre or so along the track. When we got out of the car, it was like walking into a sea of animosity, the reaction against the uniform. All cops know the feeling, that brew of resentment, unspoken disdain: shutting down a party that's become too loud, or stopping someone for speeding, or walking into a domestic confrontation. People hate you until they need you. Down there in the forest, the protesters definitely needed us, but they still resented us. They assumed that we were on the loggers' side, on the side of big business, which wasn't true. We were on the side of the law, and the law said the loggers had a licence to fell trees in the state forest. That wasn't our call, it was the decision of the politicians in Sydney, but of course you'd never see them here in the muck and the mire, trying to enforce the peace, dressed in their double-breasted suits and Italian silk ties and morocco leather slip-ons.

'Bit late, Simmo,' a bloke said to me. His red hair was long and matted under a mud-caked beanie and his face was half hidden by a beard. The skin that was visible was smeared with blood. I had to see past the hair and the grime before I recognised him: Mike Norfolk. A childhood friend, same year at school. Back then he'd been clean-cut and a rugby player; now he looked like a red-headed Charles Manson, in need of a bath and a haircut and possibly delousing. I nodded my recognition, nothing more.

'You lot got a leader?' asked the Sarge. 'A spokesman?' He lifted his belt and sucked in his gut, pumping himself up. It didn't help much; he was still only up to my shoulder and fifteen kilos over fighting weight.

'Spokesperson,' said a young feral with dreadlocks, gender indeterminate. 'Over there.'

We walked across to where a middle-aged woman was sitting on a log, bandaging the wrist of a younger woman.

'Where we at?' asked the Sarge. 'Still brawling?'

'Half-time,' said the woman. 'Good chance it will start up again when they bring more logs out.'

He pulled a notebook and a pen from his pocket. 'What happened?'

She looked around her, as if seeking authorisation from the forest to speak on its behalf. 'We knew they were heading in here. Set up a roadblock, same as most days, tried to stop them coming through. Pretty hard to stop a logging truck by holding hands.'

The Sarge said nothing at first, then, 'Go on.'

'A few of us lay down on the track. Peaceful, legal protest. Done it before. Stopped the truck.'

'What then?'

'Stalemate. Like most days. Usually the drivers get out, lift us off. Bit of drama for the publicity.' She indicated a bloke with a scraggly grey beard hovering in the background, nursing an expensive-looking camera. As though on cue, he lifted it to his eye, took a frame of us standing there talking. 'Then a van arrived, not a logging truck—just a van with snow chains on the back to get it through the muck. Knew straight away we were in strife. Half-a-dozen blokes got out. Big guys, not locals; no one I'd seen before. Most had masks on—you know, bandanas over their faces, a couple wearing ski masks. In the past, the drivers simply carried us off the road, them doing their job, us playing our parts. All part of the drama. We've gotten to know most of the blokes. Some of the trucks are local, from the mill, Cathcarts. But you don't hide your face to drive a truck.' She took a deep breath, trying to steady herself, a quiver in her voice. 'These thugs came around the side of the logging truck, just over there.' She pointed, indicating the spot. 'They ran right at us, stretched out on the road; didn't try to negotiate, just started laying in, boots and all. No warning, no chance for us to react, no chance for us to get out of the way. They were wearing gloves, big boots, steel-capped. Kicking us. Punching us.'

'Weapons?' asked the Sarge. He'd been writing all this down. 'Sticks? Batons? Knuckledusters?'

She shook her head. 'Not that I saw, but it's possible. Not that it matters much; they weren't holding back. Some people tried to get up, signalled they were moving, but that didn't save them. They got hit all the same. Some of us ran to help, but we got beaten as well. They were too strong, the six of them in a bunch. Like a pack of rugby forwards. Well trained.' She turned to me, held my gaze. 'Lasted a couple of minutes at most. Maybe less.'

The Sarge regarded the gathering, all eyes on him, the results of the violence written on the faces and the bodies of the protesters, in the grim expressions and the bloodstained clothes. 'And they didn't say anything to you?'

'Nothing memorable. Just swearwords, calling us cunts and vermin and ferals. When they were done, one bloke, maybe the leader, told us to fuck off and not come back.'

'Or it would be worse next time,' said the young woman with the bandaged wrist.

'They said that?' asked the Sarge.

A chorus of affirmation came from the group. They sounded hurt. And indignant.

'Any of your people further in? Anyone follow them?'

'No, not that I know of,' said the spokesperson.

'What are your plans now?' asked the Sarge.

The woman was grim-faced. 'Can't say.'

'Might be an idea to call it a day. Don't confront them on the way out. Live to fight another time.'

But the spokeswoman remained defiant. 'No. You're here now. They can't hit us if the police are here to witness it. To protect us. To uphold the law.'

The Sarge sighed, hitched his belt up again, upholding his gut. 'They have a licence to operate here. If you try to impede them, we'll need to clear the road.'

'Yeah, but you won't be beating us up. Not like that.'

The Sarge looked around, made sure his words carried. 'I don't want to do it, but we will arrest you if we need to. We can't allow this to escalate any further.'

The bloke with the camera and ratty beard stepped forward. He was wearing the uniform: green anorak, jeans, a hand-knitted beanie and expensive hiking boots. He was pointing his camera at us, a Pentax. It had a professional motor-wind, whirring away as the shutter fired.

The Sarge glared at him. 'Put that down for a moment, please, sir.'

The man complied.

'You get any shots of the melee?'

'You bet. Two rolls.'

'You want to hand them over?' asked the Sarge. 'Could prove useful.'

The man refused. 'I'll develop them. Give you prints.'

The Sarge considered this, assessing the situation. I thought he might confiscate the camera. 'Thanks,' he said instead.

I took the man's details. Fox Talbot. No phone number, but he said he was camping with the others at Arnie Cocheef's stone fruit orchard just north of the forest, that I could find him there.

We drove on, leaving the protesters in the forest, sullen, nursing their wounded pride and their injuries. Maybe a kilometre further in we emerged from the trees into a clearing—not a natural clearing, but a wide expanse of clear-felled forest. It went on and on, all the way up a nearby hill, all the way to the horizon, like it had been carpet-bombed. Along its edges, a series of fires were burning, consuming offcuts and debris. It looked ugly, smelt beautiful: eucalyptus and wood smoke. All around us there was the whine of chainsaws, revving and pitching and pausing, the sound of trucks and the grunting of bulldozers, a chorus of industry. Of destruction. Even as I watched, I saw two trees come down within seconds of each other. They weren't mucking about, those blokes.

I parked next to the site office: a couple of demountables flanked by portaloos, not far from where the track emerged from the forest. The demountables bore the name of the logging company: GREENFIELDS. We asked around, found the foreman as he was coming back from supervising operations.

'Officers,' he said, a challenge in his voice.

The Sarge got straight to the point. 'You have every right to be here, but you have no right to assault protesters. If we find the culprits, we will arrest them.'

The foreman took a step forward, chest inflating with aggression, like a front-bar drunk, stabbing his finger towards Obswith's chest. 'We wouldn't need to touch them if you lot were doing your job. You should be here, clearing the road, arresting anyone trying to block our way. Do your job, enforce the law; it's on our side.'

The Sarge was a head shorter, but he didn't step back. Instead he moved forward, so there were mere centimetres between them. 'Don't tell me my job,' he said quietly. 'If there is any more violence, you'll be charged along with your thugs.' He looked the man straight in the eye. 'We'll shut you down.'

'Is that right?' sneered the foreman, but I could see he was surprised by the Sarge's obstinacy.

I almost smiled. The Sarge was short and red-faced and carrying too much weight, but he wasn't one to be intimidated. I could almost see his calculation, whether he should put the foreman in cuffs then and there, throw him in the back of the four-wheel drive, make an example of him. But that calculation was never going to add up; we were here to pour oil on troubled waters, not to set them on fire. There were too many loggers nearby. I didn't doubt they would take us if they had a good enough excuse. I put my hand on my gun, almost to reassure myself I still had it, but both the Sarge and the foreman saw my movement. Luckily the gesture had the right effect, defusing rather than escalating. The foreman took a step back.

'You have a new crew in?' asked the Sarge.

The big man considered his words before answering. 'Yeah, head office sent them. Unhappy with our productivity. Few fellows from interstate.'

'You got a number for head office?'

'In the book,' said the foreman.

The Sarge gave him a stare that could lift paint, then sighed. 'Here's the deal,' he said. 'We'll help keep the peace. Do what we can to get you and your crew in and out without trouble. But you need to keep your men under control. The protesters can protest, that's their right. But you need to ignore them.'

The foreman seemed ready to argue, but maybe something in the Sarge's demeanour discouraged him, and he acquiesced. 'Provided we can go about our business, there'll be no more biffo from us.'

Back at the barricade, the Sarge tried to negotiate a truce, asking the protesters to let the trucks pass. 'Yell all you want. Throw paint at the logs. Make a racket. Just don't lie in the road.'

That afternoon, three protesters lay down: the old girl, Mike and the girl with the bandage on her wrist. The Sarge and I had little choice; we arrested them, pushing them into the back of the car, the bearded bloke in the green anorak taking photos every step of the way, the shutter chattering like a bird.

'Sorry, Mike,' I said to my old schoolfriend.

'Me too, mate,' he said. 'Me too.'

But the protesters didn't fight us, and we didn't need to use force. They got what they wanted, the loggers got what they wanted, the Sarge seemed resigned.

We didn't bother taking the three into custody. We just drove them back to the crossroad in The Valley and let them go, after taking their details. The Sarge told them they could expect to receive a fine, maybe even a summons, but I reckon he was just trying to put the wind up them.

— —

Later that night, after we'd returned to Saltwood, the Sarge pulled me to one side at the end of my shift.

'I need you to go back down, stay in The Valley. Set up an office, try to keep the peace.'

'By myself?'

'You can take Tom.'

'Tom?' Tom was a probationary constable, keen as mustard, but on the job for less than three months. Looked so young I wondered if he'd started shaving yet.

'All I can spare,' said the Sarge. 'Sorry to lay it on you like this. I know it's not perfect, but your local knowledge might help. You know the people there, the lie of the land.'

'You want me to chase up that photographer?'

He sighed. 'Only if you feel you have to. I want you to dampen things down, not inflame them. And don't get hurt.'

chapter five

TOM AND ME, WE SET OURSELVES UP AT THE OLD POLICE STATION. IT HAD BEEN abandoned years before, after the mining stopped and the sawmill downsized, but it was still on the books; maybe it wasn't worth selling. More likely the bureaucrats in Sydney had forgotten it existed. There wasn't much to it. I guess it was originally a house, and that's what it looked like from outside; the POLICE sign had been removed when it was shut. But the caretaker had done a reasonable job, and the power was still connected. We got the phone reconnected and I brought a bar fridge down from my mum's place in Saltwood. The front half of the house had a reception area, and behind that was an office with two desks, a more private office and a toilet. Not even a kitchen. That was in the accommodation part: one bedroom, a lounge, a dining area, plus a bathroom and a kitchen. But there was nothing in there: no carpets, no furniture, no fridge. No bed. Just a few dusty curtains on the windows and a wood stove. Out the back, the original garage had been turned into a holding cell, good for an hour or two but lacking a toilet or water. The Sarge suggested I stay at the pub with the force picking up the bill. That was good enough for me.

Still, I needed supplies, and that's how I met Eliza Tomsett. Or met her again. She was behind the counter at the general store. I barely recognised her. When I was a teenager, living there, she was just a kid and I never paid her any attention. Why would I? But now, here she was, behind the counter. She had a mischievous glint in her eyes and a freckled nose.

'You're still here?' I said, immediately feeling stupid.

But she smiled, not taking offence, an amused challenge in her voice. 'What's that supposed to mean?'

I shrugged, trying to make a joke out of it. 'Most people leave, soon as they get the chance.'

Her smile withered. 'Can't. My dad's crook.' She seemed to search my face, but I didn't know what she was looking for. Sympathy, I guess. 'There's just him and me left,' she added.

'That's tough,' I said.

Later on, when we knew each other better, Eliza told me her mum was dead and her two brothers had shot through to Sydney or wherever and that she never heard from them. I remembered them; one, Darryl, was in my year at school. Dropped out as soon as he turned fifteen, a violent bully whose party trick was popping lids off longnecks with his eye socket. If the other brother was anything like Darryl, she and her dad were better off without them.

— —

After a couple of days in The Valley, life settled into a pattern: sleeping at the pub, working out of the old station, driving down to the forest every morning and afternoon to shepherd the logging trucks past the gauntlet of greenies. Dropping into the general store to chat with Eliza.

This was 1990. There was no internet back then, and mobile phones were a new thing. We had phones installed in some of our patrol cars, although the nearest tower was at Saltwood, and The Valley was a black hole. Still, the old station was in a good position, just along from the crossroad, next to the Memorial Park, on the Valley Road linking the forest to the south with Cathcarts sawmill to the north, so it gave us some presence. We'd park the squad car on the road out the front, making a statement that the law was back in town.

I stayed in a room behind the pub, nothing fancy, with a single bed and a communal bathroom along the corridor. Still, there was hot water and plenty of it. Tom commuted in each day from Saltwood. His mum wasn't well, so that made sense, and he was very punctual, always there on time to see the trucks through. He was a nice young bloke, but overly keen, forever asking questions I didn't know the answers to. I was only twenty-two and had been on the force for three years, but he treated me like I was Sherlock Holmes, so I was glad when he headed back up the escarpment each night and I could get some time by myself.

One problem with setting up in The Valley, the display of visibility, was that I became the magnet for every grievance that people had been storing up for who knew how long, the sort of things that were too minor to bother reporting up to Saltwood but that they were more than happy to unload on me, especially those who knew me from when I was a kid. Mrs Stroud lost her dog three times in four days, and then a couple of farmers wanted me to adjudicate the positioning of a fence line, and an old dear was convinced hippies were growing marijuana up on the escarpment, even if she was unable to say where.

After almost a week without confrontation, I was beginning to think the logging situation had stabilised. The protesters were there when Tom and I escorted the trucks past, but still licking their wounds and subdued, and the loggers weren't stupid; they weren't about to lay into the protesters with the police there as witnesses. I really couldn't see why they'd bothered in the first place; they'd just about finished clear-felling their concession. They'd only be there another month or two before moving further south to the next place, Tarantula Creek, where Toobarra State Forest bordered the Wellington Falls National Park. It was an unsteady peace, but it seemed to be holding. I doffed my hat to the Sarge; I was pretty sure if Tom and I weren't there to supervise, the confrontation would have flared again.

The second week I was down there, I was having dinner in the pub. Back in the old days, it had been called the Commercial, but a new owner was in the process of tizzying it up and had rebranded it as the Bushranger Hotel. That's why I was out the back; the entire upstairs was being renovated. It didn't bother the locals what the official name was, they'd just go on calling it 'the pub', the way they'd always done. It was the only drinking hole for forty kilometres, so no one was going to get it mixed up with somewhere else. I'd just ordered a beer and a steak, and was about to enjoy it, when Arnie Cocheef sat down with me, nursing a beer. I'd known Arnie for years: he wasn't much older than me, mid-twenties, but he'd already inherited the family farm on the Valley Road, not far from where the forest started. Stone fruit. Seemed to be making a go of it.

'This logging blue,' he said. 'Going to last long?'

I found the question strange; he would know as well as me that the concession was almost logged out.

'A couple of months and it'll be all over. Why?'

'Let a couple of protesters set up camp in my bottom paddock, next to the stream. Pretty young sheilas. Now I've got a couple of dozen there.'

I laughed. 'You want me to move them on?'

He appeared to think about it, then he shook his head. 'Nah, let 'em stay. Not a bad mob. Just that I'll need the space if I get some fruit pickers in. Season's not far off.'

'All settled then,' I said. 'But one other thing while you're here. Is that photographer still camping with them?'

'Old bloke? Beard and a fancy camera?'

'That's him?'

'No. Haven't seen him since the biffo in the forest. Reckon he's shot through.'

'Okay. Thanks for that.'

But Arnie wasn't moving. 'Someone's been digging stuff up,' he said all of a sudden. 'Fuck knows why. Protesters reckon it's not them.'

'What sort of stuff? Your trees?'

'Nah, not damaging anything, just digging.'

'Sure it isn't wombats?'

'Nah, shot all the wombats.'

I laughed. 'Don't tell me that. They're a protected species.'

'Fuck. Are they?'

'You know they are.'

'Too late now. You going to arrest me?'

'Not if you don't shoot any more of them.'

'Reckon it might be prospectors. Saw a couple with one of those metal detectors.'

'I'll keep my eye out.'

Arnie wandered off and I went back to eating, concentrating on my food, trying to avoid making eye contact with anyone lest I attract another complainant. Then a hush fell upon the room, conversation stopping, with just the sound of the TV above the bar and a few rattles from the kitchen. I looked up, and there they were, Francis and Teramina Hardcastle, entering the pub arm in arm, like they were on a red carpet, expecting to be photographed. Francis was spruced up, wearing a sports jacket and a cravat, cream moleskins and glistening riding boots. Teramina wore an emerald dress and ankle boots, a pearl necklace, a silver brooch and an antique wristwatch. They paused, as if holding a pose, and then the silence broke. Francis greeted some men he knew, Teramina walked towards the bar, onlookers turned away and restarted their conversations, pretending to be unimpressed in the way country people do.

It was the first time I'd set eyes on Francis Hardcastle, but I recognised her, of course: Teramina Cloverton, owner of Ellensby, heir to the family fortune. She saw me and walked over, holding a glass of wine.

'Simmons. Nice to see you back here. Doing good work I hear.'

'Thanks, Miss Cloverton,' I said, unsure how exactly I should be addressing her.

She seemed amused by my deference. 'You can call me Teramina; you're not a kid anymore. Besides, these days I'm Teramina Hardcastle.'

'I heard you'd married. Congratulations.'

'Six months ago. Yes. That's my husband over there. Francis.'

I knew that. Everyone knew that. 'Not a local then?'

'No. Brisbane. Not long back from the US.'

She sat down then and started talking, like we were old friends, even though she must have been almost twenty years older than me. And all the time, I was studying her face, trying to work her out. She wasn't beautiful, but she was still striking; not pretty, more handsome, with a prominent jaw. It was her eyes that I found disconcerting: they darted about the place, never resting for long, and she blinked incessantly. I told her about the death of my dad, my mum working odd jobs to make ends meet.

'It must be difficult,' she said.

'She's okay.'

She grew serious, leant in close. 'Listen, Simmons, this is just between you and me, right? Confidential.'

I tried to control my smile. She sounded conspiratorial, like she'd been reading too many thrillers. She'd always been a bit like that, a bit dramatic. She reminded me of Kate Bush singing 'Wuthering Heights'. Mum always said she was half-mad, the way only rich people can afford to be. Have enough money and you're eccentric; the rest of us are just barmy. Mum told me once that Teramina had undergone electric shock treatment after her fiancé jilted her, but I never knew if that was right, or if it was just Valley scuttlebutt.

'Of course,' I told her. 'Confidential.'

She leant in closer. 'Francis and I are reopening the Gryphon Mine, up on the escarpment.'

I knew that as well, just like everyone else. I had moved to Saltwood, but I was still connected to The Valley and its grape-vine. People from The Valley were always up in the big town on the highway, at the school or seeing the doctor or dentist, or eating in a proper restaurant or drinking coffee in a proper cafe. Conducting their business and chewing the fat. In those days, if you wanted to do any banking you needed to go to a bank, and the closest was in Saltwood. The Valley still had a footy team and a cricket team and a netball team, but they needed to get up the escarpment to find someone to play against.

And I was familiar with the mine: like every kid who had grown up in The Valley, I'd been up there, swum in the lake, wondered at its imposing steel doors, welded shut. There was one summer when Lucas and Mike and I rode our bikes up most days to go swimming and tell horror stories about what lurked in the depths of the mine. There was an old road, more of a track after decades of ill repair, that ran off the East Road and wound its way up the escarpment beside Watershine Creek. 'I thought the mine was played out,' I said, knowing it was but acting dumb, wanting to hear her version.

'That's what my family told everyone when they shut it down in 1932, in the Depression. But it ran for almost forty years before that. They hauled a fortune out before they closed it.' She gestured around her, taking in the pub. 'It's what built this place. And your police station and the primary school and the Miners' Institute. It realigned and sealed the road up to Saltwood, and a lot more besides.' There was passion in her voice; it surprised me a bit.

'So what's changed?'

'The price of gold—and technology.'

'You're saying there's still gold down there?'

'Of course there is.' Again she peered about the bar. To be honest, I found it a little comical. The idea of keeping anything secret in The Valley, let alone something as newsworthy as a goldmine, struck me as ridiculous. And yet her voice was barely above a whisper. 'Francis is a geologist. He's been back through the company records. He says it wasn't the lack of gold that closed the mine; it was the cost of getting it out. There was a lot of seepage, water leaching into the mine, and it was difficult to pump out; they didn't have mains electricity, were relying on steam-driven pumps. Now there are lightweight diesel pumps, the sort irrigators use. And the reward is so much greater.'

I could see the sense in the project but I was also aware of something else: her enthusiasm, her excitement. Gold. It was tantalising. Infectious. This was a time when interest rates were at record highs, inflation was climbing, the dollar was falling against the American currency, and a lot of people were talking about gold as a hedge. That had even filtered through to me, reading the newspapers in the Saltwood squad room at lunchtime. It explained the fossickers at Arnie's. 'Why are you telling me?'

'The private road up the escarpment,' she said. 'It's on my land.'

'That's yours?'

'My family's. Ever since the mine. The land on top of the escarpment, the road, the old works and Watershine, the manager's house in the valley.'

'The road is still passable?'

'Barely. We'll need to fix it up. Trouble is, we've had trespassers.'

'Kids,' I said. 'Heading up to explore. Or some of the hippies, wanting to swim in the lake.'

She grimaced. 'Francis says the padlocks have been cut off the gate, and people have been up there on dirt bikes.'

'Could be fossickers,' I said. 'Heard you've got gold. Arnie Cocheef just told me he saw some on his land with a metal detector.'

She shook her head. 'Whoever it is, we don't want them there.'

It was then that Francis sauntered over, like he owned the place. He looked me in the eye, shook my hand, unleashed a smile as broad as the Nullarbor. 'Francis Hardcastle,' he beamed. 'And you must be Simmons Burnside. I've heard all about you.'

I couldn't help it; I felt flattered. His handshake possessed neither the exaggerated firmness of a try-hard nor the limpness of the under-confident. 'We are grateful to have you here in The Valley at this time,' he said. His eyes held mine, as steady as his wife's were skittish. He wasn't a big man—was rather slight, in fact—but there was a composure about him, a magnetism that attracted people to him.

'I'm very pleased to meet you,' I managed at last.

He smiled again. His hair was combed back and he had a pencil moustache, but it was his eyes that kept drawing you back. 'Has Teramina confided, then? Informed you of our little project?'

I stumbled for an answer.

'I'm sure she has,' he continued, apparently unperturbed.

'You have a problem with trespassers?' I asked.

'We do. Nothing we can't manage, of course, but I wonder if you might come and take a look for us?'

'It would be a pleasure,' I replied, and told them I'd check out Watershine and the road the next day. Except I never did. Because the next morning it all went ballistic.

—–

It was a beautiful morning, with that stillness you get there on the floor of the valley, the mist lingering, magpies chortling. I was eating breakfast in the pub; back in those days I could demolish a full English breakfast, the whole catastrophe: eggs, bacon, sausages, grilled tomatoes, the lot. You can get away with it when you're young. Or you think you can. All seemed right with the world. Then the Sarge rang the pub, looking for me. I took the call in the deserted bar.

'Seen the papers?' he asked, and I could hear the edge in his voice.

'Not down here.'

'Try the general store. The *Sydney Morning Herald*. Tom is on his way; he has a copy with him. I'll head down myself as soon as I put out a few spot fires up here.' And he hung up, without even telling me what was going on.

I tried to play it calm, finish my breakfast like a gunfighter in a movie, or Francis Drake playing bowls, but it was no good: I needed to know what the Sarge was on about. I left what remained of my breakfast to coagulate on the plate and walked the fifty metres to the general store. It was seven forty in the morning, and when I got to the store there were no *Herald*s left.

But Eliza was there, wide-eyed. 'I kept one for you,' she said, extracting a paper from under the counter. 'Shit's hit the fan.'

She wasn't wrong. LOGGING WAR RAVAGES PARADISE screamed the headline. The story was by some journo called Max Fuller. He became a big shot later on, but back then I'd never heard of him or heard of any journos coming into The Valley. But it wasn't his by-line that captured my attention or even his copy. The front page was dominated by a photo of a man in a balaclava, wielding a baton, caught in the moment of swinging it, a young woman cowering beneath him, one arm in defence, anticipating the blow. The same young woman, the one with the bandaged wrist, whom the Sarge and I had arrested. The image must have been taken that same day, a few hours before the Sarge and I had arrived to restore the peace. It made my stomach churn: maybe because of the violence depicted; maybe because I now knew more was likely to follow.

There were more images inside, a double-page spread. Colour was relatively new in papers back then, and the inside pictures were in black and white. And there, mixed in with the others, were pictures of the Sarge and me, arresting protesters, with nothing to indicate they were taken that afternoon, hours after the violence. The implication was clear: we had aided and abetted the loggers with their brutality. Shit. No wonder the Sarge was busy putting out spot fires.

Suddenly I understood why the demonstrators had been so compliant since my arrival: it wasn't because of our presence, or my efforts, or anything like that. It was because they had known this was coming, because they knew the real battle wasn't on some obscure track in Toobarra State Forest but in the suburbs and lounge rooms of middle Australia. This was perfect fodder for their cause: peaceful protesters being beaten by violent thugs supported by the police. And assessing the photos, it was hard to disagree. Taken by the man with the Pentax, the man who had promised the Sarge and me copies of the photos but had never delivered them. I found a photo credit: Stan Cimati. The bastard had even palmed me off with a false name.

Once my outrage had subsided, I was able to examine the images more closely, and one thing struck me as strange even then. I'd done some basic photography training, mostly learning how to take crime scene photos and mugshots. I recalled some of the lessons about focal lengths, how it changed the perspective, so that a photo taken through a telephoto lens appeared flat, while a picture taken through a normal lens would display a lot more depth. Get even closer, use a wide-angle lens, and there was so much depth it got distorted. I studied the images again with that in mind. The photos were up close and personal. The old bloke with the Pentax had guts, I had to give him that, and he knew what he was doing. Maybe he was a former press photographer, which made sense given the quality of his gear. But it also made me wonder: here were these thugs giving the protesters an absolute lathering, covering their faces so they couldn't be identified, but doing nothing to prevent the violence being documented. I looked again at the pictures. There was no doubt: the photographer had been right in there, in among the melee. So why hadn't the thugs beaten him up as well? Or taken his camera? Smashed it?

I walked as quickly as possible to the police station. My squad car, left outside as part of the show of force, had been vandalised. There was paint all over it. PIGS. CORRUPT. STOOGES. The same orange paint that had been sprayed on the logs that first morning. That made me mad, realising that all the efforts of Tom and myself had come to nought. I wanted to scrub it off there and then, but it could wait. I went inside and got on the phone straight away, called the Sarge, told him I'd seen the papers.

'What's it like down there?' he asked.

'Peaceful enough in The Valley. When Tom gets here, we'll head into the forest, get to the protest line.'

'All right. I'll be there as soon as I can.'

'Sarge, the photos. I've got a bad feeling.' I explained about the photographer acting with impunity.

'What are you suggesting?'

'That we've been played like a fiddle.'

chapter six

I TOOK MY TIME GETTING BACK DOWN INTO THE FOREST. I WASHED THE PAINT off the squad car, for a start. It wasn't as bad as I'd first thought: it was some sort of water-based acrylic, not the enamel paint I'd feared. It took a little elbow grease, but there was no lasting damage to the vehicle. Tom came steaming in ready to go, but I told him to calm down. I was in no rush to protect the protesters, not after what they'd done to us. If they wanted to lie on the road, that was up to them; they could suffer the consequences. But I suspected that there would be no violence that morning: the environmentalists had achieved what they wanted, while the loggers would be trying to work out what to do next and were unlikely to make things worse by resorting to violence.

Sure enough, when we got into the forest, there were only three or four die-hards on the protest line. The rest must have been back at their camp, enjoying their victory, cutting the photos from the *Sydney Morning Herald* for their scrapbooks. The old biddy was there, still fired up, still committed. 'You saw what they did, but you didn't arrest them,' she said.

'We might have if we'd received the photographs we were promised,' I retorted.

'You've got them now.'

I didn't bother replying. Tom drove on.

The mood at the logging camp was subdued. While Tom had a look around, asking after the thugs, I entered the foreman's office. He had the newspaper spread out on his desk.

'Never knew it was this bad,' he said.

'That so,' I said. I was trying to play it cool, emulating the Sarge.

'I've asked about. Don't know who they were, these blokes.'

'That's hard to believe.' I was studying the foreman's face, but I couldn't detect any subterfuge.

'I'm not saying they were interlopers. They had access. Credentials. Said head office had sent them.' He looked at the paper, then up again.

'You need to tell me where they are,' I said.

'I don't know. Seriously.' He really did appear bewildered. Either he genuinely didn't know or he was wasting his time in the forest: he should have been on stage. 'I'm as much in the dark as you are. If head office authorised violence they didn't tell me.' He held his arms wide in the universal expression of inno-cence. 'It doesn't make sense. We're almost done here. Another six weeks or so and we'll be moving down to Tarantula Creek. Eight months there, and we'll be gone from the valley for good. Why would we incite this?' He gestured towards the newspaper. 'What's in it for us?'

'What are you saying?'

'Think about it. Who wins here? Us or the greenies? Not us, that's for sure.'

'You're suggesting this was a set-up?'

'I am.'

'Any evidence?' I was thinking of the photographer, of course, this Stan Cimati, but I wasn't about to share my suspicions.

He was silent then, and I didn't think there was much further I could take it. But it didn't mean I dismissed what he was saying.

Driving back out, I got Tom to stop at the protest line.

The old biddy regarded me with contempt. 'Just you? No arrests? Thought so.'

'The blokes who beat you up aren't there,' I told her. 'Don't know where we could find them, do you?'

'Me? How the hell would I know that?' She appeared puzzled. And irritated.

'What about the photographer. What's his name? The bloke with his shots all over the *Sydney Morning Herald*?'

'George?'

'George? Is that what he told you?'

'That's his name, as far as I know. Why do you want to talk to him?'

'Chain of evidence. Need a statement from him verifying when the photographs were taken, that sort of thing.'

'Long gone. Not one of us anyway.'

That threw me. 'What do you mean, not one of you?'

'Not a protester. Came here to take some pictures. Said he was a freelancer.'

'Thanks,' I said. That explained his fancy gear.

Back in the car, I checked the paper. All those photographs, potential prize winners, taken by Stan Cimati. A freelancer. Who'd told the protesters his name was George, and had told me his name was Fox Talbot.

——

It was mid-morning by the time we got back to the old station. I figured it was late enough in the day for a journalist to be out of bed and at work, so I rang the *Sydney Morning Herald* and asked the switch to put me through to Max Fuller. I heard the beeps on the line—thank goodness the phone was set up to allow long-distance calls.

The bored-sounding switchboard operator connected me.

'Max Fuller.' The voice sounded confident, businesslike.

'Max, this is Constable Simmons Burnside calling from The Valley.' I could hear him suck in a breath; it sounded a bit laboured. I put on the voice of authority, deeper than my natural voice. 'This entire conversation is off the record, got it?'

'I guess,' he responded, sounding curious.

'Here's the deal. I'm after information. If you can help me, then maybe I can help you.'

'Information? What do you want?' I could tell he was interested.

'First things first. This morning's story. You had extensive quotes from the environmentalists. Nothing from the logging company. Nothing from the police. Why not?'

'You're in The Valley?' he asked.

'I told you that.'

'You've only got the first edition then. We had quotes from the logging company and from the police in all the major editions.'

'Right. What did Greenfields have to say?'

'They claimed they had no pre-knowledge of the incident, whatever that means, and will conduct their own inquiry. They apologise if anyone was injured, but they're not ready to accept responsibility.'

'And the police?'

'You don't know?'

'I don't know.'

'I spoke to Public Affairs. They put me on to Sergeant Obswith at Saltwood. He denied police were present at the time of the confrontation. Said that the photos containing police were taken later in the day.'

'That's true. I was there. So was he. You corrected that in the later editions?'

'I quoted Sergeant Obswith saying that, yes.'

'And did you put that to the photographer?'

Suddenly there was nothing on the line, just static.

'You still there, Max?'

'Yeah, I'm here.' He no longer sounded so sure of himself. 'It was late. I couldn't get on to him.'

'And this morning?'

'No. I left a message. Probably on his way back to The Valley.'

'I seriously doubt that.'

More static. 'Why do you say that?' His voice had dropped almost to a whisper, as if he suspected what I was about to say.

'You pay him?'

'No. He's an environmentalist. Committed.'

'Not according to the protesters. They say he's not one of them. Claim he was a freelancer, eager to record their struggle.' I let that sink in. 'You ever know a freelancer who doesn't want to get paid?'

This time the static lasted even longer. 'They're trying to protect him.'

'Don't think so. I want to prosecute the thugs who beat them up. The photographer can testify to it. A key witness. Potentially *the* key witness, able to help identify the aggressors. It's not in their interest to hide him.'

'What are you saying?'

'What name did he give you? Stan Cimati?'

'That's right.'

'Funny. He told me his name was Fox Talbot. Lied to a police officer. You know who Fox Talbot was?'

'Sorry, I don't follow.' He sounded confused.

'I looked it up in an encyclopedia. Fox Talbot was the father of photography, back in the nineteenth century.'

Silence. Just static and background noise.

'And Stan Cimati? It's an anagram. For Instamatic. You know, Kodak's low-cost camera.' I let the static run its course. 'You've been had, Max. Played. Whatever his real name is, he'll be having a good laugh right now. At your expense.'

'Bullshit.' But I could hear it was empty bravado.

'Give me his phone number. The one you were trying him on.'

'I'm not sure I can do that.'

I put on my sympathetic voice, the one I reserved for informants and other low-life. 'I get it, Max. You want to protect your source. But this bloke is no source; he's a bullshit artist. He's taken you for a ride. Played you for a fool, splashed across the front page of your paper. You owe him nothing, let alone loyalty.'

No comment. I knew he was still on the line, though; I could hear a telex and a typewriter and someone shouting, a radio playing.

'You give me his number, Max, and for now, this remains between you and me.'

'This could destroy me, if it gets out.' I could hear panic in his voice. And honesty.

'Give me the number. And if it does get out, it won't be from me.'

He gave me the number.

I rang it. No answer. I rang it again. Still no one answered, but at least it was still connected. I called through to police head-quarters in Sydney and asked for a reverse phone number search. They promised to call me back.

But when they did, I wasn't just disappointed—I was dumbfounded.

They told me that I was not authorised to know the identity of the number.

And then I had a call from the Sarge. 'Special Branch,' he said.

chapter seven

2024

SIMMONS BURNSIDE.

That's the name they give Nell. A former cop: grew up here in The Valley, was working out of the Saltwood station at the time of her birth twenty-nine years ago. Wolfgang Burnside's father. Her father. And still alive, semi-retired, living down the coast near Batemans Bay. Not much more than an hour's drive.

Through the window of the Miners' Institute, she can see Ivan on the phone outside, pacing across the grass, talking, listening, gesturing. She's not sure who he's talking with, not sure she cares. Simmons Burnside. She resists the urge to google him. It feels tawdry: googling your own father, like searching for a bargain on eBay. And Wolfgang Burnside. A brother, four years older than her. Alive, all these years, up until two nights ago. And now gone, gone forever, so that she can never talk to him, never see the light in his eyes, never know him. What karmic conspiracy is this? Drawn together because she is investigating his death. His murder.

Ivan enters, holds his phone out. 'Plodder,' is all he says. He places the phone on the table. 'Okay, boss, you're on speaker. Nell is with me.'

'Nell, how you holding up?' asks the head of Homicide.

She shakes her head, even though he can't see her. 'Not so good. It's the surprise; just so unexpected.'

There's a pause. With Plodder, there are always pauses. 'What would you like to do next?'

'How do you mean?'

'Take leave?'

'No.' She says it immediately, without thinking. 'No,' she repeats.

'You sure about that?'

'Yes.'

Another pause from Plodder. And in that pause she starts to reflect on her situation. This isn't just about her and how she feels; she's part of an investigation into the murder of her own brother. Of course the hierarchy will want her to recuse herself.

'I want you to stick with it,' says Plodder.

'You would?' she asks, surprised, looking to Ivan, her eyebrows raised.

'I do. I've spoken to Ivan. He's very supportive, as you know.'

Ivan nods.

'Thank you, sir,' she says. 'But is that wise? Under the circumstances?'

'Probably not,' says their boss. 'But the situation is somewhat delicate.'

Nell doesn't answer. Ivan shrugs, his face suggesting he's as much in the dark as she is.

'Okay, I'm telling you this in confidence. I've had representations. People insisting we need you there. People who don't want the investigation handled by the locals.'

'The detective from Queanbeyan seemed pretty competent,' Nell volunteers.

'No doubt,' says Plodder.

'Why?' asks Ivan. 'What's going on?'

'Wish I knew,' says Plodder.

'Where are they coming from? These representations?' says Ivan. And then, 'We should know—forewarned is forearmed,' he says, then winces, as if he might have overstepped the mark.

'The commissioner?' asks Nell.

Plodder's laugh comes quickly, then stops just as abruptly. 'No. I think we might leave the commissioner out of this one.' Another pause, as though their boss is carefully calibrating his words. 'Actually, it's your old mate from Professional Standards: Nathan Phelan.'

'Feral Phelan?' Ivan says, incredulous. 'He asked for us?'

Nell has the same reaction. Phelan is part of the force's internal investigation unit tasked with rooting out corruption and misconduct in the force. At various times he's threatened to end both their careers. 'Why would he do that?' she asks.

'Trusts you, would be my guess,' says Plodder.

'So he suspects the local detectives are what, exactly?' asks Ivan.

'Didn't say. You know Professional Standards. Power unto themselves. Don't share anything they don't have to.'

'Okay. He doesn't trust the locals. Fair enough. But why us? You could send a team from Sydney. Or leave me here and sub

Nell out. Send Kevin.' Ivan and Nell have left their colleague Kevin Nackangara minding the shop in Dubbo.

'No can do,' says Plodder. 'Kevin is on his way to a triple homicide up near Bourke, and all the teams here are working multiple cases. The gangland wars have kicked up a gear. There's dead coke dealers from Parramatta to Penrith. And anyway, Phelan was worried the local detectives would think it suspicious if we replaced you now and a Sydney team came in over the top.'

'But we're not investigating the local dicks,' says Ivan.

Plodder sighs. 'Look, I know it's not ideal, but I need you to stay on the case. Tread carefully.' Another Plodder pause. 'Nell, you will want to meet your biological father, I understand that. Explore your past. Of course, you have my blessing. Our blessing. But it can't contaminate the investigation.'

'Sir?'

'You must respect Ivan's judgement when it comes to investigating the murder of your half-brother. He decides when to include you; when to exclude you.'

'I see.' But if she's honest with herself, she doesn't see at all. Her relationship with Wolfgang might not impede the investigation, but it could jeopardise a prosecution. A canny defence lawyer could paint her as lacking objectivity. But she doesn't have to tell Plodder Packenham that. 'Thank you, sir,' she offers instead.

'Just be guided by Ivan,' he warns her again. 'Don't be going off by yourself.'

'Like a loose cannon, you mean?'

A chuckle on the line. 'Your words, detective. Your words.'

They finish the call and for a while the two detectives say nothing, the weight of the conversation staying with them.

'What have we got ourselves into?' Nell asks at last.

'All the hallmarks of a shitshow.'

'And Feral Phelan?'

'Seems he's drawing a bead on the local cops.'

'Lucky them. Should we call him? Find out what he knows?'

Ivan shakes his head. 'If he's not telling Plodder, he won't be telling us.'

'So we just suck it up,' she says. And then laughs. 'I guess I should be grateful. I know my father's name.'

'How you feeling about that?'

'Honestly? I don't know.'

'I need to speak to Wolfgang's parents anyway. You want to come? Or I can handle it by myself.' Ivan's concern is evident in his expression, in the tone of his voice.

'No. I'll come.' She stands, reaches for her jacket. 'The bloke in the general store said Wolfgang's mother lives up the top of the valley, near the pass. Eliza.'

Ivan looks at his watch. 'No. Let's get down to the coast. Interview Simmons Burnside. We should be able to make it before dark.'

'Okay,' says Nell, but she doesn't feel okay at all.

— —

Simmons Burnside lives in a neat weatherboard home three streets back from the ocean in Surf Beach, a suburban extension south of Batemans Bay. The grey-green lawn, some sort of hardy salt-resistant strain, is closely mown, the edges sharp. There is a double carport with a four-wheel drive in one side, a boat on a trailer in the other.

Simmons himself is a fit-looking man in his mid-fifties, his hair an echo of his lawn: strong and grey and closely clipped. He opens the door, welcomes them in. He is trying to sound measured, but Nell can hear the fault lines in his voice and see the redness in his eyes. The lounge is small, dominated by a huge television and a large feature window. The window provides a view out over neighbouring rooftops to the distant sea, the last light of the day catching the waves. The cricket is on the television, the sound muted. Instead there is folk music filling the space. A collie dog is all eagerness and curiosity, tongue out and tail wagging, a cheerful exception to the pall hanging unseen over the room. The place is spotless, but Nell knows Ivan has rung ahead, giving Simmons the opportunity to tidy it up. Or maybe he's been hard at it, something to occupy him while he grieves, some subliminal attempt to make things right; she's seen it before, more often with women than men. On a sideboard a series of family photos, many featuring his son: Wolfgang as a child, at school, graduating from university. His first wedding. His second. The grandchildren.

Simmons sees her interest. 'The grandkids love it down here. The beach.'

She and Ivan sit on the lounge, Nell biting her lip, studying the man's face while Ivan talks, then looking away again, then looking back: it's like an itch that demands to be scratched, searching for signs in his face, in his movements and gestures, searching for signs of herself.

On the coffee table is a pitcher of iced tea, prepared just for them.

'It's very kind of you to make the effort,' says Simmons, before Ivan can formalise the interview. 'I'm not sure there's a lot I can tell you that wouldn't have been just as easy on the phone.'

Ivan sets his phone recording, goes through the formalities: place, time, those present.

'When was the last time you were in The Valley?' asks Ivan.

'Last month. Visiting Wolfie. Last time I saw him. I try to get up there every few months. I was always welcome to stay with him and Tyffany. And at Ellensby with Janine and the kids.'

'You can verify your whereabouts Tuesday night?'

Simmons blinks, the former cop, knowing the ins and outs of police procedure. 'I was here. Alone. I'm always alone. But I had my phone, I was on the internet from the study. You're welcome to check with the service provider.'

'Thank you,' says Ivan. 'You understand these questions are just routine.'

'I was never a detective, but I know the score,' says Simmons.

Ivan continues the interview while Nell watches. The same questions as always: did Wolfgang have any enemies, had he expressed concerns over his safety, did he have any anxieties about his business, how was his mood. Everything Simmons says reinforces the picture she already has of the victim: a go-getter, an optimist, generous, single-minded. But she also hears something else in the answers: Simmons Burnside's love for his son.

'Do you know if he had any run-ins with the local police?'

'No. Why do you ask that?'

'No reason.'

'Right,' says Simmons, beginning to frown.

'What about him mounting a challenge to Hannibal Earl? Backing an independent candidate?'

The frown deepens. Simmons takes his time before responding. 'I wasn't aware of that.'

Ivan hesitates. It occurs to Nell that this isn't easy for him either; it makes her appreciate him all the more. Ivan stops the recording. 'That's enough for our investigation, but there is also a personal matter.'

'What is it?' asks Simmons, appearing perplexed.

Nell swallows, not sure how to broach the matter of her paternity. It's better to be direct, she decides. 'There is a close relationship between the DNA of your son Wolfgang and my own,' she says, trying to sound matter-of-fact. 'The indications are that you are my father.'

Simmons stares, blinks, clearly shocked. His mouth opens; he tries to talk, then shuts it again. He stands, turning his back to them, gazes out the window towards the far-off ocean. The sun is setting and the sea is now in shadow, but above it the clouds are glowing orange and pink and white. Simmons doesn't move, not for long moments. Then he looks at Nell, brow furrowed, studying her. She knows he's now doing what she's been doing ever since she first entered his home: seeking a likeness, seeking an echo.

'Who is your mother?' he asks, voice wavering.

'Her name was Amber Jones. I've recently turned twenty-nine.'

Simmons continues to scrutinise her, but ever so slowly begins shaking his head. 'Amber?' He looks across at the sideboard, giving the impression he's checking if her image doesn't reside there with other members of his family. 'Amber. No. I don't think so.'

'You remember her?' asks Nell. 'My mother?'

'Yes. Of course. She was very pretty, very sweet. Very brave. Strangely naive, strangely wise.' He draws a shuddering breath. 'She came to The Valley one summer. I was a cop, working from Saltwood but living in The Valley.' He turns towards the window, the colours in the clouds deepening, and Nell wonders what he might see there, what memories. He turns back. 'I'm sorry, Constable Buchanan—Nell—but I can't be your father. I knew your mother, but not like that.' And then, to emphasise the point: 'I never slept with her.'

Nell doesn't know what to say, can't meet his eye.

Ivan interjects. 'I know this must be difficult for you, but would you be willing to take a paternity test?' he asks Simmons. 'DNA? Would clear it up once and for all.'

But Simmons is just staring into space. And then his face reddens with anger. 'That hypocritical bitch.' He spits the words out, mouth twisted, like he's swallowed something distasteful.

'What?' says Nell, thinking he's referring to Amber.

'Eliza. That fucking bitch.' And then he collapses, eyes flooding, frame shuddering. 'I loved that boy,' he wails. 'I loved him. He'll always be my son.'

Before they leave, Ivan again suggests the DNA test, but Simmons declines, says he's too upset, and they don't insist. He's still weeping as Ivan and Nell find their own way out.

chapter eight

FOR THE FIRST HALF-HOUR OF THE RETURN TRIP FROM SIMMONS BURNSIDE'S home Nell remains tight-lipped, Ivan giving her space. It's not until they're halfway up the coastal range that she feels her equilibrium returning. Only then does she break the silence, commenting on the night, the possibility of rain, the need to concentrate on the murder investigation.

It's left to Ivan to broach the question of Nell's paternity. 'Do you believe him?' he asks.

'I believe Blake,' she replies. 'If he says Simmons Burnside is my father, then he must be.'

Ivan says nothing, negotiating the hairpins and switchback corners of the Clyde Mountain. As they top the range and descend the other side, the night is fully dark. They pass through the foothills, rainforest turning to gum forests and then to open fields. Ivan drives past the turn-off to The Valley, heading towards Saltwood.

'Where are we going?' Nell asks.

'Thought we could get some takeaway. There's a pizza place.'

'We could eat at the Bushranger,' says Nell.

'We could,' says Ivan. 'But I want to call in on Eliza Burnside this evening. See what she has to say. Her house is at the bottom of the pass. On the way.' He gives it a few seconds before continuing. 'I need your mind on the case. Let's see what she has to say, then hopefully we can move on.'

And Nell finds herself agreeing. 'Yes. We should.'

While Ivan is getting the pizza, Nell takes the opportunity to ring her grandmother, Amber's mum, hoping she might be in range. The phone rings, a promising sign, but then goes through to voicemail. Nell tries to keep her voice upbeat without really understanding why. 'Hi. It's Nell. Can you call when you get a moment? Nothing urgent. Love you.'

She stares out the car window. *Nothing urgent.* A man emerges from the restaurant, carrying a pile of flat pizza boxes and two large bottles of soft drink. As she watches, he drops his phone. He swears loudly at the world, venting at the gods, before placing the boxes on the pavement, retrieving his handset and checking it for damage, swearing all the time in a steady stream. She can't help but stare at him: such anger generated by such an insignificant incident.

Her phone rings. Her grandmother. Nell attempts to be cheerful, but it doesn't work.

'Nell, what is it? You sound worried.'

Her voice cracks as she explains that she has found her biological father. She finds herself fighting back tears.

'Your father? Who is it?'

'His name is Simmons Burnside. A former policeman.'

There's a pause, full of questions.

'There's more. I had a half-brother. Same father.'

'Had?'

'He's dead.' Another pause, a new wave of emotion welling. Nell struggles through it. 'Amber left the forest. She came up to where I am now. The Valley, in New South Wales. I'm pretty sure it's where she met my father. Where I was conceived.'

'My God,' says her grandmother, and now Nell can hear the distress, the reciprocal threat of tears. 'I never knew she'd been away.' And then: 'I would like to meet him. Your father. He could tell us so much.'

— —

The darkness deepens as they descend into The Valley, the rainforest of the pass blocking the sky. To Nell, the night seems more profound at the bottom, even when they leave the trees behind. Wolfgang's mother lives in a small house snuggled in behind the corridor of poplars that leads from the pass. Caught in the sweep of their headlights, the house appears almost suburban, a new brick bungalow, part of a subdivision, one-hectare blocks, a row of solar-powered lights illuminating her driveway. The oversized lawn is well maintained; Eliza Burnside has either a ride-on mower or a contract gardener but such details barely register with Nell. Should she really be doing this? Without a night's sleep to process it all? She grits her teeth, decides she wants to see it through, that Ivan is right, best to get it out of the way.

He rings the bell.

A woman answers the door. She's not as old as Nell might have imagined, mid to late fifties, but the creases engraved into her face haven't been left by smiling, and there is flint in her eyes. She wears a pinafore; she has the sausage fingers of arthritis.

Ivan introduces himself, then Nell, offering their condolences before explaining that they're investigating the death of her son. He asks whether they might come inside, talk with her.

'Yeah. 'Course. Anything to help.'

She holds the door while they enter, leads them into a lounge room. The furniture appears both new and out of date, as if she has finally been able to afford the setting she desired thirty years ago. She offers tea and biscuits.

'That's okay, Mrs Burnside,' says Ivan. 'We won't be long.'

'Not Burnside,' says the woman. 'I've reverted to my maiden name. Tomsett. Since that bastard left me.' She says it without apparent spite, giving the impression she's repeated the words so often they've been leached of venom.

'Of course. Sorry, Ms Tomsett.' Ivan places his phone on the table, seeks permission to record the interview.

Eliza Tomsett acquiesces and Ivan begins the interview. But Nell finds her mind wandering. Did she know Nell existed? Did she know Amber? Like her grandmother, Nell had believed her mother had never left the forest; they'd assumed that Nell's biological father had found her there. Now, she's trying to reimagine Amber, but doesn't know where to start. She keeps trying to pull her attention back, tries to concentrate on the interview, but finds it difficult. Eliza doesn't make it easy: her answers at first are curt and defensive. It's only when she starts talking about her son that she becomes more fulsome, recounting how wonderful Wolfie was, generous and supportive, how he'd subsidised the store, making sure she had everything she needed. How he'd given her this place, made sure to keep it aside for her, one of the best in his subdivision, how he paid for the house and a car.

When Ivan asks about the night of her son's murder, Eliza again becomes subdued, confides she's been incapable of sleep since learning of his death, unable to comprehend how she had slept so well on Tuesday night when her only son had been lying dead in the Broken River. She thought she should have sensed something, had believed that mothers always could, but she hadn't, nothing at all.

'I haven't cried yet,' Eliza says, forehead creased, eyes still hard.

'That's not unusual,' says Nell, the first time she's spoken. 'Give yourself time.'

'You have support?' asks Ivan. 'Family?'

'My cousin is coming. She's arriving tomorrow.'

Ivan casts Nell a quick look, concern on his face. *Here it comes.* He lowers his voice. 'I'm sorry, Ms Tomsett, there is something else.'

The woman frowns, looking from Ivan to Nell and back again, studying their faces.

Nell fills the silence. 'We've run DNA testing on your son's body.' She swallows. The woman has narrowed her eyes, is peering directly at her. 'They show that he was my half-brother. Same father.'

For a moment Eliza Tomsett says nothing, does nothing, her face could be carved from stone, unmoving, unflinching, eyes locked on Nell. But then her expression begins to curdle, her mouth turning down in disgust, her forehead creasing into familiar lines. 'How old are you?' she asks.

'I just turned twenty-nine. In March.'

Eliza sneers in derision, then stares off into the distance, before returning her gaze to Ivan, not to Nell. 'That sleazy bastard. Always playing the martyr, always holier than thou. Should have known. Couldn't wait to move on.'

'So you were still married?' Nell asks.

'We were,' says Eliza, contempt evident. 'But separated. Now I know why.' She shakes her head, communicating her disbelief, then gives a bitter little snort. 'Glad I went ahead with it. The divorce.'

Nell feels shaken by the reaction, not sure what to say, what to do. What to think. Her voice quavers and breaks, but she presses on, the need to know too strong. 'My mother's name was Amber Jones.'

The flint eyes narrow again, but now instead of peering into Nell's own they're ranging over her face, then her torso and breasts, before returning to her face, studying Nell like an object, not a person. 'Amber. Yeah, I remember her. You don't look that much like her, but I can see it now I know. She was here, in The Valley. Should have realised he'd be chasing her, pretty young thing that she was.' She gazes around as if she wants to spit, to expel her disgust. 'Simmons. That fucker.'

Ivan appears uncomfortable, but Nell isn't prepared to stop. 'She was here? You're sure?'

'Yeah. Not for very long. She lived in Teramina Cloverton's place—Teramina Hardcastle's. Not the big house, not Ellensby, but the old mine manager's house out on the East Road. Spent a few months here. Late summer. Autumn.' She examines Nell. 'Never knew she had a kid, though. Maybe that's why she left.' And then, for a moment, that rocky visage softens. 'I'm sorry, love. She's dead then? Amber?'

'Yes. A long time ago.' Their eyes meet, the unity of loss. 'Thank you,' Nell says. 'I am so sorry to upset you at this time.'

The woman's nostrils curl, the connection breaking. 'Nah, love. You've done me a favour. Confirmed what I always suspected.'

— —

That night, the spaciousness of Nell's room helps no more than the softness of the bed or the hot water and bath salts in the claw-foot tub. She can't sleep. She has that in common at least with Eliza Tomsett.

It's not until the first light is seeping through the curtains that exhaustion overpowers her and she finally sleeps.

chapter nine

1990

LATE THE SAME DAY AS MAX FULLER'S FRONT-PAGE HATCHET JOB, THE STATE government caved and declared a moratorium on all logging in the forests in the southern part of The Valley. The graphic coverage in the *Sydney Morning Herald* was whipping up a media storm, dominating talkback radio, and the government had wanted to act quickly and decisively, or at least be seen to be acting decisively, so that its reaction, and not the photos, dominated the evening news. At least that's the way the Sarge explained it to me.

He reckoned that was why the premier held his press conference at five pm, so there was enough time to get on the six o'clock news, but not enough time for the Opposition or anyone else to get their own heads on the television.

The Sarge had come down to The Valley to watch the evening news with me and assess the situation. We sat in the middle of the Bushranger, among commiserating loggers and surly sawmillers. We wore our uniforms, just to make it perfectly clear we were still on the clock and wouldn't be putting up with any shit—and, I guess, to show we had nothing to be ashamed of. Fortunately, the only greenies we saw were in the bottle shop and not the front bar, reducing the possibility of a confrontation. They were having a big celebration at Arnie Cocheef's farm, with a bonfire and keg of beer and a vegetarian feast, so they didn't linger at the pub. But the loggers claimed they had nowhere else to go, and the sawmill workers said this was their fucking valley and their fucking pub and they were entitled to drink themselves to oblivion anytime they fucking liked and anyone who didn't approve could go fuck themselves. Or words to that effect. I reminded myself to buy Arnie a beer next time I saw him. He'd cop a lot of shit for helping the greenies, but right now he was doing us all a favour by keeping them out of the pub and out of harm's way.

'Logical decision for the government,' the Sarge explained. 'Makes 'em appear in control.'

I listened intently. I was still trying to work through what had happened, still smarting that Special Branch had somehow orchestrated the made-for-media confrontation. 'What do they do?' I asked. 'Special Branch, I mean.'

The Sarge chuckled. 'Whatever the government wants them to do.'

'Really? But down here?'

'Don't trouble yourself,' he said. 'It's above our pay grade.'

'But there's only six weeks' worth of work left there. They were almost done anyway.'

'On that concession, yes. But this moratorium covers the entire valley, including Tarantula Creek.'

I looked at the big blokes at the bar, still in their high-vis. 'So no future, then?'

The Sarge seemed amused by the way things were playing out. 'Nah, they'll be right. You watch, the loggers will get another concession somewhere else. It's a big state; there's plenty of Crown land.' He took a chug of his beer. 'The pollies are hooked on the revenue.'

I was distracted for a moment. I saw Eliza at the bar, standing next to a bloke I didn't recognise, helping him carry the drinks he was ordering. She glanced across, caught me looking at her and waved, and I waved back. The Sarge indulged me with a smile. The man missed nothing. Then she was gone, out the back into the beer garden with her drinks and her friends.

'You don't want me to poke around, ask a few questions?' I suggested.

'Fuck no. Let sleeping dogs lie. But good work figuring out something was wrong. Shows initiative.' He finished his beer. 'Your shout.'

When I got back from the bar with a couple more schooners, I continued the conversation. 'So with this moratorium in place, you want me back in Saltwood?'

'Thought you liked it down here.'

'I like the travel allowance,' I said.

He laughed at that. 'Things a bit tight then?'

'Not so bad. But you know how it is.'

The Sarge nodded. 'In that case, I reckon you should stay a little longer. Forget about Special Branch and all that malarkey; they'll be long gone. But see if you can discover what the protesters are planning next. Find out if they're going to pack up and move to the next big thing, or if they intend staying around.'

'Why would they stay?'

'It's only a moratorium. The government will want to appease the logging industry, keep the royalties coming in. The protesters know that. They may want to stay, keep the issue in the public eye.'

I didn't argue. The Sarge had served for a long time in Sydney before transferring to Saltwood; he knew all about the push and pull of politics and money. That's one reason I liked it in The Valley; it seemed a world away from all that. I glanced across to where Eliza had been standing, but her place had been taken by a couple of rough nuts. Giles Duneven was there, the manager from the sawmill, buying his workers a round of drinks. Politics of another kind, I thought. I wondered who Eliza was with, the big bloke shouting drinks.

'Listen,' said the Sarge, as if reading my thoughts, 'if times are tough there might be a bit of part-time work here. A few extra dollars in your pocket.'

That caught my interest. Having a second job was commonplace in the force; half the cops in Sydney drove cabs on their days off. The rules were simple: the work couldn't clash with or compromise police work, and you needed the authorisation of your supervisor. Given the Sarge was my supervisor, it sounded promising.

'I'm all ears,' I said.

'Very good.' He looked around the bar, taking his time. 'This valley, you care about it, don't you—the people who live here?'

'Sure.' I'd grown up there, after all.

'Well, it's heading into hard times. The whole country is. We're already in the deepest recession since the war, and I reckon it's going to get worse before it gets better. Those fuckers in Canberra don't know their arse from their elbow. Paul fucking Keating and his Italian suits.' He sucked on his beer, as if to emphasise his point. 'The big logging companies, they'll move on. They're exporting to Japan, so with the dollar tanking, their profits will only go up.'

I pretended I understood. I didn't know much about economics, but the Sarge seemed to be all over it.

'Isn't that a good thing?' I asked.

'It is for the loggers. And for the governments; the state collects royalties, the feds claw a bit back from their trade deficit. But the loggers will abandon The Valley, move further south. The tip is Coolangubra or Tantawangalo, down near Bega, closer to the chip mill at Eden. Probably spell the end for the sawmill here.'

This shocked me, even though as he said the words, the truth of it was self-evident: no logging, no mill. Cathcarts had been in the valley for generations, a pillar of local employment. I looked across to where Giles Duneven was standing drinks for his blokes; I understood why now. And why those blokes seemed resigned, compared to the aggression of the loggers: because they could feel it slipping away. I'd gone to school with some of them, with the kids of some of the older workers.

'You reckon it's inevitable?' I asked the Sarge.

'Makes sense, doesn't it? The big loggers are only interested in volume, getting the timber to Eden and off to Japan. It was only politics that kept the mill operating here. Another political compromise. Old Lenny Johnson cut a deal when he was still the local state member, and Terrence Earl has kept it going since taking over the seat: the mill gets first dibs whenever logging is approved and can take out any rare or exotic timber, leaving the blue gums and the rest of the eucalypts for the chippers. Worked well until now; the mill gets the high-value logs suitable for furniture making and joinery and whatnot, and the loggers have been happy to be rid of them: reckon they're little better than weeds.'

'Can't the mill bring in trees from further afield?' I asked. 'I mean, if individual logs are worth that much?'

The Sarge shook his head, sure of himself. 'Long way to bring them. They'd need political support. Terrence Earl is a good local member, I'm sure he'll do what he can, but he can't work miracles. The mill needs to be viable and it's hard to see that if it stays here.'

I sat on my beer, even as the Sarge chugged his down and waddled over to the bar for a 'tweener'. By the windows a couple of the loggers and mill workers were commiserating together, sculling shots of Tia Maria and beginning to sing, off-key and maudlin. I could see Roddie Game sitting by himself, staring into a full schooner. He was stopped, appeared disconsolate. I'd known Roddie my entire life. When I was a kid, he'd coached my cricket team and my footy team and had been one of those who'd rallied around Mum when my dad died. He was the one who'd persuaded me to finish school, arguing that manual labour was for mugs. It was like his own words were coming back to haunt him: he knew the mill was on borrowed time. Of course he did.

'There's still the stone fruit,' said the Sarge, returning to our table. 'A bit of dairy. That doctor from Canberra with his vineyard. Few hobby farms, a few tourists filtering through. Recession will end eventually. The place isn't dead yet.'

'Doesn't sound much of a future,' I said. 'Not like the old days, with the mill and the mine. The primary school and the police station. The churches full. Feels like the place is dying from a thousand cuts.'

The Sarge nodded, as though considering the wisdom of my words. 'You heard about the plan to reopen the Gryphon?'

'Yeah, I heard. Teramina Cloverton. Hardcastle. She was in here last night with her new husband.'

'He speaks highly of you, you know,' said the Sarge, eyes on me. 'Francis Hardcastle.'

'He does?'

'Sure. Told me he'd heard good things. You and Tom keeping the peace down here. That he was impressed when he met you. You'd offered to check up on trespassers.'

His emphasis was strange; I didn't respond immediately.

'My grandfather worked at the original Gryphon, back in the day, after he got back from the Great War,' said the Sarge.

'I thought you were from Sydney?' I said.

'Yeah, that's where they headed when the mine shut in '32. The Depression. Tough times; makes what we're going through now seem like a picnic. I grew up in Sydney, joined the force there. But the old folks were always banging on about The Valley. You'd reckon they'd been evicted from the Garden of Eden.'

I sipped my beer, then took a bigger swallow; I didn't want him to think I was a wimp. It was unprecedented this, the Sarge discussing himself and his family. Maybe it was because we were away from the station, away from the office, away from Saltwood, down in The Valley. Or maybe it was the impact of the day, knowing we had been so thoroughly played, pawns in someone else's game. But it was curious him being so open. We all knew he was married, had kids, but I didn't even know his wife's name;

he had never mentioned it. He kept his professional and personal lives totally separate.

'I've invested some money down here—not that I have a lot. Put it into the mine.' He seemed to be talking to himself as much as to me.

'Really?'

'Yeah. That Hardcastle, he's smart. Knows his shit. He's already getting some good samples out. Nuggets. They're planning to ramp it up: they'll get the access road repaired, get the mains power put through, install modern machinery.'

I studied his face. 'What's that got to do with me?'

'The second job I mentioned. Security guard. Just to keep an eye on things while they're in the development stage. Good money. And who knows? Once the Gryphon is producing, there might be a permanent job. A step up from police work. It'd be smart to get a foot in the door.'

He drained his schooner, left me thinking while he went off to take a piss and buy more drinks. This time I made sure I'd finished my beer by the time he returned.

'Okay,' I said, when he placed the new round on the table. 'Why not?' It seemed harmless enough. Back then it did.

We clinked glasses, toasted to the success of the Gryphon reborn, to the prosperity of The Valley. I was on the slippery slope and I didn't even realise it.

chapter ten

BY THE NEXT MORNING, MY MIND WAS MADE UP: I'D TAKE THE EXTRA WORK AT the mine. There was no downside. And if anyone was bending the rules, it was the Sarge, not me. And I was tempted by the extra money. I was set to meet Francis Hardcastle that afternoon; the Sarge had lined it up.

But for the moment, I had more immediate concerns. I went over to the police station, not knowing quite what to expect. Emotions were running high, but I couldn't identify a likely source of trouble. The moratorium had left the greenies happy, the mill workers resigned and the loggers confident of more work further south. Then I got a call from Giles Duneven at Cathcarts: his workers had walked off the job and were picketing at the front gate. I was just collecting my gear when Tom rang, said he'd heard it on the radio driving down from Saltwood, that he was heading straight there.

In my mind I was imagining violence and confrontation, the return of the logging thugs, men in balaclavas, people injured.

More front-page photos in the *Sydney Morning Herald*. Instead, when I arrived Tom was already there, having a cup of tea at the gates. If anything, there was almost a party atmosphere; the workers seemed happy to be taking matters into their own hands.

'We're barricading the mill: nothing in, nothing out,' said Peter Rudd, a two-metre tall slab of a man, the best rugby forward between the coast and the capital. 'I've been elected shop steward.'

'Viva la revolution,' intoned Roddie Game, lounging in a picnic chair, raising a sardonic fist.

Giles Duneven was also there, the managing director sitting with his men, sipping a tea and smiling. 'Walked off the job,' he said and gave me a wink. 'Came out in solidarity.'

I got it then: management and the workers were colluding to attract some media attention, drum up a bit of sympathy and maybe even some government largesse. Losing a day or two of production wasn't going to hurt; their supply of logs was going to grind to a halt in a few weeks anyway. And of course they wanted a police presence: for set dressing.

'You want me to arrest anyone?' I offered sarcastically.

'Be grateful if you thumped a few of them,' said Giles. 'I can suggest a couple, if you want. Just make sure the camera has got some film in it.'

I looked about. Sure enough, there was Giles's office manager Judy with an Instamatic. She was no Stan Cimati and her camera was no Pentax, but she smiled, glad to be doing her bit.

'Heads up, here we go,' said Roddie Game, and I took a step back as a station wagon plastered with the garish decals of commercial television pulled up.

A few of the blokes stood up, started chanting as the camera team got out and started recording. *'What do we want? Wood! When do we want it? Now!'*

'Can I have a private word?' I asked, catching up with Giles, who was slinking off to one side, not wanting to spoil the made-for-television moment.

'Sure.'

We walked until we were out of shot, along the mill's wire security fence. Behind it, smoke was rising gently from a high chimney, the only sign of life. The place appeared rundown and sad, like it knew what was coming.

'How serious is it?' I asked.

Giles shrugged, laconic as always. 'Oh, we're well and truly fucked. At least, if we stay here we are. It's move south or perish.'

'So what's the point of all this then?' I asked, gesturing over towards the picket line.

'Angling for a bit of government assistance. A relocation grant.'

'You reckon the moratorium will be made permanent then?'

'That's what I'm hearing from Sydney.'

I regarded the protest, the workers waving their placards and moving on to another repurposed slogan: *'Hell no, we won't go!'*

'So those blokes, they'll relocate as well?'

'Those that can.'

'Not good for The Valley,' I said.

'Not good for anyone if we stay here and go bankrupt.'

'Fair call,' I conceded.

When we got back to the men, the cameraman had filmed enough and buttoned off. The workers had sat down again. The young journo sauntered over to me. I recognised him from the telly, a handsome guy with a preppy haircut and an impressive chin who was constantly gabbing to the camera with Parliament House in the background. He'd had enough sense to ditch the suit and put on some jeans and hiking boots, although his Ray-Bans placed his salary well above those of the mill workers and me.

'Any chance of an interview?' he asked after introducing himself. 'On camera?'

'Sorry,' I said. 'I'm not authorised to speak to the media. Best talk to Sergeant Obswith in Saltwood, or public relations in Sydney.'

'Fair enough,' he said, no doubt anticipating my response. 'What's your assessment? You think it could flare up again? More violence?'

Nearby, the men on the picket line were sharing a joke, the cows had returned to grazing, a slight breeze was blowing. 'Veritable tinderbox,' I said, then pointed to Giles. 'See that bloke over there? That's the mill manager. You should talk to him.'

The journo smiled. 'Cheers, mate,' he said. 'Appreciate it.'

I was walking back to the squad car when Roddie Game caught up with me. 'Giles tell you what they're thinking?'

'Relocation? Sounds unavoidable.'

Roddie stared hard at me, then at his feet, kicking at the ground with one of his steel-capped boots.

'What is it, Roddie?'

'Can't do it. Can't move. House is here, kids are here. Grandkids. Mortgage is here. Interest rates are killing us. Reckon my mortgage is more than what the place is worth. The wife's crook. I'm fifty-five. Can't do another relocation. Who'd buy my house? Who'd rent it?'

His desperation was obvious. 'What'll you do?' I asked.

'Don't know.' He laughed, cracking hardy. 'I could just about scrape by on the dole, if it wasn't for the fucking bank breathing down my neck.'

I considered his face, the forty years of slog written there: the lines, the scars, the watery blue eyes. 'You hear about the mine?' I asked. 'This bloke Hardcastle is planning to restart it.'

'Yeah, I heard,' he said. 'Already thrown my hat in the ring. Says he can't promise anything, not yet.'

'I'm meeting him this afternoon. Finding out what his plans are. You want me to put in a good word?'

He seemed disconcerted: the world had turned so far that I was helping him, after all those years when he had supported my mum. 'Sure,' he said. 'That'd be good.'

— —

Francis Hardcastle was waiting for me when I got back to the police station. He was a dapper bloke, quite small and self-contained, but with the ability to fill a room. He had a sharp haircut and nice clothes and a way of looking you in the eye. Tailored pants with pleats, a business shirt, a lightweight sports jacket that fitted him properly: nothing flashy, but somehow letting you know he was loaded. He had a small moustache and plenty of confidence. There was a freshness to him, as though he'd just that minute dried himself off from a shower. His eyes were hooded: made him look like the love child of Robert Mitchum and Marlene Dietrich. He possessed a sort of slow charisma, a kind of unhurried nonchalance.

He shook my hand, that same confident handshake. 'I can't tell you how glad I am to see you here in The Valley,' he said. His voice was softened by the remnants of an American drawl.

'That so?' I said, trying to imitate the aloof authority that the Sarge carried off so well.

'Of course. A police presence. The thin blue line.' He smiled, and it was a good smile, open and honest. His teeth were like his clothes: nothing ostentatious, yet nothing out of alignment. 'Put yourself in my position: starting up a goldmine with the nearest cop shop half an hour away in Saltwood.'

'Been a while since we had bushrangers,' I said, making light of it.

'Don't be so sure,' he said. 'Gold retains its ability to warp people's judgement, even in this day and age.'

'So they say,' I said, wondering at the small talk. 'Sergeant Obswith said you might have some work for me?'

'He mentioned that, did he? Good man, your sergeant.'

'What do you have in mind?' I asked.

'You familiar with the mine, know the lay of the land?' he asked.

'Sure. Not underground, of course. But the track up the escarpment. We used it as kids, to swim in the lake.'

'Well, not much has changed. The mine itself is secure. You'll remember the large steel doors? They're locked. Even if someone did break in, there's not a lot to steal. Not yet. But once we get mains electricity put through, we'll start moving equipment in: generators, pumps, mining equipment, cabling and lights. Build some new sheds, service buildings. We've already repaired the retaining wall, regulating the flow from the lake, started clearing the processing works in the valley. It's a bit of a concern, because it's so remote up there. Could be targeted by vandals, or by thieves. Even competitors.'

'I was talking to your wife two nights ago, when you were at the pub. Teramina said you'd had trespassers. I thought they might be prospectors.'

'Maybe, but there's nothing to find up there; all the alluvial gold went last century. We don't want anyone poking around once we start bringing in expensive gear.'

'You won't hire someone full-time?'

He smiled, a slow smile that began small and widened, as if he was reading my mind and liking what it told him. 'Certainly. In time. As the mine becomes operational, our cash flow turns positive and our budget expands. The stock market beckons. We'll end up with a full team. Well paid, well equipped. Good benefits. But for now, a part-timer who is also a police officer would be perfect.' He smiled again, weighted his words. 'In on the ground floor.'

'What does it actually involve? I wouldn't want to jeopardise my police work.'

'Of course not. Last thing I would want. Right now, I don't expect you'll have to do much at all. Just your presence should be deterrent enough until we start producing.'

'I'm definitely interested,' I said. I was already imagining the security team, *well paid and well equipped*, with me heading it up. *In on the ground floor.*

'We had someone cut the lock off the lower gate, where the road up the escarpment branches off the East Road. Not sure who did it or why. The gate was left open for a long time, so people might have thought it was a public road. We've put new locks on and erected signs, making sure people know it's private property.'

'So what do you want me to do?'

He outlined my duties. 'Keep an eye on the gate, and for anyone heading out the East Road who isn't a resident, take a trip up to the mine most days, make sure it's secure.'

'Sounds good,' I said.

He mentioned a salary then. It was a good two-thirds of my police pay, much more than I'd imagined. I was so stunned, I didn't respond immediately.

Perhaps he thought I was hesitating. He tilted his head slightly, like he was trying to see me better. 'One more thing. There's an old house close by the road. Watershine. You know it?'

'The old mine manager's house?'

'Would make sense if you lived there. It's rundown, in need of repairs. We could pay you for that as well. A bit of weekend work: the general store has some basic hardware supplies. And you could live in the house rent-free. Handy location, well placed to keep an eye out.'

I was doing the calculations: my police salary, the pay from Hardcastle, my police travel allowance, all while living rent-free, dropping in to see Eliza at the general store.

'I reckon I'm in,' I said, trying to emulate his calm.

'Great. That's great,' he said. And he reached into the pocket of his well-cut coat. 'Here, take a look,' he said, pressing something into my palm.

It was a small piece of quartz, about the size of a ten-cent piece, smooth on one side, jagged on the other, with a bright streak of gold running through it, like magic through a river. I'd never seen anything to compare with it. I held it up; the gold sparkled back at me, like a lover's promise.

'Got it out just last week,' Francis said. 'Not even mining, just scoping out the shafts, some exploratory blasting, deciding which ones to work first. Imagine how much more there must be.'

I studied the nugget, the quartz dull, the gold shimmering. When I went to give it back, he held his hand up.

'You keep it,' he said, eyes smiling. 'Gold, Simmons. Look at it, hold it, cherish it. This is the future. This will save our valley.'

And in that moment, I believed him.

It was only later, after he had left me alone and I was revelling in my good fortune, that I realised I'd forgotten to mention Roddie Game to him. But there was plenty of time to help my mum's old benefactor, I reassured myself. I was in on the ground floor.

chapter eleven

WHEN I WAS A KID, IN THE SUMMER BETWEEN FINISHING PRIMARY SCHOOL IN
The Valley and catching the daily bus to high school at Saltwood,
my friends and I discovered the old mine on top of the escarpment.
Mike Norfolk and Lucas Trescothic and I would ride our bikes out
along the East Road, pass them over the gate of the mine access
road, then ride as far as we could along the track winding up the
escarpment. It was like the Tour de France, climbing Alpe d'Huez,
except we walked most of it, wheeling the bikes. The pay-off came
at the top: we could bike through the forest to the lake, and afterwards freewheel down the cliff track, braking almost the whole
way. At the top was a spectacular view out across The Valley:
it made us feel we were kings of the earth. And there was that
mountain lake below the mine, sitting close to the precipice, filled
with clear cool water. Like God's own infinity pool.

We were twelve, I guess, on the cusp of adolescence, knowing the
world was about to change, that our lives were about to change, but
still kids nevertheless, on the edge of something larger. I remember

it as being hot that summer, a real scorcher, and the lake a kind of magic retreat.

One afternoon, after swimming ourselves to near exhaustion, we were sunbathing on the rocks next to the water, eating our sandwiches.

'You reckon there's still gold up there?' asked Mike, indicating the old mine entrance above us. He was a real redhead, always sunburnt no matter how much sunscreen he put on.

'Must be,' said Lucas, acorn brown and contemptuous of lotions.

'What if you found some?' I asked. 'A big fat nugget. What would you do with it?'

'You first,' replied Mike. 'You asked the question.'

'Give it to my mum,' I replied. 'She needs it.'

I could see my answer resonated with Mike. 'I'd save it. Put it in the bank. Live off the interest.'

'Fuck that,' said Lucas. 'I'd get a hot car and a hot girlfriend, and leave The Valley forever. Wouldn't see me for dust.' And he stood up, let go a Tarzan yell, and pelted towards the lake, executing a perfect running dive. Mike and I laughed, and then plunged in after him.

I thought about that sometimes, after I accepted the part-time job, when I'd travel up that same track to check on the mine, look at the lake. It was only ten years after that summer, and the track and the lake and the mine entrance hadn't changed that much, but we sure had. There's a hell of a difference between twelve and twenty-two. Mike had left school at sixteen and joined the navy, and Lucas had gone travelling and worked in the mines. I was the only one who finished high school, then I joined the coppers. Six months at the college in Goulburn, my probationary year at Cowra, a few months out of my depth in Sydney, then to Saltwood. None of us had thought we'd be coming back, and yet the other two were already there when I returned.

As part of the agreement with Francis, I got to work fixing up Watershine, mainly on the weekends, although it was already October and daylight savings had kicked in, so I was keen to do a bit in the late afternoons and into the evenings. The old house had been vacant for a couple of decades, sinking into its foundations as if from despondency and neglect. All those years she was living at Ellensby, all the years she was gallivanting about overseas, Teramina had just left it sitting there. She hadn't thought to maintain it, or rent it out, or do it up. I wondered what it might be like to have so much money you could be that cavalier. But it was a wonderful old place and I liked it. And I sure liked living there rent-free.

I was constantly going back and forth to the general store for bits and pieces. I liked that as well. The store sold food and basic supplies: bread and milk and laundry powder and soft drinks and ice creams and boxes of breakfast cereal. Nothing flash. Ham and bacon and blocks of cheddar the size of house bricks, but not much in the way of meat or veg or anything fresh. Most people in The Valley would head up to Saltwood once a week to do a big supermarket shop, and to Canberra if they needed clothes or furniture or whitegoods. The fruit pickers were very frugal. But the general store also had this little annexe stocked with basic farm supplies, fishing gear and some hardware. Not power tools or anything expensive or specialised, but screws and hinges and putty and silicone and tap washers. Bloke's stuff. Francis had given me the green light to shop there, opening an account for me. But

I was careful: I only used it for hardware; I made sure I paid for my own groceries.

Eliza was cute. She was also bored, which meant she was always glad to see me. Or anyone. Underneath the boredom I thought I saw a sadness, a type of low-level despair. Or frustration. Or resignation. And I soon understood why. She was stuck there, duty-bound, caring for her dad, while her youth fizzled away. When I mentioned one time, feeling flush with police pay, Gryphon pay and free accommodation, that I thought The Valley was a wonderful place to be, she regarded me with contempt. 'Easy for you to say. You can leave anytime you want.'

The first time I asked her to have a drink with me at the pub, she declined. Same the second time. When I asked the third time, I offered to buy her dinner too. I didn't mean to phrase it like that, I wasn't being cunning or strategic or whatever, it just came out that way, but when she said yes, I realised something. It wasn't because she wanted me to pay; it was because she couldn't: she had no money.

Once we became closer, she explained the situation. Her dad was unwell. His health was failing and he was weighed down by regrets. And so he was trying to set things to rights before he died. He wanted to make the store a goer, something he could leave her; her absent brothers would get fuck-all. This meant that he poured every spare cent he had into the mortgage, trying to reduce what he owed the bank, but he was swimming against the tide: interest rates were going up and up and up, so he wasn't making any headway. People weren't spending. Eliza suspected she and her father were actually going backwards. All they ever ate were store goods that had passed their use-by dates, a few homegrown vegies and eggs from their chooks. When she told me that, I understood a little more why she hated The Valley.

But I was happy to buy her a counter meal at the Bushman's Bistro, as the pub called it. That and a few drinks. She was grateful, but didn't abuse it: the fanciest she ever got was a gin and tonic; most times she was happy to sit on a draught cider. It made me feel good to see her enjoy herself, to see the tedium ease from her, to hear her laugh, to see a sparkle in her eye and discover she'd been hiding a wicked sense of humour. She was a good flirt, lots of fun.

We weren't alone. Mike Norfolk was back in The Valley. He'd been on the picket line in the forest, but he knew I had nothing to do with the violence and never held it against me. Lucas Trescothic had also returned to the district, and Suzie Cocheef would sneak into the beer garden and join us despite being only sixteen. When I was out of my uniform, I was happy to turn a blind eye. Her brother Arnie, who was a few years older than us, was pretty relaxed about it; they'd had a hard time since their parents died. There were a few others, but that was the main group. It was still spring, so there weren't many young people about yet; the backpackers and itinerant fruit pickers wouldn't arrive for another month or two.

Lucas was working on the old Miners' Institute. He was an apprentice carpenter, in his final year, doing most of the work while his boss stayed up in Saltwood. The boss would come down every few days to check on progress and issue instructions, but other than that Lucas was left to his own devices. The floors needed replacing—not just the floorboards but the joists as well—and some of the window frames had become warped by rain and needed to be repaired. Lucas said some money had come through after

Francis Hardcastle cut a deal with the local council, matching them dollar for dollar. 'Giving back to the community,' he said, which I thought was pretty generous as the mine hadn't started producing yet.

Lucas was sort of squatting in the Institute while he worked on it, the same way I was semi-camping in Watershine. He was full bottle on carpentry and had proper power tools and was happy to lend them to me and give advice. If he had any heavy lifting to do I'd help out, and he'd do the same for me.

The other thing I admired about Lucas was his attitude. He wasn't interested in buying into the whole greenies versus loggers divide, which set him apart from just about everyone else in The Valley. 'Live and let live,' he'd say. 'Life's too short.' He was a handsome guy, reminding me a bit of that singer James Taylor, back when Taylor was young and still had hair and was singing 'Fire and Rain'.

Lucas and Mike were mates as well. Mike was a devout conservationist and would often try to persuade us to join the cause, but never took offence at the fact that neither Lucas nor I really cared. He found a more willing ear in Suzie. Mike was also a beneficiary of the mine. Francis had put him on, which we teased him about, being such a greenie, but Mike said it was better to be inside the tent pissing out rather than the opposite. He said Hardcastle was committed to making the mine environmentally sound, so Mike was happy to help. We thought we'd done well the three of us, getting steady jobs at a time when unemployment was nudging one million.

Towards the end of October, Lucas spent a couple of weekends in a row helping me put a new corrugated-iron roof on Watershine:

one side the first weekend, the other side the next. Mike helped out too. On the second weekend, when we'd finished, we decided to drive up to the lake. The road had been repaired enough to provide access, thanks to Mike; he was good with earth-moving equipment. We tried swimming, but the lake was still freezing. I reminded them of the question I'd asked ten years before, the one about the nugget, but neither of them could remember it. Funny how people recollect different snippets of the past.

And all the time, I was getting closer to Eliza, getting to know her better, summoning up the guts to ask her out on a date. A proper date, not just drinks with everyone else at the pub. When I finally gathered the gumption to ask her up to Saltwood to see a movie, she positively beamed and asked what had taken me so long.

So we drove up, through a sun-shower sunset, a rainbow glowing against the grey skies, to a film night in the Belair theatre.

On the way home, she told me more about the store. Her father was losing hope; the logging moratorium and the imminent closure of the sawmill weighed on him, and only the prospect of the mine kept him going.

'Will it be enough?' I asked.

'Don't know.'

'Will you stay?' It was the enduring question of The Valley, the one generations of young people had asked each other. The place was a paradise, but if you were under thirty and single, it felt like living on the dark side of the moon, even if you could find work. At times, when I was feeling unsure of myself, I wondered if that was the only reason Eliza had been so keen to go out with me: there was no one else.

Anyway, the two of us finally got it on. I thought I had it made, even while I knew it couldn't last. I lacked the devil-may-care spirit of someone like Lucas. And I was right. I just didn't predict the speed with which everything would fall apart.

The first thing that happened was the government decided it would extend the logging moratorium indefinitely. And not only that, the new precinct, the one a little further down the river at Tarantula Creek, was declared an extension to the Wellington Falls National Park. Which meant it also couldn't be logged. Ever.

The greenies had won. That evening at the pub, there were tears and there were arguments and there were fights. I copped a black eye trying to break up a brawl. Not between loggers and greenies, but between two loggers too pissed to care who they hit.

That same night, as she bathed my wounded face, Eliza confided that she was scared shitless. She reckoned her dad was suicidal, said she wouldn't be able to sleep. So I did the right thing and stayed over.

chapter twelve

2024

THE NEXT MORNING, WHEN NELL AND IVAN WALK ACROSS THE CROSSROADS from the pub, there's a car parked outside the Miners' Institute. A top-of-the-line Tesla. Tyffany Burnside emerges from the driver's seat as they approach.

'I tried calling,' she says by way of greeting. 'I have something for you.'

After her near sleepless night, the last thing Nell feels like is Tyffany's brash dynamism, but Ivan invites the widow in. Nell pauses outside a moment and gathers herself, realising she has a choice to make: she's either part of the investigation or she's not. So she calms herself and adopts a professional demeanour. She's no good either to Ivan or herself if her mind isn't on the job. Time to park her personal strife and leave it for later.

Inside the Institute, Tyffany doesn't take the seat offered by Ivan. Instead, she reaches into her tote bag. Nell suspects it's one of those incredibly expensive fashion statements, the latest incarnation of the Birkin bag, but she doesn't recognise its pedigree and has no idea of its price tag.

'Thought you should see this,' says Tyffany. And she drops a small rock on the table with a thud. But like her bag and her car, this is no ordinary rock. It's quartz, laced through with a sliver of gleaming yellow metal.

'Gold?' asks Ivan.

'Gold,' confirms Tyffany. 'I have an eye for it.'

'What's its significance?' asks Nell, and she feels her mind, derailed by yesterday's revelations, shifting back on track. This feels important.

Tyffany plucks the stone off the table and passes it to her. 'Take a gander,' she says.

Nell smiles, can't help it. She realises something about Wolfgang Burnside's second wife: she likes to mess with people's expectations. Most nouveaux riches try to cultivate refined accents; Tyffany Burnside is the opposite: highly educated, worldly, from a well-established family, but putting on bogan airs, like some sort of pantomime.

'This valley was opened up by goldmining; it was its lifeblood for decades,' Tyffany continues. She makes an extravagant gesture, eyes to the ceiling, arms extended, channelling a showground magician. 'Behold. The Miners' Institute.'

Nell feels she's listening to a rehearsed performance. Ivan sighs, exasperation apparent.

Tyffany carries on regardless. 'Then the gold ran out. The mine closed. Dullsville returned.' She points to the nugget that Nell has placed on the table. 'I found it among Wolfie's things. In his carry-on bag. He'd packed his luggage, ready to meet me in Sydney.

You remember he was planning to join me? This was in there, with some toiletries and a book and his spare laptop. Intriguing, don't you think? Gold, here in The Valley, after all this time.'

'He could have got it from anywhere,' says Nell, playing devil's advocate. 'Sounds like you two were always travelling.'

'Yes. But he'd packed it to bring it with him. To show me, I expect.'

'He hadn't mentioned it at all?' asks Ivan. 'On the phone, in emails?'

'No. Not a word.'

'Maybe he's had it a long time,' counters Nell. 'From before he met you. Or he found it in a Saltwood antique store.'

'More likely he only just received it while I was away, just in this past week, and decided to surprise me. Received it—or found it.'

Ivan takes the stone from Nell, studies the glimmering line. 'Any idea what it's worth?'

'Three-fifths of fuck-all, I imagine,' says Tyffany, clearly excited, on a kind of high.

'And in dollars that would be?' prompts Nell.

'Who knows? Hundreds. Couple of thousand tops. But that's not the point, is it? There might be more where this came from.' She smiles, teeth gleaming, eyes wide. 'Gold, baby, gold. Bonanza. Eureka. Jackpot.'

Ivan appears annoyed by Tyffany's barrel-girl elation, but Nell knows that grieving people react in strange ways. She's more intrigued than irritated. 'So where do you think it came from?'

'Couldn't say for sure, but I could hazard a guess from something Wolfie said a week or two ago.'

'Go on then,' says Ivan.

'The Gryphon Mine.' She looks first at Ivan, then at Nell, then back to Ivan, perhaps anticipating a response.

'What about it?' asks Ivan, with a hint of exasperation at having to ask the question.

'I thought I told you. He was investigating repurposing the lake up by the mine. Planning to use it for pumped hydro, part of his power grid scheme.'

'You think that's where he found it?' asks Nell. 'In the lake?'

'It's possible,' says Tyffany. 'He was a certified diver. I can't imagine where else he could have got it from. He was back here in The Valley for most of the last month.'

'Do you know if he accessed the mine itself?' asks Nell. 'Or was trying to?'

'No. Can't see why he would. As far as I know, it's all locked up. Not part of our plans at all.'

Nell shakes her head, not quite able to bring the threads together. 'Okay. He finds some gold. One piece. How would that be connected to his murder?'

Tyffany looks at her blankly. 'You're the detective.'

Ivan moves sideways, transferring weight from one leg to another. Nell interprets it as a sign of impatience. 'What more do you know about his plans for the lake?' she asks.

Tyffany shrugs. 'He was having difficulty tracking down the owner. Getting their permission.'

'The owner?' asks Nell.

'It was held for decades by the Clovertons, the family that developed the mine, owned all the land. Up on the escarpment. The mine and the lake and the forest, and the house and the settling ponds on the valley floor, with the stream that flows into the river. Same family that built Ellensby. But the last of the family, Teramina Cloverton, died thirty years ago. She bequeathed it all to someone called Amber Jones, but we can't find hide nor hair of her. Teramina's lawyer, Willard Halliday, is still alive, has a practice in Saltwood. He's been searching for her for years, holding it in trust for her. But apparently she disappeared off the face of the earth three decades ago.'

Nell feels Ivan's eyes upon her and the earth shifting under her. She's lost for words. Eliza Tomsett had said her mother lived in the house called Watershine, but not that she owned it. And if Amber owned the house and land, then now Nell must: the land with an abandoned mine and a lake and a stream flowing into the river where her half-brother's body was found. The land where he might have found the gold nugget.

'What?' says Tyffany, unhappy to be the one wrong-footed. 'What did I say?'

chapter thirteen

ONCE TYFFANY HAS LEFT, NELL SITS AT HER DESK, STARING AT THE SCREEN of her computer, feeling dazed. Just when she'd committed herself to re-engaging with the investigation, suppressing questions about her lineage, they reassert themselves. The world feels like it's conspiring against her, playing some strange game, entangling her personal life more and more in the case. First the revelation that Wolfgang was related to her, and now the discovery that he may have found gold on a piece of land once owned by her mother and, in all likelihood, now owned by herself. Her eyes remain on the screen, but it remains blank.

'What do you want to do now?' asks Ivan, who's been sitting at his desk, apparently working but looking up every few seconds to check on her. 'Talk to the lawyer? Halliday?'

'About the land?' She shakes her head. 'No. We need to prioritise the investigation. The land can wait. You think we need to update Plodder?'

'No. It's not going to change his mind,' says Ivan.

'Let's check out this lake. Might be the source of Wolfgang's gold nugget.' And she gives a disembodied laugh. 'Might belong to me.'

Ivan stares at her, that focused gaze of his. 'Tyffany mentioned he was an accomplished diver. They went scuba diving on their holidays. You think maybe that was where he drowned? The body moved later?'

'Possible. If he was thinking of using it for pumped hydro, makes sense that he would want to check it out. That sort of hands-on approach sounds like his personality all over.'

'Cyanide,' replies Ivan. 'Blake says Wolfgang had it in his system, but just trace amounts. Isn't it used to process gold ore?'

Nell feels herself smiling: the quest to find Wolfgang's killer has reasserted itself; her demons are back in their box.

— —

The two colleagues determine what they need and set out along the East Road. It's a good feeling: escaping the office, heading somewhere with purpose.

'Slow up,' Nell says as they approach the escarpment. There's a rusted gate on the right-hand side, hidden behind a massive gum tree. A faded sign hangs from it, lopsided. WATERSHINE. She points to it, says to Ivan, 'This is where Tyffany said the land starts. There's a house through there somewhere.'

'You want to check it out? Might be yours, after all.'

'No, let's keep going.'

They continue on, pass over a creek, water flowing strongly after recent rains. They find a second gate and Ivan pulls up. There's a solitary sign—TRESPASSERS PROSECUTED—but the peeling paint and rusting metal deprive it of authority. They have boltcutters if they need them; if it's her land, there's no need for a warrant. But the gate isn't locked, just kept in place by a chain with a circular clasp of grey metal. It's slack on its hinges and Nell needs to heave it across. There are signs where it has bitten into the dirt; someone has come this way in recent weeks. She wonders if it was Wolfgang, investigating his plans for pumped hydro.

The road follows the creek, winding up a small valley and into a ravine the stream has carved into the escarpment. Off to the right, the water flows through a series of pools, some natural, some displaying the straight lines of human construction. The track folds away to the left, leaving the creek, and starts to climb. Immediately it begins to deteriorate, runnelled with erosion, and Ivan slows the vehicle to a walking pace. The trail starts to turn back on itself, tight corners, running back and forth across the slope, struggling to find purchase, threading its way through patches of trees clinging to the incline.

They come around a corner and a wallaby stands curious, dark and thick-furred, looking right at them fleetingly before bounding away. They come across a fallen tree, can see the signs where someone has chainsawed it clear. Nell jumps out, inspects it. 'Not so recent; a month or two,' she declares as she climbs back in.

They ascend further, until the landscape lurches up once more, the trees thinning enough to see the escarpment rising above them, sandstone cliffs, imperious and timeless.

'Some sort of road,' says Ivan, inching the four-wheel drive forward in low range. He manages to get around one more hairpin, and then is forced to stop. A three-metre segment of the track has been washed out completely. 'End of the penny section,' he sighs.

They've anticipated this might happen; they'll hike the rest of the way.

'We're not the first,' says Nell, collecting her equipment from the back and gesturing towards the side of the track. Tyre tracks reveal someone has turned a vehicle around, a multi-point turn.

They leave the car, proceed on foot. They have backpacks, water, hats, sunscreen. They scramble over the gap in the road. It must have gone some years ago; there are signs where kangaroos and other animals have made their way across.

'Easy enough on a dirt bike,' says Ivan, pointing to tyre marks beyond the gap. 'What do you think? Pretty recent. Days? A couple of weeks, tops.'

'Yeah, fair bit of rain around these parts,' says Nell.

Their conversation peters out as they climb higher and higher. Nell finds herself breathing hard, despite the winding nature of the route. The trail narrows further. It's eroded and overgrown in parts, though still easy to follow. There are a couple of small bridges, made out of tough hardwood, hardy enough to walk on, or ride a trail bike. Maybe strong enough to support a car, maybe not.

There's a final section taking them towards the south, cutting across the face of the cliff itself, buttressed by hand-cut masonry, a masterful piece of nineteenth-century engineering. A waterfall is flowing from the top of the cliff, fluming white, catching the light breeze, spraying them with relief. With the trees thinning out, unable to establish a foothold in the vertical sandstone, Ivan and Nell can see out across the valley. There are the orchards and vineyards, there are the roads, the pub and the Miners' Institute and the park where Wolfgang was found on the Broken River, not far downstream from where the creek from Watershine flows into it. Ivan brings out his phone, taking multiple photos. He will like this, Nell knows, being able to get The Valley into a single frame, the pattern of life available to scan and examine and contemplate.

The track climbs over the top of the cliff, between two pillars of rock. Ivan pauses, places his hand on one. 'This is strange. Granite. The cliffs are sandstone. Must be some kind of anomaly.'

The track leaves the bare rock behind and takes them into a forest. Ivan pulls up Google Maps on his phone; despite the feeling of isolation, the signal is strong up here, four bars of 4G. The track isn't marked on the app; according to the map, they're standing in a solid patch of light green. He switches on the terrain function. It shows a sharp circular rise between them and the blue shading of the lake.

'Big hill just there.' He points through the trees, where Nell can just glimpse a rise. 'Must be the mine. My guess is the track winds around the back of it in a semicircle, comes out above the lake.' He switches to satellite view, uses the 3D function. The hill is evident, with a road and signs of the mine, standing above the lake. 'All good?' he inquires.

'Yes, let's push on.'

Ivan's supposition is correct. The track heads into the forest of gums, then begins to wind to the right, a slow circle, as the ground gradually ascends, an easy climb after the exertions of the escarpment itself. There is a beauty in the forest—the trees aren't tall or densely packed, just box trees—yet Nell feels a sense of tranquility here. She can't help but wonder: could this really be hers?

They are about halfway around the rise when the forest comes to an abrupt halt and Nell's wonder with it. There, spread out before them, is a desecrated landscape, clear-felled so that nothing is left but thistles and weeds, with no apparent attempt at replanting or rehabilitation.

'Holy shit,' she says.

'What a mess,' says Ivan.

'That fucking lawyer,' says Nell. 'Holding it in trust? More like pillaging it for all he can get.'

'Not Wolfgang?'

Nell shakes her head. 'Not his style. Not the clean-and-green image he wanted to project. And not his land.'

'How could they get the logs out?' asks Ivan. 'Not down that track we climbed, that's for sure.'

'Must be another way. Out across the plateau.'

They continue walking into the desolation. It must be some months since the loggers were here, and yet it still feels barren. Nell can see regrowth here and there, a sapling fighting upwards from a patch of blackberries. But there are bare patches of dirt and naked stone, an indication that the soil is poor and thin. Not that the loggers would have cared.

Without the trees, the two detectives have a better view of the peak standing above them: an old volcanic core. The road continues climbing even as they circle the hill. And as they hike higher, the better their view of the devastation. Only to the west, by the cliff edge, is there a thin band of natural vegetation, the timber workers leaving a veneer of the natural forest to disguise their plunder from those in The Valley.

The detectives come to a small ridge and the track forks: the right path continuing upwards towards the mine, the left dropping towards a lake. At least the water seems clear enough, reflecting the blue sky. The sight makes Nell thirsty. It must be at least thirty degrees, the humidity rising. She drinks more water from her canteen.

They climb first to the mine. There are steel doors sealing the entrance, covered with graffiti, like a Sydney commuter train, with a metal sign welded above the entrance: THE GRYPHON MINE 1866. There's no evidence the doors have been breached: there are steel chains, brass padlocks the size of a man's fist, all still in place. Ivan checks them, takes photos with his phone, zooms in on some of the results.

He shakes his head. 'Haven't been opened anytime lately.'

'You think this is where the gold is from? Inside?'

'I want to eliminate the possibility.'

'Let me check.' They're a long way from anywhere, but the elevation is providing them with a strong signal. She finds the number, calls the lawyer, but the phone rings out. She tries again, getting through on the second attempt.

'Halliday Lawyers,' states a bored young voice. 'Ollie speaking.'

'This is Detective Senior Constable Narelle Buchanan. Can I speak to Mr Halliday, please?'

'I'm not sure he's available right now. He hasn't been feeling well.'

'I see,' says Nell. 'We're up at the Gryphon Mine. Would you be able to ask Mr Halliday if Wolfgang Burnside had access to the interior of the mine? Also, ask him who holds the keys to the locks on the mine entrance.'

'Can I call you back?' asks Ollie.

'Yes. Please do.'

They walk back down to the fork, and from there descend to the shore of the lake. There are signs others have been here during the summer. A camp fire: a ring of stones with charcoal. Empty bottles. A few pieces of plastic. Nell stoops, collects some, places them together with a rock on top to prevent them blowing away. She is aware of Ivan watching her, not talking but understanding her impulse, her desire to care for the land.

As they draw closer to the water, the pristine illusion falters. Nell can see banks of silt where the creek enters it, flushed off the landscape after the trees were felled. More damage.

'Good place for a swim on a hot day,' observes Ivan.

'Not if it's full of cyanide,' replies Nell. She takes a flask, collects a sample for Blake.

Ivan is looking around, searching. 'If he died up here, drowned, how would they get the body down?'

'Maybe the same way the loggers got the timber out.' She frowns. 'If this lake is contaminated, then there must be a good chance the Broken River is as well. What do you think? Looks like the lake flows over the edge, forms that creek that carves down through the ravine, past the house and into the river. So maybe he did die there after all.'

Ivan stares at her. 'You think that's why he was killed?' He gestures at the lake. 'He realised that felling the trees had destabilised mine waste, allowed it to be washed into the lake, and from here down into The Valley?'

'So the killers are?' asks Nell.

'Whoever logged this land?' Ivan suggests.

They lock eyes, minds working. Nell feels they're getting some-where, as if the trip up the escarpment has been worth it.

They continue to search, but can find no evidence anyone has been by the lake in recent days. They find tracks left by a trail bike, similar to those on the road up, but they seem too old, and there are no signs a larger vehicle has been here.

'Seen enough?' Ivan asks eventually.

'I reckon,' she says.

They're working their way back across the barren landscape when her phone chimes. It's the young man from the lawyer's office: Ollie. 'Mr Halliday says Wolfgang Burnside did not ask for the keys to open the mine. But he has them here in the Saltwood office and you are welcome to call by and collect them.'

'What about the house—Watershine?'

'I can check, if you like.'

Nell wants to ask about the destruction of the forest, but realises she would be quizzing the office assistant. Instead, she thanks him and ends the call. She's tempted to drive to Saltwood and give Halliday an earful, although she has no evidence the lawyer knew anything about the logging.

Once they've descended the escarpment and regained the car, Ivan drops Nell at the gate leading to the old mine manager's house. She thanks him, says she'll call when she's done, or she'll walk back to the Miners' Institute. It's only a couple of kilometres along the East Road.

She approaches the house following the drive, through the trees. The path is overgrown, with puddles of water from recent rains. The grass here is a lush green, trimmed by animals. She sees a ring of mushrooms, reminding her of childhood superstitions, of fairies and bewitchments. It's a beautiful spot; she's sure the fairies would approve. She reaches a bridge, tilting precariously. The water beneath it looks cool and clear and clean, apparently untainted by the ruined landscape above the escarpment. She pauses, edges down to the stream, resisting the temptation to cup her hands and drink. She wonders if her mother ever did: stopped here in this spot, drank from this stream.

She finds the house perched on a rocky outcrop, like a castle, set on higher ground. It's lopsided, paint peeling, a creeper climbing one side. But the roof is intact, the windows undamaged, with no signs of vandalism. Had her mother really lived here? Was this where Nell was conceived? Did it now belong to her? She ponders the possibility of that, at all these possibilities revealing themselves to her now, making her wonder if they have been waiting here patiently all these years; waiting for her. It's only two years since she learnt she was adopted, learnt the identity of her biological mother, Amber Jones. Father unknown. Until now. She climbs stone steps, slippery with moss and lack of use, and wooden stairs, becoming precarious with age. She tries the door, finds it locked. Hopefully the lawyer will have the keys; she'll need to return.

Ivan phones then, interrupting her musings, urgency in his voice. 'Where are you?'

'At the house. Watershine.'

'There's a letter addressed to you. Arrived in Dubbo.'

'Who from?'

'Wolfgang Burnside.'

chapter fourteen

1990

LIFE BECAME SWEET, SPRING RUNNING INTO AN EARLY SUMMER. THE PROTESTERS drifted away, followed by the loggers. Smoke still wafted from the chimney at Cathcarts; I found myself constantly checking if it was still rising, knowing sooner or later it too would stop forever. And yet, despite all the dire predictions, the mill kept going, working its way through the logs it had in storage, the specialty wood drying in kilns or the less valuable timber out in the yard. Giles Duneven explained it to me one night at the pub: the rarer and more valuable the wood, the further away he could source it, transport it to the mill and still extract a profit. He was considering accessing logs from further south, where the loggers had moved, or from private holdings, from farms and bush blocks where the owners would never countenance clear-felling but were willing to sell a tree here or a copse there. Duneven was offering hundreds for the right trees.

'We'll have to scale back, but there's a chance we can survive.' He smiled. 'Terrence Earl is helping us to tap into government funds.

We're rebranding. Boutique. Green. Artisanal. Environmentally sustainable.' He was a clever man, Giles Duneven: ahead of his time.

But it was the mine that sustained the community, not through work or money or new-won prosperity, but through hope: the prospect that it might again become a going concern. There was no warning of impending disaster.

With The Valley calm once more, the rationale for me to remain there eroded day by day. So I made the most of it. I still put on my uniform each morning, still started each shift on time at the old police station, but I was clocking off earlier and earlier, working on the house at Watershine and dallying in the general store. Tom no longer came, so I was pretty much free to do as I pleased. I was diligent about keeping an eye on the mine, driving up every second day, but I knew that at any time the Sarge would ring to tell me my furlough in The Valley was over. I think it was that, the knowledge that it all must come to an end, that made me value it all the more. Like the mill, I was living on borrowed time; unlike the mill, I stood little chance of remaining in The Valley. Not unless a full-time job at the Gryphon materialised. I confess: I was much more conscientious about attending to the mine than I was about fulfilling any police duties.

But instead of recalling me, the Sarge decided to keep me there longer. I was delighted, of course. He drove his private car down one Sunday, wearing his civvies. He wanted me to take him to the mine, to check it out. So we drove up together.

At the lake, we could see where work was underway to harness its water and the flow down into the valley. A small dam had been repaired between the lake and the settling pool below, and another low dam where the pool itself emptied into the creek and ran over the cliff, forming Watershine Falls. I explained it to the Sarge the way Francis Hardcastle had explained it to me: the ore would initially be crushed below the lake, then the gravel would be washed and sent down a race to the cisterns near the house, where it would be pulverised and chemical separation could be conducted.

The Sarge cast an eye over the works, apparently satisfied with my explanation. But when he turned to me, he had a steely cast to his eye, that steady and calculating and perceptive gaze of his. 'I want you to keep an eye on him,' he said.

I knew the Sarge had invested money in the mine, knew what he was asking me. 'You're concerned?' I asked him.

'Not really,' he said. 'But The Valley. People have a lot riding on him.'

'Same as with you, then?'

'Yes. Me included.'

I didn't see a lot of Francis Hardcastle, but he seemed to be present even when he wasn't. He'd become a sort of saviour, a prophet leading The Valley towards a promised land. No one ever questioned it; it was like it had been ordained, and to question the viability of the mine was to question the viability of The Valley itself. If any of the local fruit growers or dairy farmers harboured any doubts about the impact a mine might have on their livelihoods, or the implications of processing gold in the man-made pools below the falls, or what these might mean for the quality of the water in the Broken River, they kept such misgivings to themselves. Or if they did talk, they didn't talk to me. But I think for the most part, Francis charmed them, or offered them shares at a discounted rate. He was generous to a fault; as well as helping to fund Lucas's work on the Miners' Institute he had contributed towards a new playground for the primary school. And I was no different: it never occurred to me to doubt him; the tantalising possibility that there might be a job for me, should the mine prove itself profitable, kept me believing. But the Sarge was a smart man and a tough man and nobody's fool. And so I agreed to do as he asked, told him I'd let him know if I detected anything untoward or out of the ordinary.

And then there was Eliza. She was always glad to see me, glad to get some relief from the constant demands of her father and the monotony of the store. The rest of it, the mill and the mine and the orchards, were simply the stage upon which this played out. I tried to cheer her up, conveyed to her what Duneven had told me about the prospect of the mill remaining. And with the mine opening, surely there were better times ahead for the store.

One weekend the two of us walked from Watershine along the main creek up to the cisterns. These were a series of natural ponds below the waterfall that had been expanded and deepened and lined with concrete. The cisterns originally played some part in processing the ore from the mine, and Francis was hoping to replicate that, albeit at a smaller scale, but when Eliza and I were there they overflowed with clear cool water, falling down the escarpment from the lake. Once, it must have been a busy place, full of noise and steam and clouds of dust, but that day we visited, it was peaceful, like a garden. The weather was hot, summer was coming, and we couldn't resist swimming. The water was icy cold, but the flat rocks beside the pool were sun-warmed and perfect for sunbaking.

'I don't think he'll last much longer,' Eliza said, referring to her dad. 'The doctor says his heart is failing. It's enlarged.'

'Sounds serious.'

'It is. He's always tired, always short of breath, always shitty.' She sighed. 'He's not much, but he's all I have.'

'You have me,' I said.

She smiled at me then. How I loved that smile. 'So I do. So I do.' And she took my hand and kissed me full on the lips. I had never felt so alive, but I tried to contain my joy. After all, we were discussing the decline of her father.

'Have you thought what you will do?' I asked. 'After?'

'After he dies, you mean?' she said.

'Yes. Will you sell the store, move away?'

She looked off into the distance. 'That's what I've always wanted, but now I'm not so sure.'

My heart leapt at that. 'It's not such a terrible place.'

'I'm not sure I can sell it,' she said, as if she hadn't heard me. 'Not now. Any prospective buyer would check out the books, see the cash flow. The amount I could sell it for wouldn't clear the mortgage.' She looked at me. 'I'm trapped.'

'Pub seems to be doing all right,' I said.

'Terrence Earl's company. Owns it outright. Not paying nineteen per cent interest.'

I wasn't sure how I should feel: sorry for her plight, or grateful that she wasn't leaving. 'So what will you do?'

She shrugged. 'Keep it going as long as I can. If the mine opens up, if the mill survives, if interest rates fall, there's a chance we'll turn the corner.' She grimaced. 'Lot of ifs.'

I nodded. 'There's a possibility I might move down here. Permanently.'

Her eyes met mine then. 'I thought you'd be off back to Salt-wood, now the logging strife is settled.'

'That's what I thought. But the Sarge wants me to stay on for a bit. And Francis Hardcastle, this work he's given me, he said it might become full-time. Running security for the mine.'

'Really? You'd move here?'

'Why not? You'd like that, wouldn't you?'

She wasn't smiling, nor was she unhappy; she just regarded me as if contemplating me for the first time. 'I thought you were like all the rest,' she said finally. 'Get what you want, then shoot through.'

I didn't know how to respond, but it cast a pall over the day. Her words made me sad. That she'd thought of me like that. That she thought of the world like that. Of herself.

— —

That day, swimming in the cisterns with Eliza, was the first sugges-tion of the hot weather to come. It was the first day I heard cicadas. There were flowers by the cisterns, and clouds of butterflies. To me, Eliza was beautiful, despite her world-weary ways. The pall lifted and life felt good again. That was me back then, glass half full.

The Valley always seemed green, then as now, but in the following days and weeks the waterfalls coming off the escarp-ment started to dwindle, and up on the plateau above the cliffs you could feel the dryness on your skin. I was driving up every couple of days and I became used to the change in the atmosphere. My ears would pop and I could feel the humidity burn away, the sun somehow harsher on my bare arms, like I was closer to the sun. There was a hint of wood smoke and I recall raising the possibility of bushfires, how it was a potential risk to the operations. Francis was sanguine, said the mine itself was a perfect shelter for personnel, and the lake provided a good supply of water. With a little warning, the pumps could be diverted to fight any outbreaks. Nevertheless, he thanked me for the observation and indicated he would put a strategy in place: installing hoses from the lake to feed sprinklers, protecting the new works he was building below the lake.

And then, as if God had flicked a large switch somewhere, the weather turned. The constant flow of weather from the west, with its arid winds, started to be interspersed with easterlies of an evening, the cooler, fresher winds coming in off the Pacific, rolling moisture across the plateau and into the valley. At first, it was a relief, the hot days and cool nights a perfect combination. Storms began to build above the coastal range, all lightning and fury and pounding rains that would sweep across The Valley, dumping water and moving on. We'd stand outside the pub, watching the light show and laughing as the first fat raindrops fell. The threat of bushfires receded; it seemed the world was returning to balance. But it wasn't, far from it.

The evening it started, we were at the pub. Eliza and me, Mike and Lucas and Suzie. Mike was working on the mine and Lucas was spending a bit of time up there as well, his work on the Miners' Institute almost done.

We were all there, talking about nothing much, when Teramina and Francis walked in. They waved in greeting, not just to us but to all the people in the pub, whether they knew them or not.

They were like royalty; they even waved like royalty. Teramina beamed: she was his queen, and he was her king.

It was the aura of the mine, of course, its potential to enrich all the patrons in the pub. It was still early days; the Hardcastles were fixing up the road and conducting studies, and it would still be many months before the mine was properly operational. And yet Francis had captured the imagination of the community. He and the nuggets he had shown people, extracted from the Gryphon Mine during a scoping study.

Francis was offering shares to a few leading citizens, giving them an opportunity to share in the dream. I don't know where they got the money from, but people wanted to be part of it, feared missing out. I don't think it was the financial projections or geological surveys that won them over; it was holding a nugget in their hand and basking in the charisma of Francis. And for those lacking the wherewithal to invest, like Roddie Game, Francis was promising employment.

At one point that evening, as I went to the bar to fetch new drinks for Eliza and myself, I found myself talking to Teramina. Maybe it was by chance, or maybe she had manoeuvred to intercept me. I rested the drinks on a table as we fell into conversation. She looked about the bar, giving the impression she was proud of what she and her husband were achieving. I remember how glamorous she appeared, how happy. She held a martini glass; I didn't even know the pub possessed them.

'Do you think it's all real?' she asked, gesturing at the happy crowd. 'Sometimes I think it's a dream.'

I thought it was typical Teramina, overly dramatic. 'Those nuggets seem real enough,' I said.

She gave me a huge smile, like I was paying her a direct compliment. 'Let's hope it really is the El Dorado we all want it to be.' And she raised her glass in a toast before taking a sip, cocking an eyebrow above its rim.

I remembered then how the Sarge had asked me to keep an eye on Francis. 'You have any doubts?' I asked.

'None,' she said, and laughed. 'I'm far too committed for that.'

'What does that mean?'

'In for a penny, in for a pound,' she quipped. And then she was away, off to talk to someone else.

I paused for a moment before rejoining the others. Had I imagined it, that she had sought me out? To tell me what? Nothing of consequence. Maybe she was just working the room, gladhanding the less important people while Francis concentrated on the investors.

Nevertheless, it was an evening to remember, like the last ball on the *Titanic*. It was the last time I saw Teramina happy; it was the last time I saw Francis alive. Outside it was already raining. We didn't even notice at first, all of us inside the Bushranger, cocooned by alcohol and bonhomie and hope. But the rain grew heavier and heavier the longer the night went on. And this time, it didn't stop.

chapter fifteen

IT RAINED AND IT RAINED AND IT RAINED SOME MORE. BY THE MIDDLE OF THE
night, the drumming on the new roof Lucas and I had installed
on Watershine was growing increasingly intense. I lay awake in my
upstairs room, listening to it come in waves: easing away, almost
stopping, then coming again with renewed strength. The wind was
picking up, angling the drops into the window. Just as it seemed
to be easing for good, and I drifted towards sleep, it returned
with renewed power, as though the storm had merely paused to
regather its strength. And there was lightning, peeling and slicing
through the sky, coming through the shutters like X-rays, followed
by thunder that shook the house, shook the foundations. It roared
and it whipped and it howled. Watershine shook with it, in thrall
to its elemental power.

I was up at first light, dawn an ill-defined transition. The rain
had consolidated into a steady downpour, constant and unremit-
ting. The wind had dropped to almost nothing, which I took as a
bad sign: there was nothing to propel the clouds away. The rain no
longer fell at an angle, but still it fell. A major front had followed

in the wake of the storm; the drumming on the roof had become constant, with none of the surges and breaks of the night. An east coast low they called it, massive amounts of moisture coming in from the Pacific, an atmospheric river. The ocean might have been an hour's drive, but as the crow flies, we were only forty kilometres inland. The weather was hitting the mountains, all that water-sodden air, lifted by the coastal range, the sky emptying upon us, flowing off the escarpment and into the valley like water flowing into a bathtub. A bathtub with no drain hole, just the Broken River, swollen and angry, overflowing its banks.

I did what I could to secure the house and then I got out of there. Even then, I barely managed to get across the home stream on the drive. The happy brook that gurgled under the bridge had been replaced by a crazy thing: foaming and spitting, no longer clear but mud brown. And rising rapidly. Another half an hour and I could have been trapped in there for days.

Out on the East Road I crawled towards the crossroad, the way treacherous. I eased over to let an orange front-end loader trundle past. As it came abreast, I looked up to see Mike Norfolk in the cab. He waved, and then twirled his fingers in a circle, signalling for me to turn and follow. Directly after him came a farm truck, driven by Teramina, a local at her side, another vehicle behind them.

She stopped next to me, wound down her window, yelled through the rain. 'Heading to the cisterns! Need your help!' It was a command, not a request.

I shouted my agreement. Only as they drove on did I question my response. Might I not be needed elsewhere on such a day? The only policeman in The Valley? But then the second vehicle was past and I needed to concentrate as I tentatively negotiated a three-point turn, taking care not to get bogged on the verges. The East Road, normally so hard-packed and corrugated, was quickly becoming unpassable; only the blue metal pebbles spread by the council on top of the gravel saved it from becoming a bog. I crept back past the gate to the house, crossed the bridge over Watershine Creek and turned right onto the mine road, then took the fork leading to the cisterns. I didn't drive all the way in; there was water flowing across the track and I wasn't confident my two-wheel-drive squad car could navigate it. And even if it did, it was unlikely to make the return journey. So I continued on foot. I was wearing wet-weather gear—a raincoat and boots, a solid hat—but I was almost immediately drenched. And it was cold; the storm front had driven summer back into Australia's interior.

As I got closer to the cisterns, the sound of the rain grew heavier, until I realised it was blending with another sound: the roar of water plummeting off the escarpment. It was too misty to see, but there must have been hundreds of waterfalls. I knew that even if the rain stopped right then, the water would continue to flood down for hours. For days. It would be the same in all directions, water cascading over the rim, down into the valley.

I reached the cisterns, and what I saw shocked me. They were no longer a series of interconnected pools; instead they had joined to form a churning brown river, foaming and twisting, a series of rapids. This newborn river had already carved a slice out of a huge mound of tailings. I remembered it from previous visits; I had thought it was a small hill, covered in shrubs and grass, part of the natural landscape. Now, with its flanks left gaping by the flooding water, I could see it for what it was: mining waste. The entire hillock was threatening to collapse into the stream, to be swept away by the rising flow. I immediately understood Teramina's concern: it might seem like gravel and dirt, but these were tailings left from the old Gryphon Mine, back in the days when environmental regulation was all but non-existent. Who knew what contaminants it could contain: mercury and cyanide, lead and heavy metals? Who knew how much had already been washed into Watershine Creek, how much had already been carried into the lower reaches of the Broken River, down into the national park? It would be a disaster for The Valley, for the clean green credentials of the fruit growers, and catastrophic for the mine, for the hopes of it winning regulatory approval.

Mike was already into it with the front-end loader, trying to clear a channel to direct encroaching water back into the torrent. At least I guessed that was what he was doing; it seemed hopeless: one man in an earth mover against the primal forces of nature. The other men were almost out of sight, clambering higher, armed with nothing more than a couple of shovels, gone to assess the risks further up.

I found Teramina supervising Mike. 'Where's Francis?' I yelled.

'At the mine. Rang last night, said he was on the way there.'

'By himself?'

Even through the rain, I could see trepidation in her eyes. 'He'll be fine. Securing the outdoor equipment. Making sure the pumps are working, feeding them diesel.'

'That road's not up to it. It'll go. He'll be stuck there.'

'He'll be okay,' she said, but it sounded like she was attempting to convince herself more than me. 'Lucas is trying to get up there. He's taking food and drink. They can always shelter in the mine. Drive the cars inside.'

The rain made it difficult to speak, difficult to hear. Difficult to understand.

She pointed at Mike, then across at a bobcat parked off to one side. 'Help him.'

The bobcat was small, tiny compared to Mike's loader. Ineffectual. It had a roof, but the cab was a safety cage, not fully enclosed. The roof provided some shelter from the rain, its impact, but I was soaked, getting cold. The keys had been left in the ignition. I fired the engine, saw the fuel gauge was near full. I'd driven farm equipment before, and it didn't take me long to work out the controls. I drove it across to where Mike was working. He stopped the loader, left the engine running, leapt out. He knew what he wanted, told me how to help.

He'd worked it out in steps. First, clear the area most under threat, then pile rocks where the water might rise to form a barrier. He pointed out the rocks, asked me to bring them over, pile them up ready for use. He was single-minded, focused, engorged with purpose.

It was touch and go, Mike carving into the slag heap even as the water continued to rise. But a tipping point came, when we started to get ahead. It was then that I realised the rain had stopped for the first time since we'd all been sitting at the pub the evening before. It gave the two of us a chance to pause our respective vehicles and shout our thoughts to each other—for while the rain had stopped, the waterfall continued to roar through the mist. The air was sodden with water, fluming out from the falls and the cascades, a heavy fog.

We were shifting protective rocks into place the best part of an hour later when the flow of water coming down the creek abruptly diminished and the level flowing through the cisterns started falling. Mike climbed out of the front-end loader and I climbed out of the bobcat, intrigued. We thought we were getting on top of it. The torrent slowed further, then almost stopped altogether. It didn't make much sense, as it had recommenced raining, albeit more gently, but we took the opportunity to push on, to use the break. If I figured anything, I figured the water had carved itself a new course down the escarpment, maybe into the home creek that ran the other side of the house, taking the pressure off us.

'This is good,' I said to Teramina, who'd come over to join us.

She just stared at me, eyes wild and sort of desperate, hair matted. 'You think?'

'Let's have a squiz,' I said to Mike.

'Be fucking careful,' he replied, but followed me all the same.

The two of us ventured up the side of the slag heap, saw where our work made sense, saw where it didn't, saw where there were gaps, where the lowering water level had exposed some concrete steps, allowing us to get lower, get a better perspective. But we went too far, ventured away from the safety of the embankment.

Mike had already turned, was walking back, when an almighty roar came down upon us, the sound like a physical thing, a monster, some mythical beast made real, from high on the escarpment. There was no way of seeing; the entire cliff face was covered in mist.

'Run!' yelled Mike.

I was only a few paces behind him, running for my life, the roar coming closer, a freight train with the two of us still on the tracks. Mike made it to the stairs, started up, two steps, four, six, almost to safety when it hit me like a wall, sweeping me off my feet, churning and tumbling. Being able to swim had nothing to do with it, not in that force. I was tumbled, a puppet in a washing machine, over and over, under and under, floundering and doomed. I tried to fight, but there was nothing to fight against; it was all around me, naked power. All I could do was try to catch snatches of breath every time I was lifted to the surface. I told myself to relax, to go with it, but how could I? I would drown, I knew, and I was helpless to stop it. Then the current slammed me into something solid and unforgiving, a rock or concrete, shoulder first. Somehow it didn't bash my head in. The water pushed me to the right, away from the main thrust of water, and I found myself caught in a back current, a swirling eddy, trapped in behind the boulder I'd been flung into. Chance and chance alone had spat me out of the current, saved me from certain death. Of course, that didn't make me safe—not yet—but my head was above water. Adrenaline surged; maybe I could survive this.

'Simmo! Simmo! Here!'

It was Mike, calling from the shore. Heedless of his own safety, he stepped into the water, knee deep, then waist deep, risking all to save me.

'No!' I shouted. I'd felt the power of the water, its irresistible surge; no one could defy it. Chance had saved me; chance could just as easily plunge me and Mike back into the maelstrom.

Teramina arrived on the shore above us. She yelled something to Mike and he turned, understood. It was hard for me to see. The water was rising and falling, in and out of my eyes, and I could barely make out what was happening. But then I caught a glimpse: Teramina had given Mike a shovel. A shovel. He grasped it tight by the handle, his other hand clutching some handhold, extending the blade towards me. I grabbed it with one hand, then two, kicking towards him, out from where I was pressed against the rock face. My feet were instantly dragged back towards the stream, the river sucking at me, as if to vacuum the marrow from my bones, the spark from my existence. And yet Mike held firm. Somehow, he managed to slowly pull me towards him. I kicked with all my might, all my remaining strength, anything to help him, no matter how little. And still the river was reluctant to surrender me, to give me back.

Then I had a foot on the ground and Mike had me: my arms were wrapped around him, not the shovel. He held me, held me tight. I couldn't stand, my legs were gone. But he held me, in that waist-deep water, held me for all he was worth, and I held on to him like I was clinging to life itself. Above us, one of the men arrived with rope. He was practically next to us, but he didn't enter the water. He lowered it and Mike looped it around me; the man dragged me out, Mike pushing from below, getting me up onto land. I only just had time to appreciate I was alive before I sank into unconsciousness.

chapter sixteen

THEY GOT ME OUT THE BACK WAY. THE BRIDGE ACROSS WATERSHINE CREEK WAS gone, so we emerged through the farms at the northern end of the East Road. The fields were so waterlogged that at one point Mike had to haul the trucks across one by one using the front-end loader. I was semiconscious, loaded into the front of Teramina's truck, the heater blasting me. They got me to the hotel, into my old room, where a hot bath and a twelve-hour sleep sorted me out. My shoulder still ached from hitting that rock, a huge bruise emerging. But the sleep, the bath and a bowl of minestrone large enough to swim laps in returned me to something approaching normal. Part of it was just being alive: you don't really appreciate how wonderful it feels until you've brushed so close to death. That minestrone tasted better than a gourmet dish in a three-star restaurant.

That next day, the rain was gone and the sun was out, but The Valley was ravaged. No one had died, the road up to Saltwood had been reopened, and somehow the power had been restored to the main spine of the community. But the creeks had overflowed, and the Broken River had flooded, bad in the northern part of the valley, growing worse as it made its way south and more and more creeks joined it. It was at its worst below the confluence with Watershine Creek. The Memorial Park was a muddy mess, the Anzac memorial rising above the water like a lighthouse on an island. There were roofs draped in tarps, downed trees, broken fence lines and stranded cattle, but the river level was falling, the peak having passed sometime during the night. The rain had stopped about the time I'd been plucked from the water. The worst had passed.

But there had been no word from Francis. The road up the escarpment had been cut by a landslip; Lucas had never made it to the mine.

The Sarge arrived as I was finishing my soup and bread, keen to hear how I was, relieved when I recounted what a close-run thing it had been.

'You sure you're up to working?' he asked.

'I'm good.'

'Let's go then,' he said. He had the four-wheel drive, the big one, kitted out for back-country rescues. He'd even put snow chains in the back, just in case we needed them to get through the mud. As we drove, he told me he'd requested a helicopter, but the demand was too high: they were winching people to safety west of the mountains—apparently The Valley wasn't even the worst hit. The Shoalhaven near Nowra wasn't expected to peak for another twelve hours.

'How are we going to get to the mine?' I asked. 'Road's been swept away.'

'Have to go the long way round.'

So we did: back up the main pass, all the way to the Kings Highway. There was no traffic; the road up the Clyde had been closed. The four-wheel drive had a car phone, so once we were within range, the Sarge called through to Dirk Stannard in Saltwood. Stannard was captain of the rural fire brigade and a volunteer with the SES. He was out, but we got a fix on his location. We found him a few blocks off the main street, chainsawing a tree that had fallen across a driveway.

'Need your help, Dirk,' said the Sarge. 'Gotta go find a bloke.'

'Bit busy right now, Sarge,' said Stannard.

'Bloke's in danger. Could be serious.'

Stannard regarded the tree, making his calculation, before delivering his verdict. 'Life and limb, life takes priority.'

The Sarge was smart, drafting Stannard that way. The firies' captain had an encyclopedic knowledge of every back road and fire trail within a fifty-kilometre radius of Saltwood. More than I did, and certainly more than Obswith, who had only been trans-ferred to the town a couple of years before.

'The Gryphon Mine, on the escarpment, east of The Valley. The road up the ravine is out. Can we reach the mine across the plateau?' asked the Sarge.

'Close enough,' said Stannard. 'Might have to hoof the last couple of kilometres.'

'Not flood-affected?' I asked.

The SES man shrugged. 'One way to find out.'

I rode in the back seat, the Sarge driving, Stannard riding shotgun. The first part was easy: along the Kings Highway, then the main road to The Valley for a couple of clicks, then a turn to the left. A council road, dirt but graded and cambered, messed up by the rain, but not so bad provided you stuck to the middle. We encountered a farm truck: the Sarge flicked on the police lights and waved down the driver. It was a young woman, the power on her farm out, off to get some extra petrol for generators and chainsaws. She said the roads were passable as far as she knew.

Getting closer, we turned off the road, negotiating a private driveway. It took us up to a farmstead. There was smoke coming out of the chimney: a good sign. In the distance, not more than a kilometre away, I could see the start of the bush. The farmer pointed the way, offered to come with us, but told us the gates were all unlocked. 'No reason to lock 'em,' he said. 'Ain't nothing past here. Just kangaroos and bunyips.'

The track through the bush was a fire trail, nothing more, not graded, not maintained. The terrain was lumpy, but the crew who had cut the way knew what they were doing: for the first kilometre or two it followed a ridge, dipping only when necessary, staying away from creeks and streams. If anything, the rain had washed it clean, exposing the underlying rock. The biggest issue was fallen limbs: Dirk and I were constantly needing to get out and haul them clear. My shoulder was aching something terrible, but I didn't dare complain. Most of the fallen branches looked recent; the storm must have been a complete fury up here. At one point Dirk was obliged to use his chainsaw.

We reached a gate with an old cattle grid.

'All used to be grazing country once,' Dirk informed us. 'This is the border between the national park behind us and the state forest.'

'I can't see the difference,' I said.

'There isn't any. Not to look at.'

The fire tracks merged and split, but Dirk knew where he was. It was like he had a sixth sense. He had maps, a compass and a handheld GPS device that gave coordinates, which he could then see on the map, but he barely referenced them. When he did I had the impression he was checking the maps for errors, not trying to glean information from them.

'Almost there,' he said. And then a few minutes later: 'Anywhere here, mate. We'll need to walk the rest of the way.'

There was a kind of bay on the right and the Sarge pulled over. It looked like others had parked there, before the storm, but it was empty when we arrived.

'Bushwalkers,' said Dirk. 'They can't have driven through the national park. Must have come from closer to the mountains.'

'Why here?' I asked.

'The lake near the mine. The view over the valley.'

It wasn't so very hard. The bushwalkers must have been frequent enough visitors to have formed a discernible track. It wasn't a straight line—where there were gullies, the growth bloomed into pockets of dense rainforest—but the track mostly kept to the high ground, circumventing the thickets, following the ridge, with its rocks and sparse vegetation. We climbed a bluff, and from there we could see the granite knob above the Gryphon Mine. There was one more difficult gully, and then we were there.

As we emerged from the trees, the sun was really beating down, barely a cloud in the sky. But the water was still rushing into the lake, leaving a long brown stain, and rushing out again, the landscape still giving up its moisture. We could see the water level of the lake had fallen from its peak: there was a ring of mud and rocks around it a metre or so high.

We gained the road and walked up it to the mine entrance. There we found Francis's truck parked by the steel doors, keys in the ignition. The mine doors were wide open. We thought of driving in, using the headlights, but we walked. I'm not sure why: I think we just wanted to take care, take it slowly, not make any mistakes.

There was no light inside the mine. There was a generator close by the entrance. The Sarge gave it the once-over, didn't try to start it. 'Out of gas,' he declared. 'Run dry.'

I tried yelling out his name: 'Francis! Francis!'

The Sarge and Stannard joined me, but our entreaties echoed away into nothing.

We had brought torches, were prepared to go all the way down if necessary. We started descending, shouting his name as we went, the sound echoing and then falling into complete silence. There is nothing as black as a mine, nothing as silent. Except maybe a grave. 'Francis? Francis!' we yelled, pausing for a response. I think we were yelling to reassure ourselves, to reinforce our purpose, not because we were expecting an answer. The silence was extreme, sucking the sound from the world.

We descended for about fifteen minutes, and then we reached the water, as black and impenetrable as the Styx. The mine was flooded. There was no sign of Francis. He was gone.

chapter seventeen

2024

NELL LEAVES WATERSHINE AND JOGS BACK TO THE MINERS' INSTITUTE, READY to push on with the investigation. She's had enough of self-reflection. She wants to find Wolfgang Burnside's killer, find out if his death is somehow connected to her, to the ownership of the land. Hopefully, the letter will begin to answer that.

'Where is it?' she demands of Ivan as she walks into their makeshift office.

'Hello to you too.'

She ignores his attempt at levity, focused once more. 'Where's the letter?'

'In Dubbo. Duty officer wants your permission to open it.'

'Seriously? Of course they should open it.'

'We thought that's what you might say.'

Nell sits, then stands again, listens as Ivan calls through, requesting the officer scan the letter and email it through to Nell.

He hangs up, addresses her. 'It arrived the same day we left. No one thought anything of it, they were going to leave it there until you got back. Then an intern noticed the sender's name.'

'An intern?' says Nell. 'For fuck's sake.'

'I know, right?'

Nell's email gives its silent notification. She opens the attachment, quickly reads it, then prints it out. It's dated five days before Wolfgang died, the Thursday.

Dear Detective Senior Constable Buchanan,

I am writing to you in relation to a significant parcel of land located in The Valley in southern New South Wales.

I wish to purchase this real estate from its rightful owner.

Records indicate the last registered owner of the property was a Ms Amber Jones.

Furthermore, I have reason to believe a) she was your mother and, if so, b) you may have inherited this land and that you are now its rightful owner.

Please forgive me if this is not the case. If you have on-sold the property, I would be grateful to learn the identity of the new owner.

I also have reason to believe you to be the majority shareholder in a company called Gryphon Number Two Pty Ltd, which may control, or have interest in, some residual infrastructure connected to an abandoned goldmine sited on the land.

I realise this may come as a surprise, and that you may harbour suspicions about my bona fides and my intentions. Let me assure you that this approach is genuine.

Please feel free to look into myself and my reputation,
using whatever means are at your disposal.
I hope to hear from you in the near future.
All the very best,
Wolfgang Burnside
CEO, The Valley Power Corporation

The signature is a flourish of blue ink: a fountain pen, stretching across half the page.

Nell reads the letter for a second time, then a third.

'Nothing we don't already know,' she says. 'But he knew. About my mother. Before I did. Do you think he had any idea that we were half-siblings?'

Ivan looks at her, eyes sympathetic. 'Sorry. There's nothing to indicate that he did.'

She again examines the sheet of paper. Written on a computer, only the scrawled sign-off to personalise it. So different from her own small, self-contained signature.

'How could he have known that Amber was my mother when I didn't?' she asks.

'Because he had a good reason to seek her out. To find the owner of the land. Someone here in The Valley might have remembered her, remembered she'd inherited it. He had money and resources, might have hired an investigator. Learnt she was dead, and that you were her daughter.'

Ivan turns to his computer, runs a search for Amber Jones, leaving Nell to re-read the letter yet again. Her initial interpretation was correct: it supplies no new information. And yet there is something unsettling about it. Maybe the fact that after so many years they were so close to connecting; now they never will. Someone killed him, denying her the opportunity.

'Here,' says Ivan, summoning her over.

It's a long feature, written two years ago by a crime reporter on the *Sydney Morning Herald*, Bethanie Glass. The feature ends:

> The resolution of the case was a huge success for Detective Sergeant Ivan Lucic, but emotionally challenging for his deputy, Detective Constable Nell Buchanan. Not only were members of her family implicated, but as a sad and dramatic twist, Constable Buchanan learnt that she was adopted, and that her birth mother, Amber Jones, had died mere days after the constable was born.

A twist of anger passes through Nell; her private affairs reported for the entertainment of the masses. But Ivan is right: Wolfgang had good reason to identify her as the likely owner of the land. Two years ago it would have been difficult, but not anymore.

And yet something still bothers her. At first she thinks it's the brutal coincidence: Wolfgang coming to find her but unaware of their relationship. But that's not it; it's something else; something that doesn't add up. And then she catches the elusive tendril.

'He was trying to find me. He was trying to buy the land. You don't imagine that's what got him killed, do you? Someone didn't want him gaining possession?'

Ivan says nothing, but his eyes have locked on hers, the way they do when he's concentrating or deep in thought.

Nell continues. 'And if Wolfgang was able to find me, why couldn't Willard Halliday? He's the company secretary. And my father, Simmons Burnside. How come they never found me? How come they never came searching for Amber?'

Ivan's gaze remains loaded with concentration, but he doesn't answer. She doesn't need him to.

'Tyffany didn't know,' he says at last. 'Remember? She said Amber owned the land. Not you. That Wolfgang had been trying to find her, hadn't been able to find any trace of her. He knew Amber was dead; she didn't. So maybe he and his wife weren't the tight-knit unit she's been claiming?'

'You think she showed us the nugget as some sort of distraction?' she asks.

'Dangerous game to play,' he replies. 'Drawing attention to herself if she has something to hide.'

Nell looks at the letter again. 'Wolfgang only wrote this last week, when Tyffany was already in Sydney. Entirely feasible he'd just found out, hadn't told her yet. Just like the nugget.'

She can see Ivan considering the possibilities before nodding his agreement. 'You want to upload the letter into the system? Could be important,' he says.

'Of course,' she replies, still unsettled by this collision between her personal interests and the homicide case.

'What about this lawyer, Willard Halliday? Pay him a visit?' Ivan asks. 'You could find out what he knows about the land, whether it's yours or not, and ask who gave authority to log it.'

Nell wants to say yes, but she shakes her head. 'Catching the killer has to take priority. Not my personal concerns.'

'You might be right. On the other hand, if Willard was the lawyer for the old owner, the one who bequeathed the land to your mother, then he's been around for a long time. Who knows what he might be able to tell us about Wolfgang and his connections?'

Nell considers this, trying to work out where the homicide case starts and her personal interests end, but is unable to determine a clear line.

Her train of thought is interrupted by a knock at the door, a businesslike rap, and it opens before the detectives can respond.

It's Vicary Hearst, appearing pleased with himself.

'Afternoon, folks,' he says jovially. 'Update for you.'

'Right,' says Ivan, shooting a glance at Nell. It lasts a fraction of a second, but after three years working together, it's enough for her to know what he's thinking, to be thinking the same herself: Plodder's reluctance to involve the local police, the cryptic warning from Feral Phelan.

'Wasn't expecting to see you back here so soon,' says Ivan. 'What have you got?'

'CCTV. In the system, but I can save you the trouble of trawling through it.'

'Thanks,' says Nell. 'Much appreciated. The lemon-coloured van?'

'The same.' Vicary takes a seat, uninvited. 'I was up most of the night, going through everything we've got.'

'What have you found?' asks Nell.

'Nothing. That's the point.'

'You want to explain that?' says Ivan. Nell can hear the faintest suggestion of irritation in her partner's words.

'Sure,' says Vicary, unperturbed. 'We know the van came from the north, and the only way into The Valley from the north is the road down the pass, leading off the Kings Highway between Saltwood and the coastal range.'

'Yes. I follow,' says Ivan.

'If the van came from the coast, it would have passed under the cameras on the Kings Highway, just up from where it branches off the Princes Highway. I've been through the footage for the previous day. Nothing.'

'There're no other roads? No back ways?'

'There are, but those are dirt tracks through the forest. You'd need a good reason to take them.'

'Like not being caught on camera?'

'Precisely.'

'And the other direction? From Saltwood?'

'Similar. We have cameras on the main street. Ninety-five per cent of through traffic is going to pass that way. There's nothing on the tape.'

'So what's your conclusion?' asks Ivan.

'That wherever the van came from, the driver was keen to circumvent the CCTV.'

Ivan agrees. 'Which is probably how you would behave if you had a body in the back.' He stands, offers his hand. Vicary Hearst stands too, shakes it. 'Thanks for coming, Vicary. That's very helpful.'

'No problem. No problem at all. I needed to come down this way, thought I would tell you in person.' He glances around the room, as if expecting the homicide detectives would have a whiteboard, the way they do on television. 'How's the case going? Getting anywhere?'

Nell can sense Ivan bristle, but her partner keeps his voice light and pleasant. 'Steady progress, thanks. Steady progress.'

chapter eighteen

1990

STANDING THERE IN THE MINE WITH THE SARGE, STARING INTO THAT INK-BLACK water, I understood what had happened during the storm; why the torrent flooding into the cisterns had temporarily paused, deceiving Mike and myself, almost costing me my life. It hadn't come from the water finding a new course down the escarpment—it was the result of the lake collapsing into the mine. And once the mine was full, it started pouring down the hillside once more, busting the dam wall and almost killing me.

I never doubted Francis Hardcastle was dead. His car was there, keys in the ignition, doors to the mine wide open. Later on, all sorts of conspiracy theories emerged, but standing, staring at that water, there was no other conclusion to draw.

'Poor fucker,' said the Sarge, and that was that.

— —

We investigated the possibility of draining the mine, but the Sarge brought in a technical expert, a mining engineer from Captains Flat, who said it was impossible: the more we drained the mine, the more the lake would fill it. We had no choice: Hardcastle's body would remain where it laid.

Teramina was broken, inconsolable. She couldn't believe it. Kept blaming herself for letting him go up there by himself. It was like some light in her had been extinguished; this new hope, this new life, had been taken from her and she had nothing left but a flooded mine and mounting debts.

It was left to me to prepare a report for the coroner. I set out the circumstances clearly and concisely: the onset of the storm, Francis calling Teramina to tell her he was heading to the Gryphon, the massive flooding over the next twenty-four hours, the long-held fears that the mine was unstable, susceptible to cave-ins, the risks involved in exploratory blasting under the lake. I set down clearly our efforts to discover what had become of Hardcastle: the disintegration of the one road to the mine, the Sarge and I walking in with Dirk Stannard, finding Hardcastle's car parked directly outside the mine entrance, the steel gateway open, our conclusion that he had drowned when the lake burst into the mine, or the possibility he had been crushed by the cave-in.

I thought I'd done a pretty good job, and the Sarge was impressed. Commended me. But he suggested I wind back the conclusion that Hardcastle was dead. 'You're right, no doubt. But leave that for the coroner. They don't appreciate having their findings pre-empted.'

I had to hand it to the Sarge; he had an uncanny ability to understand those in power and how they operated.

Preparing the report would be my last job in The Valley, I knew that. The forestry wars were over, the national park declared, and now there was no possibility of the mine ever becoming productive. The mill might survive, but it was downsizing; there was nothing to justify me remaining in The Valley. Nothing except Eliza, of course.

I went to see her, to tell her, but she already knew.

'I'll come down to see you every weekend,' I promised.

'Sure you will.' She smiled indulgently.

Strangely, after that our relationship entered a golden period, we knew it was coming to an end and we were both determined to make the most of it. Her dad's health was deteriorating rapidly. She said that he was unlikely to last the year. You could see the sadness in her eyes, but also a kind of relief that what happened next had been taken out of her control. Like me, she understood that her time in The Valley was almost over. Her father would die, she would declare the estate bankrupt and leave it to the administrators to clean up the mess. She'd have no money, but at least she'd be free.

— —

After some weeks, Teramina's grief solidified into something harder, more resolute. She was in debt and she needed her husband to be declared dead. She wasn't being callous, she said, just practical. She explained it to me, her desire to move on, saying she wanted to wind up the company, distribute the remaining funds to shareholders. She'd invested a lot of her own money and she needed it back. But she couldn't access it, not until she had his death certificate. I suspected she was driven as much by emotional need as the financial necessity: the need for closure, the need for someone in authority to confirm her husband really wasn't returning. I assured her it would all be okay and that the process would be straightforward.

But it wasn't. Like everyone else, I'd assumed the coroner's finding was a foregone conclusion. Instead, she delivered an open finding. There was no body. According to the Sarge, that was always a red flag at an inquest. And no one had actually seen Hardcastle enter the mine, or even pass up the road that night. There was only the late-night phone call to Teramina. To us, it was open and shut: he had good cause to rush to the Gryphon that night and had rung to inform his wife of his intentions. But the coroner wasn't convinced. A rumour had emerged, from where I have no idea, that Hardcastle had embezzled funds and been planning to flee with shareholders' money. It was uncorroborated, there was no evidence, but it was enough to sow a seed of doubt, to raise the possibility he wasn't dead, that he had seized the opportunity to take the money and scarper. That's all it was, a suggestion, a whisper, an insinuation, but it was enough to sway the coroner. She declined to declare Hardcastle dead.

The Sarge was angry and dismissive. 'Arse-covering,' he steamed. 'Bitch doesn't care about the widow or the workers, just making sure she isn't exposed. Fucking fence sitter.'

Teramina wasn't angry, but she was visibly upset, in a quieter, more intense way than the Sarge. Without a death certificate, without the official declaration, it meant there was uncertainty over whether Francis was in fact dead. But instead of arousing her hopes, it played on her mind, raising the spectre of betrayal, that he had in fact taken the money and run.

She started going downhill after that. Her grief turned into something more malignant, more damaging. Her mental health started to fracture. She locked herself away at Ellensby and it was left to me to call in, conduct welfare checks. She was becoming more and more distressed. She couldn't wind up the mining company; she didn't have the authority, despite being the one who had invested the most money. The majority of shares were held in the name of Francis Hardcastle. That had been their trade-off. She could apply to take control of the company, but that would be expensive, and for the first time in her life she found herself short of money. That shocked her, I could see, as if it had never occurred to her that wealth was a finite resource, that it wasn't a continual, everlasting flow.

I knew all of this because I became her confidant. Maybe it was the uniform; more likely it was because she had no one else. She'd always held herself above the community, one of our 'betters', but now she was alone, fraying at the edges, isolated in her grand homestead, a queen without her king, a monarch without a kingdom. She was only in her forties, but her gait and her mannerisms began to resemble those of an older woman. She told me she couldn't sleep, her mind torn between possibilities: he was dead; he was alive, perhaps kidnapped, needing her help; he was alive, and had run off with some buxom twenty-year-old. She described it as a type of purgatory. She asked me to investigate: she wanted the matter settled once and for all. She even offered me money, money she was increasingly short of, and invited me to stay at Watershine for as long as I wished. One day, when I called by Ellensby, there was an antique dealer there, appraising the furniture and artworks.

I realised some heirlooms were already gone: she was pawning her heritage.

I didn't take her money, but I stayed on at Watershine, living rent-free. It didn't bother me. She still had Ellensby, and she still had her fancy car and elegant clothes. Maybe it was wrong of me, but I thought she was crying poor, that compared to Eliza and her dad she was doing just fine, that the source of her distress wasn't her bank account but the spectre of her lost husband.

I asked the Sarge about her money. He was a shareholder, after all. He said it sounded like bullshit to him, but he put me on to the lawyer, Willard Halliday, who was the company secretary, who put me on to Fred Wallington, the company accountant. Wallington informed me that there were certainly irregularities in the books, that Francis had displayed an unfortunate tendency to use the company funds as his own. Groceries, expensive dinners in Saltwood, repairs to Ellensby, drinks at the Bushranger, trips to Sydney and Melbourne and overseas, he and Teramina living the high life, their wedding and honeymoon. Even the account he had set up for me at the general store to buy hardware.

'The important thing is this,' Fred Wallington summarised. 'I can account for every cent that was spent. Most of the expenditure was totally appropriate, some of it wasn't. But none of it is missing. If Francis Hardcastle is still alive and on the run, he hasn't taken any company money with him.'

That was good enough for me. I went and told Teramina. She was grateful. Stoic. If she cried, she waited for me to leave first.

I didn't do any more repairs at Watershine: there was no more money for it, and I knew I would be leaving soon. But it gave me some satisfaction that I'd done enough to ensure the house would last for many years yet. The new roof Lucas and I had put on had survived the storm without leaking. If it could repel that, it would repel anything. My last job was building a new bridge across the home creek. The council were constructing a new bridge over Watershine Creek out on the East Road, concrete and steel, and they were more than happy to give me the old timbers from the original bridge.

Towards the end of my time at Watershine, I walked up to the cisterns, the first time I'd ventured there since I almost drowned. It was almost unrecognisable from that day: the water was placid, ducks were floating on the ponds. The slag heaps were still more or less in place, although large sections had collapsed into the works, into the cisterns. I wondered if they would clear again over time, or remain buried. Not that it mattered. They weren't going to be of any use now.

Then Teramina asked me to vacate Watershine, told me she was going to move in herself, that she could no longer wait for me to leave The Valley. She was renting out Ellensby to a production company eager to use it for an upcoming feature film, and then she was going to put the homestead on the market. She couldn't afford to keep it.

'You'll get a pretty penny for it,' I told her, a feeble attempt to cheer her up.

She was wasted. She'd lost a lot of weight and her skin was pallid and loose on her, just as her once-stylish clothes now hung on her frame, two sizes too big.

'Ellensby has been in the family since it was built in the 1840s and rebuilt in the 1880s,' she said. 'I thought the mine would secure it forever. Instead, it's been its undoing.' Her eyes had withdrawn into their sockets. 'My legacy.'

'I'm sorry,' I said, knowing the words were inadequate, feeling guilty all over again.

'I'll need every cent to clear my debts,' she said. 'And Sergeant Obswith says it's time for you to return to Saltwood.'

'Yes. It is.'

I went to break the news to Eliza. We'd known our relationship was coming to an end, that I'd always been keener than she was. Sometimes it felt as though I were just an entertainment, something to relieve the boredom of her days and the drudgery of caring for her father. But those last weeks had been good, given me some hope. I went to her, thinking she might come with me, join me in Saltwood once her father had succumbed.

And that's when she told me that she was pregnant, that we were going to have a baby.

chapter nineteen

FRANCIS HARDCASTLE WAS DEAD OR MISSING, THE MINE RECEDED INTO HISTORY
and The Valley returned to stupor. The loggers left, the mill
struggled on, the orchards and dairy farms recovered from the
floods. Eliza's dad died and Wolfgang was born. I wanted to quit
the force and move down to The Valley to be with Eliza and Wolf,
to be a real family, but we couldn't afford it. Eliza showed me
the books, and her logic was irrefutable: the only way we could
save the store was with my salary. So I commuted up to Saltwood
each day. I picked up weekend shifts at the sawmill and driving
fruit trucks. It was hand-to-mouth at first, but gradually we started
to make headway. Australia emerged from the recession we had to
have and interest rates on the small business loan fell from a high
of nineteen per cent to just a little over eight by 1994. We still didn't
have much money, but our heads were back above water and we
could see the shoreline. The weather was kind and the farmers
were doing well, spending a little more at our shop each quarter.
One of the wineries won some big prizes, and land became more
valuable as other winemakers followed. The annual agricultural

show was revived, rebranded as a weekend harvest festival, with a pop concert at the cricket ground on the Saturday night for the backpackers and the fruit pickers and returning locals.

But as one year folded into the next, and then the next, and then another, Eliza and I found ourselves fighting more and more, until we reached a point where we resented each other. There were nights when I'd just stay at Saltwood, but then I would miss my son and head back down. That's what united us: our love for Wolfgang; we never would have stayed together if it wasn't for him. We buckled under, committed to making the store work and the marriage too, just for him. Sometimes, when she'd had a few drinks and she lowered her guard, I could see gratitude in Eliza's eyes, that I had stayed, and sometimes I saw the contempt, that I would bother with her. I didn't really understand it then, that damage, that lack of self-esteem. What a monster her father must have been, what a cruel and lonely childhood she'd endured.

— —

After Teramina sold Ellensby, she left The Valley. Her debts were erased, but that seemed of little consolation to her. She was anxious and she was depressed, ashamed at losing her family seat, grief-stricken for her husband, haunted by the rumours he was still alive and had betrayed her. Whatever the reason, she went off travelling, leaving Watershine vacant. I'd call in every now and then if I was out on the East Road, just to make sure the place was okay. One weekend, Mike and Lucas and I took the last of the timbers from the old East Road bridge and made the road up the escarpment passable. Willard Halliday asked us to do it, said as company secretary of Gryphon Number Two Pty Ltd he was authorised to make minor expenditures, up to a certain limit. He thought there was some equipment up there that the company could sell off. That made sense: Francis had moved some air compressors and generators inside the mine before his demise.

Teramina eventually returned from her travels and moved back into Watershine. At first she seemed better, her health restored. She told me she'd thought of selling it, the house and the land, but realised if she did, then she would have nothing left. It was her one remaining anchor. She told me she'd journeyed overseas, but international travel had lost its allure and so she came back. She said she'd drifted, contemplated killing herself. She told me that in a matter-of-fact manner, like suicide was the most normal thing in the world. All her born-to-rule entitlement had been stripped away and replaced by something more honest, more fundamental. Whereas she had once seemed skittish and erratic, she became brutally honest; whereas once her eyes had darted this way and that, she now looked me in the eye and held my gaze. She confided that she and Francis had been trying for children, even considered adopting. She laughed at herself, deriding her own aspirations, her desire to continue the Cloverton line, to have someone to pass it all down to. I appreciated some of her grief then, how deep it ran, knowing how much I loved Wolf and how fulfilling I found it to be a father.

One Tuesday night, after a fight with Eliza, I was drinking by myself at the pub when Teramina found me there. She was alone and already a little drunk. I was feeling sorry for myself, so we made a good pair. We got to talking. And the more we drank, the more we talked, the more we unburdened ourselves. She recounted how she'd hit rock bottom down on the Murray River. She'd been thinking more and more of suicide, of ending it all. Instead, she'd stayed there for more than three months, saved from herself by a young woman called Amber living a subsistence life in the forest all by herself, without vanity or ego, unworried by what others might think of her, uninterested in material possessions. Through the example of her existence, she had led Teramina to realise that wealth and privilege and social standing were nothing but illusions.

I didn't see it then, not trapped as I was in the world of mortgages and children and trying to get ahead, but I listened. I still thought it was a luxury that the rich could afford, this rejection of the material. Nevertheless, I could see that Teramina had recovered during her time away: she'd regained her weight and her skin was clear.

But when I commented on it, she seemed to smile and frown at the same time, a sadness in her eyes. She became listless, and over the following months, her health again began to deteriorate. It was not as bad as before her travels, but noticeable nevertheless.

'Have you ever been back up there?' she asked. 'To the mine?'

'Once or twice. When we fixed up the road.'

'I have. Until recently, I'd go up every now and then. I think if Francis was in the graveyard, I would have visited him there. Instead, up by the lake, I felt somehow closer to him. I'd walk around, thinking of what might have been, appreciating his innovations, understanding his plans.'

'Until recently? Have you stopped?'

But she didn't answer. 'I have a favour to ask,' she said instead, changing the subject. 'I'm preparing my will. Willard Halliday is writing it up. I'd like you to be executor.'

'Of course,' I said. 'You're not ill, are you?'

'No. Not anymore. It's just a precaution.'

Again, I thought of wills and estates and executors as belonging to that other world, the world of the wealthy. If I died, or Eliza, all we would be leaving each other would be debts. Still, I persisted. 'Is there anything wrong?' I asked.

'My accountant died three weeks ago. Fred Wallington.'

'So I heard.'

'I have a new person. A woman in Goulburn: Juanita Malakova. She's very thorough.'

'I see.'

'She thinks there's money missing.'

'Missing? From where?'

'My accounts. She thinks Fred Wallington syphoned it off. She's trying to work through it.' Teramina looked like she was about to break down in tears.

'I see,' I said. But I didn't, not yet. 'What about the company? Wasn't there still money in there?'

'Juanita is trying to find out. But it's been more than three years. I don't hold out much hope.'

'You want me to investigate?'

She smiled wanly at that. 'Wallington is dead and my money has gone. I'm not sure there's a lot you can do about it.'

'He had access to your accounts?'

'Most of them, yes.'

'Most? Not all?'

'I didn't think so.'

'Who else knew the details?'

'Just me,' she said. 'Just me and Francis.'

— —

That Friday, Teramina came to the store and gave me a copy of her new will, 'just in case'. It was sealed. She said she was leaving Watershine to a dear friend, but needed someone she could trust to see it implemented. I didn't realise it at the time, but she was putting on a brave face. She was more desperate, more despairing, than I realised. It was the last time I saw her; she killed herself not long afterwards.

We buried her in the little graveyard behind the church. It was a sad affair: Terrence Earl had bought Ellensby and denied permission for her to be buried in the family plot on the property. I went up to see Willard the next week, told him I knew I was the executor. He said he was glad to see me, grateful that Teramina had thought to inform me, and we set about contacting her heir: Amber Jones.

PART TWO

PART TWO

chapter twenty

1994

THE CROWD SWIRLED AND SHIFTED, RISING AND FALLING IN WAVES, MOVING in time with the music. Amber felt she was at sea, floating in the swell, embraced by euphoria, the band a lighthouse, the stage a headland, the crowd an ocean. She had never seen the sea, yet she believed she could taste the salt on her tongue, see blues and greens where she knew they could not exist, the dope and the alcohol and the mushrooms inciting an artificial synaesthesia, accelerating her senses, then slowing them again, like a tidal surge. There was heightened awareness, then an easing into the soporific, a vibration deep and mellow within her, a bass note counterpointing the band's treble, a riding of the current, a submission to the undertow. Another sensation came to her, the smell of cinnamon and mint, and then it was gone, fleeting, leaving a residual sense of wellbeing. Her second night in The Valley, and she felt herself aligning with the landscape, like stars in the sky.

She had never seen so many people, let alone been engulfed by them. And these were her people, her destiny, her crowd, these straggly strangers and anonymous shapes, backpackers and fruit pickers and vagabonds. She swayed with the music, letting it take her, move her, feeling the gravity of their mass. There was a young woman of a similar age, twirling and gyrating, near naked from the waist up, painted breasts beneath a string vest, a sarong tied around her waist, lost in her own world, dancing to her own music. Amber realised it was Suzie, her new friend. A young man joined her, his hair long and red, his beard fuzzy sand, dancing like a bird in plumage, courtship hips gyrating, but Suzie had her eyes closed, was unaware of the man's attention.

The current pulled, the crowd moved, and Amber was carried forward, closer to the stage, into the vortex, arms above her head, waving not drowning. The band stepped it up, louder and louder, more and more passionate until, reaching a mighty crescendo, it came to a stop. There was a roar of approval from the crowd, the band left stationary, almost bewildered by their accomplishment, until the lights faded and the last smattering of applause sputtered and died. Amber breathed out. She had never experienced anything comparable in her twenty years; nothing even close.

The audience ebbed away, a receding tide, leaving her standing alone, eyes closed and not wanting it to end, a warm breeze playing on her skin, smooth like a silken shift. No longer carried by the crowd, she too moved from in front of the stage, and began giggling to herself with the pleasure of this new existence. She walked towards the cricket ground latrines, red-brick and pungent, rendered magical by candlelight and lanterns and the substances flowing within her.

Afterwards she wandered aimlessly while roadies shuffled about, setting up for the next act. She searched for Suzie, but her friend was gone. So Amber stumbled off towards the darkness, seeking a patch of solitude. She lay on her back, eyes closed, away from the stage, away from everyone, drawing circles with her open palm, feeling the texture of the new-mown grass, the first hint of dew, its taste imagined on her tongue, the greenness passing smooth shapes through her mind.

She sensed someone sitting beside her and she sat up, opened her eyes.

It was a man, hair ruffled, thick and messy and expressive. He was watching her.

'You have impressive hair,' she said.

He laughed and she felt warmed by the sound of it: like bells in the sunshine. There was something golden about this person, even in the half-light. Maybe because of the half-light. She decided he must be a kindred spirit without knowing why.

'Good band,' he said.

'Great band,' she said.

'Saw you dancing,' he said.

'And?'

'You're very pretty.'

'Good drugs,' she said.

'Great drugs.' He laughed, again the purity of bells.

They fell into silence then and he began to roll a joint, concentrating, not speaking, half in and out of the light from the stage, darkness and the bush behind them. She liked that, this lack of talk, the man just sitting there, assured. The colour of gold deepened, becoming coppery. She could smell his sweat and his empathy. A good man.

'What's your name?' she asked.

'Lucas.'

She tasted it, felt it, and it seemed right, part of his alloy, a part of the night.

'Amber,' she said, her name both strange and familiar.

'That's beautiful,' he said, and he lit the joint. 'A name as old as humanity.'

She laughed. 'I'm not so old.'

He drew deep on the reefer before breathing out. 'The ancient Greeks worshipped a sun god, Helios, who had a son and seven daughters. When the son died, his sisters wept tears of golden sunlight that were hardened by their grief to become amber.'

She stared at him. 'How could you know that?'

He handed her the joint. 'When I was a kid, in one of the houses where I was fostered, there were only half-a-dozen books. One was about Greek mythology.' He looked away, up at the starfield hanging over them like Christmas decorations. 'I loved that book.'

She drew on the glowing joint. She enjoyed the drug, had taken it before; it somehow melded her senses, mixed them together into a more eloquent palette, helped incite the synaesthesia.

The music started again, a folk duo, singing songs nicely dated, as though they had shed a couple of decades and were back in the 1970s. She imagined she saw the notes flowing into the sky, white like doves, watching as they blended with the stars. Above them, the Milky Way was painted across the sky, shimmering in time.

'What are stars?' she asked, the joint finished, the duo pausing between songs.

'Billions and billions of suns,' Lucas replied.

She smiled at the image. 'Suns?'

'Same as our own, some bigger, some smaller, just so far away that they seem tiny. Just pinpricks of light.'

'I heard they were the souls of the dead,' she whispered. She wondered if Teramina was up there, a tiny prick of light. Which one?

He laughed. 'No. Some aren't even single stars but whole galaxies, billions of stars, but so small they appear to be a single star.'

'But the dead,' she whispered.

She stood then, the stars swirling, dancing to unheard music, spiralling, and she understood she had consumed too much, stood up too quickly. Dope and cider and a hot dog and mushroom juice sluicing inside her. The stars spun more quickly and she felt ill. A bitter taste came into her mouth; she recognised it only too well: the unwanted flavour of reality. Her head was spinning as well now, in a different direction from the stars, so that she was out of synch, and the inevitability of vomiting occurred to her.

'Nice to meet you, Lucas,' she managed, bowing formally, before hurrying away, stumbling towards the anonymous dark of the surrounding bushland, beyond the boundary fence, beyond the circle of light.

——

She woke much later, lying out there at the edge of the cricket ground, being gently shaken, someone holding her arm.

'Are you okay?' It was a man's voice, his face in silhouette, backlit from the showground lights. The music was finished. There was only the soft hum of a generator.

'What time is it?' asked Amber. She needed water and her neck hurt. So did her head.

'Late,' said the man. 'Or very early.'

Amber tried to sit up, accomplished it at the second attempt. The showground was all but empty. 'It's over?'

'Well and truly.'

She remembered him then: Lucas, all gold and promise, half a memory and half a dream. She looked back to the man, saw now it was Simmons Burnside. 'What are you doing here?' asked Amber.

'Making sure you're okay,' he replied. 'Let's get you home.'

chapter twenty-one

AMBER JONES HAD LEFT HER HOME IN THE FOREST BEFORE, BUT NOTHING LIKE this. Since her grandfather had died almost six years before, her mother had been away more than she'd been at home, leaving Amber to live alone in the family's shack on its island by the river, keeping to herself, a teenage hermit. She'd been happy there, but as the years passed, she'd become increasingly aware of the wider world and what it might hold. She'd taken it upon herself to venture to nearby towns, either by bike or hitchhiking—not just Tulong for supplies and Boonlea for library books, but across the Murray to Echuca, where she'd sneak into the movie theatre if the weather was too hot or too cold or too wet. She'd see groups of teenagers laughing together and wondered what it might be like to experience such companionship. At the railway station she'd watch the trains arrive and depart and wondered where they might take her, knowing the tracks led to Melbourne and even to the sea. She'd become increasingly restless, dreaming of sallying forth, and so the lawyer's letter seemed to be delivered by fate and not just Australia Post. It was the catalyst she needed, requesting her attendance at his office in Saltwood.

And so she had studied maps, counted her cash, asked for advice at the Boonlea library, decided on her route. First, she took a bus to Albury, then the train to Goulburn, amazed at the length of all those carriages strung together, astounded at the power of the locomotive. She was suspicious of the smell of diesel and the railway pies, but open-eyed and curious about her fellow travellers. There was an old man, as crumpled as his suit, and a mother with children she was unable to control no matter how much she beseeched them, and a young man with a guitar, long hair and a beard so wispy it seemed spun from the finest cotton. She had an old backpack of her grandfather's and a swag and a little stove. She had some money, but it was unfamiliar enough for her to regard it with respect, a last resort, not something to be squandered. She didn't know how long she might need it to last. She still found it difficult to anticipate prices, bewildered at times by the arbitrary value the world chose to demand for different commodities.

She feared she was running late, that she wouldn't reach Saltwood in time. The lawyer's letter had languished for weeks at the general store-cum-post office in Tulong until she'd eventually ridden her bike there to buy essentials. She'd read it at once, then spent the rest of the day re-reading it, pondering its meaning from every possible angle before making the decision to travel north. She read it again on the bus and again on the train. At first, she'd found it difficult to get beyond the news that Teramina Hardcastle had died, one of her very few acquaintances from beyond the forest. But by the time she'd set out on her journey, she'd moved on to the implications the letter held for her future. It seemed that Teramina had bequeathed her property.

She left the train at Goulburn, watching it recede as it gathered pace, heading towards Sydney, another magical name, long imagined. Goulburn was a country town, she knew that, but to her it seemed a metropolis, and she was glad she had chosen to take this route instead of transiting through Canberra. People described the capital as nothing more than a large country town, but that seemed unlikely to her. As it was, Goulburn railway station was a revelation, as Albury's had been: long and cool and beautiful, all that stone and brick. It impressed her, and made her feel somehow proud, that people had built such things. She wandered the town, studying buildings and faces and fashions, unperturbed by the occasional frown she attracted, aware that her clothes were outdated and her hair wild. It bothered her not at all.

She'd lived her life in the forest, but that hadn't rendered her ignorant. In her solitude, she'd become a fervent listener to the radio, and would emerge from the forest once a week to hitchhike to Boonlea and borrow books from the library, becoming a voracious reader of everything from fantasy novels to encyclopedias, or finding stories in newspapers that more fully explained matters which had piqued her interest on the radio. Her second-hand knowledge of the world grew to be exceptional, even as her first-hand experience remained impaired. And it was this curiosity, as much as the lawyer's request, that saw her embark on her journey towards Saltwood. It was what she wanted: to explore the world, like her mother before her, to witness its richness and experience its wonders. Whether Saltwood was the place to find either, she had her doubts, but how could she know without going there? The letter had given her purpose, granted her permission.

That night in Goulburn, instead of pushing on to her destination, she decided to sleep by the river. There was a sign stating NO CAMPING, so she climbed a fence and set up her swag in the golf course instead, in among trees beside a fairway, where she lit her little stove and ate her dinner and slept undisturbed, except for the exotic punctuations of the night: trucks changing gears, the thunderstorm rumble of freight trains, car horns and police sirens, so that she might close her eyes and imagine that she had set up her swag in New York's Central Park and not the golf links of a country town. But there were also sounds more comforting and familiar: the hoot of an owl and the squabbling of possums and the chorus of frogs from the golf course dam. She felt happy: this was an adventure and she was on it.

The next morning Amber returned to the railway station, where she found a shower with hot water, which seemed a wonderful gift for travellers. She inquired about a bus to Saltwood, and when told it didn't depart until mid-afternoon, she decided to hitchhike instead. The woman at the information counter was kind, tearing off a town map from a large pad of them, showing her where to find the road south.

The weather was fine but not yet hot, clouds white and puffy and somehow happy to float in their blue expanse. It seemed to her the weather in Goulburn was not so very different from at home, and she was able to read it with ease: no rain for at least a day. And certainly luck was with her: no sooner had she reached her setting-off point than a middle-aged couple in a russet Volvo picked her up. They were heading towards Saltwood, and from there on to Batemans Bay and a holiday at the coast. The woman was mostly silent, and seemed disapproving, but her husband regaled Amber with stories from the couple's youth, when they had spent a summer hitching through Europe. Amber had difficulty at first reconciling the man's balding pate and his wife's double chin with such adventures, but listened intently nevertheless. By the time they reached Saltwood, she was almost tempted to continue on with them to Batemans Bay to see the ocean for herself.

Upon reaching the town, she went directly to the office of the lawyer, Willard Halliday, on the main street, the highway. The meeting struck her as strange, even without any yardstick to measure it against. She'd read *To Kill a Mockingbird* and had imagined her own Atticus Finch, but Willard Halliday reminded her more of the old Western films that used to play as mid-week matinees at the cinema in Echuca. The lawyer had a handlebar moustache and a silk waistcoat and a string tie, like a gunslinger from the American frontier, albeit missing a revolver and spurs. He wore polished riding boots and a belt with an ornate silver buckle, and he smoked pencil-thin cigars. The bakelite phone on his desk seemed a reluctant concession to modernity. Amber wondered if lawyers were required to dress this way and thought probably not. A personal affectation, then.

'Congratulations,' he said, blowing a celebratory smoke ring.

'Why congratulations?'

He explained. Teramina Hardcastle had died childless, with no close relatives. She'd bequeathed to Amber her worldly possessions. 'Do you know why?' asked the lawyer, eyebrows raised in curiosity. 'Why you?'

'Perhaps,' said Amber, without volunteering anything more. If Teramina hadn't shared her reasons with the lawyer, she wasn't sure she should break her friend's confidence. Her reticence was a characteristic inherited from her grandfather, who'd distrusted an intrusive and curious world.

'Right,' said the lawyer, ashing his cigar and shuffling papers. 'When do you turn eighteen?'

'Two years ago,' said Amber.

'All yours then,' said the lawyer and smiled, canines yellow with nicotine. 'Shall I take you through it?'

'Please.'

He began by offering his services in conveyancing, changing title deeds and whatnot, all for what he described as a modest fee. She had no idea whether the amount was reasonable, but it sounded an awful lot.

'What is it that I now own?' she asked.

'Not a lot of money, I'm afraid. Only two thousand dollars or so.'

It seemed an enormous amount to her, but she did her best to hide her astonishment. Apparently, the money was in a bank here in Saltwood. He would take her across directly, help her set up her own account. She asked if it would be better to simply with-draw the money, hold it in cash, but he warned her that might be risky. She could feel his eyes upon her then, studying her more closely, taking in her clothes and the mess of her hair. Assessing her. Drawing conclusions. She didn't like him examining her and her discomfort grew. She wasn't sure she cared for this lawyer.

'What else?' she asked, wanting to move the conversation along.

'Shares in a mining company, Gryphon Number Two, and land. A significant amount of land.' He seemed to be expecting some reaction, but she wasn't sure what to say. He continued. 'The shares are all but worthless, at least for now. The mine is flooded and cannot be worked. But there is the land and a house, the house where Teramina lived these past few years. Watershine, it's called. In what condition, I couldn't say, but it must be habitable. The land is forested, but most of it is difficult to access and unsuitable for farming. There's a lake and the abandoned mine, but I doubt it's worth very much. I'm not sure who would want to buy it.'

'How much land?' she asked.

'Four thousand acres.' And then, perhaps seeing her puzzled expression: 'About sixteen square kilometres.'

She tried to summon an image of how that might look. Maybe four kilometres by four kilometres, or perhaps eight long and two wide. Her island was tiny by comparison, big enough for the shack and not much else. 'Am I rich?' she asked, the idea dawning on her all of a sudden.

The lawyer smiled and arched an eyebrow. She wondered if he had practised the gesture: seen it in a movie and then perfected it in front of a mirror. She'd done that herself, studying her reflection, mimicking some expression or other she'd seen at the cinema or in a magazine.

'No,' the lawyer said in answer to her question. 'Not particularly rich. It's rugged country, full of ravines and cliffs, the soil thin and sparse. Not much you could do with it.' He leant back in his swivel chair, drew on his cigar, and considered her face, as if assessing her prospects, like a cattleman valuing a calf. 'The timber might be worth something, although I'm not sure how you could extract it. Not a subject I know much about. You could sell the land, I suppose, but I can't really say what it might be worth. I could look into it if you wish.'

'Why do I have to do anything with it?' she asked.

'Well, you don't. But you will be required to pay council rates. They're not massive, the land is not developed, generates no income, but they'll still need to be paid. Six hundred and twenty dollars per annum.'

She thought of the two thousand dollars she was about to receive. 'So I don't have to make an immediate decision.'

'Not at all.'

He showed her a map then, a survey map, covered with green contour lines, swirling this way and that, like op art. It took her a little while to grasp it, to understand the scale, the meaning of the contours, but once it had set in her mind, it was easy enough. It was different from her home on the Murray River, where the land was dead flat.

The lawyer pointed with his silver-nibbed fountain pen to a spot where all the green lines swarmed together to form a solid swathe. 'That's a cliff, where the plateau falls away into the valley. An escarpment, four hundred metres from top to bottom. The house, Watershine, is here, below it. Access is from The Valley.' He circled it with his pen. 'Close by the house, there's a road that runs alongside this creek, winding up onto the escarpment. Dates back to the days of the original mine. More of a track by now, but it should be accessible: I know Teramina and her husband repaired it to some degree. But it's a private road, your road, so not maintained by the council.'

Amber stared hard at the map, and as though responding to her intensity, it began to surrender more of its secrets. 'So most of the land, it's not in the valley but above the cliff?'

'That's right. Ninety-five per cent of it. Just a few acres at the bottom of the road surrounding the house, a foothold in The Valley.'

'And this road? That's the only way up?'

The lawyer examined her, took a drag on his cigar, considered its burning ember. 'As far as I know. Most of the high country is national park or state forest. Your land is squeezed between the two. There must be fire trails, but again, it's not something I know much about.' He smiled once more, teeth like aged ivory.

'And here?' Amber pointed to the map. 'A lake. Sitting above the cliff edge. Is it real?'

'I believe so.'

'It looks like it flows out, down this creek, into the valley.'

'So it does,' said the lawyer.

'A waterfall,' and an image came to her, a torrent of white, tumbling from the cliffs. There were no waterfalls where she was from, and the idea of it gave her a thrill. She examined the map even more closely. There was a second stream, also coming down from the high ground, flowing in front of the house before joining the larger creek. And up on the clifftop, concentric circles of contour lines next to the lake. She pointed. 'What's this? A hole?'

The lawyer extracted a magnifying glass from a desk drawer, leant in close, still smoking his cheroot, a cloud passing across the imagined landscape like a storm front. 'No. A mountain, I would think. A hill, at least. A knob. It's the location of the old mine. Gold.'

'Gold?' she asked.

'Closed for sixty years. Teramina Hardcastle and her husband Francis were attempting to revive it. Thought they could make a go of it.' He took a drag on the cigar. 'That's why they were fixing the road.'

She remembered Teramina then, when they had first met, traumatised by the loss of her husband, fractured and threatening to split apart. Teramina had mentioned the gold, the failed attempt to revive the mine.

Willard continued. 'But it all came to nothing. Francis Hardcastle died more than three years back.'

Amber frowned. 'How old were they?'

The lawyer shrugged. 'Your benefactor was forty-six. Not sure about Francis; perhaps a little older. He drowned when the mine flooded.'

'And Teramina?' She asked the question with trepidation; the lawyer's letter had informed Amber that her friend was dead, but not the circumstances.

'Her own hand. Leapt from the clifftop.' He stated it as a fact, but she could feel his eyes upon her, judging her reaction.

'I see,' she said, a tremble passing through her, knowing her anguish must be clear to see. She recalled her friend, so troubled but so full of life. Seemingly recovered after her months in the forest with Amber. She didn't want to look at Willard Halliday, so she stared at the map, eyes drawn to the merging of the contour lines, the precipice nearby the lake, close by the waterfall.

'And did they find any gold?' she asked, trying to escape the image of Teramina's final act.

'I believe so. I saw a nugget once. Impressive.'

'Is the mine beyond salvation, then?'

Willard Halliday laughed aloud, and sucked on the remnants of his cigar, smoke curling past squinted eyes, before stubbing it out in a cut-glass ashtray. 'The mine is flooded, inaccessible. Any gold is submerged. Gone forever. And Francis Hardcastle has not been officially declared dead, so his shares technically still belong to him.' He considered the contents of his ashtray, before looking up. 'If you're interested in gold, I could have the land surveyed. You never know.'

There was a strange taste in her mouth. Probably the smell of the cigar. 'I'll think about it,' she said.

'Forget about the goldmine,' said Willard then, not unkindly. 'But there is one more thing you should know.'

'Tell me.'

'Teramina appointed an executor, a person tasked with ensuring the instructions in her will are realised.'

'You?' asked Amber.

'No. We felt it better to have a disinterested third party. Simmons Burnside. A good man. Police officer. Works in Saltwood, lives in The Valley. He'll be able to help fulfil the terms of the will.'

— —

Amber stayed in Saltwood overnight, in a century-old hotel, half demolished and half renovated, full of ghosts and character. The room seemed overly large for one person, high-ceilinged, the brass bed too big and too soft. She'd intended to camp, but her weather eye had deserted her. Rain had started coming in, a storm rising over the coastal range, moist air from the sea, lightning playing like a steel drum, the front coming from the east, the weather

CHRIS HAMMER

pattern unfamiliar and catching her unawares. She decided it was a message, pushing her towards an unexpected future. After meeting the lawyer, she knew she could afford the hotel's shelter. She had money; for the first time ever it was more than she could carry in her pocket. It was in a bank, with a passbook to prove it. It was strange and intoxicating. She ventured downstairs, ate in the bistro. She ordered a glass of wine; her grandfather had loved wine, and she drank a bottle every now and then from his collection. It was her twentieth birthday and she offered herself a quiet toast, sitting alone at a corner table, and whispered a silent thank you to Teramina. Tomorrow she would go to The Valley.

202

chapter twenty-two

THE FIRST TIME AMBER DESCENDED INTO THE VALLEY—THE DAY AFTER MEETING
Willard Halliday and two days before the night of the concert—
she couldn't believe it, dropping unexpectedly over the lip of the
mountains, sinking from a bright autumn morning into rising mist,
plunging into beauty, into a greener version of the world, with trees
she'd never seen before, with ferns the size of cars, with creepers
and vines and strings of purple flowers. The road changed from
asphalt and straight lines to hairpin corners of mud and gravel,
the sky obscured, the overhanging limbs creating a sun-flecked
tunnel. Never before had she experienced this sense of altitude.
The sound of the wind sweeping the grassland plains had been
replaced by a stillness emphasised by the tolling of bellbirds and
the melodic call and response of parrots. It was like descending
into paradise.

She'd hitched a ride in a peach truck, the driver a girl, Suzie, just
a few months younger than Amber. She had a spirited personality
and was happy for the company, happy to chatter away, a stream-
of-consciousness commentary, not demanding anything in return.

She'd told Amber that her family were fourth-generation stone fruit farmers: peaches and nectarines, some oranges on the side; that she and her brother Arnie, nine years older, now ran their holding between them. Amber had warmed to the girl's easy-going manner, the way she handled the truck effortlessly, one arm out the window. The way she'd asked Amber to hold the steering wheel for her, not slowing down, while she'd rolled a cigarette. Amber decided she should learn to drive. What freedoms might that bestow?

Only when they started the descent into the valley itself did Suzie quieten, place two hands on the wheel and concentrate. She wrestled with the steering, spinning it constantly one way then the other, her forehead creased with concentration and sweat as the truck dropped lower and lower, Amber's ears popping. They came to a break in the trees, a lookout, and Suzie stood on the brakes, bringing them to a stop, just so Amber could see. The Valley spread beneath them, the mist rising in patches, the sun catching the western escarpment and the valley floor below it, painting the pastures and tree lines with dappled light. It looked like it was lifted from the pages of a fantasy book, with a waterfall coming off a cliff face far in the distance, the wind transforming the falling water into a white veil. She'd heard of The Valley, read a description, but she'd lacked the reference points, the context to imagine it. And now here she was, and the air tasted so cool and clean it was like drinking water. The breeze caressed her skin and entered her mind, interpreting the landscape for her and filling her with hope. As if hope was a spell and the landscape the conjuror.

Back in the truck, they were forced to wait as a truck laden with milled timber came steaming up the hill, engine straining, the driver performing a three-point turn on the hairpin below the lookout. Only after it had crawled past were they free to continue their descent.

The peach truck reached the bottom of the hill and entered a corridor of poplars, leaves autumn gold. Suzie relaxed once more, moving the vehicle back out of low gear, and Amber exhaled with relief. If this was the main road and that was the pass to the outside world, the one maintained by the government, then Amber held out slim hopes for her own road up the escarpment. She remembered Halliday's map and realised she'd not fully grasped what it represented, how significant those green contour lines were.

Once they emerged from the poplars, The Valley spread out around them: lush fields of constant green, cows sluggish in their contentment. They passed an orchard, trees covered in white netting to protect the fruit. Yellow dandelions dotted the pastures and there was a sweetness to the air, which was noticeably warmer here, thicker. More moist.

'Where you want to be dropped?' asked Suzie.

'General store, please.'

'You after work? Fruit picking?'

'Maybe,' she said, unsure why.

'Bit late in the season. We've already got a full crew on, but they can be unreliable. Come see me if you're interested. Cocheef's. Down the end of this road, just before the forest.'

They passed a church, a sprinkling of houses, more orchards and a cricket ground bearing a hand-painted sign. HARVEST FAIR.

BAND SATURDAY NIGHT. THE LOVELORN LOSERS. TICKETS AT THE GATE. $10. FOOD AND GROG FOR SALE.

'See that?' said Suzie, pointing to it. 'This weekend. Only happens once a year. Every fruit picker and backpacker in The Valley will be there, uni students down from Canberra.'

To Amber, it seemed propitious. Only once a year. She'd never seen a proper rock band, though she'd heard plenty on the radio: Nirvana and Queen and The Beatles. She knew the Lovelorn Losers wouldn't be in the same league, but she wanted the experience, irrespective of quality.

Suzie pulled in at the general store. Beyond it, Amber could see a pub, two storeys, sitting at a crossroad, with some sort of institute diagonally opposite. She thanked Suzie, climbed out, lifted her pack from where she'd stowed it in the back of the truck.

The store was made of weatherboards, askew with age, the corrugated-iron roof painted green, powdering from the seasons. There was a red mailbox outside and Post Office signs, as well as hoardings advertising Coca-Cola and Bushells Tea. A large plastic Peters ice-cream cone, the sort that lit up at night, extended out above the entrance.

Inside was cooler and darker. Amber liked the feel of the floorboards; they felt soft with use, with the passage of time. There was a young woman behind the counter, pretty in a hard-edged sort of way. A toddler was busying himself in front of the counter, smashing at coloured blocks with a wooden mallet, gurgling with delight.

Amber approached, lowering her backpack and leaning it against the counter. She smiled at the toddler, who kept bashing away, oblivious.

'Help you?' inquired the woman.

'I'm looking for Simmons Burnside,' said Amber. 'I was told he lived here.'

'No luck, darl. At work in Saltwood. Be back this evening.'

'Right,' said Amber, wondering what her next move might be.

'Anything I can do?' asked the woman.

'I hope so,' said Amber, smiling, but letting the expression drift away when it wasn't returned. 'My name is Amber Jones. I've inherited some property here in The Valley. From Teramina Hardcastle.'

The woman's eyes widened, even as her eyebrows closed above them in a frown. 'What's that got to do with Simmons?'

'Her will. I'm the beneficiary, he's the executor.'

'She leave him anything?' the woman asked, an edge in her voice.

'No. Sorry.'

'That'd be right. Typical Simmons. Always doing shit for free.' The woman examined some paperwork on the counter, as though Amber was no longer worth talking to.

'But he'll be back this evening?' Amber persisted.

'Better be.'

Amber wasn't sure how to react. The toddler was staring at the blocks with a look of puzzlement.

'I'm told there's a house,' said Amber. 'Watershine.'

The woman gave a derisive snort. 'Yours now, is it?'

'So I'm told.'

The woman shook her head, as if at some perceived injustice, then looked down at Amber's pack with a sigh. 'You got a car?'

'On foot,' said Amber.

'Lucky it's not far then. Simmons should have the keys. Let me check.'

The woman went out through an internal door. Amber squatted, smiled at the toddler. 'Hey there, fella.'

The toddler beamed like a maniac. 'You pretty,' he said and whacked another block, demonstrating his skill.

The mother returned with the keys: three modern ones, Yale and Lockwood, and one old-fashioned key, with a circular steel shaft, a circle at one end and a sawtooth square of teeth made of brass at the other.

The woman handed them over, talking as she did so. 'You come from Saltwood, down the pass?'

'Yes. Got a lift.'

'Okay, it's pretty simple then. You were on the main road. The Valley Road. Takes you down into the forest, the national park. So don't go there. But right outside here, just near the pub, there's a crossroad. Road to the right is sealed. That's the West Road. Road to the left is unpaved, called the East Road. Not very imaginative, I know, but saves confusion. Your house is on the East Road.'

Amber waited, but the woman offered no more information.

'How far?' she asked.

'Maybe two kilometres. Easy walk. Gate on the right, just before the road swings north. Close by the escarpment. One of the keys on the ring will get you in if the gate is locked.'

'Thanks. Sounds good.'

The woman appraised her once more, scanning her up and down unapologetically. 'You want to buy some supplies while you're here?'

Amber thought that a good idea. She bought food, and toilet paper, and candles and matches. Not too much. She could always come back when she didn't have to carry her pack.

She paid and thanked the woman, who made a harrumphing noise. As Amber left she could hear her scolding the toddler, still bashing away. 'For fuck's sake, Wolf, give it a break.'

Amber was glad to be out of the store, back in the open air. She walked to the crossroad. The pub sat prominent, a couple of cars outside, but no sign of life. Diagonally opposite was a solid-looking building. MINERS' INSTITUTE 1874 said the lettering on the fascia under the eaves. A young man was out front mowing the lawn, wearing shorts and work boots and gloves, but no shirt or hat in the autumn sun. His body was lean and tanned. He saw her and waved; she waved back.

The East Road crossed a river just after the crossroad, then ran straight out through fields dotted with dairy cows towards cliffs of towering sandstone, trees in the gullies, fringed at the top with more trees, like a ragged haircut. She walked along, happy with the thought of discovery, the bags of groceries not so heavy, her pack comfortable enough, bothered only by the persistence of the flies. They were much worse here than at home; it must be all the cows, she concluded. Before her, the escarpment rose higher and higher the closer she approached. Not far from the bottom of the cliffs, she could see a single-lane bridge—no passing, no overtaking—above a creek, just before the road curved to the left. She wondered if this was her stream, emerging from her property, heading for the river. She looked about her, saw an old man gum tree with a milk-can mailbox, corroded and leaning precariously, by its side. Tucked in behind it was a five-bar gate, steel rusted to brown. And on the gate, a sign, grey-green with moss, hanging by fencing wire: WATERSHINE.

The gate was closed but unlocked, a steel chain gathering it to a post. A massive padlock was clamped to nothing more than a loop of steel. She lifted the catch, swung the gate open, walked through and closed it behind her.

The way into Watershine wasn't a driveway so much as a track, winding in and out of trees, giving the impression they had been there first and the builders of the house had respected their prior claim and declined to clear them. The heat of the day was beginning to build, but not here, where the shade was thick and ferns abounded. She could hear the sound of water, like laughter. She recalled the lawyer's map again, streams coming off the escarpment. She followed the track up a low rise, the first suggestion of the cliffs to come, and down again, to a sturdy wooden bridge, wide enough for a car but no more than that, extending across a stream.

She left her pack and the groceries and crept down beside it, was greeted by a cloud of butterflies. The water was as clear as gin, tumbling over small rocks. She'd never seen water so clear. She crouched, splashed her face, the liquid cool. She cupped her hands, lifted some to her mouth and sampled it: as pure as rainwater, such a contrast to the murky rivers of home. She had not yet reached the house but already the land was drawing her to it. Teramina. God bless her.

The house was of wood, sitting atop a rocky outcrop like a caterpillar on a mushroom, slightly off kilter. It was two-storey, weatherboard, once painted blue but the colour mellowed by years, faded here, peeling there, hosting lichen in its corners. There were sash windows, generously sized, and shutters, some of them closed, some of them open in welcome. The roof was corrugated iron; it appeared to be new. A climbing vine grew up one side, and she wondered if that might damage the underlying wood. An early job, she thought, although the creeper appealed to her and it would be a shame to remove it. Perhaps it could stay.

She carried her pack up steps carved into the stone of the outcrop, and then up wooden stairs onto a porch. She felt somehow like she had come home. She regarded the surrounding trees: there was no view, no distant vista, just a sense of elevation and the canopy breathing around her.

My God, she thought to herself. *It's gorgeous.*

The door was locked. It was the old-fashioned key made of steel and brass that opened it. Inside, she found a higgledy-piggledy sort of house, bent this way and that by the years, so that it lacked even one straight vertical. Amber saw a light switch, flicked it on. Nothing. So instead she walked to the windows, released the clasps and lifted the sashes, opened those shutters that had been closed, and pulled up the windows, letting light and air into the house, pushing out the mustiness.

The lawyer had told her Teramina had died two months before, and yet her presence was everywhere: in the kitchen and the well-cared-for utensils, knives of fine steel and saucepans with heavy bottoms; in the lounge, the piles of books, the fireplace set for a winter still months away; in the art on the walls and the heir-loom rugs on the floor; in the furniture, stylish and antique; in the upstairs bedroom with a wardrobe full of clothes; and in the study, with papers still on the desk and shelves bursting with books and papers. Amber closed the door on the study, leaving it for some future day, and decided she might do the same with the bedroom, at least for the moment. She took the third room upstairs, seemingly unused, to be her bedroom instead.

In the kitchen, mounted on one wall, she found a map, drawn by hand in an old-fashioned style, crosshatched, like something from an eighteenth-century atlas. It showed the land—her land— labelled *Watershine* in elaborate cursive. It held echoes of the map the lawyer Halliday had shown her, but this was more functional. She wondered who might have drawn it, searching closely for an identifying signature and finding it in the bottom right-hand corner. *A.K. Cloverton, 1922.* The orientation was not north–south but east–west, with the house at the bottom, below the cliff line, with the escarpment itself stretching horizontally across the page. The driveway was marked, including the bridge and stream, and now she could see more clearly that there were two creeks, one much larger than the other, both falling from the escarpment. She had crossed the smaller of the two on the driveway. The larger one—Watershine Creek—flowed to the north of the house through a series of ponds, marked on the map as *The Cisterns*, before the two streams joined and flowed under the East Road and from there into the Broken River. She traced the lines on the map and realised, with some pleasure, that she was again living on an island, or at least a peninsula.

And I have waterfalls, she reminded herself, and the thought gave her a sense of wellbeing. According to the map, above the house, up on the escarpment, there was a lake, also on her land, feeding Watershine Creek and the waterfall. There were other details as well, mining works, the road winding up the cliff and then circling the mine itself.

She spent that first day, and the next, cleaning. The act of clearing out the house, of wiping and rearranging, helped make it feel more like hers, that she belonged. She found a fuse box on the porch. There was one primary switch; she turned it on and suddenly she had electricity. It was still connected. She scrubbed out the fridge, admired the flush toilet, discovered a vacuum cleaner and worked out how to operate it. She found herself revelling in the bath, the water made miraculously hot. Outside there was a shed, full of old woodworking tools and packing cases and a pushbike. The bike's tyres were flat, but otherwise it was not so different from the one she'd left at home, just fancier, with gears. She knew bikes, how to fix them. Her mother had taught her to ride and her grandfather had taught her how to repair them. She pumped up the tyres and oiled the chain, and the general store seemed much closer.

— —

It was only on the second evening that she returned to the letter, the message from Teramina handed to her by Halliday. She'd read it in the hotel room in Saltwood, yet reading it here, in this house, made it seem more real. Perhaps this was where Teramina had written it: here on the kitchen table.

My dear girl,
      The demons are back, stalking my days and haunting my nights. I thought I was rid of them, that I was cured,

that we had banished them during those curative days in your forest.

I am doing all I can to resist them, and hope and believe I can vanquish them once more. But if you are reading this, then I am lost, and they have won.

Why you? I know that is what you must be asking.

It is simple and sad, but it is the truth: there is no one else. No one as deserving as you. I have no relatives. Only distant twigs on the branches of a failing family tree, people I have never met, scattered across Europe. And Francis and his family remain a mystery to me. So there it is.

But please don't think you are merely the beneficiary of last resort. After all, there are charities and worthy causes aplenty—but none of them have touched my life the way that you did, down in that haven of yours. I will never forget your kindness, your generosity of spirit, the way you took me in and cared for me and showed me support and love when I was at my most vulnerable, and you a girl and me a grown woman. And never once did you ask for anything in return.

Perhaps you didn't realise it fully at the time; I was putting on a brave face. The truth is you only just found me in time. I was very close to the edge, becoming obsessed with leaping from it.

It was only three months, I know, and you little more than a child, and yet somehow you restored me, or the forest restored me, or some alchemy between the two of you achieved it.

I remember how much you cared for the forest, for the trees and for the animals, how much you loved the river. And so, in deciding who should inherit Watershine, I thought: what better custodian than you?

I hope it repays you better than it has repaid me. Care for the land, so that it might care for you.

With my everlasting love and gratitude,

Teramina

She was still holding it, this tenuous link with her benefactor, when she heard a knock on the door. It startled her. Amber hadn't heard a car; she hadn't heard anything.

The knock came again. She tucked the letter away in its envelope and went to see who it was.

She inched the door open hesitantly, relieved to find a policeman standing there.

'Yes?' she said, opening the door a little wider.

'Amber Jones?' He seemed quite young, with sandy hair cut short and an open face.

'That's me,' she said.

'I'm Simmons Burnside,' he said. 'The executor of Teramina Hardcastle's will.'

'Of course. Please come in.'

'I won't right now. I need to get home. I just wanted to make sure you'd made it okay. That you have what you need.' He held out a basket. It had a few grocery items, nothing fancy, but complementary to those she had bought at the store.

The gesture touched her. 'Thank you,' she said.

'I'll be back when I have more news, and more time, but every-thing is in hand. I'm meeting Willard Halliday to make sure all the paperwork is in order.'

She watched as he walked back down the stairs and out along the drive. He seemed nice, she thought. And wondered what he was doing with the hard-eyed woman at the store.

chapter twenty-three

2024

NELL IS RUNNING THROUGH HER MARTIAL ARTS ROUTINES AT THE CRICKET ground the next morning, enjoying the coolness of hour. The sky is bright blue directly overhead but the sun is not yet above the eastern cliffs, the dew still thick on the turf. Her phone chimes, joining a chorus of warbling magpies. A text message from an unknown number, sent to her and Ivan.

Might have something for you. Meet Halfchurch crossroad. 9am. Vicary H.

Before she can respond, a message from Ivan appears.

I'll call him. See what it is.

She resumes her movements, trying to return to her meditative zone. She's almost there when her phone rings.

'He's not answering,' Ivan says.

'That message didn't come from his police phone number,' Nell notes. 'I put it in my contacts when we met.'

'Seems a bit suss,' says Ivan. 'You reckon it's him?'

'Where's Halfchurch?'

'Little village about ten minutes east of Saltwood.'

'Either it's not him, or he's being very secret squirrel,' she says. 'You in the Institute yet?'

'No, out running. You?'

'Cricket ground.'

'You want to handle it?' he asks.

'Sure. I'll run the number through the system, see if it's attached to anyone. Try the number he gave me.'

'Good thinking.'

— —

Half an hour later, showered and changed and caffeinated, Nell is on her way up the escarpment towards Saltwood. The reverse number register has given her nothing: the phone number is a pay-as-you-go SIM. A burner phone. And Vicary's own phone is either turned off or out of range.

Halfchurch is just a few houses, barely deserving of the description of village. There is no church and even the crossroad isn't a crossroad, just a three-way intersection.

She arrives with fifteen minutes to spare, but almost an hour later, there's still no sign of the Saltwood sergeant.

She rings Ivan. 'Vicary's a no-show.'

'Right. You think it really was him?'

'No idea. I'll call past Saltwood, see if I can learn more.'

So instead of returning south to the highway, she drives west, an easy drive on a sealed road.

At the police station, no one has seen Vicary Hearst.

'Rostered on, but haven't seen him,' says the constable at reception. 'Not answering his calls.'

Nell thanks the young officer and heads out. She texts Ivan, telling him what she's learnt, then decides not to waste her trip. She walks along the main street, Google helping her find the office. Even from outside, there is something archaic about the setup, the wood-framed windows, the gilt writing—*Willard Halliday—Attorney-at-Law*—in an old-fashioned font, the letters somewhat tarnished with age. Inside, Nell finds a large man hunched over a small desk, hair plastered to one side, strands defiantly breaking free.

'Help you?' says the man. Nell places him in his mid-twenties at most.

She flashes her badge. 'You must be Ollie. We spoke on the phone.'

'That's me,' the young man replies, taking his time to scrutinise her identification, exhibiting a childlike fascination.

'I want to speak to Willard Halliday,' she says.

'Let me see if he's free,' says Ollie.

Only when he gets to his feet does she get a full sense of his size. Two metres at least, fleshed out without being fat, a lumbering Lurch-like presence, a gentle giant. He knocks on a door to an inner office, enters without waiting for a reply, and closes the door behind him.

Nell takes a look about her. There is a telephone on the desk, but that's the only concession to modernity. There's a manual typewriter, filing cabinets, bookshelves. If there are any computers or printers or scanners, they must be hidden in some other room.

Ollie emerges. 'All good,' he says, gesturing for her to enter.

Willard Halliday is shrivelled and wizened, his face more jaundiced than tanned, leathered like a pharaoh, embalmed by decades of smoking and drinking. He sits in a wheelchair behind a desk, dwarfed by the furniture, fragile in contrast to its Victorian-era solidity. An oxygen tank sits next to him on a trolley, clear tubes resting on the desktop, ready for use. A cut-glass ashtray on the desk already contains a couple of butts. There's a heavy-looking lighter, some paperwork and an antique brass bell with a wooden handle. He smiles up at Nell, his lower teeth sharp and stained a brownish yellow, his upper teeth flat and white and artificial. The contrast is disconcerting. Ollie hovers, awaiting his master's instructions. Willard waves the young man away, dismissing him.

'A police officer?' Willard asks, voice wheezy. 'Could that be correct?'

Nell shows him her badge. 'Detective Senior Constable Narelle Buchanan,' she says. 'Homicide.'

Willard gestures towards an empty chair. 'Well, you'd better sit down.'

Nell does so. Around her, the office seems ancient, like a museum. Faded qualifications in lacquered frames, a Leica camera on a shelf, another manual typewriter. A pair of opera glasses, looking suspiciously like ivory. She wonders if it's a deliberate aesthetic choice or the accumulated evidence of decades of neglect. No, not neglect: it's too artfully curated, too dust-free.

'We're investigating the murder of Wolfgang Burnside,' she says.

'Wasn't me,' says Willard, gesturing at the wheelchair and oxygen tank then chuckling at his own joke, before his laughter transforms into a wheezing cough.

Nell waits for him to recover his composure.

'How long have you been practising here?' she asks.

'Close enough to forty years,' says Willard. He's smiling, but his eyes are wary. There is intelligence there. His body might be ravaged, but Nell suspects the solicitor's mind remains sharp.

She resists a natural inclination towards sympathy, reminding herself why she's here. 'So you were practising back at the time Francis Hardcastle and Teramina Cloverton were attempting to revive the Gryphon Mine?'

Willard considers his response before answering. 'I thought this was about Wolfgang Burnside's death?'

'Please answer the question.'

Willard nods, again exposing his yellow and white teeth, as if in appreciation of her attitude, but is not easily swayed. 'What is it you want, detective? My time is short—literally.' He gestures at the tank once more. 'What is the connection with Wolfgang Burnside's death?'

'I was hoping you might be able to help me there.'

'I know of no such connection,' says Willard. 'It's been more than thirty years.'

'Did you act for Amber Jones?'

He turns his head to one side, regarding her out of the corners of his eyes, as though to appraise her better. 'I did. Initially, at least.'

'Can you take me through that, please?'

'Why?'

She leans forward. 'Because I'm interested in your answer.'

He smiles, but the expression has lost its amusement. 'At your service, I'm sure,' he says, followed by another wheezing laugh in appreciation of his own mock civility. But he answers nevertheless. 'Teramina Hardcastle wrote her will only a month or so before she killed herself. Sat in this office while she instructed me; sat where you're sitting now. Left her estate to a young woman I'd never heard of. A Miss Amber Jones. I drew up the document, Teramina returned a few days later, and we had it signed and witnessed.'

'And then?'

'After she died? I wrote to Miss Jones, informing her of her good fortune. She travelled here to see me, also sat in that same chair.' He steeples his hands. 'A lot of people have sat in that chair over the decades.'

Nell isn't sure, but she senses something of a threat behind the words.

'And she inherited what, exactly?' she asks.

'The land, an old house called Watershine, and some shares in the mine.'

'Some shares? Not all of them?'

'The majority.' Willard peers at her, intelligence playing in his rheumy eyes. He takes a couple of deep breaths in through his nose, a fluting sound. 'In Australia, mining rights are separate from the land. For example, you and I are permitted by law to wander onto someone's private land and stake a mining claim. Goes right back to the gold rushes of the nineteenth century. Technically, the minerals belong to the Crown, not the landowner.'

'Who owned the mining rights?' asks Nell.

Willard frowns. 'Why would you want to know that?'

'Indulge me a moment more, and I'll tell you.'

Willard squints, concentrating, like a card sharp reading the table. 'The original company was wound up in the 1930s, so Francis and Teramina Hardcastle were able to stake a fresh claim and work towards applying for a mining licence. They formed a company, holding a clear majority of shares between them, but also selling shares to other investors. A very common way for a mining company to raise money.'

'You know a lot about it,' Nell remarks.

'I was the company secretary.'

Nell blinks. 'Who were the other shareholders?'

'Local business identities, that sort of thing. None had holdings of more than a few per cent.'

'You did the accounts?'

'I'm a lawyer, not an accountant.'

'So who did?'

'A local. Fred Wallington. But he won't be much use to you.'

'Dead?'

'Thirty years.'

'Okay, so Amber Jones inherits the house and the land and shares in the mining company, right?'

Willard frowns, like he's chasing a memory. 'Yes. But the mine was flooded. The shares were worthless.'

'So what happened to the company?' asks Nell.

The lawyer stops for a breather, takes a drink of water, then extracts an antique hip flask of brass and silver from a desk drawer and takes a swig, swilling the liquid back and forth through his teeth like mouthwash. Nell can smell alcohol, whisky.

'It was wound up eventually.'

'What happened to its assets?'

Willard stares at her for a moment, takes another swill of whisky, gasps in a little oxygen, takes care to set the mask well aside before lighting a thin cigar using the desk lighter. 'My apologies,' he says, sighing with satisfaction before another cough comes upon him. 'I really shouldn't, but it's a bit late to stop now.' He takes another drag from the cigar, lets the smoke waft out from his mouth and nose, clearly relishing the sensation, then stubs it out, regret in his eyes.

Nell waits for him to finish, then persists. 'What happened to the assets?' she repeats.

'There weren't any to speak of. A little cash that was distributed to shareholders, a few pieces of minor equipment sold off.'

'Were you a shareholder?' asks Nell.

Willard beams, apparently amused by the question. 'Me? Only a very minor one.'

'What happened to Amber Jones? I'm told Wolfgang Burnside was trying to contact her.'

The lawyer slowly begins to nod. 'Ah. Now I see the connection. Why you're so interested.' Nell thinks he seems relieved. 'Amber Jones left The Valley thirty years ago. Vanished. Despite my best efforts to locate her, I never could.' He looks at her, a challenge in his eyes.

'Why did she disappear?'

'I don't know.'

'Why was Wolfgang Burnside able to track her down and you couldn't?'

'I wasn't aware that he had. He was a very well-resourced individual, with a strong incentive to find her.'

'He came to you?'

'He did.'

'And what did you tell him?'

'Same as I'm telling you. That Amber Jones owns the land. She must be about fifty by now.'

'She's dead.'

Willard frowns. 'Is that a fact? I didn't know.'

'Twenty-nine years ago.'

'No. Really? That's very young. But it would explain why she never responded to my letters.' He taps his finger on the side of the ashtray. 'How sad,' he says, almost as an afterthought.

Nell doesn't respond, but she feels a fleeting anger. It seems insincere, this expression of sympathy. She remembers the devastated landscape, the clear-felled forest. 'So if you weren't ever able to contact Amber Jones, who authorised the felling of the trees on her land?'

He smiles, that same reptilian grin. 'Why, me, of course. Acting in her interest. As I have these past thirty years.'

'Where is the money?'

'In a trust account, being held for her.'

'Minus your expenses, I assume.'

'Naturally.'

'But Wolfgang Burnside, he wasn't prepared to deal with you? Didn't recognise your authority?'

'Why would you say that?'

'I told you. Because he was trying to find Amber Jones.'

'Well, I dare say if she was dead, he didn't fare any better than me.' There is a touch of assertiveness in Halliday's voice, and the smile has grown thin on thin lips.

'You didn't try to contact her, did you?' Nell presses.

'I most certainly did.' He lifts the bell, rings it with a feeble shake. The clerk comes in. 'There is a file, Oliver. Amber Jones. Please bring it here.'

The young man walks out.

The lawyer continues. 'I still don't see your interest. Wolfgang Burnside was seeking the owner of the land. So what? You think the events of thirty years ago have some connection to his death?'

'I want to make sure we investigate all possible avenues,' she replies. And displays her own mouth-only smile, hoping to return some of the lawyer's insincerity. Two can play at that game.

The young man returns, carrying an archive box, like a large hollow book, designed to sit vertically on a shelf. Willard opens it, gesturing at the contents. 'I've written numerous times, and each time they are returned unopened.' Inside the box is a series of envelopes.

The sight of the letters seems so sad. 'How did you know where to write?'

'It was the address that Teramina gave me when we constructed her will. It was where I wrote to alert Miss Jones of her inheritance, a letter she obviously received. I guess her early death explains why they were returned unopened.' He smiles, forehead creased. 'I'm sorry, but what does this have to do with your investigation?'

'I'm Amber Jones's daughter.'

Willard doesn't move, a tic playing at the corner of one eye. 'You don't say.'

'I do say. I want to see your trust fund. See the wealth you have garnered from her land. My land. My inheritance.'

'Not so fast. You have proof of this? There's a birth certificate?'

'Yes. With her clearly stated as my mother. And another, when I was adopted and my name changed.'

'And her death certificate?'

'Yes.'

'And a will?'

'No. She died too young for that. I'm her only child. Her mother is still alive.'

'And your father?'

'What does that matter?'

And now the smile returns, oily and smirk-ridden. 'That might prove problematic. For you.'

'How so?'

'He's still alive?'

'I believe so.'

'They were married?'

'No. And he's not listed on my birth certificate.'

Willard recovers his thin cigar from the ashtray and lights it. He inhales, eyes closing with momentary pleasure, before he coughs, smoke billowing. He gathers himself, returns the cigar to the ashtray. 'If he can establish a de facto relationship was still current at the time of her death, or that they were emotionally committed at the time she acquired her wealth, then he may be able to establish a superior claim.'

'I doubt that very much,' says Nell.

'Not up to you. Not up to me,' says Willard. 'That will be a matter for the court, if he decides to pursue it.'

'Can I see the company records?' she asks. 'I *am* her daughter.'

Willard shakes his head. 'But not yet her heir.' And he lets his smile fade to nothing. 'If I were you, I'd find your father. Be nice to him. Ingratiating. In the meantime, please send me a certified copy of the death certificate. Until then, I will continue to act in the best interests of Miss Amber Jones.'

chapter twenty-four

1994

THE DAY AFTER THE CONCERT, AMBER WAS OUT OF SORTS. HER BODY DIDN'T feel like it belonged to her, and her mind kept distancing itself, as though she were entering a dream. Only her stomach, with its spasms and its nausea, and the aching in her limbs anchored her to reality. The drug-induced synaesthesia had gone; her previously heightened senses now seemed blunted: colours were muted and sounds were muffled. It was lunchtime before she left her bed, and only then to sit on the porch and stare into space. It took two pots of tea and three slices of buttered toast for her to feel she was coalescing into a single entity once more.

There was still much to do in the house, cleaning and repairing, but she couldn't face it. Instead she sat on the porch and stared out into the treetops until the sun, now well and truly clear of the eastern escarpment, found her exposed and forced her to move. So she collected a hat and her sandals and went walking, thinking that it might help her recovery.

She followed a path towards Watershine Creek. The trail led her up the same low rise her driveway traversed and then along to the creek itself. The stream seemed in a convivial mood, flowing freely, gurgling and laughing over the rocks. It wouldn't always be so genial, Amber knew: she could see how the waterway had carved its own miniature valley, where the remnants of foliage remained stuck in tree branches. She understood then that flood must be a risk: not the rising waters of her home on the Murray, but flash floods, walls of water pounding downwards off the escarpment. She appreciated why Watershine had been built high on its rocky outcrop.

The path ran alongside the stream towards the escarpment. Emerging from the trees, she found herself near its base, where the creek had expanded to form a wide pool below a wall of concrete and rock, clearly man-made. She walked up the right-hand side of the pool to a natural rock platform. She was clear of the trees now, and above her she could see the water careening down off the escarpment, not a single waterfall but several cascades, winding out of a cleft in the cliff face, a narrow ravine carved from the rock. To its left, high on the precipice, she believed she saw a steel safety barrier, part of the old road connecting the valley with the mine and its surrounding uplands.

Closer at hand, there was a series of three pools, thirty metres square, concrete-lined, water flowing from one to another, like linked swimming pools. They were half filled with sand, washed in over the years. She climbed another level, a couple of metres higher, concrete steps combining with those cut into the rock. A rusting machine, three metres tall and twice as wide, stood beside the water, steel turned orange, caked in splintering rust. She guessed it had been an ore crusher, massive pistons connected to a crank, designed to pulverise rock. And behind it, the matching bulk of a steam engine, bolted to a concrete block, the crusher's power plant. This was the treatment works for the old mine, she realised. They must have brought the ore here for crushing, to wash out the impurities, extract the gold. She wondered at that, the chemicals used, trying to remember what she had read in the library at Boonlea. Quicksilver. What was that? Mercury? Or perhaps they'd used cyanide. Both were poisonous, she knew that. She stared into the water. It seemed so clean, so pure. Surely after sixty years any residual toxins would have been leached away, or at least buried deep within the sediment. How had they brought the ore down? she wondered. By the road? Or somehow sluiced it down, built a race descending the narrow ravine? It was more than six decades since the mine had fallen silent, yet here were its bones, the steel skeletons of an enterprise that once moved and lived and breathed.

She felt a certain awe for the ruins; they had an atmosphere to them, like the fallen gods of a Grecian temple. These had been industrial shrines to a different god, built in the worship of gold, and industry. She closed her eyes, tried to imagine the place as it was in the 1920s, the sound and the fury, men yelling, the roar of the steam engine, the glow of its furnace, the incessant pounding of the crushers, ore hurtling down the race. Machines belching smoke and dust, a haze everywhere, filling eyes and throats. She opened her eyes once more; everything so peaceful, so silent, just the gentle sounds of flowing water and birdsong.

She climbed to the final level, this time finding steps cut into the rock, and here was an even larger pool, perhaps fifty metres by fifty metres, a small waterfall melding the natural to the man-made, the place where the two joined. The water seemed deep, three metres or more. As she watched, a fish circled beneath her. Sand and sediment had built up in the opposite side of the pool, forming a beach, emerging from the water and creating a dune. The sand wasn't white but a kind of honeyed brown, sandstone from the cliff face. She had her own beach. Her own swimming pool. She peered into the deep water. There were plants swaying in the current. She saw another fish and then, to her amazement, a native water rat, a rakali, with its white-tipped tail, unperturbed by her presence. She wondered at nature's power, its ability to recolonise, to claim back its territory. The map in Watershine's kitchen referred to these structures as the cisterns—a prosaic term for such an evocative place.

The day was hot; she was alone. She stripped off, eased herself in, the water cool and medicinal, clearing her head of its residual wooliness, as if the cisterns had been built for that purpose, awaiting her arrival so that they might restore her.

— —

Back at the house, she began to consider what she should do next. There were still elements that needed attention: a shutter hanging by one hinge; a broken stove element; a loose banister on the stairs. She sat out on the porch and considered her presence here. Was she staying, or should she return to her forest shack on the river down south? Her mother had been gone for more than a year this time, who knew where, but sooner or later she must return and expect Amber to be there waiting.

She felt an obligation to her absent mother. Was it that, or merely the longing to see her again, to hold her once more and be held by her? She wouldn't want to miss that. Strange: at twenty she felt almost like the adult, while her mother, at forty, was more like the child, wandering the world, feckless, unable to settle.

But she felt at home here. It held the promise of a different future, while the forest offered only more of the past.

chapter twenty-five

AMBER WAS SITTING ON HER PORCH THE NEXT MORNING, BREATHING IN THE day and listening to the magpies warble, when she heard the sound of an engine. And soon enough a truck appeared: a small Toyota flatbed, a tradesman's toolbox anchored to its tray, winding its way through the trees before coming to a stop below the house and its outcrop. Suzie stepped out from the passenger side. 'Brought your bike,' she said. And so she had: there it was, lashed to the back of the truck. Amber had forgotten about it after she'd ridden it to the concert at the cricket ground.

She descended the stairs, expressing her thanks as she came.

A young man emerged from the same passenger side, long red hair and side choppers. And then, from the driver's side, Lucas, last seen in the half-light at the concert. Amber's heart did a double beat, like a syncopation, and she thought she heard a jazz chord, a final echo of that night's melding of her senses.

'Hi there,' called Lucas, smiling and raising his palm in a cursory wave.

In the morning light, without the music and the dope, he didn't seem quite so golden, not so much a god as a handsome mortal, but she still found his brown eyes engaging. She'd been vulnerable at the end of the concert, wasted by too much drugs and alcohol, yet he hadn't taken advantage—hadn't tried to kiss her or touch her.

'This is Mike,' said Suzie, indicating the redhead. 'And Lucas.'

'Hi, Mike,' she said. 'Hello, Lucas.'

'Thought we might go swimming,' said Suzie. 'Check out your inheritance.'

Amber smiled at that. So they knew. Probably everyone in The Valley knew. Of course they did.

She thought of the cistern below the waterfall, but that wasn't what the trio had in mind. 'Apparently you own a lake,' said Lucas.

She remembered the map, the lawyer's statement. 'Yes. Up on top of the escarpment.'

'C'mon,' said Lucas. 'We'll show you the way.'

'I worked up there,' said Mike, 'when your aunt and uncle reopened the mine.'

'Not my aunt and uncle,' she corrected, but her interest was piqued. They knew the way, Mike knew where everything was. She didn't have to climb the escarpment on foot. 'Can we make it in that?' she asked, tilting her head towards the Toyota.

'With a bit of luck,' said Lucas.

'Yes,' she said. 'I'd love to see what's up there.'

— —

Lucas's truck was small, a single cab with a bench seat. He was driving, Mike on the passenger seat with Suzie squirming on his lap, Amber sandwiched in the middle. It was a new experience for her, this proximity, being confined, pressed together so closely with strangers. Unprecedented. She was used to not seeing people for days or weeks, not speaking, let alone touching. She found the experience both confronting and intoxicating. Her arm and her leg were pressed against Lucas and she could smell his scent. In the heat of the morning, she felt him infiltrating her senses. She glanced across, examined him: the clear line of his chin, bristles dark and invoking the feeling of sandpaper; the hair on his bare arms, soft like wool, brown and blond on the dark skin. A thin bracelet of multi-coloured thread. A tattoo on his left wrist, a trident in blue ink.

They made their way back out along her driveway, over the home creek and through her gate onto the East Road, turning right, crossing the single-lane bridge over Watershine Creek, but going no more than a few metres before stopping at another gate. There were signs, still relatively new: PRIVATE PROPERTY and NO THROUGH ROAD and NO ACCESS and PRIVATE ROAD and, in the largest letters, red and bold: TRESPASSERS PROSECUTED.

Suzie then Mike then Amber clambered out. Amber had the key ring she'd brought from the house. She had the right key, or thought she did, it was neatly labelled, but the lock refused to budge. Lucas joined them with a can of penetrating oil. 'Give us a go,' he said. He worked the lock and the key, applying the oil liberally, until a minute or two later it turned and he unshackled the gate with a satisfying click.

'Bravo,' said Mike.

They drove through some low trees, and Amber could see the cisterns, or some sign of them, over to their right. They were travelling alongside Watershine Creek, on the other side from the house. And then they diverted to the left, entering a ravine and beginning to climb.

It was a nerve-racking ascent, the track twisting and narrow, traversing makeshift bridges and half-buried pipes carrying water under the road. They fell silent, all except Lucas, who whistled as he drove, happy to negotiate the tight corners and rutted surface, to change gears in time to some unheard metronome. She admired his confidence, his competence; it made her feel safe. She started to relax and enjoy the sensation of the truck bouncing as it climbed. The higher they went, the more the view opened up, The Valley laid out below them. Watershine was hidden by outcrops and trees, but she could see the East Road, the crossroad, the pub and the general store, noticing for the first time THE VALLEY painted in white lettering on the store's green roof.

And then they were at the top, driving over the lip, between twin granite pillars, onto the high plateau and into the trees.

'The old mine is through there,' said Mike, pointing over to their right. 'Granite and quartz in among the sandstone. The road winds around the base. We'll see it when we get to the lake.'

They moved through the forest, tall trees and ferns, the route covered in leaves, the light dappled. Amber was grateful for the shade, the cab having grown hot under the sun. Around them the bush became low and khaki, a hardier breed of gum tree, exposed to the wind, the land rockier, the soil more granular and eroded, the ferns and the undergrowth becoming sparse, large termite mounds dotted here and there. They emerged from the trees and the road split, the right-hand fork leading upwards—to the mine entrance, Mike said—while the left-hand track, less well formed, sloped downwards beside the lake.

They parked by the water. Amber could see where people had been there before: the stone rings of camp fires, empty beer bottles, a metal grille for the fire. Mike didn't wait: he stripped off, so scrawny he was like a skinned rabbit, except with a tuft of red hair in the centre of his chest. His willy was a funny little thing, a worm, but he seemed proud of it, making no effort to cover it or turn away. He ran towards the water, white bum flashing, galloping into the lake, until the water grabbed at his feet, tripping him forward into a dive.

Suzy and Amber undressed behind the truck, Lucas giving them space. The sun was warm and the water was cold. Amber could hear wind in the trees, but down in the lake there was little breeze. She could hear water tumbling in the distance.

There was a rope. Mike was swinging out. He really was proud of his willy. Suzie was laughing at him, encouraging him.

'We should leave them,' said Lucas.

'Yes,' she said.

He led the way. They swam out towards the centre of the lake. Amber dived down, eyes open, into the deepening blue, such a contrast to the opaque turbidity of the Murray River. She dived deeper, until the pressure in her ears and nose was too much, and yet she still could not see the bottom. She didn't linger too long, but allowed herself to drift back to the surface, feeling the water's embrace. Who knew how deep the lake might be?

'You okay?' asked Lucas.

'I'm fine,' she said with a laugh, treading water. She was a good swimmer, used to negotiating the currents of the Murray. The still waters of the lake were no trouble.

'Let me know if you need help.'

She was tempted. She imagined him next to her, arms supporting her. 'I'm okay for now,' she said, regretting the words even as they left her lips.

After their swim, the four of them sunbaked, Amber feeling at home. She enjoyed this, appreciated being with people. In this place. Her place.

She turned to Mike. 'Tell me about the mine. Tell me what happened to Teramina and her husband.'

'Francis and Teramina?' said Mike. 'It's quite a tale.' He gazed over the lake, gathering his thoughts, before turning back. 'They were seen as saviours in The Valley. Our very own power couple: Francis smooth as silk, Teramina with the gloss of old money. They were just what we needed. The logging was finished, the mill was contracting. The mine seemed heaven-sent.'

He paused, looked at each of them in turn, a born storyteller.

'They were good to me. Took me in, gave me a job. I'd been protesting against the logging in the forest, so I was never going to get a job at the mill. The recession was in full swing and work had dried up, so I was thinking of maybe heading to the mines in WA or Queensland. Instead, Francis and Teramina gave me work and I stayed. They dreamt of reopening the mine and they thought I could help, make sure the new operation was environmentally sustainable. They were big on that.'

'Was there always gold here?' asked Amber. 'Other mines? Or was it just the Gryphon?'

'Gold was what really opened up The Valley. Before that, in the 1830s, the 1840s, it was all wooded, inhabited by local people. The Walbunja. Must have been amazing, a natural wonderland. Imagine it. That's when my family first arrived, freed convicts.

Those early settlers started clearing the land, turning forest to pasture, a gradual transformation. There were maybe a dozen families; the Clovertons had the biggest landholding, Teramina's family.

'Then the gold rush arrived. The 1860s. Gold fever ran through the colonies like the plague. They chased it up the river, coming from the coast. Got into the valley, panning and scraping. They call it a rush, but it was a frenzy, men driven crazy by the idea that the next turn of the spade could secure their future.

'They cut down the remaining trees, all of them, drove off the blacks, cared nothing for the farmers and their settlements. They dug up the entire valley, every last blade of grass, seeking gold. They excavated the graveyard by the church, the blackfellas' burial grounds, they didn't care. They dammed the river, diverted it into races, altered its course and dug up its bed, panning and sifting and scrounging. That's how it got its name: the Broken River. When it rained, the entire valley became one massive quagmire, a breeding ground for mosquitoes. Men died of typhus and cholera and dysentery. And still they dug, a scene from the Somme, blasting at the rocks when their picks wouldn't bite or when they couldn't wait. They chased it up Watershine Creek and up the escarpment, up the ravine, cutting a path where the road is now. And when they got here, they found the source of the gold, up on the hill there. The main seam. The motherlode. And then they chased it underground, forming the Gryphon company. Fortunes were found and lives were lost. Year after year they went deeper and deeper, bringing more and more gold to the surface.

'And on the surface, the valley returned to its former state, the prospectors off to the next big thing, Majors Creek or Captains Flat or down into Victoria. The diggings grew over, the grass returned, the farmers reclaimed their lands, the soil as deep and rich as ever, the Broken River repairing itself and finding its course again.'

'Why was it called the Gryphon Mine? Do you know?' asked Amber.

It was Lucas who answered. 'The gryphon is a mythical beast. Half lion, half eagle. Famed throughout antiquity for guarding treasures, particularly gold.'

Amber looked up at the hill above them. 'Sounds appropriate.'

Mike continued his narrative. 'The mine's heyday was the end of the nineteenth century. There were other mines, but this was the most important one, the one that followed the main seam, the one that employed people, that bankrolled the pub and the Miners' Institute and the churches and the old bank and all the rest of it. While The Valley recovered, and the grass returned, and the dairy cattle came back and the fruit trees were planted and the sawmill got its start, the mine continued. Right up until the Depression, 1932. That was the end of it. Until Francis Hardcastle arrived.'

Mike saw he still had the other three in his thrall, and kept going. 'It was never quite clear why the Clovertons closed it: if the gold had run out, or it was just getting too expensive and too dangerous to continue. The seam had twisted and turned and split. At the last, they were pursuing it below the lake. All the ground under us, where we're sitting now, is honeycombed with tunnels and shafts. I explored many of them when I worked here; some looked like they were excavated yesterday, while others were collapsing in upon themselves, full of cave-ins and rotting timbers. And those old miners, they didn't just go down, they went sideways, they went upwards, wherever the gold led them. More and more water was seeping in, the workings were going down and down, and the pumps needed to work harder and harder to clear it. They were steam-driven. Only right at the end did they have diesel pumps, but it was problematic running them underground. The carbon dioxide build-up. It's heavier than air, settles at the bottom of mines. No lightweight breathing apparatus in the 1920s. The pumps spooked the miners instead of reassuring them. There were a few close-run things.

'Whispers began, fears emerging. There was a cave-in, a blasting gone wrong. Two men died, buried in a slurry of rock and water. Some of the workers foresaw a disaster and insisted on more money, unionising and striking. But there was no more money; the gold was petering out. The miners were a superstitious bunch, and some of them refused to work on the newest tunnels and shafts, the ones reaching out under the lake. So in the end, the Clovertons shut it down.'

Amber is intrigued. 'So why did Francis and Teramina think they could succeed, if there was no more gold?'

'Francis didn't believe that. He was a mining engineer. He'd worked all over the world. Knew his shit. Thought the mine might still be viable, convinced Teramina to investigate the possibility. It was her mine; passed down through her family. It's not the only place it's been happening. There's been quite the push in recent years, particularly in Victoria, re-evaluating old mines, seeing if they're viable.'

'The gold price,' interjected Lucas. 'It was locked in at thirty dollars an ounce for decades. That's what they would have been getting in 1932, maybe less. Nowadays it's more than a thousand bucks US.'

'That's right,' Mike concurred. 'And there were the changes in technology. Francis was organising to get mains electricity put through. We could run proper lighting, run ventilation fans, power excavators. No carbon dioxide. A completely new game. That was part of my job too: working out how to lay in the lighting, how to get power to the machinery.'

'It sounds so promising,' said Amber. 'Teramina approved?'

'Oh God yes,' said Mike. 'She was flying. It gave her purpose, somewhere to direct her money, a way to revitalise The Valley. And she was in love with Francis. Blind Freddy could see that.'

Amber looked out across the lake, remembering her friend, so fractured and hurt by the loss of her husband. So damaged. So unsure. Amber found it hard to imagine her happy and fulfilled, but it made her glad to think that had been the case, no matter how fleetingly.

'We were still in the development stage, when it ended,' said Mike. 'A hundred years ago, dozens of miners worked shifts there, but the Hardcastles were starting small, wanted it to be sustainable. Half-a-dozen of us tops, still laying the groundwork for when we got the electricity through and upgraded the road and built a new race down the escarpment. But we were on to something, no doubt about that.'

'How can you be so sure?' asked Amber.

'Saw it with my own eyes,' said Mike. 'Some small nuggets, glitterings in the walls of the mine, in among the quartz. Right at the bottom levels, the shafts under the lake. Plucked some of them out myself. We did some exploratory blasting, and there it was. We had good diesel pumps, new generation, running up on the surface, powerful enough to lift the water. We did some more blasting, chasing the gold, up under the lake, and there was no question: the seam continued.'

'Were they making money?' asked Amber, captivated.

'Not as much as they were spending,' said Mike. 'To make more, to make it a going concern, they'd need to attract investors. The reward would come when they started mining commercially. That was the plan. They were going to list on the stock market.'

No one said anything; they all knew what was coming next.

'There was a cave-in; the lake poured in, flooded the mine. Francis was down there. The old miners were right after all; it was too dangerous, too risky. If you ask me, that's why they closed the mine in 1932. Not because they'd run out of gold, but because extracting it had become too hazardous.'

'How awful for Teramina,' said Amber. 'So there's no doubt he died?'

'Drowned or crushed in the cave-in,' said Mike. 'Coroner delivered an open finding, but that's only because there was no way of recovering the body.' He gestured towards the mine entrance. 'In some ways it was fortunate that he was alone down there. There was a huge storm and the rest of us were at the bottom of the hill, at the old crusher site, trying to stabilise the slag heap and the tailings, prevent it being eroded by a flash flood and capsizing into the cisterns. If we weren't working on that, more of us could have been underground. More of us could have died.'

Lucas spoke, voice grim. 'I tried to get up here, to the mine. Teramina sent me. But the road was gone, swept away by the rain. There was nothing we could do.'

'And this was only three-and-a-half years ago?' asked Amber, remembering what the lawyer had told her.

'That's right.'

She took in the landscape. Her's now. It all seemed pristine, almost untouched. She thought of Teramina, so distraught, so damaged. Now Amber was here, it seemed that much more real.

It was Lucas who broke the silence, speaking to no one in particular. 'The gold price has doubled again since then.'

Mike laughed. 'It's no use, man. Mine's flooded. The only bloke who could dig down there is Jacques Cousteau.' He laughed at his own joke, but Lucas was not laughing.

Amber contemplated the mountain, and felt something cold and subterranean, like there was ice water in her veins.

chapter twenty-six

2024

NELL IS ACROSS THE FAR SIDE OF THE KINGS HIGHWAY, THE MAIN ROAD BISECTING Saltwood, getting a coffee, when she sees an ambulance ease up outside Willard Halliday's office. There is no siren, no sense of urgency, but it still catches her attention. Has she somehow exhausted the lawyer, overextended his reserves of energy? Or has the news she is Amber Jones's daughter incited some sort of seizure?

Curious, she starts across the road, getting halfway, but having to wait as a long line of traffic snakes past in front of her: Canberrans heading to the coast; she can tell by the licence plates. Through the gaps in the cars, she watches as Halliday is trundled out in a wheelchair, a huge orderly in a white jacket steering the chair, another man with him. Nell frowns. They resemble hospital attendants, not ambulance officers. She can't recall seeing that before. Suddenly Halliday, spotting her through the magic lantern of passing cars, lifts his arm, waving frantically and attempting to yell, his shout subdued by his damaged lungs, but Nell is less than ten metres away, she can see the mouthing of the word: 'Help!'

The orderly sees Nell, and slaps Halliday hard across the side of the head.

Nell drops her coffee, liquid splattering on the bitumen, and reaches for her gun. The traffic is bumper to bumper, no gaps, but moving slowly. The man guiding the chair swears, and now his companion sees her as well. Nell has no choice: she moves into the traffic, stepping in front of a car; hand out, palm open, ordering the driver to stop. He sees her; slams on the brakes. Behind him, a horn blares. She hears the driver swearing at her; she doesn't care, doesn't look.

The man handling the wheelchair pushes it towards the ambulance while his companion sidles the other way, to his left—and withdraws a sawn-off shotgun. *Jesus*. A shotgun, it's real. Before Nell can bring her Glock to bear, he fires off a shot. Most of it goes over her head, but a stray pellet or two, unconstrained by the shortened barrel, ping off the side of the car.

She flings herself backwards, sheltering behind the engine block, realising as she does so that she may be putting people in danger. She hopes the gunman won't shoot into the car, hit the innocents inside. She looks up, over the bonnet, holding her weapon tight, but it's no good; she can't start a gunfight in the main street of Saltwood. She's just as likely to hit Halliday or some passer-by as his abductors; they're just as likely to return fire indiscriminately. She glances inside the car, the driver sitting horrified, mouth open, a child in the passenger seat, her phone out and filming, as if this is some sort of made-for-Insta moment.

Across the road, the first man has lifted Halliday from the wheelchair and is manhandling him towards the back of the ambulance, doors now open, the gunman standing with the shotgun pointed straight at her, eyes trained on her, the threat unmistakable. Stalemate.

She places her gun on the ground, holds her hands up. She hears a child screaming somewhere. Willard is struggling, trying to break the grip of the orderly, but the man has almost succeeded in shoving him into the back of the ambulance. A siren starts up a couple of blocks away; someone has called the police. The man with the gun doesn't move, just yells at his colleague to hurry the fuck up, and fires another shot into the air above Nell's head. She crouches back down, but when she again steals a glimpse above the car bonnet, she sees movement from behind the gunman. Out from Willard's office staggers Ollie, the lumbering office assistant, glasses gone, his face a bloody mess, like a pink balloon smeared with tomato sauce. He has a rifle.

'Fucker,' he swears, voice calm but emphatic, as though he's been here before.

'No!' yells Nell, a moment too late, as the orderly with the shotgun begins to turn. Ollie shoots him calmly in the leg at point-blank range, and the man collapses, still holding the gun as he goes down. Nell crosses the intervening few metres in no time, smashes her boot onto the man's wrist, wrestling the shotgun from his grasp.

Ollie stands motionless, staring, still holding the rifle, pointing it at the man on the ground. There's a roar as the ambulance engine revs, then tyres squeal as it pulls out, cuts through the line of traffic, speeds south on the wrong side of the road. Ollie, back with it, casually raises his gun and puts a couple of bullets into the retreating vehicle.

'Drop it,' says Nell.

Ollie blinks once, twice, then places the gun on the ground. Willard is lying on the footpath with no apparent physical injuries, gasping like a beached fish. Somehow, he's managed to struggle free.

A police car pulls up, an officer is out, holding his service pistol in front of him. Nell is standing over the injured gunman but lowers the shotgun, pointing its barrel towards the ground, not wanting to cause confusion. 'Police,' she says. 'Homicide. My gun's over there. Middle of the road.'

The officer nods, comprehending but vigilant. 'Gun on the ground. ID.'

She does what she's told, flashing her badge.

'All good,' he says, visibly relaxing. He retrieves Nell's gun, brings it over, hands it to her.

'Thank you,' she says, then points south. 'That way. An ambulance, maybe stolen. At least one perp, probably two. Most likely armed, definitely dangerous.'

'On it,' says the officer.

Nell yells after him as he climbs back into the squad car. 'I need backup. And paramedics.'

For half a moment, she stares down at the wounded man, writhing with pain. She slides the shotgun further away with her foot, all the while keeping her own gun trained on him. Blood is pumping from his leg, but she's not willing to drop the Glock and help him, give him the chance to overpower her. Then she sees another officer running along the street, gun out.

She holds her gun aloft, lifting her badge with her other hand. 'Police!' she yells.

The advancing constable calls his understanding. 'All good!'

'Keep your gun on him,' she instructs when he reaches her. 'I'll try to stem the bleeding.'

She sees the car she ran in front of, the one she sheltered behind. It's still stopped, the driver still gaping, the kid in the front still filming. 'And move them along!'

She's trying to staunch the bleeding when a real ambulance pulls up, the paramedics in uniform. On the ground, the big man is drifting into unconsciousness.

Another policeman arrives, then another. Nell flashes her badge once more, her hand bloody, addressing them. 'Detective Senior Constable Nell Buchanan. That man there, the wounded man, fired on me. One of you go with him to the hospital, keep him under guard. And arrest him.' She points to the shotgun. 'Evidence. He fired two shots. I've handled it, but try to preserve it as best you can.'

The first officer, a senior constable, assigns the ambulance to one of his subordinates, delegates the shotgun to the other. Only then does he turn to Nell. 'You okay?'

'Sure. Bit rattled, that's all.' She holds up her hand, the one covered in blood. 'Not mine.'

'No, I think you're bleeding,' he says, gesturing under his chin.

She doesn't feel a thing, but when she touches her neck with her clean hand, it elicits a wincing pain. When she withdraws her hand, she sees more blood. A shotgun pellet. Could've taken her eye. Didn't. 'He'll need to be charged with that as well. Actual bodily harm.'

'Who is he?' asks the uniformed man.

'Don't know.'

She looks at Ollie, still bleeding and dazed. And Willard, now sitting up, his face pallid, wheezing like a steam train. Nell walks across to the abandoned wheelchair, gets it across to Willard. 'Give me a hand,' she says to the officer. They get the lawyer into the chair.

'Wouldn't mind a hit of oxygen,' says Willard with a snakish smile. 'Big day.'

Anger flares in Nell. She's about to deliver a riposte, but Ollie interjects. 'It's all right. I'll take him.'

Nell stares at him, his face a bloody mess. 'You okay?'

'I'll live.' He sounds tougher than he appears. Maybe she's underestimated him.

'Let's get him inside,' she says. 'And then I need statements from both of you.'

'I'm sorry, officer,' says Willard. 'Ollie and I are suffering the after-effects of a brutal assault. I fear any statement we give at this time might prove unreliable. Inadmissible.'

Nell touches her neck again. 'Bullshit. I almost died coming to your assistance. You looked right at me, yelled for help.'

Willard starts coughing.

'I'm getting him inside,' says Ollie.

'I'm coming too,' says Nell.

'Suit yourself.'

— — —

Inside, the outer office is much the same, just some drops of blood on the floor next to a set of broken eyeglasses. 'Is this where they assaulted you?' she asks Ollie.

Ollie defers to Willard, who gives his permission.

'Yep. Walked in. Asked politely if Mr Halliday was available. When I asked their business, they laid into me. Caught me totally unawares. Knocked me out. Cowardly fuckers.'

Ollie doesn't wait for the next question, but pushes Willard through to his office. Nell follows. Ollie concentrates on hooking his boss up to his oxygen bottle, ignoring her. The place has been trashed. Or partially trashed. A line of books has been swept from a bookcase, the glass front of a cabinet has been shattered, a framed oil painting smashed across one of the client chairs facing the desk.

'Who are they?' asks Nell.

'No idea,' says Willard, but the smile has left his eyes, replaced by fear and anxiety.

'What did they want?'

'Beats me. They didn't say. Presumably they were going to broach that subject after they'd captured me.'

She stares at him, irritation bubbling, convinced he knows more than he's letting on. 'Can you think of any reason why anyone would want to kidnap you?'

'None whatsoever. I am an officer of the court.'

Nell examines the broken office. A small-town solicitor, a modest office. 'Do you want police protection? I can ask them to provide someone, even if it's just to safeguard you through the night.'

Willard coughs, shakes his head. 'I've got Ollie.'

Nell glares at the assistant. 'I should arrest you right now.'

'It was self-defence. Or defence of Mr Halliday.'

'Is that gun licensed?'

'Yes.'

Nell stares hard at him, and then at Willard. 'Those men. We'll find out who they are. Why they came after you. You know that. Sure you don't want to get ahead of the game? Tell me what you know?'

Willard wheezes, shaking his head. 'I wish you luck with your inquiries, detective.'

Nell is caught by indecision. Her phone buzzes in her pocket. She checks the caller ID: Ivan. She answers.

'You all right?' he asks, sounding breathless. 'I heard something about a gunfight.'

'I'm fine. Two thugs tried to abduct that lawyer, Willard Halliday. One of them is on the run, the other's in hospital. He'll need surgery.'

'You hit him?'

Nell is surprised to hear herself laugh. 'No. Shot. Not by me.'

But Ivan isn't laughing; he still sounds like he's catching his breath. 'They've found Vicary Hearst.'

'Is he okay?'

'No. In hospital in Canberra. Found lying beside a road out beyond Halfchurch. Serious enough to warrant a chopper.'

'Jesus. You heading to see him?'

'Not unless he regains consciousness.'

chapter twenty-seven

1994

THE DAY AFTER AMBER HAD VENTURED TO THE LAKE ON THE ESCARPMENT WITH her new friends, Simmons Burnside visited her at Watershine, again arriving unannounced. She'd heard no car; he must have walked. This time he was out of uniform, dressed in jeans and a slightly tatty shirt. Somehow it made him appear more human. She knew he was the same age as Mike and Lucas, that they'd all been in the same year at school, but even in casual clothes he seemed older, more responsible. Maybe it was because he was a police officer, or perhaps because he was married, had a son. 'Not good news, I'm afraid,' he said, standing on her doorstep, looking uncomfortable, shifting from one leg to the other.

'You'd better come in then,' she replied.

He sat on a sofa, casting his eyes about the room. 'Did I tell you that I lived here for a while?' he said.

'Really? I thought Teramina did.'

'That was later on. I was here when she and Francis were still living at Ellensby. She moved here after the mine flooded, when she was forced to sell the homestead.'

'I remember now,' she replied. Amber recalled the anguish of her friend, as she slowly unwound her past in the shack by the Murray, how upsetting it had been for Teramina to sell the Cloverton family home.

'You remember?'

'Yes. When we met. She was very upset about it.'

Now Simmons seemed unsettled, or maybe angry; she could see a scowl on his face. 'Did she tell you why she had to sell?' he asked.

'Only that she had no choice.'

'That's true. She had mortgaged Ellensby to help finance the Gryphon Mine.'

'I see.'

Simmons continued. 'The sale of Ellensby cleared the debt, with a significant amount left over. It wasn't just the house she sold; it was the entire estate: a large tract of prime farmland. It left her a wealthy woman. It should be yours. But it's gone.'

'Willard Halliday told me she left me two thousand dollars. I have it in a bank in Saltwood.'

'That's right. That's all that's left.'

'There was more?'

'A lot more. Teramina had an accountant, Fred Wallington. The same accountant they used at the mining company. He died less than a month before Teramina. After his death, she engaged a new accountant, Juanita Malakova, who discovered Wallington had stolen all of Teramina's money. I've been trying to investigate. Juanita's been helping, but we've hit a dead end. There's no obvious way to find out where the money went.' Simmons studied his hands. 'I'm sorry.'

'What made you think there was money missing?' asked Amber.

'Teramina told me, the night she asked me to be her executor. She said Juanita Malakova had discovered the theft.'

'What about the mining company?' Amber asked. 'Willard Halliday said there were shares.'

But Simmons was shaking his head even as Amber finished speaking. 'I went to see Willard Halliday yesterday; he was the company secretary. Between the two of us, we were able to convince the bank to open up the company accounts, told them what Juanita Malakova had discovered with Teramina's own affairs. It was the same thing—the money was all gone. Wallington had been siphoning it off even before Francis drowned.'

'Francis didn't suspect?'

Simmons turned away, off towards a window, hesitating, before framing his next statement. 'There are signatures. Obvious fakes. But there is one that appears genuine, a large withdrawal, countersigned by Francis—a week before he died.'

'He was in on the theft?'

'Impossible to say.' He looked at her then, his discomfort clear. 'I'm sorry, Amber. I don't think there is anything more I can do.'

She felt dismayed—not for herself, as the land and the house and the money had never really been hers to begin with—but on behalf of Teramina. The widow had been treated appallingly, robbed and abandoned. Amber couldn't imagine how terrible that must have been, to lose the person you love, the person you trust, and then to lose your inheritance. And afterwards, when she was at her most vulnerable, humiliated and brought low, this man

Wallington returned again and again, until there was nothing left. No wonder Teramina had been so devastated, no wonder she had done what she had done.

'What about Watershine? Is it safe?' she asked Simmons.

The policeman smiled for the first time. 'Yes. We've confirmed that, at least. The land and the house and the two thousand dollars are yours.'

She felt a sense of relief, grateful that not all of Teramina's possessions had been plundered. 'Thank you,' she said. 'For everything.'

His smile broadened, and she realised she quite liked his smile.

'The house is sturdy,' he said, standing. 'I fixed it up while I was living here. I put a new porch on, and Lucas and I replaced the roof.'

'You and Lucas?'

'Yes.'

'I'm in your debt, then. I would much prefer Teramina's house to her money.'

He frowned at that, like he was struggling to understand.

— —

Lucas came by the next afternoon. She heard the truck and walked out onto the porch, watching as it appeared through the trees. There was a canoe strapped to the vehicle's back tray.

'I brought you something,' he said, almost shyly, after climbing the stairs. He handed her a solid disc, wrapped in aluminium foil.

'What is it?' she asked, unable to conceal her pleasure at receiving a gift.

'Siena cake. Made it myself.'

'Thank you,' she said. 'That's very kind of you. You want to come in? We could sample some.' It felt heavy, more robust than the cakes she made herself, and she was curious.

'Maybe later,' he said. 'I want to show you something first. Up at the lake. We can have cake and tea afterwards.'

'Okay.'

It was a clear autumn day, the sky a deep and cloudless blue, no wind to speak of, The Valley basking in late-season warmth. The prospect of a journey up the mountain with Lucas appealed. She felt perhaps a swim might lift her, clean away some of the residual anger and sadness left from her meeting with Simmons. 'Swimmers?' she asked.

'If you like.'

When she got into the truck, she gestured towards the tray with the canoe. 'For the lake?' she asked.

'Uh-huh.'

They climbed the track, the truck bouncing merrily, Amber able to enjoy the view now she had the passenger window to herself. She watched the valley fall away, every shade of green and some in between, punctuated by the yellows of the poplars, starting to turn, and a smattering of reds and burnt oranges from other imported trees. She could see a truck moving slowly through an orchard, the fruit pickers like tiny dolls, going about their work. This time, some of the track was familiar, and the journey up didn't seem to take so long or seem so precarious.

After circling through the forest on top of the escarpment, Lucas took the left-hand road at the fork, taking them down to park beside the lake, the same spot they'd come with Mike and Suzie two days before. He manhandled the canoe from the back, then she helped carry it to the water and float it in. He held it steady while she clambered into the front. 'Quite the mystery,' she said.

He laughed. 'All will be revealed.'

They paddled out towards the centre of the lake. She'd spent her life in canoes, knew she could handle the craft better than him, but she demurred, sitting in the front while he did the majority of the rowing, interested to see how competent he was. Not too shabby, she concluded. He understood it, the flow of a craft through water.

Towards the centre, he stopped paddling, the canoe drifting forward with the momentum. When she turned to look at him, he pointed to the far shoreline. There was a ring about it, new growth, about a metre higher than the current surface. 'See that high-water mark? The lake level used to be higher, not so long ago. I reckon back when Francis and Teramina were reviving the mine.'

Amber studied the marks. He must be right; they couldn't have endured since the mine closed in 1932. 'So the water level dropped when the mine was flooded?' she said.

'That's what people believed,' he said. And she remembered Mike's story: that there had been a cave-in, that the lake drained into the mine, that the water level had dropped as a consequence. 'But the lake is as full as it can get. It's emptying out, down the falls and into the cisterns.'

'Yes, I've seen them,' she said.

'So after the mine was filled with water, why hasn't the water level risen back to where it was before?' asked Lucas.

'Do you know?'

'I think so, but let me show you something first. Two things, actually.'

He brought the canoe to a complete halt with a couple of deft strokes, gathered up his canvas backpack and pulled out a small leather case. He opened it and extracted an instrument the size of an alarm clock, glass-faced, like a compass or perhaps a barometer. It appeared to be old, made of brass. 'An altimeter,' he said.

'Altitude?' she asked.

'Yes. Height above sea level, measured in feet. Uses air pressure.'

'Must vary from day to day then,' she said.

He studied her then, perhaps surprised at her insight. 'So it does. I calibrated it at the crossroad, just before I left. Five hundred and twenty-five feet above sea level.'

'And now?'

'One thousand, seven hundred and seventy feet.'

'Intriguing,' she said, voice teasing. And yet it was. He had drawn her in.

Undeterred by her amusement, Lucas again rummaged around in his backpack, and this time he withdrew a calico sack. 'Second thing,' he said, grinning. This looked homemade: just a length of twine with knots at regular lengths, and a lead weight tied to one end. 'Plumb bob,' he said. 'Watch.'

He lowered the weight gently over the side and into the water, letting the string out gradually as the weight sank, counting the knots as they passed through his fingers. She understood immediately; he was trying to establish the depth of the lake.

'You might be in a shallow place. An outcrop, a sunken tree. Hardly scientific,' she offered. But she recalled how deep the lake had been when they had swum here, how she had been unable to detect the bottom.

'Correct. But in this instance, near enough should be close enough. We're pretty much in the centre of the lake.'

The string began to slacken; the bob must be on the bottom. He hauled on the string until it was taut again.

'A knot every six feet,' he said. 'Each fathom.'

She laughed at the archaic expression, like something from a pirate tale, and he grinned back, pleased with himself.

He hauled up the bob, counting the knots again as it ascended. 'Seven fathoms,' he declared, once the bob was back on board. 'Just over forty feet.'

'Deep,' she said.

'Profound.' He laughed.

'Which proves what?'

'I'll show you.'

The canoe was beginning to drift again with the slight current, and Lucas now helped it on its way, propelling the narrow craft towards the escarpment. He pushed the canoe to the bank, onto a small beach stretching between two stone outcrops. There, she leapt clear, helped pull it further up the bank.

They were on the north shore of the lake, under the looming presence of the mine entrance, not far from where he had left his truck.

'You've done this before,' she asserted.

'Yesterday,' he replied. 'Something Mike said when we were here made me wonder, so I came up and checked it out. I wanted to be sure before I showed you.'

'Showed me what?'

'This way.'

They threaded their way through a thicket of tea-trees and along an animal path to where the lake tumbled down through the opening in a broken dam and formed a small cascade, bubbling into a wide pool, a natural feature eroded out of the sandstone. At the end, it flowed out through a gap in a second wall. Another man-made dam.

'You see?' he said. 'The lake emptying.'

She nodded.

'Pretty benign now,' said Lucas, 'but it must really roar through after a big storm.'

She thought of the ravine the creek had carved out of the escarpment. She knew how powerful a force water could be.

'What are the dams?' she asked.

'From the original mine. Built to feed the race, carrying ore down to the cisterns at Watershine.'

They moved alongside the lower pool, on smooth stones, towards the second dam, breeched in the centre, and signs of concrete blocks, stone work, some iron posts, rusted and twisted after sixty years. Lucas was in front and he pushed through some low shrubs, closer to the water. He led her on, towards the escarpment. It was not a sheer cliff, not yet, the land falling away, then levelling off for a few metres, before the precipice proper began.

Lucas pointed. 'See it?'

At first she couldn't. He stood behind her, one hand on her shoulder, pointing with the other. She could feel his breath on her neck. Smell him. And then she saw it: a shadow darker than the rest of the shadows. An opening in the cliff face.

'What is it?' she asked.

'I'm pretty sure it's a ventilation shaft. From the mine. Not used for access, just to get air in and out.'

'How can you be sure?'

'I'll show you.'

They scrambled down. She almost fell once, saving herself by grabbing at a boulder, skinning the palm of her hand, though she didn't let on. She had grown up in a pan-flat landscape; she wasn't used to such elevations. And as she approached the cliff edge, Amber felt the thin air of the precipice calling to her, inviting vertigo. And a terrible question came to her: was this where Teramina had ended herself, where she had leapt into oblivion? After pausing a moment to steady herself, determined not to show any weakness, she caught up with Lucas as he stood above the opening. The hole was less than a metre wide, and it plunged down, almost vertical. She could see the marks in the rock, where it had been worked.

'Here, show me your face,' he said. She did what he asked and he took his water bottle, wet a cloth and gently wiped her cheeks. 'Stand over the opening.'

She did as she was instructed, and felt the suggestion of wind on her face, and a smell, dark and moist. 'Airflow,' she said.

'And this,' said Lucas. He extracted the altimeter once more, showed her the dial: sixteen hundred and ninety feet. 'That's eighty feet below the surface of the lake, and almost thirty feet below its bottom.'

She understood what he was demonstrating, saying it aloud. 'If the story Mike told us was true, that the mine caved in and the lake flooded it, there should be water pouring out of this hole. The water level of the lake should have dropped to this height.'

'It's not even close,' he said. 'Maybe the mine is not flooded after all. At least, not from the lake.'

She stared at him. 'What exactly are you saying?'

'That maybe there never was a cave-in. That maybe we can access the gold.'

— —

The next day, the two of them returned to the mine once more, this time equipped with keys, two torches and a lantern as well as the altimeter. Lucas had again calibrated the instrument at the crossroads, and to make double sure they measured beside the lake. It gave exactly the same altitude as the day before.

The entrance, the main one, was four hundred and thirty feet higher than the surface of the lake. They unlocked the doors, crept into the darkness. It was so silent, so devoid of life or movement. They whispered; their voices seemed so loud. To Amber, it felt like trespass. Like Howard Carter in Egypt, defying a curse.

There was equipment inside the door: a modern generator, some hard hats, gloves and goggles. Not from the original mine, but from almost four years earlier, when Teramina and Francis had been here. A shiver ran down Amber's spine at the sight. Had Teramina and Francis worn these hard hats, these gloves? A rail line curved into the darkness, easing down a spiralling descent. It was profoundly dark, the beams of their twin torches like a life line. She reached out without thinking, took Lucas's hand. He squeezed hers reassuringly. 'C'mon, it shouldn't be so far,' he said.

They made their way slowly forward, slowly downward. Here and there were side tunnels, some no more than indents, others snaking away into the dark. There were markings on the walls, labels. The shafts were named, Big Sur and Eureka, Klondike and Eaglehawk, with dates: 1868, 1874, 1888, the lower the level, the more recent the year. At some places the walls glistened with moisture, at others they were dry and grey. After a while they saw layers in the rock, reflecting the light like dull glass.

'Quartz,' said Lucas, his voice echoing ever so slightly despite his quiet tone. 'They were following the seams, chasing the gold.'

'Down and down,' said Amber, imagining the effort, decade upon decade, blasting powder and picks and shovels, the ore carts on the tracks hauled up by hand or by donkeys and horses. There was no great mine wheel, no steam-driven elevator, certainly no electricity.

They descended further.

'Hold up,' said Lucas. 'Here we are now. The same level as the lake surface.' He shone the torch on the altimeter to demonstrate the truth of it and then directed the beam into the distance. There was no water.

They followed the ore cart rails. Down. Further. Almost on tiptoe, trying not to breathe too loudly. For a long moment, Amber wondered if the mine was flooded at all, if perhaps the water had drained away in the intervening years. But soon enough they reached it, the surface still and black and impenetrable. Lucas read off the altimeter.

'We're a good one hundred and seventy feet below the surface of the lake and one hundred and thirty feet below its bottom. They can't be connected. There might have been a cave-in, and there might have been flooding, but not from the lake.' He was speaking more loudly now and there was excitement in his voice.

'So what happened?' asked Amber. 'How did it flood?'

'I think I know.' His smile was meant to be reassuring, but in the artificial lamplight his face was sallow and his eyes looked mad.

She shook her head, dismissing the image, a trick of the light.

——

Outside, back on the surface, the perfect day was still perfect and she breathed long deep breaths of relief, feeling like she had been released from a prison. He took her back to the place where the lake spilt out into the valley.

'There,' he said, pointing.

Amber could see it now. The level in the lake had been higher, contained by the top dam, had dropped at the time of the accident. That's why the authorities had believed there'd been a cave-in. Lucas pointed to the wall, where it had collapsed near its centre.

'They dammed the creek, lifted the level. Used it to help wash through the crusher. Hardcastle must have patched it up, but not well enough. The day he came up, there were huge storms. Massive. I remember it like yesterday. I tried to get up here, see if he was safe, but the road had been washed out. The lake must have been completely full, water overflowing the makeshift dams, the creek and the waterfall raging. Then the dam collapsed, releasing a massive wave of water. And see.' He pointed to the ventilation shaft. 'If the flow was strong enough, high enough, it would have poured through there. Enough to fill the mine. And with the dam breached, the level of the lake dropped permanently.'

Amber felt herself sharing his conviction. 'There was no cave-in.'

Lucas was bouncing from foot to foot, excitement on his face. 'And now there is no water flowing into the mine. What we saw down there just now, that's what's left from three-and-a-half years ago. We can bring in pumps, empty the mine. Find the gold.'

She could see his logic, could feel his exhilaration. Gold. Money. Enough to fix up the house, enough to pay her bills—enough to honour Teramina's legacy, enough to build a new life.

chapter twenty-eight

2024

THE ADRENALINE HAS LONG WORN OFF. NELL IS SITTING IN A HOSPITAL LUNCH room, fluorescent lights too bright and no windows, a clock ticking on the wall above her. She's waiting for the gunman to come out of surgery. She's just finished another call to Sydney, filling in the media team, when Ivan appears at the door, eyes focused and forehead creased.

'Your neck?' he says, hand moving to his own throat.

'It's nothing,' she says. 'Stray shotgun pellet.'

'You're kidding.'

'It's fine. Superficial. You?'

'Borrowed a car from Wilhelmina at the pub. Went up to Halfchurch. Doorknocked the locals.'

'And?'

'No one saw anything.'

He sits next to her, checking they're alone and not being overheard. 'Pack of journos outside. Gunfight in Saltwood. The way they're whipping it up, it'll be bigger than the OK Corral by morning.'

'Terrific. Just what we need.'

'Might have to start calling you Wyatt,' says Ivan, cracking a smile, starting to relax. 'They're calling you the hero cop.'

'What? Really?'

'Kid in a car filmed it all.'

'Jesus.'

A wiry-looking doctor, hair like steel wool, wire-framed glasses, metal braces on his teeth, walks in, not bothering to knock. 'Patient's out of surgery, in recovery. Stitched up. We've got him stabilised and he should improve from here. Too early to say if there will be any nerve damage but he won't lose his leg.'

'How long before we can speak to him?' asks Nell.

'He'll be conscious any time now. We'll let you know.'

Once they're alone again, Nell asks Ivan. 'Vicary Hearst? How is he?'

Ivan shakes his head. 'Induced coma. They've had to relieve swelling on the brain. Scans don't show anything obvious, but we'll have to wait. It'll be a few days yet.'

'He wanted to meet us there. Halfchurch.'

'Good place for a rendezvous, coming along different roads. Unlikely to be seen.'

'Someone saw him,' says Nell.

'No sign of his phone,' says Ivan. 'They left everything else.'

'So he was bashed?'

'Injuries consistent with being hit by a car. Lucky to be alive.'

'Jesus.'

It's another hour before a nurse gives the detectives the all clear: the man is conscious and lucid.

'You take the lead,' says Ivan. 'You were there.'

'Thanks,' she says.

The gunman is sitting up in bed, face creased with annoyance. At being shot, at being in hospital, at being in custody. It's not a handsome face; even forty years ago it would have struggled to be passable. That would have been before the scars to his left cheek and chin, the broken nose and the cauliflower ear, before his hair fell out, he shaved his skull and the tattoo started creeping up his neck. His irises are a startling blue, but the whites are bloodshot and tinged with yellow. Nell places him in his mid-sixties, with every one of those years seemingly leaving some trace.

'Nah, fuck off. Not talking. Want me lawyer.'

'We can call one,' says Nell, already wondering why she waited all this time.

'Don't bother,' he says. 'They'll be on their way.' And then he draws a line across his lips with pinched fingers, zipping it shut, and doesn't say another word. His hand is gnarly and the knuckles are out of alignment, evidence that he's hit too many things too hard over too many years.

'He's a pro,' says Ivan as they leave the room. 'Seasoned crim. You can see where he's had tats lasered off.'

'Reformed?' asks Nell.

'Not judging by today,' says Ivan.

Nell frowns. 'How old do you reckon he is?'

'Early sixties. Face like a drover's dog, but in pretty good nick. Must work out. What about his accomplices? You get a good look at them?'

'One of them. Similar age, similar build. Short-cropped hair, a goatee, wraparound sunglasses. There must have been a driver, but I didn't see them.'

——

Ivan leaves his borrowed car at the hospital and they drive together to the Saltwood police station. It's past sunset, getting dark, but the gathering of media outside the main gate is obvious enough. Nell feels her heart sink; Ivan wasn't joking.

'Had a call from your journo mate? Scarsden?' she asks, hoping some banter might relieve her sense of foreboding.

Ivan laughs. 'Not yet.' And then he points. 'But it can't be long. Look.' There's a television journalist talking to a camera, lit up by a battery of lights. 'Doug Thunkleton.'

'Wow, the circus really is in town,' says Nell.

She parks at the rear of the station, and the two detectives announce their arrival to an intercom. The door clicks open and a young constable comes to greet them, taking them through to the officer in charge: Senior Sergeant Alice Wheelright.

'Detectives,' she greets them. 'Busy day.'

'You could say that,' says Ivan.

'What's the latest from the hospital?' Wheelright asks.

'Out of surgery, doing fine, not talking. Lawyering up.'

'Not surprising,' says the senior sergeant. 'We'll need a statement, but I'm assuming you'll want us to lay the charges, oversee the prosecution. Not really one for Homicide.'

'Provided we get unfettered access,' says Ivan.

'Oh. I wasn't aware the shooting was connected to your investigation,' says the officer. 'I thought it was coincidence.'

Nell is unsure how to respond to this.

'Detective Buchanan interviewed Mr Halliday shortly before the assault,' Ivan volunteers, but Nell hears the hesitation in his voice. No doubt he's thinking the same as she is: Feral Phelan and Plodder Packenham not trusting the local police for unstated reasons. Was it just the detectives in Queanbeyan, or were the uniforms in Saltwood under the same cloud of suspicion?

'Have you had any luck finding the other two?' asks Nell, deciding to change the subject. 'The ambulance?'

'We've found the vehicle, abandoned and torched, on a side road five kilometres out of town. A passing motorist saw the smoke and called it in. It had been bleached then set alight. Don't like our chances of finding any forensic traces.'

That infuriates Nell. Stealing a car is one thing, but ambulances are expensive and time-consuming to kit out. They save lives. She feels a primal desire to nail the offenders.

'And those who stole it?' she asks.

'Shouldn't be long. Our man in hospital was carrying a fake South Australian driver's licence. Quite convincing, enough to get past a random traffic stop. Facial recognition software has come up blank. We got some blood from the surgery and are running DNA and should have a result tomorrow. Depends if he's on file.'

Nell frowns. 'Fingerprints?'

'You won't believe it. The database is down. Something to do with a systems upgrade. They're promising it will be back online any moment. But they've been saying that for the past three hours.'

'What can you tell us about Vicary Hearst?' Ivan interjects. 'What was he doing out at Halfchurch?'

Wheelright scowls. 'I thought he was working with you. That he'd been seconded.'

'He was helping, that's right,' says Ivan.

Wheelright's scowl deepens and she seems to hesitate before responding. Maybe she's heard the half-truth in Ivan's words. 'He was spending a lot of time examining CCTV footage, I know that,' she says eventually.

'Do you know where exactly it was from?' asks Nell. 'Would anyone here?'

'You believe he found something?' asks Wheelright.

'If he did, he didn't tell us,' says Ivan.

'I'll see what I can find out,' says the senior sergeant. 'But as you might have noticed, we've got a bit on.'

— —

Outside the station, the night is fully dark. The journalists have drifted away, off to file their stories, or eat, or drink.

'I'm calling Phelan,' says Ivan.

'Is that wise?'

'What harm could it do?'

Nell listens to the one-sided conversation. It doesn't last long. 'Just tell us who we can trust,' she hears Ivan say at one point, a note of frustration in his voice.

After the call is finished, she asks him the same question. 'What did he say? Anyone we can trust?'

'Vicary Hearst, apparently,' says Ivan, shaking his head.

'Phelan knows who Vicary is?' says Nell. 'Professional Standards really must have Saltwood under the microscope.'

Ivan's about to respond, when his phone rings. 'Yes, it's Ivan Lucic,' she hears him say. And then: 'You're sure?' Followed by: 'We'll be right there.'

'What?' she says.

He stares, thinking, sounding stunned when he does speak. 'Graverobbers. In The Valley. Possibly connected.'

chapter twenty-nine

1994

AMBER FELT ALIVE. SUDDENLY, HER LIFE HAD PURPOSE: SHE WOULD DRAIN THE mine, search for gold, unearth treasure. And with the wealth, she could fix up Watershine, care for the land, govern her own domain. She would be able to honour Teramina's legacy.

She had friends; for the first time in her life, she had friends. She hung out with Lucas and Suzie and Mike, she'd drop in to the store and talk with Simmons, even Eliza, but mostly she was with Lucas. He was getting away from work early and helping at the mine as they prepared to start up the pumps Francis had stored inside the mine entrance, offering advice, bringing tools and expertise, making himself indispensable.

Simmons took her up to Saltwood to see Willard Halliday, the strange lawyer with his cowboy boots and string tie and a silver belt buckle the size of an ashtray. They asked him if the law permitted her to revive the mine.

'Interesting question,' said the lawyer, lighting a thin cigar with a fat lighter. 'Technically, the company still holds the mining rights, and Francis Hardcastle still holds the majority of shares, despite the overwhelming evidence that he drowned in the mine. As I told you, the coroner declined to declare him officially dead.'

'So I don't have the legal authority?' asked Amber.

'Maybe, maybe not. There's the law, and then there's the way the law is applied.'

'What does that mean?' asked Simmons. 'The law is the law.'

'True.' Willard smiled a vulpine grin, and ashed his cigar. 'But if you proceed, who would seek an injunction? Not Francis Hardcastle, not Teramina Cloverton. And not me. I'm still the company secretary.' He took a satisfied drag of his cigar. 'So I suggest you go ahead, and in the unlikely circumstances that someone challenges us, then I will declare that I was acting in good faith as Francis's proxy.' He blew another cloud of smoke. 'But keep what we're doing to yourself, as much as possible. We don't want to attract the attention of mining inspectors.'

Amber wasn't stupid, she realised they were bending the rules, but the lawyer assured her it was ethically correct. Simmons was in favour. He was a policeman, so if a policeman and a solicitor both thought it the right thing to do, who was she to disagree? And so with the lawyer's blessing she set to work, helped by her new friends.

Simmons, who was much better at paperwork and forms than she or Lucas, investigated getting mains electricity connected. Francis had begun the process, applying to the council and the power company, but it had stalled before anything had been decided, let alone built. Francis had wanted the power lines to come in through the national park, running off existing transmission lines, but that had encountered bureaucratic opposition almost immediately, so instead he had decided to bring power up the escarpment next to the road. Approval had finally come through three months after his death, and so nothing had been done. Simmons was trying to reactivate the approval, and to estimate the cost. Amber was learning councils, governments and private companies did nothing quickly, and nothing for free, and she didn't have much money; on the other hand, Lucas said the outlay, the investment, would be a game changer: with electricity, they'd have the ability to run lights, drive ventilation fans, power mining equipment and air compressors. And most importantly of all, they could run the pumps, those on the surface and those underground, without concerns over carbon monoxide. If they were right about what had really happened in the flood more than three years ago—and everything suggested they were—they could pump the mine clear of water.

She and Simmons and Lucas were making the same calculations that Francis and Teramina must have made: plentiful electricity and modern technology combined with the towering gold price meant there was every chance of reviving the Gryphon. But they simply didn't have the finances to get the power put through, so they decided to pump out the water using the diesel pumps Francis had installed on site. Amber spent most of the rest of her money ensuring the road to the mine was safe: Lucas and Simmons and Mike had made it passable after the flood, but only just.

Progress was slow, but it had a unifying effect on the group of friends. They would often gather together in the evenings, sometimes at Watershine, occasionally at the Bushranger, once or twice in Saltwood. Mike was a fount of information, having been involved in the first attempt to resurrect the Gryphon.

The day arrived when they started the pumps. It wasn't easy getting the diesel tanker up the road, but Mike had cleared the way with a front-end loader borrowed from Suzie's brother Arnie, and he and Lucas had ensured the small bridges across the rivulets were sturdy enough. It took a whole day to get the two pumps set up. Lucas backed his truck into the mine, they loaded them onto the tray, and then he slowly descended the ramp. He positioned one pump a little way down the spiralling mine, the second closer to the water. He ran inlet pipes down to where the water began, and outlet pipes out the mine entry and down the hill towards the lake.

Mike arrived to help, and there was a great deal of discussion about fumes and ventilation. They set up fans, powered by a generator on the surface, to suck air down the ventilation shaft and back towards the main entrance. Amber insisted they buy a carbon monoxide detector. There was also the threat of pollution. Amber loved the lake and didn't want it despoiled, but Lucas convinced her the water in the mine would have settled over the intervening years, that it should run clear. And, he added, with water constantly flowing into the lake from the east, and running out into the pools, through the broken dams and off down the escarpment, it was self-flushing and self-filtering. Mike, the dedicated environmentalist, supported Lucas's judgement, so she reluctantly agreed.

Finally, when they were all satisfied, Mike and Lucas started the pumps.

They took some time to prime, but once they were chugging away, she could see Lucas had been right: the water flowing down the slope looked as clear as Watershine's tank water.

With the pumps slowly draining the mine, there wasn't that much to do inside the mine, not yet. They could plan for the exterior works: repairing the dams, building a new race down the escarpment, working out how to process the ore at the cisterns. But all that was hypothetical; there was no money. They needed to empty the mine and establish there was gold in economic quantities. Until then, any further spending would be profligate.

They had to rearrange the feeder pipes every couple of hours, to extend them lower as the water level fell, and to refuel the pumps. She came to realise that the fall in the water was unpredictable: when it was just the main shaft being emptied, it fell about a metre each hour, but when there were branch tunnels and supplementary shafts to clear, the water might fall by no more than a few centimetres all day. It meant they needed to check progress regularly, to make sure the pipes were still in position.

Lucas was spending much of the time underground remapping the mine, the small detours and blind alleys, as they were cleared of water. He had a map left by Hardcastle, but it was half-hearted and messy. Lucas concluded that Hardcastle had done very little to explore or chart these old workings. His focus had been the very bottom of the mine, the new tunnel snaking out under the lake. Chasing the seam.

Amber was growing uneasy. The water from the mine did run clear and cold at first, but as the level receded, the pumps began to stir up sediment and their outflow was turning murky. She became increasingly concerned about the quality of water in the lake. She'd seen fish in there, turtles, even a platypus. Kangaroos and wallabies and every type of bird, from magpies and parrots to cockatoos and kookaburras, came there to drink. And she thought of the fish and the rakali in the cisterns.

Lucas suggested pumping the water out through the ventilation shaft they had discovered below the lake, swearing he should have thought of it before. It took some doing to feed the pipe down the shaft, and he and Mike moved the pump to sit beside it. It was an elegant solution: the pump didn't need to lift the water nearly so high, and now they could bypass the lake and pipe the water all the way into the pond between the bottom of the lake and the broken dam, establishing it as a settling pond, with the excess water flowing through the broken dam, through the series of cascades and down the escarpment, getting filtered as it went. Every few days Amber would walk from Watershine to the cistern to check, but she could detect no change in the purity of the water.

While Lucas mapped the mine, Amber explored the rest of her land above the escarpment. She was much happier there, above ground, surrounded by nature. There was bush and rocky outcrops and ravines and gullies. She found fence posts, marking the boundary of her land, placed there who knew when. A hundred years ago?

One day she discovered a group of three bushwalkers, come to see the lake. They explained how they had gained access, walked her along the mine road and showed her the path out. She thanked them, and left them to go on their way. The next day she walked it herself. It was a beautiful track, barely there, leading from her land into the national park and across to a fire trail.

To the west was the escarpment. To the north was the national park and to the south was state forest. She found another fire track, traversing the edge of her land, gates at either end to mark the boundary, closed but unlocked.

She discovered another creek, heading down into a ravine on the southern edge of her land, full of ferns and flowers. There were black cockatoos, their eyes and tails bearing yellow blazes, their cries like those of pterodactyls, feeding in among a thicket of banksia trees, and then, a little further down the ravine, a small clearing within a grove of trees, leaves almost iridescent, aglow with beauty. The trees were old, ancient, of a kind she had not seen before. She wondered if they might be cedars. She stood in silence, worshipping in nature's chapel.

— —

One week passed, then another, and still the pumps chugged away.

Amber was visited at Watershine one evening by Simmons Burnside. He said he had an update on Teramina's will, good news and bad. The good news was the land transfer had gone through and she was now officially the owner of Watershine and the land. The bad news was the mining company, Gryphon Number Two. 'The company can't borrow money. No bank will extend a loan with the major shareholder missing.'

'So how can I finance the development?' she asked.

'I guess you could find some gold,' he said. 'Or Francis Hardcastle.'

It hit her then, the thought that had been circling all the time, one she had pushed away from conscious consideration, perhaps the reason she felt uncomfortable underground: if Hardcastle had drowned, as almost everyone except the coroner believed he had, then his remains would be somewhere in the depths. The idea made her shudder. But she also realised the truth of the matter: if they found him, he could be declared dead and control of the mine would pass to her. The company might no longer have any money, but it did control the mining rights. And as Simmons explained, if she legally controlled the company, she would be able to borrow against its assets.

A few days later, Lucas announced they were getting very close to draining the mine. He was very happy with their progress. Whenever they turned the pumps off overnight and returned the next day, he would take a reading with his altimeter, and there was no sign that the water level had risen during the night. He was convinced more than ever that the Gryphon was a closed system; that it had been flooded in unique circumstances and there was no new water seeping in. As for Amber, she didn't like being underground, but she was more than happy to imagine the riches that might flow from the mine. In that sense, Lucas's obsession had become contagious. She started checking the newspapers on the stand at the general store, reading the gold prices. And she started imagining a future. She decided they didn't need an industrial-scale mine; that she didn't need to borrow vast amounts; that connecting the electricity, building a race, constructing a new crusher weren't necessary. They had no debt and didn't need any. They could mine the Gryphon as a cottage industry, working slowly, hiring people they liked and only as required. They could be self-sustaining.

——

And all these days, she and Lucas grew closer. At first it was shared glances, unspoken confidences, then a brush of hands, a look of longing. And then a kiss, his hands brushing her hair, his eyes alight.

One glorious blue-skied day, after he had set the pumps working, she led him to the grove of cedars hidden away in its own small valley, the stream running through it before tumbling into a gorge and over the escarpment. Autumn was well advanced and the foliage was turning yellow and orange, so that the sun streaming through it was infused with a golden light. The wind had gathered fallen leaves in among the buttressing roots. She kissed him then, and he kissed her back, and without words they lay on the soft beds of yellow and orange and red and made love. It seemed perfect to her, wondrous, as if ordained, so natural within nature's embrace. She felt herself welling with emotion and wondered at it, the majestic and the ordinary, the physical and the spiritual, all combined in that one messy and animal and transcendent act.

It bonded them. Passion and love and belief, united in common purpose. Amber felt elated: she had embraced a new life and it had embraced her back.

— —

One evening at Watershine, Lucas laid out a map, explaining to Amber that this was the one part of the mine Francis had recorded in some detail. 'We're almost fourteen hundred feet down now, almost at the bottom. Three more days should do it. Maybe even two.' He pointed. 'There is a long shaft here, reaching out in the direction of the lake. You can see why they might have thought it was a cave-in that flooded it. It rises as it extends, so the low point isn't the end, it's where it branches out from the main shaft.'

Amber studied the cross-section, and a terrible image came to her. 'So Francis Hardcastle. If he was at the end of the tunnel when the water started flooding down the shaft, it would have blocked his exit. He would have been trapped.' She imagined the scene. Trapped down there, with just his torch, in the dark. Perhaps he raced back, saw the water rising. What did he do? Attempt to swim out, diving into the blackness, trying to feel his way forward, torch failing, current pushing against him, until he ran out of air and succumbed? It drove a shiver through her, hard and cold. 'Will he still be there?' she asked Lucas. 'Will we find him?'

Lucas nodded solemnly. 'Yes. I imagine. What's left of him. I don't know what the water will have done; helped preserve the body or hastened the decomposition. I just don't know.'

'How horrible,' said Amber, and her excitement over the gold suddenly seemed petty and selfish.

'True,' said Lucas. 'But we'll be able to retrieve the body, give him a proper burial. Lay him to rest beside Teramina in the church-yard, with a proper headstone and a proper funeral. We'll make it right.'

— —

And so the day came when the pumps coughed their protest, when there was air in the pipes, when the mine had at last been emptied.

Lucas said he would go alone, then Mike said he would accompany him. They thought of calling the police in. Instead, they rang Simmons, up at the police station in Saltwood, and informed him of what they were doing.

At the last moment, Amber decided she should go with them. She wasn't entirely sure why, but it had something to do with respect, with honouring Hardcastle, with bearing witness. It felt like her responsibility; she was the owner of the mine. And Francis had been her predecessor, the one who'd had the vision to breathe new life into the Gryphon, a vision which had the potential to benefit them all, but no one more than her.

And so she went with Lucas and Mike. First, they secured the pumps. Lucas took his altimeter reading: eight hundred and twenty feet above sea level, the mine's lowest point, almost fourteen hundred below the steel doors of the entrance. There were still larges puddles, shin deep in places. Then at the very bottom of the mine, they entered the shaft out under the lake, the way slowly rising.

With grim expressions and thumping hearts they moved into the narrow passage, barely wide enough to pass through, forced to crouch: the fatal bottleneck. The rock was seeping water, dripping, and for a horrible moment Amber thought they had got it wrong, miscalculated, that the lake was looming above, that a plug of some sediment had blocked the water's ingress but now, with no water to press back, that plug could give way at any minute. She decided she wanted to stop, to turn back, to wait some more days until they were absolutely certain. The lights of those ahead were starting to distance her. Soon she would be alone.

A torch beam spun around, catching her in the eyes, blinding her momentarily.

'You coming?' It was Mike.

'Right behind you,' she said, suppressing her fears and moving forward.

She'd just reached Mike when she heard Lucas's voice, slightly distorted by the strange acoustics of the tunnel. 'Jesus Christ.'

He wasn't shouting, he wasn't whispering, but the silence of the mine, the silence of the tomb, brought his words to them as clear as a bell.

She and Mike moved forward, the tunnel opening up a little, allowing them to stand abreast.

And there he was, the horror of him. Francis Hardcastle, slumped against the wall, clothes still largely intact, flesh falling from his skeleton in plasticine blobs. There was no smell, not really. That was one of the things she would remember, all those nights when she was trying to forget. And the sight she could never erase: the grinning skull, the empty eye sockets and the bullet hole dead centre in his cranium.

PART THREE

PART THREE

chapter thirty

1994

I WENT DOWN THE MINE THAT DAY WHEN LUCAS, MIKE AND AMBER DISCOVERED Francis Hardcastle, shot through the head. The Sarge took me with him, and Lucas guided us into the lowest depths. If I close my eyes, I can still see the body. The obscenity of it. The liquid flesh, the skull, the bullet hole. See something like that and it never leaves you. Every cop has stories; that's one of mine.

I wasn't so big on the pub, not in those days. Eliza and I tried to limit it to once a week tops. We were still trying to save money, knock a hole in the mortgage, and if we both went, it meant taking Wolf. Not that he minded. He thrived on the noise. He must have been three by then. Eliza was more unpredictable than he was: often she would be reluctant to go, worried that people would be judging her, judging us, but once she was there and had a few drinks on board, she'd end up enjoying herself, dancing and flirting and talking to strangers. Sometimes I'd get a bit jealous; sometimes I'd get a bit embarrassed. Sometimes I'd just collect Wolf and take him home. In summer, with the windows open, I could still hear the music and the voices and the laughter coming from the Bushranger, and wonder what she was up to. And I'd berate myself for being so possessive, so old-fashioned and boring. Conservative—at least compared to my old classmates, Lucas and Mike. Lucas and Amber had become more than just mining colleagues by then, and Mike and Suzie were already solid, but they weren't married, they didn't have a kid, and they didn't have a mortgage.

But that night, after Francis's body was found, Eliza and I had to be there. The whole valley was, full of dark stories and conspiracy theories and speculation. Only Amber and Lucas were missing, them and Mike.

The Sarge had been to Saltwood and back, still wearing his uniform. We spoke out on the verandah, away from the crowd.

'What's the consensus?' he asked me. 'What are people saying?'

I shrugged. 'Some reckon he shot himself,' I offered. 'Mine flooding, no way out.'

'Could have,' he said. 'But why take a gun down the mine? Why would he be right at the bottom?'

'Worried about thieves, maybe,' I suggested.

'In the middle of a storm?' The Sarge drank some beer. 'You were working security. You ever know him to carry a gun?'

'Sure. Frequently. Insisted I carry one as well.'

The Sarge frowned, thought that over for a moment. 'Your police weapon?' he asked.

'Yes. You going to reprimand me?' I said it with a smile, and he smiled back.

'Bit late for that,' he said. 'What about thieves? Were there any?'

'No, not that I ever came across. Not since I started. But Francis was extra vigilant. Always kept those big steel doors locked when he wasn't there. Didn't want any scavengers getting in.'

'And no one ever tried cutting the locks?'

'No.'

'What about CCTV? Did he have any?'

'No. I asked him about it, and he reckoned that would be a priority once he got the electricity through.'

'Makes sense, I guess.' He took another slug of his beer. The Sarge really could put it away. 'Harder for us to investigate, though.'

'So the gun,' I said, serious once more. 'The one with him down the mine. It was his?'

'Yeah, almost certainly. We'll have that confirmed tomorrow, I would imagine, if he registered it.'

'So what are forensics saying: suicide or murder?' I asked, already anticipating the answer.

'I haven't heard. But you saw what I saw. My money's on murder.'

Murder. The word hung in the air between us. 'By whom?' I asked eventually.

'Teramina.'

That unsettled me; he said it with such conviction. 'Why would she do that? She was besotted with him.' The memory came again of them that evening in the pub, the night the rain started, the night he was killed, waving like royalty, the world at their feet.

Instead of answering me, he asked his own question. 'After he disappeared, when you were preparing the report for the coroner, did you come across any suggestion that Hardcastle wasn't quite right? That there was something wrong?'

'You mean mentally disturbed? Unbalanced?'

'No. More like he was hiding something. Maybe something from his past.'

My beer was growing warm and flat, so I took a draught, giving myself time to consider this. 'No,' I answered honestly. 'The night before the flood, I saw them together here. Teramina was happy, full of optimism. There was no sign she suspected anything was wrong.'

'You're sure?' asked the Sarge.

'Not back then. Not before he died.'

'And afterwards?'

'Definitely. Just a few months ago; not long before she leapt. After Fred Wallington had died. Said her new accountant reckoned the books weren't right. There was money missing. But even then, it sounded like Wallington had taken the money.' I sipped the beer again. 'But that was years after Francis died, not beforehand. She never said anything, not back then.'

'That was her money that Wallington took, right? From the sale of Ellensby?' the Sarge asked. 'Not the mine money?'

'Yes. But you know all this. Willard Halliday and I gained greater access to the company records, after Amber Jones inherited. It appears Francis Hardcastle may have embezzled a substantial amount of money a week before he died, or attempted to. But Teramina never even hinted she knew that before he disappeared.'

'Well, she wouldn't, would she?'

'What do you mean?'

'If she was planning to kill him, she wouldn't be confiding in you, a police officer, would she?'

That made me stop and think. 'I guess not. But I was with her, so were others, when the mine flooded.'

The Sarge shrugged. 'True. But we only have her word for it that Francis went up there in the middle of the night, and that he went alone. I mean, what was he doing right down in the depths, if he was meant to be securing the mine and the equipment? Why leave his car outside, when he could have driven it into the mine?'

The Sarge could probably see the doubt on my face, so he continued. 'What if she went up with him, after the rain started, telling him she was going to help with the mine? She could have killed him then. She would still have had plenty of time to get back down to The Valley before the road gave out. Plenty of time to arrange for you and Mike and the others to be with her at the cisterns, to lay the groundwork for her alibi.'

'But she couldn't have anticipated the mine flooding.'

The Sarge scrutinised me, then his beer. 'Couldn't she?'

'What are you suggesting?'

'Thanks to Amber Jones and Lucas Trescothic, we now know there never was a cave-in. How can we be sure the flood was a natural event?'

— —

Later that night I walked along to the park, sat in the dark by the Broken River and thought. Teramina had been good to me; so had Francis. So had the Sarge, for that matter. But the whole thing rested badly with me. The report I had written for the coroner was wrong. I knew that now.

As I sat in the park, I remembered back to that day, the day the mine flooded, working at the cisterns with Teramina and Mike, the rain pouring down, the creek a wild torrent, a foaming rapids. And then that terrible pause, when the flow had subsided for a while, when Mike and I had foolishly put ourselves in danger. When I'd almost died. In the days after, I'd come to believe—we'd all come to believe—that the pause in the flow was caused by the cave-in; that during that short, terrible interregnum, all the water was teeming into the mine. And then what? The mine had filled and then, only then, after the lake had refilled, the dam gave way, sending the wall of water down the hill: that tsunami which had almost killed us. It all made perfect sense at the time, but I now knew that was not how it had happened: there had been no cave-in.

So what could explain that chain of events? First, the interruption in the flow: water pouring into the mine—but how? Lucas and Amber said it was flooded when the dam walls collapsed, directing a torrent down a ventilation shaft. Could it be that simple?

I was trying to work my way through it, to visualise what had happened, but I was distracted. I heard laughing, giggling. I knew that sound, that voice. Eliza. I thought she'd come to find me, that she must be drunk. I started walking towards her, but then I stopped dead in my tracks. She was with someone. A man. I was unable to move for a moment, then I turned and slunk away before they could see me, back into the shadows, back towards the pub. I collected Wolf and went home.

Only afterwards, lying in bed, staring at the ceiling, did I regret not staying a little longer to see who it was she had been with. Wondering why I hadn't confronted them; wondering why I hadn't confronted her before.

chapter thirty-one

1994

AMBER KNEW THE WHOLE OF THE VALLEY WOULD BE AT THE BUSHRANGER, swapping information, trading rumours, generating gossip. But she couldn't face it. She was getting better at being with people, but the thought she might be the centre of attention, that people would quiz her about finding the body, left her cold. So she locked herself away at Watershine. Lucas stayed with her, lighting a fire even though the night wasn't cold. She was glad for his company; she could see he was as badly affected as she was, knew what she had experienced.

He held her close on Teramina's antique sofa, the light from the fire bathing them, and she folded herself into him, gaining some measure of comfort from his strength and his tenderness.

'I should have anticipated it,' Lucas whispered at one point. 'I always believed he'd run off with Teramina's money.'

'Really?'

'Yeah. I knew there was a chance we might find him, though. But drowned—not like that.'

It was thirty seconds before she responded. 'What do you think happened?'

'I don't know,' Lucas said.

'The police think it was murder.'

'They said that?'

'Yes, Sergeant Obswith.'

— —

Later, as he made dinner, she stared into the fire and recalled her conversation with the Saltwood sergeant. She and Lucas had driven down from the mine together, Mike making his own way. They'd driven in silence, eyes glazed, not knowing what to say to each other, rendered speechless by their discovery, knowing only that they needed to report the body to the authorities, to shift the responsibility from their own shoulders and pass it to someone more capable. They'd rung from the phone booth at the Memorial Park. The police had come from Saltwood, and Amber met them at the gate on the East Road, Sergeant Obswith with Simmons Burnside. The sergeant had appeared determined to remain steadfastly professional, following protocol, as though a skeleton with a bullet hole in its forehead could be taken in his stride. But Simmons had seemed shaken; had extended his hand and touched Amber's arm, a gesture of understanding. Of solidarity.

'You okay?' he'd asked.

'No,' she'd replied.

She and Lucas had driven back up to the mine, the police following in their four-wheel drive.

'It must be Hardcastle,' Lucas said, eyes on the track. He was driving more slowly than usual, cavalier attitude absent. She thought maybe he was being extra cautious, shaken by the proximity of death, or perhaps he was delaying revisiting the scene.

'Has to be him,' she said. It was obvious, but saying it out loud helped somehow.

At the mine, the police allowed her to stay at the surface. She was grateful, had thought that maybe, as Teramina's heir, the putative owner of the mine, she would be obliged to revisit the pitch-black tomb. No longer a goldmine, but a charnel house. And so she stood by herself outside the entrance, the steel gates somehow more sinister. *Abandon all hope . . .* The fact that it was a beautiful autumn day, glowing and warm, made being there all the more difficult. The lake looked at peace, reflecting the drifting clouds. So much beauty, she thought. But beneath the surface, was everything tainted, was that the way of the world?

Eventually the men returned above ground, a grimness attached to them, bringing it to the surface, as if contaminated. Simmons used the police radio to call for an ambulance and to alert the detectives in Queanbeyan.

Sergeant Obswith came across, stood with her. He was no longer matter-of-fact. He too appeared unnerved. 'It's Francis Hardcastle,' he said. 'Not much doubt.'

'How can you be sure?' she asked.

Obswith looked away, distress in his eyes. 'I checked, as best I could. There was a watch, the remains of a wallet.' He took a breath then, like he'd forgotten how for a moment, and breathed out again. 'But we'll get the experts in. Get it officially confirmed.' He frowned. 'I'm sorry, but we'll need to seal off the mine until they're finished. Keep the doors closed. Don't want any animals getting down there.'

She felt herself shudder; felt the urge to step back, to distance herself from the hands that had searched the corpse.

'Was it suicide?' she asked.

The sergeant studied the lake, trouble rippling across his face like the wind on the water's surface. 'A possibility, I guess. If he found himself trapped in that final chamber, with no way out. But off the record, I think it more likely that he was murdered. The position of the body, the nature of the wound.'

That scared her. Murder. How could someone do that: hold a gun, fire a bullet, end someone? She'd killed plenty of animals in her time in the forest, hooking fish and snaring rabbits, but that was for food. Despite the warmth of the sunlight, she found herself trembling. 'Who?' she asked.

Obswith sighed. 'My guess would be his wife. Teramina.'

Amber shook her head. She didn't believe it; couldn't believe it. Not her friend, not her benefactor. 'No. Never.'

Obswith regarded her with apparent compassion, but didn't resile from his opinion. 'There's evidence he embezzled money about a week before he died, planned to clear out. She must have found out. It was her money, after all, that was bankrolling every-thing. She was the one who had mortgaged Ellensby.'

Amber saw the sun on the lake, the wind stirring the trees. This beautiful land, now tarnished, the mine contaminated, her friend smeared. Surely not. And yet Teramina had been so clearly troubled, fragile and struggling against dark thoughts, doubting her husband, questioning his motives. If the sergeant was right, it was all defiled: the land, the mine, the house. She wished she'd never agreed to reopen the mine. Why would Teramina bequeath her something so corrupted? Because she had believed her murderous deed was hidden forever within the flooded mine?

It was like the sergeant was following her thoughts. 'After Hardcastle disappeared, she was in a terrible state. A mental breakdown. Depressed and suicidal. Most people attributed it to grief. I thought it was because he'd drowned. Others speculated it was because he'd betrayed her, run away with the money. Now I'm beginning to think neither theory was correct: if she murdered him, that would definitely explain her mental fragility.'

'Didn't she make a submission to the coroner?' Amber said. 'Want him officially declared dead?'

'You know about that?' Obswith asked.

'She told me herself.'

The sergeant scowled, assimilating what she'd said. 'Yes. She wanted to inherit his shares in the mining company. To get her money back and find out what he'd been up to. After the coroner handed down her open finding, Teramina left. Disappeared for over a year.' She felt his eyes upon her before he spoke again. 'Is that when you encountered her?'

'I guess it must have been. I found her lost in the bush, starving, out of her mind. Ranting and despairing and suicidal. I nursed her. What else could I do?'

It had been mutual: as Teramina had healed, had come back into herself, she had begun to fill a hole left by Amber's own mother, off on her endless travels. It hadn't just been Amber rescuing Teramina; the older woman had repaid the service in kind. But Amber didn't reveal anything of that to Obswith.

'So it was you: you who saved her from herself,' the sergeant observed. 'Explains why she bequeathed all this to you.' He gestured at the land below them.

Amber said nothing. Her eyes were drawn to the meeting of land and sky, where the escarpment plunged into the valley. Where Teramina had leapt.

Up in the sky, she could see an eagle soaring above the escarpment, riding the thermals rising from the valley. Above it all, triumphing over gravity. She wondered what that might feel like. Right now, she felt the opposite, like the world was pulling at her, dragging her down.

Obswith said nothing for a long period, his tone more business-like when he did break the silence. 'It's a good thing you found him. Makes things easier. Not now, but in the future.'

That confused her. 'How so?'

'Now we know for certain he's dead, it will help clear things up. Your ownership, your control, it can no longer be doubted. You can start mining, unhindered by the past.'

Amber regarded him blankly. 'Maybe.'

'You should,' he said. 'If there's gold in there, then maybe you can make something good from the tragedy.'

'Do I have to stay up here?' she asked.

'No. You can go. Simmons and I will wait for the ambulance and the forensics team. We can take a statement later, if necessary.'

— —

Later that night, after Lucas had left for the pub, gone to monitor the gossip, she sat by herself before the fire. All she wanted to do was lock the door, curl up on the sofa and close out the world. But she knew that wasn't possible; the world wouldn't allow it. The memory of Teramina wouldn't let her. She felt a new obligation: not just to push ahead with the mine, but to somehow work out what had really happened to her friend, what had driven her to take her own life.

chapter thirty-two

2024

THE SOLITARY HALF-HOUR DRIVE TO THE VALLEY GIVES NELL TIME TO REFLECT.
The kidnap attempt was brazen: steal a vehicle and abduct a
sedentary man in a wheelchair. Just walk in and take him, in
broad daylight, on the main street of a busy town. But it would
have worked if Nell hadn't been there or if the criminals hadn't
misjudged Ollie. Still, it irks her, the gunman lying in the hospital,
receiving care from the very community whose ambulance his
accomplices have just trashed.

The moon is rising and at any other time it would be beautiful,
bathing the countryside. There's a stillness to the scene, the landscape looks like it's carved out of dark stone, yet she hardly notices.
She's in her own world now: the world of the homicide detective,
where everyday life becomes increasingly extraneous and the tunnel
vision of catching killers becomes all-consuming.

She thinks as she drives. Wolfgang Burnside was found murdered, Willard Halliday has been attacked, Vicary Hearst is in hospital in Canberra. It's like a pebble has been dropped into a pond, and the ripples are spreading out. And a second pebble plopped into the same pond, not far from the first: the mystery of her own blood ties to Wolfgang, the ripples overlapping, setting up interference patterns. There must be connections there, she feels there has to be, but she cannot see them. Not yet. Too many questions and still no satisfactory answers. Too many variables. She's no closer to knowing if they form part of some larger truth, or are just a fractured series of events connected by nothing more than geographical proximity.

She reaches the bottom of the escarpment and is relieved to arrive at the church on the Valley Road, just before the cricket ground. St Barnabas, a single street light creating more shadows than illumination. The church is tiny but made of stone, as if solidity can compensate for its diminutive size. There's not a lot to see from the road: just a pocket-sized car pulled up outside. As she pulls in, Ivan gets out of the car.

'Nice wheels,' she says.

'Beats hitchhiking,' he replies, looking about. 'I think this is the right place.'

They find their way around the back. The scene that greets them could be a television set waiting for the actors and crew to arrive: police tape around an open grave, an excavator next to it, a stand with LED lighting, glaring bright in the surrounding darkness.

'Francis Hardcastle,' says Ivan. 'Happened last night, not discovered until this afternoon. Took the whole lot, coffin and all.'

Nell stares into the black hole, the gaping wound. 'Why? He's been dead thirty-four years, buried for thirty. There can't be much of him left.'

'You wouldn't think so.'

She considers the light, wonders why it's been left turned on. Perhaps the local police have left it that way while they eat dinner, to make sure no one accidentally falls in. 'Maybe it's not him they were after,' she suggests. 'Maybe he was buried with something. Something else in the grave?'

Ivan looks unimpressed. She knows how much he dislikes speculation, preferring his facts cut and dried and irrefutable, trusting in methodical investigation and the process of elimination.

'Or maybe it has to do with identity,' says Nell. 'Checking to see if he was really who he claimed to be.'

'DNA?' For all his innate scepticism, she can see Ivan is interested.

'Technically possible to extract, even after all these years.'

'What are you thinking?' he asks.

'Who identified the body back then? And how did they know it was him?'

'You think the corpse in the mine, the one buried here, didn't belong to Hardcastle?' asks Ivan.

Nell shrugs. 'Just canvassing the possibilities.'

'How do you think we should proceed then?'

She feels grateful for the question; he's still including her, supporting her, even as she knows he'll have his own ideas.

'I should jump online, check the records,' she says. 'Find out if there was any mystery about him.'

Ivan looks at his watch. 'Okay, but first you need to eat. Have a shower, take a break. Power nap if you need it.'

'I'll be fine. I'd prefer to push on.'

Ivan appears doubtful, studying her closely. She feels the harsh light of the LED on her, like she's a specimen, there to be examined. She reaches for her neck, an involuntary gesture, touching the bandage.

'Nell, I'm not going to stop you probing Francis Hardcastle and his past—or your connection with Wolfgang Burnside, for that matter—but I want you to rest first. Wash. Eat something.' His tone is caring, but behind it she can sense his authority, the sergeant addressing his subordinate. Not pulling rank, but quietly insistent. 'The records aren't going anywhere.'

'Ivan, I'm fine.'

'When did you last eat?'

She thinks back, recalls her coffee hitting the road in Saltwood. Why didn't she think to eat something while she was waiting at the hospital? 'Breakfast, I guess.' And she recalls: a coffee and a banana. Yet she doesn't even feel hungry. She frowns, wonders if she might be dehydrated.

'The records will still be there in an hour or two,' he says.

— —

Ivan proves to be correct. She returns to her room, takes a quick shower, changing the dressing on her neck. When she lies on her bed, she thinks it will be for a couple of minutes at most. Yet when Ivan rings her an hour later, she's been fast asleep. And now she's ravenous. Downstairs in the bistro, she demolishes a huge serving of lasagne. While she eats, she brings Ivan up to date on the events in Saltwood.

'You don't think we need to charge Willard Halliday's assistant?' he asks.

'I think some sort of action is required, but let's leave that with Alice Wheelright. She's promised to keep us fully informed.'

'I agree,' says Ivan. 'We can't be everywhere.'

After eating, the two of them traverse the crossroad to the Miners' Institute, and Nell starts searching for information about Francis Hardcastle, grateful for Wolfgang Burnside's high-speed optic fibre internet.

First, she seeks out the police files at the time of Hardcastle's disappearance, and then finds them summarised in two reports to the coroner.

The first is dated 1990. She sees it was prepared by Constable Simmons Burnside. Her father and the father of Wolfgang Burnside. She's not sure what to make of that: small towns, always so many coincidences, so many interconnections. She parks the temptation to speculate and reads the report. It details the huge amount of rainfall that hit The Valley over a twenty-four-hour period, the extensive flash flooding, bridges out, roads unpassable, electricity cut. It quotes from the police statement made by Teramina Hardcastle, given shortly after her husband had gone missing, saying he'd called her at home the night the rain set in to tell her he was heading to the mine to secure equipment. She stated that it had been about eleven pm and that she'd thought her husband had just left the pub and had called from the phone booth at the Memorial Park. The report notes that was the last time Hardcastle was seen or heard alive. It then recounts how the storm washed out the road leading up the escarpment to the mine, and how two days later Sergeant Cornell Obswith and Constable Simmons Burnside hiked to the Gryphon, guided by local fire chief Dirk Stannard, where they found Hardcastle's car abandoned outside. Entering the mine, they discovered that it had been flooded and concluded that Hardcastle had drowned, and recovering the body was not possible.

Nell takes a note. Who is Sergeant Cornell Obswith? She wonders where she might find him, and whether she should talk to him. She wonders if he might know about any relationship between her mother and Simmons Burnside.

She reads on, finds that the coroner declared an open finding, unwilling to declare Hardcastle dead without a body and without a witness to place him in proximity to the mine. In her finding, the coroner referred to 'speculation about malfeasance by the missing man'. What did that mean?

She finds the second document from four years later, after the body was recovered. A new report to a new coroner, this time prepared by a different constable, Tom Sievers. It recounts the discovery of Hardcastle's body by Amber Jones, Mike Norfolk and Lucas Trescothic after they had drained the mine.

Nell stares at her screen. Amber Jones. Her mother. She'd pumped out the mine, been the one to find Hardcastle? For a moment Nell imagines the horror of the scene, deep underground, in the claustrophobic dark, finding the man's remains.

She again sets aside the temptation to speculate, stronger now that both of her parents are connected, and continues. The report says that Amber and her colleague Lucas had earlier established the mine could be pumped clear and had set about draining it with the intention of searching for gold. This had led to their discovery of the body. Gold. Nell thinks of the nugget Tyffany handed to them. Could gold possibly be a linking factor?

She digs deeper. The report states that Hardcastle was found at the lowest level of the mine, at its furthest extension, the last tunnel excavated, sloping up under the lake. The man had been shot in the head. There are photos, gruesome even now, thirty years later. The fatal wound is clearly evident, a bullet hole in the skull. The images stir Nell's scepticism: the body is beyond easy identification. And yet while the report confirms who found the body, she can't find who identified it. The report simply states that it was Hardcastle, even as it describes the body as being in an advanced stage of decomposition, and notes that it deteriorated quickly once the water was removed. It does say that artefacts belonging to Hardcastle were found on the body, including a watch and his wallet. The clothes were his. But nowhere can she find in the coroner's report, or in the police reports, evidence of who formally identified the body and by what means. She considers ringing Blake, to find out what the proper procedures might have been in 1994, but it's already gone ten o'clock at night. She decides to leave it till tomorrow.

She takes a break, makes herself a cup of tea. Ivan comes back in; he's been out walking. He seems almost light-hearted; there's a spring in his step.

'How's Carly?' she asks.

That stops him. 'Good, thanks. Sends her love. How about you? Find anything?'

She tells him about the lingering question over who identified the body and how.

'If the body was that far gone, it would either be dental records or maybe DNA,' says Ivan.

'I'll start on it.'

She does, as Ivan sets to work on his own computer. Nell isn't sure what he's searching for and doesn't ask: she suspects he's returned simply to demonstrate his support.

But then he proves her wrong. 'Holy shit,' he says. 'Listen to this.'

'What is it?'

'Hardcastle's murder. Says here a preliminary investigation was conducted by homicide detectives Sergeant Dereck Packenham and Senior Constable Morris Montifore, who then assigned it to a cold case team.'

'Plodder? You're bullshitting me.'

'Wish I was,' says Ivan, voice incredulous.

'We should call him.'

Ivan stares at her, blue eyes focused. 'No. Let me call Morris.' He glances at his watch. It's late, but not too late. He makes the call. Doesn't put it on speaker, but doesn't leave the room either. Nell can only hear half the conversation.

'Yeah, yeah. I know. I'm unreliable, you know that . . .'

Two seconds.

'No. Not social. Professional.'

Two seconds.

'I'm in The Valley, near Saltwood, with Nell Buchanan.'

Maybe five seconds.

'Yeah. Local bloke, Wolfgang Burnside. Might be a link to a murder back in 1990. Francis Hardcastle, body found down a mine in 1994, bullet hole in his forehead . . .'

Fifteen seconds.

'So you and Plodder. Says here you handed it off to cold cases . . .'

Almost a minute.

'Thanks, Morris. And I promise, we will drink that beer, we will catch that fish.'

He ends the call, eyes squinting with concentration.

'What?' she prompts him.

'They didn't hand the case off. It was taken from them. They were ordered back to Sydney, despite their protests. Case assigned to Queanbeyan, not cold cases.'

Nell says nothing for a long moment. 'That's why Plodder wants us here. Doesn't want the same thing happening again.'

'Sounds like it. Let's push on for now. I'll call him if I think it will help.'

They resume trawling the internet, and at last Nell finds a mention, one short sentence: 'Dental records match.' But nothing to say who matched the records, what dentist held them, or what police officer was involved. All she has is that the initial identification was made by Sergeant Cornell Obswith. That name again.

Having exhausted the police and coronial records, Nell starts searching the net more widely, seeking open-source information about Francis Hardcastle. There's no shortage from the time he was in The Valley, with news reports that he and Teramina Cloverton had married, that they were redeveloping the mine. According to the reports, Hardcastle had recently returned from the United States, where he'd enjoyed a stellar twenty-year career as a mining engineer and a company director. And there are photographs from his time in The Valley. She meticulously copies them and pastes them into a new file. He appears elegant, always well dressed, always smiling, not her image of a stereotypical miner, with his pencil moustache, wavy hair slicked back and well-defined cheekbones. There's one with Teramina by his side, seeming happy and confident and full of life. Nell takes time to examine it.

She searches further, finds a record of Francis Hardcastle graduating from the University of Queensland with a degree in geology in 1966. So far so good, and when she searches in the United States, she finds more records. A mine in Utah, another in Wyoming. And in Colorado, a goldmine. It all seems authentic. Until she finds the photograph, the photograph that gives the lie. An obscure annual report, a long-gone mining company in Colorado, Francis Hardcastle listed as chief operating officer, the head shots of senior management. But this Francis Hardcastle is tall not short, fair not dark. With a bald head.

'Ivan. Come here.'

chapter thirty-three

1994

THE NEXT DAY, AT THE STATION IN SALTWOOD, I TOLD THE SARGE I WAS BOTHERED by what had happened at the Gryphon the day of the flood; his suggestion at the pub that the mine had been deliberately flooded. He told me to leave it to the experts, the forensic technicians and the homicide detectives from Sydney. When I tried to persist, he took me to one side.

'Mate, we don't want to be anywhere near this.'

'Why not?'

'Why not? Because you were taking money from Francis and from Teramina. I authorised it. And Francis had made me a shareholder.'

'I thought you bought those shares?'

'I did. On favourable terms. We don't want to draw attention to ourselves, believe me.'

'What's any of that got to do with murder?' I asked.

'Nothing. Don't be dense. But if the detectives come across anything that appears untoward, they'll be duty-bound to inform Professional Standards.'

I saw his point. 'You think Francis did it on purpose? That he was trying to cultivate us? Compromise us?'

'Doesn't matter what he was trying to do. What matters is how Professional Standards would see it.'

'Shit,' I said, as the precariousness of our position dawned on me.

I could see the relief on his face. 'We good?'

'We're good. And thanks. I probably would have stumbled right in there.'

But it nagged at me. I saw the two Sydney homicide detectives, serious-looking men with shrewd eyes and furrowed brows, wearing well-cut suits and an air of superiority. I was tempted to tell them what I knew about the day of the flood, what I'd experienced, what Teramina had told me before her death. But then I thought of Wolfgang, and what might happen to him if I were to be caught up in an unethical conduct investigation. So I kept my thoughts to myself. Or at least that's how I rationalised it.

Instead, to satisfy my own curiosity, or to assuage my guilt, I decided to return to the mine the following weekend, on my own time, as a citizen, not a policeman. I knew the forensic team was finished, the body had been removed and the site returned to Amber. I thought I should call in at Watershine, seek her permission, given she now owned the road and the land. And I was curious to learn if Teramina had ever said anything about Francis to her.

The drive still wound through the trees, the same as it had always done, the same patterns, the same fall of the light, filtered by the canopy, unchanged, the same as when I lived there. I drove over that last rise, around that last bend, and there it was: Watershine. Not a grand house, not like Ellensby, but a beautiful house, self-contained and unpretentious, weatherboard not stone, impressive in its way, two storeys raised into the canopy on its outcrop of stone. It made me think: maybe those few short months minding the old house, fixing it up, were my best months, when life was simple and the future was rich with possibilities. Then I rejected the thought. Life was harder now, more demanding, money still tight, but I had Wolfgang and I had Eliza. The memory came back from the park, Eliza giggling in the dark, but it was already in the past, not worth dwelling on.

I parked the car, climbed the stairs, knocked on the door. Once, twice. Yelled, 'Hello?' I was about to give up, or try around the back, when I sensed some movement inside. A few moments later the door opened.

'Yes?'

It was Amber. Framed in the doorway of the old house, she seemed so very small, so very vulnerable. So very young. She'd been crying, her eyes red, her hair unkempt.

'Simmons?' Her eyebrows tilted ever so slightly downwards, the beginnings of a frown.

'Would you mind if I came in? I want to talk to you,' I said.

'About the body in the mine?' she asked.

'Yes. About the body.'

She saw my clothes. 'Is this official? We've been through it with the detectives.'

'No. Not official.'

'Oh. I see. You'd better come in.'

She led me into the lounge and I sat on the sofa with Amber seated across from me, clearly disconsolate, wringing her hands. I thought of the skeletal remains, of what a shock it would have been for her. We had that in common, that image etched into our retinas.

'You were close to her?' she asked. 'To Teramina?'

I took a long breath. She had somehow identified the heart of the matter. 'She was generous to me. So was Francis.'

'She must have trusted you,' Amber continued. 'She made you the executor of her will. Did she ever tell you why?'

'No, not really.'

'Did she confide in you at all?'

'At times,' I said. 'After Francis disappeared. When her new accountant discovered the money was gone.'

'Yes,' she whispered, and I thought perhaps she might start weeping. She was very controlled in one sense, very subdued, but made no attempt to hide her emotions. 'Do you think that we're the only ones who care what happened to her?'

I wasn't completely sure what she was alluding to, but I said, 'Yes.' In that moment, it seemed like the correct thing to say, the sympathetic and supportive thing, but once the word had passed my lips, I realised that it was true. I did care. 'Yes,' I repeated, and felt something shift in me. I wasn't really one to care about things, about people. I think it was part of my upbringing, my dad being a bastard and then dying young, my mum doing it tough, hiding her feelings. I thought it was just the way people were. Lucas and Mike and all the other people I knew seemed the same. But I knew I was changing. Part of it was Wolf; I wanted so desperately for him to be loved and accepted, for his childhood to be different from mine. Maybe that's what triggered this evolution in me. It was true that life was more simple when I lived at Watershine, but this seemed more grounded, more real. So I sat on that sofa in Watershine and looked Amber Jones in the eye and felt a connection with her, a bonding.

I took another breath, bracing myself, then spoke again. 'I was helping the Hardcastles, part-time. That's why I was living here. I was here the day the mine flooded. With Teramina and Mike and a couple of others, out at the cisterns, trying to stabilise the tailings. I went up the top two days later with Sergeant Obswith. Hiked in, through the bush. We were the ones who discovered that the mine was flooded, Francis Hardcastle's car by the entrance, no sign of him. Some people thought he'd drowned, some people thought he had run off with the money.'

Amber had become very still, concentrating on what I was saying, each word. 'So why come here today?'

'I want to work out what really happened,' I said.

She said nothing, but her eyes never left my face.

'How the Gryphon flooded,' I continued. 'I wrote in the report to the coroner that there had been a cave-in, the water from the lake flooded through into the mine. That was the technical advice, from a mining engineer. But we know that's not right. There was no cave-in.'

Amber was becoming more distressed by the minute, as if she understood where my questions were leading. 'Lucas and I think it flooded when the dams burst.'

'Do you think that could have been done on purpose?' I asked.

She replied by asking her own question. 'Do you think it's possible that Teramina killed him? That's what your sergeant thinks.'

'I'm afraid that's what they're going to conclude.' I hesitated to continue, but I said it anyway, believing I needed to be honest with her. 'Sometimes, with the police, it's easier to lay the blame on someone who can't defend themselves.'

She looked horrified, but she seemed to accept the truth of that. 'How can I help?' she asked.

'Let me get up there. See what I can find. Work out what happened.'

She smiled then, a wan and fragile expression, and I saw the gratitude in her eyes. 'Of course.'

We were interrupted by the sound of an engine, a car door shutting, feet on the steps. It was Lucas, entering without knocking. 'Hello, Amber?' he called, walking into the lounge, seeing me on the sofa. 'Simmo. Hi, mate. Saw your car.'

I stood up, shook hands, greeted him, my blokey persona back in place.

Amber was still sitting. 'Simmons wants to check out the Gryphon,' she said. 'He has some concerns about the flooding.'

'Let me take you up,' offered Lucas. 'Show you what we found. How we drained it.' He sounded proud of his accomplishment. He spoke to me, but then deferred to Amber, seeking her permission. 'Okay?'

'Yes,' she said. 'Take him up. Explain what happened.' She might have been young, but she spoke with authority. The weeks in The Valley seemed to have matured her; the shy girl I'd first met had become more assertive, more self-assured. We'd only been talking for a few minutes, but I still felt that connection, that I knew her better, and that I liked and admired her more.

We drove up in Lucas's truck. On the way, he explained about finding Hardcastle, the gun, the state of the body. What an awful shock it was. I had seen what he'd seen and didn't really want to revisit it. But they say it can be a good thing to talk about traumatic incidents, much better than bottling them up, so I said nothing, let him talk.

It took a while to reach our destination, Lucas forced to slow to a crawl around the hairpins and switchbacks, but eventually we were up the top of the escarpment, winding our way around the base of the mountain. At the fork in the road, I couldn't help looking up towards the mine entrance, but there was nothing to see, the landscape unaffected by the drama of the past week.

Lucas parked near the shore of the lake. The surface was placid: more than three years after the flood, it too seemed unchanged, the same as it was when we were kids. We left the car, following the shoreline, Lucas leading the way, walking towards where the lake emptied out and flowed towards the escarpment.

At one point, before the end of the lake, he pointed across at the far side. 'You can still see where the water level dropped.'

It was true. There was regrowth, but the evidence was still there, three-and-a-half years on. 'That's why everyone thought of the cave-in: the lake level dropping, flooding the mine,' I said.

Lucas smiled. 'Sure. Made sense at the time. Doesn't make sense anymore.'

I nodded, understanding. Once the mine was filled, the lake should have risen back to the previous level.

He took me to the end of the lake. The dam wall was still there, with a huge gap in the middle, where it had failed. Water trickled through the gap into a large pool below it, sandstone augmented by concrete. I imagined the lake, filling to capacity during the flood, up to the high-water mark still evident on the opposite shore. And then the dam had collapsed, sending that massive wave of water into the valley, the torrent that almost killed Mike and me.

Lucas scrambled on ahead, so we were parallel to the old dam wall. He pointed down the slope. We were above the secondary pool now and I could see it properly. I realised it also had a dam wall, also breached in the middle, possibly destroyed by that first surge when the upper wall failed.

'What are the walls? Why were they damming the lake?'

'Goes back to the original mine. They built a race down the escarpment, used the water to flush the ground-up ore.'

He pushed on and we scrambled through a thicket of tea-trees, so we were close by the lower wall. From there he pointed out the ventilation shaft. 'See it?' he asked.

It was easy to spot, with black plastic tubing leading out of it, and winding down the hill. 'What's the pipe?' I asked.

'Where we were pumping the water out, clearing the mine,' he explained. He turned, pointed up the hill towards the entrance of the mine, more than a hundred metres higher. 'Daft to pump all the way up there only for it to flow back again. More efficient to do it here.'

I compared the entrance to the shaft with the height of the failed dam. The shaft was below the height of the dam, but off to one side. And not far beyond it, the edge of the precipice. Where Teramina had thrown herself to her death. She'd told me she was coming up here maybe once a week to commune with her dead husband. Had she found the ventilation shaft? Suspected something?

'It's how I worked out there had been no cave-in,' he said. 'The opening of the shaft is below the surface level of the lake, but there was no water flowing from it.'

'So how did the mine flood then?' I asked. A bad feeling was starting to crawl up my back.

'Way I figure it, when the dams gave way, the amount of water coming through here would have been unbelievable. Enough of it went into the shaft to flood the mine almost completely. Makes sense, if you line up the levels.'

And it did make sense. Except for one thing, something that Lucas didn't know about. The pause. If the dam wall had collapsed and the water had come flooding through, some of it down the mine, but most of it over the falls and onto the cisterns, then there would have been no pause: just the opposite.

'You say you used that ventilation shaft to pump water out from the mine,' I said, trying to keep any emotion out of my voice, 'but just for argument's sake, if you wanted to flood the mine, could you pump water *into* the shaft?'

He stared at me then, mouth opening, but no words coming. He understood exactly what I was suggesting. But when he did speak, his response surprised me. 'You wouldn't need to pump it in. A siphon would work.'

I understood what a siphon was; every country kid did. 'From the lake?'

'Sure. Or from the lower pool here, if the dam was still in place.'

And then I knew. I knew what had happened. Or I thought I did.

chapter thirty-four

AFTER WATCHING LUCAS AND SIMMONS LEAVE TO VISIT THE MINE, AMBER WAS left sitting on Watershine's porch, staring into space. It was another sunny day, bright and still, taunting her. She still wasn't sure what she should be doing with herself: planning for the reopening of the mine, or preparing to leave The Valley and return home.

The allure of the gold had insinuated itself into her thinking, she realised that. Once the seed had been planted, she'd begun to imagine what she might do with her wealth: she could restore the house, renovate it, upgrade the road, bring power. She could preserve the trees on her land, preserve them forever. She could bestow gifts on her community. On her new friends: Lucas and Mike and Suzie, Simmons and Eliza. Help their boy, little Wolfie.

And she acknowledged that it wasn't just the gold; it was the idea of ownership, of control, that had attracted her. At her home by the Murray, she owned nothing, her mother owned almost nothing, only the tiny island, just big enough for the shack. Even that could be taken sooner or later, by a flood or by the authorities. The rest of that forest belonged to the government. But here, the land was hers. She realised that the idea had seduced her.

And yet it was more than that. It was the sense of belonging, the sense of community that she'd found in The Valley, being part of something. A place where people knew her name, seemed to care for her, asked how she was faring and told her of themselves. Who gave of themselves. She thought of Simmons. He had seemed distant at first, a policeman fulfilling his duty, but now she felt she had made some sort of connection with him. Everyone else seemed so focused on the gold, or on what the death of Francis Hardcastle meant for the mine; he was the only one who seemed to care about Teramina and what had happened to her. The image of Francis Hardcastle came again: the skull's hollow eye sockets, the bullet hole in the cranium. She wondered for the first time if any danger lingered, whether she could be under threat. The two policemen, Simmons and his sergeant, both thought Hardcastle had been murdered. But why kill Francis Hardcastle? And who was the killer? Why was the Sergeant Obswith so ready to accuse Teramina? And if she wasn't the murderer, then who was?

Amber found herself questioning whether she should stay here, if she should make the move permanent. It had all seemed so wonderful: friends, a community, a purpose. It had made her previous life in the southern forest feel so small, so insignificant. But now, she missed her island refuge: the security, the clarity, the ability to order the day exactly as she wanted. There were no surprises in the forest: no heartbreak, no accommodating others. It's what had shaped her—that landscape, not this one— all those years with her grandfather. But he was dead and who knew where her mother might be. Amber had been happy there, alone in her solitude, but now she contemplated whether she could ever be satisfied with such a simple life, whether she was now spoilt, if returning to such isolation was still possible or if she had grown beyond it. There was a community here, and she'd believed she could become part of it. Not just part of it, but a benefactor, the owner of a goldmine, bringing some measure of prosperity and employment to The Valley. A person with status. She pondered whether there was an obligation there, a duty, or whether the only duty she owed was to herself.

But what if she might in some way be the beneficiary of violence, of murder? If Teramina had killed her husband then bequeathed the wealth to her, then surely that inheritance was tainted? And yet, it was clear that Teramina had not benefitted financially from the death of her husband: quite the contrary. Her assets had been plundered. She'd been forced to sell her beloved Ellensby, bringing only remnants with her to furnish Watershine, and then her remaining wealth had also been stolen. It didn't make sense to Amber: why would Teramina have killed her husband if it cost her so much? Maybe she'd miscalculated, anticipating that Francis would be declared dead, that she would win control of the company, get her money back. Amber was aware she didn't know much about people, had very little first-hand experience of their dealings and their motivations, but she'd read enough to know that people were often illogical, and that murder could be a crime of passion and not a crime of reason. After all, what reasonable person would ever kill another?

She felt the questions nagging at her, the doubts growing, her thoughts losing their clarity, becoming murkier. Restless, she descended the steps, walked to the home creek, hoping physical activity might bring some semblance of perspective. She followed the stream to where it joined Watershine Creek, and from there up to the cisterns. The water appeared just as clear and inviting as when she'd first swum there. Lucas had been right about that at least; there was no sign of pollution. The vale seemed so peaceful, so serene. For a moment she considered diving in, then suddenly the idea repulsed her. The water from the mine still flowed here, some miniscule part from the past weeks' pumping, water tainted by contact with the body of Francis Hardcastle. The thought sent a shiver through her. She regarded the beach and its strange dunes, man-made she knew, the tailings from the original mine, partially collapsed and washed into the pools by the flood more than three years before. Leached before that by decades of rain and river flow, looking pristine. But what might that soil contain? All those pollutants used to extract gold: mercury and cyanide and other poisons. How could it appear so beautiful? She again wondered if the whole world might be like this: a beautiful exterior, a veneer of nature, hiding a poisoned and malformed substructure, the cascading impact of humanity. Or perhaps the opposite: just as nature healed the trauma of the past, maybe human society was the same, new generations able to shed the sins of the past and create a new and better world. She thought of Mike's story, how The Valley once resembled a battlefield, dug up from one end to the other by the gold-rush miners, and yet now here it was, a land of Tolkienesque beauty.

She made her way above the cisterns to where a waterfall came tumbling from the escarpment into a pool, entirely natural, devoid of concrete and brick. Surely a beautiful and pure place, predating the mine, and destined to outlast it.

She sat on a rock and tried to conjure up memories of Teramina, what she'd been like when they'd first met. It had been cold, winter, and Amber had been checking snares for rabbits; she much preferred trapping them to shooting them. She'd found the older woman half-mad and suicidal by the Murray River, freezing, her hands blue with the cold, her eyes wild, her hair matted and unkempt. Amber remembered placating the woman, cajoling her, persuading her to return to the shack. Warming her by the pot-belly, firing the wood-heated bath, feeding her broth, encouraging her to sleep.

At first the woman had been without speech, but over the following days she'd come back to herself, thanks to Amber's ministrations. She'd been able to tell Amber her name—Teramina—and a little of who she was: the scion of an old-money family, from a place called The Valley. She spoke of her home, Ellensby, and how the roses bloomed nine months out of twelve and the sheltering trees had been there for more than a hundred years. She told Amber of her schooling and her university degree in fine arts, of an early engagement to a British aristocrat, broken off for unspecified reasons; another lover whom she had adored but who had died; and a third, a local, from an up-and-coming family, who'd only wanted her for her social cachet and had turned abusive and vindictive. Amber let Teramina talk, realising it was her role to listen, not interrupting, only prompting every now and then. And she came to understand that Teramina was circling the truth, trying to find her way towards some traumatic event, working out how to broach the cause of her heartache.

It began to surface one night, the forest dark, a bitter wind blowing, a rare easterly coming off the snow-covered mountains.

At last Teramina told Amber what had happened. She recounted how she'd resigned herself to spinsterhood, until one day a man came to her door at Ellensby. The man had worn a fine three-piece suit of lightweight wool, a watch of some quality and well-polished brogues, like an upper-class Englishman. But when he spoke, it was with a soft American burr. He explained he had a proposition for Teramina, wondered if she might invite him in. And so she did, for there was nothing threatening about him; he was well groomed and well spoken, rather slight. But it was his smile, open and generous, accompanied by a twinkle in his eyes, that was his most appealing feature. There was an understated humour to him, a gentle playfulness.

He had told Teramina his name was Francis Hardcastle, and that he was Australian but had spent many years in the United States, working as a geologist and engineer, and eventually as a mine manager. He'd returned to Australia recently to tend to elderly parents, and had found himself bewitched by the possibilities he saw in the landscape and read of in the trade papers. He spoke of a new phenomenon sweeping America: the reopening of goldmines considered spent but made viable once more by the soaring gold price and new technology. The same thing was happening in Australia, at places like Bendigo and Ballarat. He'd researched the history of the Gryphon Mine, read some reports on its geology, and thought it bore the hallmarks of just such an opportunity. He said he could make no promises, but he asked politely if he might investigate underground. He suggested the prospect of it being financially attractive was small but real, perhaps twenty per cent, but it would cost very little to find out. He claimed he had some savings, that he would pay for any laboratory analysis, but for the main, he was capable of doing the work himself.

Teramina had found herself spellbound. Bewitched by Francis Hardcastle, bedazzled by his talk of gold, as if he were a magician. By the time he left that afternoon, Teramina had given him the keys, and within days he'd opened those huge steel doors and entered the mine. And declared, after some weeks, that a Sydney laboratory had found the samples he'd sent it were ambiguous. He apologised for having wasted her time. He said he wanted to blast in one last section, near where the original miners had been working before the Gryphon was closed. And so he did. And two days later, he presented her with a nugget. A small piece of quartz, grey and white, with beads of gold interlaced. Later, he'd had it cut and polished, and presented it to her as a pendant. Teramina had shown Amber the jewellery, a flat disc of quartz laced with gold, held in place by a gold setting fabricated from a second nugget.

That was as far as Teramina got that night, cocooned in the shack with Amber. She still hadn't arrived at the heart of the matter, but Amber sensed that Teramina was getting close. And so she did, some days later, when they had taken the larger of two canoes and ventured to a field of new grass, and sat while kangaroos grazed off along the tree line. It was a clear winter's day, cloudless, and the absence of wind allowed the sun to gift a little warmth. The trees reflected in the still water; it was like the forest was holding its breath.

Teramina explained how the two of them had started a company, she and Francis. She'd invested her money and he'd invested his expertise. There was so much work to be done: the road improved, arranging electricity, buying equipment, seeking government approvals and licensing, making the mine safe with new shoring.

But it was a time-consuming process. Nothing was easy and interest rates were reaching new peaks monthly. Teramina hadn't told Francis, but much of the money she'd invested was borrowed. She'd mortgaged Ellensby, so keen was she for the mine to work, for the Cloverton fortunes to be restored. To save The Valley. And she was equally keen for Francis to stay, not vanish like her previous lovers. For that is what they had become: not just business partners and fellow dreamers but lovers. Teramina felt herself floating through life, wondering at times whether she was a fool and deciding she was happy to be so. He'd proposed, they'd married.

Amber thought she was almost there, but again Teramina hesitated. They sat in silence, Amber giving her new friend space, and eventually the older woman continued her story, recounting how she'd finally broken down and told Francis that she was overextended, that she'd mortgaged Ellensby. Francis had seemed appalled by the news, devastated, and immediately offered her his own money, cash, but it wasn't nearly enough. He told her they should leave the Gryphon to the creditors and the other investors, have her investment refunded. Eliminate the risk. They would save Ellensby then take the remaining money and leave The Valley behind. And the magician had conjured a new spell, a vision of the two of them, travelling the world unfettered. And then the storm had come and he was lost, drowned as the mine flooded.

'He died?' Amber asked, understanding at last the grief that consumed Teramina.

'So I believe.'

'You're not certain?'

'There was an inquest. The coroner delivered an open finding.'

Amber was confused. 'There's a possibility he's alive?'

'I don't know. I don't know if he is drowned, or gone.' And then, as tears ran down her face: 'I sometimes think I'd prefer it if he was dead.'

'No,' Amber said. 'Surely not.'

'People in The Valley say that he took my money and ran.' A huge sobbing had racked her then.

Now, sitting alone near the waterfall, with Lucas and Simmons up at the mine, Amber wondered anew at what had wreaked such devastation on Teramina's mind: the uncertainty of not knowing if he had died or the possibility he had fled with her money. For a moment, Amber considered the third possibility: Obswith's assertion that Teramina had shot her husband, and that's what caused Teramina's downward spiral into mental instability and depression. But it was too horrid to contemplate; Amber couldn't believe it.

And now she knew for a fact what Teramina never had: Francis hadn't conned his wife, hadn't stolen her wealth. Instead, he was dead. Murdered. And almost certainly not by Teramina, given her uncertainty about her husband's fate. Nevertheless, it did make Amber wonder if that was some part of the reason Teramina had been so distraught, that she'd suspected there was some truth in those rumours that he had stolen her money and abandoned her.

Amber stood up. She realised she had a decision to make. Did she leave, or did she stay? And if she stayed, did she try to make do, barricade herself away in Watershine, or should she seek the truth: find out what really happened to Francis and to Teramina— and to Teramina's money? She was still trying to determine a path forward when Simmons and Lucas returned.

chapter thirty-five

2024

IVAN AND NELL STARE AT THE SCREEN IN THE MINERS' INSTITUTE.

'This has to be why they dug up the body,' she says. 'Someone else suspects, the same as we do, that Hardcastle was not who he claimed to be.'

But Ivan is frowning, shaking his head. 'But why? To what end? Whoever it was in the grave, they've been dead for decades. And if the graverobbers found what you've unearthed, why would it be necessary to dig him up?'

'All we've established is that he wasn't the real Francis Hardcastle,' says Nell. 'Maybe they were trying to find out the same thing we need to ascertain: who he really was and why he was impersonating Hardcastle.'

Ivan stares at her, and Nell lifts one questioning eyebrow. She returns her attention to the computer, contemplates the screen. How can she advance this? How could the events of the 1990s possibly be connected to the murder of Wolfgang Burnside? Burnside wasn't even born when the man in Francis Hardcastle's grave had been shot in the forehead. Wolfgang's father—her father—Simmons must know more, at least more detail. Maybe he's worth another approach? From Ivan, though, not her; keep it professional.

Ivan's phone rings. Nell checks her watch. It's twenty to eleven at night.

'Blake?' says Ivan, addressing his handset. And then: 'She is,' and then, 'Okay. Will do.'

He taps at the phone, places it on the desk between them, speaks towards it, voice loud and clear. 'Okay, you're on speaker. Nell is with me.'

'Nell, it's Blake. Carole is here with me. You can hear all right?'

She frowns. What is this? 'Yep. All good.'

'Two pieces of information you should know about. The first is the gold nugget that Tyffany Burnside says she found in her husband's luggage. It's a fake.'

Ivan sounds sceptical. 'Pretty convincing fake. Looked genuine to me.'

'It is real gold,' says a woman's voice. Carole. 'That's the problem: it's too real. It's nearly one hundred per cent pure. The nugget's been fabricated out of refined gold.'

'Why would someone do that?' asks Nell.

'Maybe to fool someone into thinking they've struck gold some-where,' says Blake.

'So part of a con?' asks Ivan.

'Could be,' says Carole.

'That would make sense,' says Nell. 'Ivan and I have just estab-lished the man passing himself off as Francis Hardcastle was an imposter. We don't know who he really was, but running some sort of con would fit.'

'There is another possibility,' says Carole. 'It could be an attempt to disguise stolen jewellery or bullion. Melt it down, fabricate a nugget, pretend it's a new find. Rebirthing it. In this case, it would have to be bullion. The gold is too pure for jewellery.'

Ivan summarises: 'So the man pretending to be Francis Hardcastle reopens a goldmine. Then he is murdered there. Decades later, Wolfgang Burnside is killed after finding a fake nugget. And then the body of Hardcastle's imposter is stolen.'

'It has to be connected—but how exactly?' asks Nell. 'And why now? How does all this become relevant more than thirty-three years after the first murder?'

'Must be the nugget,' says Ivan. He takes a breath. 'Thanks, Blake. Thanks, Carole. I'm not entirely sure why, but this feels significant.'

'What's the second piece of information?' asks Nell.

Carole answers. 'It's personal, Nell. About your father.'

She looks at Ivan, sees that he's baffled, that he hasn't been told in advance. 'What is it?' she asks.

'We've found him,' says Carole. 'It's not Simmons Burnside after all. It's a man called Lucas Trescothic.'

Lucas Trescothic. One of the men who was with Amber when they discovered the body at the bottom of the mine. 'How'd you find him?' she asks, thinking they've done something clever, triangulated a genealogy database or something. 'How can you be sure?'

'He's on the police database,' says Carole. 'I'm sorry, Nell. He's a convicted criminal. A killer.'

'Oh.' It's all she can summon, just a small exhalation. Her father, a killer.

'There's no doubt?' asks Ivan.

'I'm sorry, none. His DNA was in the database all along.' Carole sounds remorseful. 'We didn't think to check. Everyone said Simmons Burnside was Wolfgang's father; we assumed he was yours as well.'

'Entirely my fault,' says Blake, contrition evident. 'Lucas Trescothic is your father. And the father of Wolfgang Burnside. The probability is as close to one hundred per cent as it's possible to be.'

Nell isn't sure what to say. She remembers the reaction of Simmons Burnside down at Batemans Bay, his denial of paternity. The former cop's protestation of love for Wolfgang regardless, his fury at his former wife. She can see now that he was telling the truth. 'Thanks, guys,' she says. 'Better to know.' She's too stunned to ask anything else.

'Where is he now?' asks Ivan, eyes on her even as he addresses the handset. 'Is Lucas Trescothic still alive?'

'We believe so,' says Blake. 'We've got an address in Nimbin. Northern New South Wales. Hippie central. You know it?'

'Heard of it,' says Nell.

'He was sentenced to twenty-two years, served seventeen,' says Blake.

'Right,' says Nell. 'Does he know about Wolfgang? That he's dead?'

There's a silence. 'We don't know what he knows, Nell,' says Carole. 'We put in a call to the local police, asked if they knew his whereabouts. They do, but he's not so easy to contact. A hermit, lives in the rainforest.'

Nell struggles to speak. 'Okay. Well, thank you. We'll take it from here.' It's easy to say, but she's not sure where she *should* take it. She leans back in her chair as Ivan continues the call, but she has trouble following the conversation, her mind spinning off in all directions, propelled by the centrifugal force of this new revelation. Blake is talking about the gold in the nugget, whether it can be traced to any particular mine or mint. Something to do with trace impurities. She barely listens, doesn't really notice when Ivan finishes the call. The elation has gone from her, the impetus that came from discovering Hardcastle was an imposter and that the nugget is a fake.

She's still staring into space when Ivan speaks, breaking through her numbness. 'Here it is, Nell. You want to see?' He's gesturing towards his computer screen.

She blinks. 'Just read it out, could you?'

'Sure. Lucas Stanhope Trescothic. Found guilty of murdering Senior Sergeant Cornell Obswith here in The Valley. And . . . shit.'

'Ivan?'

'Found guilty of murdering Senior Sergeant Cornell Obswith here in The Valley—at Watershine.'

'When Amber lived there?'

'We'll have to check, find if there's a court transcript.'

'Surely there would be?'

'Maybe not. Says he pleaded guilty, didn't appeal. Might only be an audio or shorthand file if it wasn't contested in court. We'll need to get it transcribed.'

'A cop killer,' says Nell, numb. 'Right. My father. A cop killer. At my mother's house. How cosy.'

'You okay?'

'Just dandy.'

Ivan doesn't speak for a long moment; she can sense him studying her, but she doesn't meet his gaze. Something deep inside her feels like it's coming apart.

Finally, he turns away, recommences reading. 'He pleaded guilty and . . .' Ivan stops, starts scrolling on his computer.

She turns to him. 'Now what?'

'Represented in court by Willard Halliday.'

'Small world,' says Nell.

'Here's another report. Newspaper. Trescothic shot Obswith dead. Witnessed by Simmons Burnside and Amber Jones. Arrested by Simmons Burnside.'

'Tiny world. Miniscule world.' She feels dazed, almost anaesthetised.

'Supported by DNA evidence. Obswith tried to fight him off.' Ivan's phone bleats again. He checks the screen. 'Alice Wheelright,' he informs Nell, then takes the call. 'Ivan,' he says.

Nell watches as he listens, nodding in understanding, or maybe in appreciation.

'That's very good of you. Could be the break we need. Thanks for getting it to us. Nell is right here. She'll be intrigued.'

'What is it?' she asks as Ivan ends the call. She feels overwhelmed: too much information, too late at night.

'The fingerprint database is back online. The man in Saltwood hospital is Trent Priestly. One of two surviving members of the Nautilus Gang.'

'The Nautilus Gang?' says Nell. The name sounds vaguely familiar, something heard long ago.

'Staged a famous robbery, the Botany Warehouse Heist, between Port Botany and Sydney airport, back in 1988. Stole millions in cash and six cases of gold bullion. Three hundred ingots. Never solved, never recovered.'

Their eyes lock. 'Holy shit,' she says. 'And two years later, in 1990, an imposter passing himself off as Francis Hardcastle reopens a former goldmine here in The Valley.'

'London to a brick he was finding nuggets,' says Ivan.

chapter thirty-six

1994

THE FOLLOWING MONDAY, AS I DROVE TO WORK IN SALTWOOD, I WAS STILL mulling over what to do about my discovery at the mine with Lucas, my firm belief that the mine had been deliberately flooded, that someone had siphoned water down the ventilation shaft. And then what? Deliberately destroyed the dam wall to disguise their handiwork? Could Teramina have done that? Could one person, acting alone?

I ran it through my mind. Hardcastle went to the mine, or was taken there, and was murdered, a gunshot to the head. When? We only had Teramina's account that he had called her at Ellensby about an hour before midnight, as the rain was growing heavier. Was it possible he had been dead for some time when the mine was flooded? But no one could have anticipated the ferocity of the storm, could they? Would they have needed to?

The Sarge was accusing Teramina, but that seemed too convenient: she was dead, unable to defend herself. And even

338

if she had shot him, it couldn't have been her that flooded the mine. I was convinced it had been inundated when she had been with me and Mike and the others at the cisterns, when the flow down the hill had paused: the water flooding into the mine had reduced the flow for that short time, lulling Mike and me into a false sense of security.

So even if Teramina did kill him, she would have needed an accomplice to flood the Gryphon. Or had someone inundated the mine for some other reason? Was it possible that Francis Hardcastle himself had planned it? After all, there was evidence he had stolen money from the company accounts in the days before his death. Maybe he was the one who set it up to give the impression he was underground. Left the car outside, keys in the ignition. Set up the siphon himself. Except someone had captured him there, taken him down the mine and killed him, then used the siphon. Maybe an accomplice, someone he'd arranged to drive him away, someone who then double-crossed him.

So I arrived at the Saltwood police station, thinking I might bypass the Sarge and tell the homicide detectives, the ones from Sydney, but I never got a chance. The place was abuzz, you could feel it in the air, that strange electricity you get when something big is happening, people talking over the top of each other, phones ringing, constables scurrying from one office to the next.

'Welcome to the shitshow,' said Tom Sievers.

'What is it? What's happening?'

'The forestry wars. They're back on.' He showed me the newspaper, that morning's edition of the *Sydney Morning Herald*. And there it was, splashed across the front page, MINISTER'S SCAM EXPOSED, and the subheading, POLICE IMPLICATED IN FOREST LAND

GRAB. It was accompanied by a photo, the Sarge and me, taken back on the protest line four years earlier. I read the caption: *Police arrest protesters, part of a series of orchestrated confrontations*. There was no photo credit, no reference to Stan Cimati or anyone else. But the by-line was familiar enough: Max Fuller, the bloke who'd originally done all the damage, the reporter who'd been duped by Special Branch back in 1990. In his photo, he appeared solemn and authoritative, and the story carried a red banner *Exclusive* and the title *A* Herald *Investigation*. But this time around, he was telling a very different story.

> A four-year investigation by the *Herald* has uncovered a conspiracy led by former police minister Terrence Earl involving Special Branch, undercover operatives, hired thugs and local Saltwood police.
>
> The *Herald* believes this conspiracy manipulated an existing confrontation between forestry workers and environmentalists in the state's south to benefit the minister and his family. It's believed the windfall was worth millions of dollars.
>
> The *Herald* has uncovered compelling evidence that Mr Earl used hired thugs to bash peaceful protesters, using an under-cover police officer—now identified as Jeremiah Fouks—to photograph the confrontation.
>
> That incident—known colloquially as 'the Battle for Fowlers Gap'—was the catalyst for the extension of the Wellington Falls National Park. Mr Fouks alleges public outrage over the violence was used by the minister to win support for the park extension.
>
> The *Herald* can reveal the national park now totally surrounds, and serves to protect, the Rainbow Mist Eco-Resort, rated five

stars by the *Good Weekend*'s Annual Weekend Getaways and described as 'gorgeous, luxurious and pristine'.

The *Herald* can also reveal that Rainbow Mist Eco-Resort, sited at Tarantula Creek, is wholly owned by Terrence Earl, police minister in the former government at the time of the confrontation.

Environmental activist Gordon Orthrite says, 'This is criminal. They beat us up, defrauded the public. We were duped. The whole country was duped. We thought we were getting a national park, but it was Earl feathering his own nest.'

The *Herald* has established that at the relevant time Jeremiah Fouks was serving as a senior constable in Special Branch. Fouks has now gone on the record, telling the *Herald*: 'I really didn't know any of the whys and wherefores. I was told to do a job, to go undercover, so I did it. I was following orders.'

Fouks says he was ordered to infiltrate a group of environmental campaigners protesting against the logging of old-growth forests near Fowlers Gap in The Valley in southern New South Wales. He told them he was a freelance photographer, come to document their protest.

'They welcomed me with open arms. They were keen to get their story out. They thought I was God's gift.'

Asked if he felt bad about lying to them, Fouks says his conscience is clear. 'I didn't know why I was being sent there. As far as I knew, it was some sort of counterterrorism operation.'

But he did know in advance of the planned confrontation. 'I knew it was coming. The blokes would know not to touch me, to let me get in and get the shots. That was the whole point.'

Fouks says he now believes the team of six men were hired thugs, but that they were led by a serving Special Branch officer, known by the pseudonym 'Sergeant Black'.

'He's a mean c**t, all right,' says Fouks. 'Former Special Forces. A hard man.'

Fouks was later dismissed from the police force in relation to unconnected matters, but denies he has come forward to seek revenge. 'You've been chasing me on this matter for four years. I couldn't talk while I was still serving, but now I can. People have the right to know the truth.'

The former Environment Minister, Chris Glumm, has denied any knowledge of the conspiracy, and says he and his colleagues were deceived by Earl. 'It wasn't just me. It came through cabinet. It seemed like politics 101: hose it down, keep everyone happy. Give the greenies the national park, give the loggers access to state forest further south. It seemed win-win, a no-brainer. We had no way of knowing Earl stood to make millions.'

He adds: 'If the allegations are true, then Earl should face criminal charges. He misled the premier, the government and the people. It's shameful.'

Mr Glumm also supports a royal commission, conceding the cabinet decision was tainted. 'Of course it's tainted. Earl was in the room. At no time did he declare his personal interest or recuse himself. That in itself should be enough to send him to prison. As for using police resources for personal gain, that's an outrage.'

Terrence Earl couldn't be reached for comment, despite numerous attempts. His son, Hannibal Earl, a member of his staff, told the *Herald*, 'What are the greenies whingeing about? They got their national park, didn't they?'

The coverage went on inside, the four-year-old photos splashed again. A feature piece and a timeline and a sidebar story, all by Fuller. The sidebar was intriguing: *How I was played—and spent four years setting the record straight.* The story was a mea culpa of sorts; I admired Fuller for that, setting out in black and white how he'd been conned. I couldn't ever remember seeing it before: a journalist admitting their mistakes. And just near the end, there was an unexpected acknowledgement.

> I wasn't able to correct the record by myself. My thanks to those honest police, in Sydney and in The Valley, who helped guide my investigation.

I hadn't even made it to my desk when the Sarge found me. 'You and Tom. Down to The Valley. Protesters are pouring in. Environmentalists and some of the blokes from the mill.'

I didn't have time to mention my concerns about the mine flooding. Instead, Tom and I were heading back to The Valley.

chapter thirty-seven

THE DAY AFTER LUCAS HAD SHOWN SIMMONS THE VENTILATION SHAFT, AMBER was still at Watershine, still pondering what to do, coming to terms not only with the murder of Francis Hardcastle, but now plagued by the possibility that the Gryphon had been deliberately flooded. Lucas was up on the plateau again. He'd said he wanted to work on planning the race, trying to see what he could learn from the original mine, see what changes Francis might have contemplated.

She found it unnerving. Here she was, housebound, practically paralysed by the twin discoveries, and yet Lucas was seemingly unaffected, intent on progressing their venture, as though all it needed was one night's sleep to erase the trauma of their discovery. She didn't want to think him callous, or obsessive, so she decided instead that different people had different ways of coping with calamity. She'd read somewhere that men were not as in touch with their feelings as women, that they resorted to compartmentalising their emotions, so she chose to attribute his reaction to that.

Then she heard the sound of his truck approaching along the drive and withdrew her allegation. Maybe he'd rethought his actions. But when the vehicle emerged from the trees, it wasn't Lucas's work truck but an old Holden. Suzie was at the wheel, Mike in the passenger seat. They pulled up, Suzie speaking even before they got to the bottom of the stone steps.

'Have you heard?' she said.

'It's on again,' said Mike, waving a newspaper.

'The talk of The Valley,' said Suzie.

'You coming, or what?' demanded Mike.

Amber stared at them, attempting to catch up. 'What is it?'

'The protests,' said Mike, again flourishing the paper. 'They're back on.'

Amber could hear the excitement in their voices, see their nervous energy. 'Come up. Explain it to me.'

Inside, Mike spread the newspaper on the kitchen table, the *Sydney Morning Herald*. The front page was dominated by a single story: MINISTER'S SCAM EXPOSED.

Suzie and Mike watched as she read, barely able to control themselves, like grasshoppers on a skillet. The story was written by a journalist called Max Fuller. He stared out from a picture by-line, looking superior and self-satisfied. There were some graphic photos from the original protest in 1990, including one of Mike, red hair longer and sideburns in full bloom, cowering under the attack, his face resolute.

'Wow,' she said to her friends. 'I know you told me about this, but I didn't realise.'

'There's a demo planned,' said Suzie. 'We're going there now. You coming?'

'I guess,' said Amber, grateful for the distraction. 'But why protest? Didn't you get the national park?'

'Not the point,' said Suzie. 'This is police fucking corruption.'

Mike was regarding Suzie with admiration. 'Too right. Well said.'

——

They drove south into the forest in Suzie's Holden, joining the protest outside the former minister's eco-resort. Amber found it new and exciting, and was immediately glad she'd come along. There was nothing for her at Watershine, and she couldn't bring herself to return to the mine. Not yet. And she felt at home among the trees, had always felt that way. She was on the side of the angels, no longer alone but back with her friends.

A picket line had been set up, blocking staff and guests from entering, encouraging those high-paying customers already inside to leave. There was some construction work underway, a new wing for the lodge, and a union official proudly declared the site black—'Nothing new is going to get built here!' he proclaimed, winning the applause of the demonstrators. Amber joined in the clapping and cheering and felt the thrill of being part of a crowd. Of having a clear and undiluted purpose. She loved the sense of unity, of belonging. Spontaneous chanting broke out: *'National park now!' Clap, clap, clap! 'National park now!'*

'Why are we yelling that?' asked Amber, as the chant fell away.

'This entire place is surrounded by national park,' said Suzie. 'We want the resort incorporated into the park.'

Not long afterwards the police arrived. She recognised Simmons Burnside, but not the other, younger officer. Simmons talked to the union organiser and one of the grey-haired environmentalists, coming across as serious and no-nonsense. She was impressed by his manner; he was conciliatory, not simply issuing orders.

He saw her and walked over. 'Taking time away from the mine?' he asked.

'Finding it a bit hard to face right now,' she replied.

'Fair enough.' Simmons looked about him, as though to ensure no one overheard them. 'Could I talk to you? Maybe not here. Somewhere more private.'

There was weight in his voice and he sounded sympathetic, attuned to what she was thinking. She felt something of the bond from their last meeting returning.

'Sure,' she said. 'Come over to Watershine when this is finished.'

It ended less than an hour later. Just as the crowd was beginning to dissipate, and the chant was growing tired, news came through from Sydney. The new government, unable to resist inflicting maximum political damage on its predecessor, had announced its intention to establish a royal commission into the actions of Terrence Earl and Special Branch, as well as the decision to expand the Wellington Falls National Park surrounding the Tarantula Creek holding of Earl's.

And, in a strongly worded statement, the new premier declared that, depending on the outcome of the royal commission, there was a real possibility that the government would compulsorily acquire ownership of the eco-resort and surrounding private property and have it incorporated into the national park.

It was a massive win for the environmentalists and Amber found herself swept up in the celebrations. Suzie invited everyone back to her brother's farm to celebrate. Amber thought of going, almost did, but at the last moment decided her heart wasn't in it.

And she wanted to hear what Simmons had to say. Instead, she asked Suzie to drop her at the crossroad, so she could walk back to Watershine.

She wasn't home long when Lucas arrived. He was as bright as ever, full of optimism, keen to get on. It was as if nothing had happened, as if they had never discovered Francis Hardcastle's rotting corpse, as if the forest victory had occurred in some foreign land. Amber studied his face, that beautiful face: the sharp jawline, the sculpted brow, the hazel eyes. Her golden man. Her lover. If he was worried, he didn't show it. Just the opposite. He was excited.

'Good news!' he said, bounding up the stairs and onto the porch. 'Have you heard?'

'What's that?'

'The government. They're going to confiscate Terrence Earl's land at Tarantula Creek, declare it part of the national park.'

'I heard.'

'Well, now the loggers are up in arms. They say Earl's fraudulent campaign cost them the concession to log that land. That none of it should have become national park.'

'It's too late for that now, surely?'

'Absolutely,' said Lucas. 'But the loggers are threatening to sue the government for compensation, so it's considering releasing another tranche of state forest instead.'

The hairs on Amber's neck stood up, some intuitive warning. 'What's that got to do with us?' she whispered.

'There's state forest on the land up beyond the Gryphon—but the only feasible way to access it is up your road.'

'My road?'

'The road to the mine.'

'But it's narrow, full of switchbacks.'

'Yeah. So the government would pay to have it upgraded enough to carry logging trucks . . . and mining trucks.'

Amber shook her head, distressed and disbelieving. 'No.'

'What do you mean no? It's win-win. They pay for the road upgrade, pay you money for the right to access it, and we get an all-weather road to the Gryphon. We can get heavy equipment in, truck the ore out, no need for the race. Make it a truly commercial venture, like in the old days, bigger and better than anything Francis Hardcastle imagined. Who knows? We could even float it on the stock exchange.'

Amber said nothing, even as Lucas continued, face animated. She thought he looked just as glorious as he had that first night at the cricket ground concert, skin perfect, teeth shining, his eyes alight. And yet she felt she had never known him. And all the while that she was studying him, he kept talking, oblivious to her reaction.

'I've been thinking,' he said. 'We need money to finance the mine, expand it. If they're logging up there, why not let them log some of your land? They'd need to pay for the right, of course, the same way they pay fees to the state government.'

Amber still said nothing, even as her heart shrivelled inside her.

'And the mill,' said Lucas. 'Rare timber. I'm sure there's some up there that would be worth a small fortune.'

'The grove?' she said at last, her voice barely audible. 'The cedar?'

'Well, maybe not all of it,' said Lucas, at last picking up on her reticence. 'Just one or two trees. A bit of thinning out might be beneficial. Foresters say that.'

'Please leave,' she said.

'What?'

'I don't want the road. I don't want any logging.'

He stopped then, beginning to understand how badly he had misstepped, becoming still where a moment before he was bristling with movement. 'But the mine. How do we finance it?'

He kept saying 'we', and she felt herself repelled by the pronoun. She didn't know what to say. Or, rather, she knew what she wanted to say but not how to say it. And then it poured out, not what she wanted to say at all, but a stream of questions.

'How do you know the loggers are interested in my land? How do you know the government is interested in my road? How do you know the mill is interested in my logs? How do you know they're considering granting the loggers a concession above the escarpment?'

He stared, words more mumbled than spoken. 'Just something I heard,' he said.

To her ears, it sounded lame, like she had caught him out.

'Please leave,' she said again, and this time she turned her back, dismissing him. It was only when she heard the engine of his truck start that she felt herself crumple, and allowed the tears to come.

— —

And that's how Simmons found her, some hours later, curled into a ball as the room darkened. It was Simmons who consoled her.

And it was to Simmons she told her story about the time she had found Teramina by the banks of the Murray.

The house was growing dark, the sun having long fallen behind the western escarpment, but still they talked.

'Do you mind if I ask you some questions—about Teramina and the mine?' he asked.

'Is this official?'

'No,' said Simmons, looking her in the eye. 'No, it's not. And it's anonymous. Off the record.' He waited for her nod of assent before continuing. 'You know what Lucas and I found up there. The more I think of it, the more I'm convinced the mine was deliberately flooded after Hardcastle was shot. Water siphoned in, down the ventilation shaft, most likely trying to make sure the body wasn't ever recovered. Afterwards, someone propagated a story that the flooding was caused by a cave-in, that the lake and mine were connected.'

She grimaced. 'Sergeant Obswith says he thinks Teramina killed him.'

'He's pushed that theory to me as well. What do you think? Could it be true?'

'No. I can't believe she would do it. To him, or to me.'

'To you?'

'Why would she bequeath me that horror show?'

'I agree,' said Simmons. 'I don't think she did it.'

'Really?' She felt a lift in her heart.

'I have a pretty good idea of when the mine was flooded. Teramina was with me at the time, at the cisterns by Watershine.'

'So she can't have done it?'

'It's still possible that she killed him, then had an accomplice flood the mine later. That's what Obswith thinks.'

'I don't believe that. I think it must have been someone else altogether. Killed him and then flooded the mine.'

'I'd like to think so,' said Simmons. 'But who?'

'You don't think it could have been Lucas, do you?'

That seemed to shock him. 'Why would you say that?'

'He said he went up there that day, tried to reach the mine. Teramina sent him.'

'That's right. I remember. He said the road was unpassable. A landslide.'

'He just seems so focused on the gold. As if nothing else matters. He was up near the lake all day today, planning the processing works. Now he's talking about logging up there, getting them to rebuild the road.'

But the young policeman shook his head. 'I can't see it. Hardcastle's body was safely hidden. Why would he want to uncover it and implicate himself? You wouldn't have worked out that the mine could be pumped out by yourself, would you?'

'No. That was all him.'

'And why would he take me up there yesterday, show me how someone could flood it using a siphon? I didn't even know that ventilation shaft existed.'

And she looked away, feeling ashamed. 'Yes. You're right. Silly of me.' She remembered all that Lucas had done for her. Why was she talking this way, to a policeman? Because she felt lost, not knowing whom to trust? An echo came to her of Teramina in the forest, distraught because she doubted Francis. 'I think it has to do with money,' she said. 'They took all her money. I think if we find who did that, then we'll know who killed him.'

'I agree,' said Simmons. 'And who drove Teramina to suicide.'

Their eyes locked, and she felt they were asking themselves the same question. She was the one to vocalise it. 'Is it possible she didn't jump?'

chapter thirty-eight

2024

AT THE CENTRE OF THE VALLEY, ALL IS QUIET. AT THE BUSHRANGER HOTEL, Wilhelmina has closed the bar early and locked up for the night. A solitary car winds its way along the Valley Road, pauses at the crossroad, then turns right and continues along the West Road. Perhaps the driver notices the lights on in the Miners' Institute, perhaps they don't. But there is activity inside the old building: Nell Buchanan and Ivan Lucic, probing the records, joining the dots, alert and hyper awake, a frisson in the air. The best part of a homicide case: when it starts coming together. For the moment Nell has parked the revelation that her biological father is a cop killer named Lucas Trescothic, and moved on to the question at hand: who killed Wolfgang Burnside and why.

It takes no time to find information on the Botany Warehouse Heist: it's famous enough to warrant an extensive Wikipedia page. Nell starts reading aloud, summarising as she goes.

'Twenty-five million dollars, most of it in cash, but also including three hundred gold bars, were stolen from a storage facility between Port Botany and Sydney airport. Gang members were able to gain access to vaults, almost certainly after obtaining inside information and pass keys.

'The robbery was going smoothly, almost complete, when a group of hobbyist tunnel explorers passing through sewers under the warehouse overheard the robbery in process through drainage grates, if you can believe that. They alerted police, who swarmed the warehouse. There was a shootout. One policeman and a security guard were killed outright, two more seriously injured. One of the gang members died, two were captured. Trent Priestly and Claus Barker.'

Ivan interjects. 'Trent Priestly. In hospital at Saltwood. You think Barker was the other one trying to abduct Willard Halliday?'

Nell runs an image search through Google. It doesn't take long to confirm Ivan's suspicions. 'Yeah, that's him. Not much doubt. The two of them, trying to track down their gold, thirty-six years later.'

'Gold that Wolfgang Burnside somehow stumbled upon,' says Ivan.

'Gold that someone posing as Francis Hardcastle was trying to rebirth in 1990,' says Nell, looking up from the screen, meeting Ivan's gaze.

'Through a front company whose secretary was Willard Halliday,' says Ivan.

'Of course,' says Nell. 'The company. Rebirthing the gold, but also using it to launder the cash.'

'Yes. Wouldn't be hard to fabricate a few sales documents.'

'There's more,' says Nell, referring back to her screen. 'Shit, what a mess.'

'What?' asks Ivan.

'The surviving gang members split up, reconvening in a shearing shed outside Goulburn. Police couldn't work out precisely what happened. They believed there was a gunfight, then a fire. The bodies burnt beyond recognition; the heat was phenomenal, the boards in the shed soaked through with a century of lanolin. Guns and bullet casings were recovered from the ashes, but no sign of the money or the gold. Police concluded one or two gang members escaped with the loot, but found it almost impossible to identify them. Priestly and Barker weren't talking, and it was never clear if they even knew the identities of other members of the gang. Police believed there were eight men involved altogether, but they weren't even a hundred per cent sure of that. They did establish that the team was led by two men, Bert Glossop and Hector "Curtains" Curtin. Glossop was shot dead at the warehouse; it's believed Curtin died in the woolshed blaze. Investigators thought it likely that the gang was put together specifically for the one-off heist, and Glossop and Curtin were possibly the only two who knew the identities of all the gang members.'

'So why were they called the Nautilus Gang?' Ivan asks.

Nell doesn't know. It takes her a few minutes to uncover the story. 'Says here Curtin and Glossop and perhaps other gang members met when they were in the navy.' She scrolls through more pages. 'The body of a man named Radovan Burke, known as Raz, was discovered about a week after the robbery, in bushland.

356

He'd been shot some time earlier and had died of his wounds. The timing matched, so there was speculation he was part of the gang.'

'Leaving?'

'One person alive and on the run.'

'A man without an identity.'

'Just twenty-five million dollars in cash and gold.'

'You think it was Francis Hardcastle?' asks Ivan. 'Or whatever his real name was?'

'Makes sense. That would give Priestly and Barker motivation to exhume the body.'

'A DNA check?'

'Pretty sophisticated technology needed,' says Nell. 'There'd only be bones left. They'd need something to compare it to. A relative. Something like that.'

There's a long pause, as Nell tries to catch up with her own thoughts.

'Okay,' says Ivan at last. 'You're the one who's good at speculating. Speculate.'

'You sure?'

'Go for it.'

Nell smiles. 'Okay. Our unknown gang member escapes the woolshed with a shit-ton of money. He's the most wanted man in Australia. Wanted by the cops, wanted by his surviving gang colleagues. So he goes to ground. Priestly and Barker are in custody, so he has time to work it through. Then a couple of years later, a man turns up here in The Valley claiming to be a mining engineer called Francis Hardcastle, wanting to reopen the Gryphon Mine. A perfect way to rebirth the gold bullion—and launder the cash through the company accounts.'

Ivan holds up a hand, interrupting. 'So we know this man passing himself off as Hardcastle was an imposter, and we think he was the fugitive gang member. So who was he?'

Nell scowls. 'Maybe he wasn't the gang member. Maybe he was a front man. A con man. An actor. Someone hired to do the job, someone who could bring it off.' She pauses as she thinks it through. 'Someone disposable.'

Ivan stares. 'Perhaps that's it. He'd rebirthed the gold, laundered the cash, so he was no longer of any use. More of a liability. So the gang member shot him, flooded the mine and made good his getaway. Leaving no tracks, no witnesses.'

'It's over thirty-three years ago,' says Nell. 'We'll never find him. We can't even identify him.'

'Hang on, we're not dead yet,' says Ivan, although he's looking less lively by the minute. 'Let's think it through. It's just one man, the surviving gang member, not even one of the leaders. He recruits Hardcastle as a front man. He can't have managed everything else, something of that scale, all on his own. Surely not, no matter how much money he had.'

The more Ivan elaborates, the more he makes sense to Nell. 'You're right,' she says, feeling her energy returning. 'Knowing how to set up a front company, launder money, fabricate nuggets. Forging documents. Bit beyond a run-of-the-mill armed hold-up merchant. Even to find and then assume the identity of Francis Hardcastle. Hardcastle had the perfect background story, exactly the right CV. But finding someone like that in 1990, pre-internet, that would have taken some doing.'

'What happened to the real Hardcastle?' asks Ivan.

'Let's see if we can find out,' says Nell.

They turn to their computers, and this time it's Ivan who gets there first. 'Here,' he says. 'A small funeral notice, in 1988, in the *San Francisco Bay Times*. No cause of death listed. Francis John Hardcastle. Forty-four years old. Born Brisbane, Australia.' Ivan keeps searching. 'It's a gay newspaper. That would have been the height of the AIDS epidemic.'

'Might explain a few things,' says Nell. 'If the real Francis Hardcastle was gay, might be why he went to America in the first place. And why no one back here missed him when he was gone.'

Ivan is staring at the screen. 'Jesus. There are pages full of these death notices. Every week. No way would this have been easy to find in 1990.'

'An impeccable cover,' says Nell.

'But finding that identity—an Australian in the US, a mining expert—and then finding this place,' says Ivan. 'The mothballed mine. And Teramina Cloverton. The fake Hardcastle was able to woo her, to win her over. Surely that can't have been by chance. Someone must have known her, identified her vulnerability, her gullibility.'

'So someone local, someone connected, who knew Teramina. Not just her circumstances, but her psychology. Possibly the same person who knew the history of the mine.'

'Yes,' says Ivan.

'Maybe the same person who shot Francis Hardcastle, or whoever he really was?'

Ivan stares, blue eyes focused on her face, the look that used to unsettle her but which she has come to appreciate.

'But that doesn't explain why Wolfgang Burnside was murdered,' says Nell. 'All that was decades ago. What's the connection?'

'The nugget?' suggests Ivan tentatively. 'It can't have been Priestly and Barker who killed him, can it?'

'And then they dig up Hardcastle, trying to find out who he is and whether they're on the right track,' says Nell, finishing Ivan's sentence for him. 'And they attempt to kidnap Willard Halliday.' She pauses. 'Willard. The company secretary. Of course.'

'Time we paid him another visit, wouldn't you say?' suggests Ivan with a smile. 'Great work, Nell. Amazing work.'

chapter thirty-nine

1994

I COULDN'T CONCENTRATE AT WORK THE NEXT MORNING, BACK IN THE SALTWOOD
police station. I felt frazzled. My mind kept wandering, drifting
off into 'what ifs' and 'maybes', a deep disquiet in my gut. Part of
it stemmed from Amber and I agreeing that Teramina couldn't
have murdered Francis and confronting the prospect that his widow
had herself been silenced. On top of that, I had prepared a deeply
flawed report for the coroner after Hardcastle's disappearance,
essentially suggesting it was all an unfortunate and unforeseen
accident, that he was drowned, whereas the whole world now
knew it to be murder.

But at the station, the discovery of the body was old news: the
talk was all about Max Fuller's revelations in the *Sydney Morning
Herald*. I could feel eyes on me, sense the whispering. Fuller had
referred to police collusion, the photographs in the paper were of
the Sarge and me. There was little comfort in knowing Fuller
was referring to Special Branch, or in his oblique thanks in his

mea culpa piece. Mud was flying and I could feel it slapping into me. And sticking.

If the *Sydney Morning Herald* was right, the Sarge and I had been manipulated, used as pawns in Terrence Earl's machinations.

My mind kept bouncing between the forestry wars and the killing of Francis Hardcastle. I'd stuffed up both of them. I was feeling like I was not suited to being a police officer, and never had been. I feared the pit in my stomach could never be filled back in.

About mid-morning, the Sarge came through. 'You okay, big fellow?' he asked.

'Feeling shitty,' I said, speaking honestly for once and not bothering with the tough-guy exterior expected of cops. 'Those forestry protests. We were played for suckers.'

The Sarge squinted at me, hitched up his trousers for emphasis. 'Don't feel so bad. We had no way of knowing; we did nothing wrong. Remember that. We did nothing wrong.'

It was a good speech, a ten-second pep talk. I guess it was what I needed. It made me feel a little better, at least temporarily.

After work I headed straight down to The Valley, gave Eliza the car. It was part of our weekly routine, her mothers' club/playgroup in Saltwood. A little bit of normalcy. She was tired after a full day minding the shop, so I took over, the way I normally did, so she could have some time with the other mums. Most times she would take Wolfie, sometimes not. Sometimes she was in a good mood, sometimes not. That was the thing about Eliza: when she was fun, she really could be fun, but when she was feeling low, or slighted, she was like a ticking bomb. On those days I had to be careful, needed to steer clear. But as it happened, that afternoon she was the happy one. She was experiencing none of the troubles that were preying on me. I was glad to have some time to myself, and I was happy she could do a bit of socialising and Wolf could play with some kids his own age. He was three by then and we had him in kindy, just a couple of afternoons a week. He loved it and he loved playgroup. He was born that way: so sociable, so good around people.

With the two of them in Saltwood, I was alone in the store, operating on automatic, even as my brain was working away, running through the permutations of Hardcastle's murder. I was so distracted that I didn't notice him when he first came into the store. He could have been a tourist, another Canberran taking the scenic route. He waited until I'd served a customer and then walked up to me.

'Simmons Burnside?'

'What of it?' I'm not sure why, but I was automatically on the defensive.

'I'm glad to meet you,' said the man, undeterred. 'I'm Max Fuller.' And then, when I didn't react, didn't know how to react, he extended his hand for me to shake. I just looked at it. 'The journalist,' he prompted.

'Yes. I know who you are.'

He lowered his hand. 'Can we talk?' he asked.

'What about?' Again, I was on guard.

He smiled, trying to sound relaxed. 'I want to buy you a beer. To thank you. For saving my career.'

I wasn't sure what he was trying to say; I didn't answer.

'Without you, I wouldn't have realised until too late that the photographer, Jeremiah Fouks, was a fraud, that Stan Cimati was a joke at my expense. A booby trap and I was the booby. Sooner or later someone would have noticed; I would have been a laughing-stock. I never would have recovered from that; I never would have had the chance to convince my editor to let me start digging.'

'Well, I'm glad it's worked out well for someone.'

He must have heard something in my voice, resentment perhaps, and his smile eased away. 'I'm serious,' he said. 'I'd like to shout you a drink. A meal. To say thanks. And to talk.'

I gestured around the store. 'Have to be later. There's just me here. We close at six thirty.'

'See you at the pub a bit after that then.' He handed me a card with his name, a phone number, an email address and a mobile number—not that the latter would be any use in The Valley; there was no mobile tower this side of Saltwood.

I was still tossing up whether to meet him or not when Eliza rang. The mothers' club was kicking on; she was going to have an early dinner with a couple of the others.

'Is Wolfie okay?' I asked.

'Having the time of his life,' she said.

So after I shut up shop, I met the journalist at the pub, this Max Fuller. I'd been thinking it over as I stocked the shelves and moved bags of fertiliser about in the trade section and served the occasional customer. I figured talking to him couldn't hurt; that it might even be useful. I wondered if maybe he could help me work out what had really happened to Francis Hardcastle. I didn't know a whole lot about the way journalists worked, but it seemed to me that an unsolved murder would be a good story. Even so, I was in two minds about telling him, mostly out of loyalty to the Sarge, who'd more or less decided that Teramina had killed her husband. I hadn't yet told my superior what I'd found with Lucas, that there was the strong possibility that someone had deliberately flooded the Gryphon, so I wasn't sure about discussing it with Fuller. I didn't want to land the Sarge in more trouble; he'd been good to me.

––

Fuller was a few years younger than me, mid-twenties, but he must have been at the *Herald* for a fair amount of time. He'd done the original spread on Fowlers Gap, and that was four years before. He seemed pretty at home in the pub, sitting on a beer and writing in a notebook, listening back to a microcassette player.

I went up and said hello and he invited me to sit with him. I'm guessing he sensed my nervousness, so instead of asking me questions, he started telling me about himself. He thanked me again for putting him on the path to his big scoop, the revelation that we'd all been manipulated by the former police minister Terrence Earl. He told me some of how he had tracked down the photographer working for the Special Branch. He'd spent the past three or four years trying to convince Fouks to talk to him off the record and, eventually, on the record.

'I got lucky,' said Fuller. 'He was never going to tell me anything, but then he fell foul of some internal inquiry. Evidence tampering. More shonkiness. Reckons he was hung out to dry, taking the fall for more senior officers. That Terrence Earl is up to his neck in it.'

'It can happen,' I said. We were on to our second beer by then.

'You ever encounter it?' Fuller asked.

'Not directly,' I answered honestly, 'but you hear things.'

'Sergeant Obswith?'

I looked hard at him. Had he heard something about the mine? 'No, never,' I said.

He grimaced. 'Listen, Simmons. I need to tell you something. Like I said, I owe you.'

'Go on.'

'Obswith was in on it. Fouks told me. I've corroborated it with a second source. They got your sergeant to go down, arrest some demonstrators, put on a show for the camera.' He paused, checking my reaction. 'All part of the plan. It wasn't my mistake in captioning the photos four years ago: Fouks had told me the photos of the thugs beating protesters and those of you arresting the victims were taken at the same time. It's only recently that he's admitted they were taken hours apart.'

I didn't respond, not immediately. I was thinking back to that day in the forest. On our way back out, after talking to the loggers. The three demonstrators lying in the road, against our express instructions. Of course we arrested them. 'I'm not sure that's how it played out,' I said. 'We didn't have much choice.'

Fuller regarded me grimly. 'The demonstrators who lay in the road, the two young ones, they were paid. A hundred bucks each. Cash.'

I stared at him. Mike? Mike Norfolk? Mike, who had saved my life at the cisterns, my childhood friend? Easy-going, environmentally concerned Mike? I started shaking my head. The Sarge I could almost believe, but Mike? Again, my mind turned back to that day. Sure, we'd arrested them, but we never pressed charges, never processed them. Left no record, just the photos in the paper. The Sarge had decided to let them go, dropping them at the crossroad.

Not abandoning them in the middle of nowhere; more like giving them a lift to the pub. At the time I was hoping they were feeling chastened, that Mike wouldn't hold it against me, but now I realised they wouldn't have been the least bit fussed. Mike and that girl would have headed straight into the bar, a hundred bucks each to spray about the place. And all the time, me driving back to Saltwood with the Sarge, feeling bad about arresting him. And the Sarge: how much cash did he have in his pocket?

'Sorry,' said Fuller eventually. 'But I think you deserve to know the truth.'

From somewhere across the bar came laughter. I looked over, thinking I had heard Mike's laugh, searching for that flash of red hair, but there was no sign of him. My mind was working, but I was feeling shit, all hollowed out. Betrayed. Again and again. For his part, Fuller was good; he just sat there, not saying a word, letting it unfold in my mind.

'You want something to eat?' he finally asked.

'Yeah, let's do that,' I said. 'And I might have a story for you.'

—–—

That night, I was a bit drunk. I think maybe Eliza was as well. The mothers' club could be like that: goon-bag wine with ice cubes to take the edge off. She'd driven home tipsy, bringing Wolfie back down the pass, which made my skin crawl, but I knew better than to pick a fight, that I should make the most of her good mood. She had a shower and I got Wolfie into bed, then I went rummaging back through my old papers. I found the *Sydney Morning Herald* from the original protest. I'd kept it, I knew that. Why? It was hardly my finest moment. But there it was, the paper brittle and dry and yellowing after just four years. I turned to the inside pages, the black-and-white photo spread, the article by Max Fuller, the photo credits of Stan Cimati. The photo of the Sarge and me, arresting the protesters. I was shown side on, concentrating on cuffing the girl, the Sarge was manhandling Mike. In the next frame Obswith was pushing him into the car, but there, on the side of his face, I could see it. Mike was smirking. The fucker.

I found that morning's edition, scanned it, seeing if I could find any more photos of Mike, more evidence of his duplicity. Most of the photos looked the same, just in colour; at first I thought they were identical to the 1990 paper. Then one caught my eye. Maybe it was just the red of the blood, making it stand out more than the black and white from 1990. I remembered; none of the demonstrators had experienced any major injuries: a cracked rib or two, a few stitches, that was about it. Nothing permanent, nothing life-threatening. And then I saw it. There was a woman's face, a close up, left of frame. She was screaming, eyes shut. And in the background, I could see Mike, arms up, protecting his face, orange hair bright. I couldn't see his expression; it was obscured. There was a man standing over him, half out of the frame, preparing to hit him, all in black. Similar to one of the shots from four years ago, but in this photo, the thug's sleeve was riding up. And there it was, clear as day. A tattoo. A trident. Lucas.

That night I couldn't sleep. Beside me, Eliza was snoring softly, sleeping peacefully. And so I was the one awake when Wolfie yelled out, fear and panic in his voice. I raced into his room, turning the light on. He was sitting up in bed, tears in his eyes, frightened as hell. I went straight to him, hugged him, cooed, soothed him. 'A nightmare, buddy. That's all it is, a bad dream.'

'There was a man, Daddy. Hurting Mummy.'

'It's okay, Wolf. Just a bad dream.'

'He took all her clothes off.'

I was silent.

'At Saltwood.'

chapter forty

THE POLICE WERE LONG GONE. IT WAS ALMOST A WEEK SINCE FRANCIS
Hardcastle's body had been removed and all traces of the crime
expunged. Even so, Amber was reluctant to go underground, even
to venture up to the mine. It had lost its mystique, its promise.
Lucas and Mike had started to survey the Gryphon without her.
If Lucas had noticed her reticence, her lack of focus, he hid it well.
He seemed obsessed with making progress and little else, leaving
her feeling like an afterthought. He seemed to have forgotten their
disagreement about logging and granting the timber company
access to her road. He'd head up to the mine early, come back
late. He still stayed at Watershine most nights, still slept in her
bed, but there was no more sex. Amber wondered if he was only
staying over because the house was close to the mine.

Mike was happy, seemingly unaffected by our discovery of
Hardcastle's body. He was knowledgeable, familiar with the layout
of the mine, able to help Lucas explore and map the shafts and
tunnels and galleries. Once Lucas was comfortable, Mike started
on the cisterns, using Arnie Cocheef's front-end loader, something

he could do without spending money, clearing away some of the silt, laying the groundwork for the cisterns themselves to be cleaned out for when the time came to build new processing facilities.

Lucas said they needed to find some gold. If there was enough, its sale could directly finance further development; if there wasn't, they could use it to demonstrate their creditworthiness.

But after a few days, and then a week and then two weeks, Lucas, initially so keen, was becoming more and more frustrated. Day after day he left Watershine full of fervour, evening after evening he returned empty-handed.

'I don't know what to make of it,' he confided in Amber eventually. 'There's nothing there—or if there is, I can't find it. Not even a fleck of gold, let alone a nugget. Even right down the end, where they were working before the flood.' He was deflated, she could see that. The spark in his eyes was sputtering, dampened by disappointment.

She asked Mike about it the next day. She walked across to the cisterns, and was surprised at the progress he'd achieved. Somehow, working alone, he'd figured out how to divert the water as he cleared the pools, one by one. But when she complimented him on the work, he pointed up towards the largest pool, the one closest to the waterfall. 'It's still half full of sand and debris. We'll need to redirect the flow down the escarpment, before we can drain it and dig it out. That must be why Francis repaired the dams up by the lake's outlet. Not just to feed water into the race, but so they could send the flow along the home creek while they cleared these out. We might need to rebuild the dams and do the same thing.'

'Might not be any point,' she said, and told him about Lucas's inability to find gold.

Mike was incredulous. 'There was definitely gold,' he said. 'It wasn't just Francis. I found nuggets; so did one or two of the others.'

So the next day Mike went underground with Lucas. After another fruitless day, and then a second, they decided on some exploratory blasting.

'Is it safe?' she asked Lucas when he told her of their plan. 'Shouldn't we be making sure everything is properly shored up? It's been underwater for more than three years. Some of those timbers must be a century old.'

'Mike says we can set a long fuse,' he said. 'Be back above ground before it detonates.'

So they blasted, nearby two spots where Mike recalled finding nuggets with Francis.

That evening the two men arrived at Watershine, clearly crestfallen.

The next afternoon they were even more despondent, covered in dirt, only their eyes clear. 'We took samples of the quartz from the blasting,' Mike told her as they stood out on the porch. 'Brought it up to the surface. Pulverised it. Turned it into powder. Washed it, treated it. Almost nothing. Just trace amounts of gold.' He appeared apologetic, bewildered. 'I'm no expert, but even I can see it isn't there in viable quantities.'

'I don't fucking get it,' said Lucas, pacing backward and forward, anger in his voice. 'I just don't. Hardcastle was finding nuggets. We can't even find flecks.'

Amber didn't know what to say. But said it anyway. 'You think maybe that's why he was shot?'

Lucas stopped pacing and looked at her, then at Mike, who shrugged, and back to her again. 'Teramina? You think she shot him?'

'No. Not her. But somebody did.' She turned to Mike. 'Do you think it's possible the nuggets weren't genuine? That they were planted.'

The question made Mike squirm, apparently unwilling to even entertain the possibility. 'No. I can't believe that. They were authentic. He was authentic.'

That night, after Mike and Lucas had washed and gone to the pub, she went upstairs and unlocked the door to the study. The light bulb didn't work, so she brought up a standard lamp from the lounge, set it up next to the desk, its top covered with dust. The room was quiet, like it was unused to human presence. She started going through the papers, records from the time Francis and Teramina were running Gryphon Number Two Pty Ltd. They'd made more progress than she and Lucas, but not that much more. They were still in the prospecting stage. They hadn't put through mains electricity, the road up the escarpment was basic, they hadn't rebuilt the race down the escarpment or installed new machinery at the cisterns. Their workforce was small and casual. They'd spent money, but possibly not that much. Maybe just enough for show. Indeed, the only things that really set them apart from Lucas, Mike and herself were the formation of the company, attracting investment, and finding gold. Claiming to have found gold.

She discovered a ledger, money in and money out, but its discipline deteriorated after just a month or two. She turned the pages, finding it almost impossible to decipher. At one point, there was a note, in red-pen capitals: COMPANY FORMED. RECORDS WITH HALLIDAY, ACCOUNTS WITH WALLINGTON. After that, the entries were few and far between. A sense of frustration swept over her. The papers were telling her nothing; she felt ill-equipped to understand them even if they could.

As she thought, her eyes wandered about the room. They settled on a portrait of Francis Hardcastle as a young man, maybe mid-twenties, wearing a hard hat with a miners lamp on the front, smiling out at the viewer, brimming with confidence. It was an oil painting, but it had the feel of something based on a photograph. She wondered when it was painted, when the photo was taken: decades ago, or was it commissioned more recently, about the time Hardcastle had arrived in The Valley? She examined it more closely; there was no way of telling. Next to it was a framed certificate from the state of Colorado, certifying Francis Hardcastle was qualified to supervise mine works in that state. It was dated 1973.

The painting and the certificate hung above a glass-fronted bookshelf, full of old ledgers and books bound in canvas and leather, dating to the earlier incarnation of the mine, when it was a proper commercial-grade operation, when the Clovertons ran it, productive for decades. When Watershine was the manager's house. It was then that she knew what to look for.

It took till past midnight, but she was confident in what she had uncovered. There were mining assays, records of production, records of ore grades. Expressed in parts per million, or ounces produced per ton of rock crushed. Detailed and disciplined, in dramatic contrast to Francis Hardcastle's erratic record keeping. There was mention of quartz seams, of other minerals, recordings of gold flecking and gold dust. Of veins of gold. But the last mention of substantial seams of gold, of native gold, of nuggets, was in 1912, twenty years before the mine finally closed. After 1912, the mine was chasing gold dust and decreasing rates of return.

So where had Francis Hardcastle found his nuggets?

chapter forty-one

2024

THE NEXT MORNING, EARLY, IVAN AND NELL TALK ALL THE WAY TO SALTWOOD, throwing theories at each other, planning how to approach Willard, rehearsing the grounds for taking him into custody, conducting a formal interview.

'Man's a lawyer,' says Nell from behind the wheel. 'He'll clam up. Say nothing to incriminate himself.'

'True,' says Ivan. 'We have absolutely no proof he knew Hardcastle was an imposter. He's bound to deny it.'

'So how did they know each other? What's their connection?' asks Nell. 'Surely it must have been Willard, or someone else local, who alerted the gang to the potential of the Gryphon Mine and Teramina. The surviving member can't have stumbled upon The Valley randomly.'

'You're right,' says Ivan. 'Before we front him, let's see if we can find anything to connect Willard to the Botany Warehouse

Heist.' Ivan says he doesn't want to go anywhere near the Saltwood police station, so instead they park on the main road, find a cafe with a courtyard out the back, and use their phones to glean all they can about Willard Halliday.

And when they find it, it seems obvious.

'Here,' says Nell. 'Willard Halliday. Officer school in the navy, back in the day. Melbourne.'

'The Nautilus Gang,' says Ivan. 'Ex-navy.'

'Is it enough to haul him in?' asks Nell.

'Let's talk to him first. Don't show our hand. Say we're investigating the blokes who tried to kidnap him.'

'But he'll have been interviewed already by the local police.'

'We tell him the truth: that we think it's linked to Wolfgang Burnside's murder.'

Nell smiles at her partner. 'Okay. Let's go.'

––

The office has been cleaned up, with no sign of the violence perpetrated by Priestly and Barker. Its polished wood still exudes the ambiance of a museum. Ollie is at the reception, smiles when he sees Nell. 'It's our saviour, come for a visit.' His face is still a mess, stitches on his forehead, stitches on one cheek, with a black eye turning yellow and purple. He seems unfazed.

'Hi, Ollie. How you holding up?'

'Yeah. Good. These painkillers are the bomb.'

'Glad to hear it,' says Ivan. 'Your boss in?'

'Yeah. Go on through. Check if he's still breathing while you're there.'

Willard is behind the desk, oxygen tubes sitting on the desktop, ready for use. It's just gone nine in the morning but the ashtray already contains a fully smoked butt. 'Officers. Have a seat.'

Nell lets Ivan take the lead, ready to inject herself if need be, but happy enough to study Willard, see if she can detect any tells or giveaways. What she sees is a crafty old man, keen for a contest of wills, amused by their presence.

'The men who attempted to kidnap you,' says Ivan. 'You know we have one of them in custody?'

'I do indeed. Thanks to my brave assistant Ollie and Constable Buchanan here,' replies Willard, grinning at Nell. 'I didn't really get the chance to thank you, my dear. What you did was very brave.'

'You're welcome,' says Nell, smiling back, hoping hers appears more convincing than the lawyer's own predatory smirk.

'Have you caught the others yet?' asks Willard. His breathing seems better today, less laboured.

'No,' she says. 'But the locals found the ambulance. Burnt out.'

Willard grimaces. 'What a waste. Stolen, I assume?'

'Yes,' says Nell.

'And you still have no idea why they wanted to abduct you?' asks Ivan.

'No,' says Willard, smile easing.

'The man in custody in Saltwood hospital has been identified. Trent Priestly. You familiar with him?'

'Can't say that I am.'

'A career criminal. Convicted in connection with shooting police in 1988. Thirty-six years ago.'

Willard shrugs, says nothing.

'A member of the Nautilus Gang.'

The smile has gone altogether now. 'I remember them. That robbery in Sydney. All that money.'

'All that gold,' says Nell.

Willard turns to her, studies her. 'Yes,' he says. 'Bullion.'

She matches his gaze.

'Is he talking?' asks Willard. 'This Trent Priestly?'

'Doesn't really have to, does he?' asks Ivan.

Willard says nothing, like a poker player, keeping his cards close to his chest, trying to glean what the detectives know.

'We think they dug up Francis Hardcastle,' Nell says softly.

'You know for sure it was them?' asks Willard.

'Unless it was you and Ollie,' she says.

'Nothing to do with me,' says Willard.

There's a pause, Willard waiting to see what card Ivan chooses to play.

He tables the trump. 'You and Hec Curtin. In the navy together. Same year. Roommates.'

Willard laughs, phlegmy and moist, no sign of panic in his voice, no sign of anything except amusement. 'Rather a long bow, don't you think?'

'You're not denying you knew him?'

'Sure I knew him. But not well. And it was more than forty years ago. I left the navy, became a lawyer, he stayed and became a clearance diver then an armed robber. We never met again.'

And just then, a terrible thought occurs to Nell. She and Ivan have assumed that Priestly and Barker, the surviving members of the Nautilus Gang, were responsible for digging up Francis Hardcastle's body, intent on establishing his identity. But what if it wasn't them? What if it was Willard? Or his well-trained assistant,

Ollie? What if they had dug him up in order to dispose of the body, make it impossible to prove that Hardcastle was an imposter?

'We don't need the Nautilus Gang,' Ivan says. 'And we don't need the body. We know the real Francis Hardcastle died in San Francisco in 1988.'

Willard is no longer smiling. 'I think I have said enough,' he says formally. 'Now, I have work to do. So either arrest me, or leave me to get on with it. Good day, officers.'

Ivan sits there. Five seconds, ten seconds. More, even as Willard proceeds to work, reading a document, or pretending to do so.

'In that case, you're under arrest,' says Ivan.

Willard looks up, surprise on his face. 'On what charge?'

'For wilfully obstructing a police investigation.'

'Bullshit,' says the lawyer. 'That'll never stick.'

'Doesn't have to,' says Ivan. 'Twenty-four hours in custody and we'll have a lot more to hit you with than that.'

'Ollie as well,' says Nell. 'We'll need to question the two of you. Doesn't matter what about. Where you were when the graveyard in The Valley was desecrated. Where you were the night Wolfgang Burnside was murdered.'

Nell stands, takes a step towards Willard, sees him reach under his desk. And withdraw a handgun. A revolver, huge and black, a glimpse of pearl inlay on the grip. A six-shooter from the Wild West, a collector's item, so large that Willard is wheezing with the effort of bringing it to bear. But even an antique can put a hole the size of an apple in your chest.

Willard pulls the hammer back with his thumb, setting it with a click, a manic glint in his eyes. 'Always wanted to do that,' he says, a lopsided smile making his face appear unhinged.

The door to the outer office opens slowly. Then Ollie enters, brandishing a rifle, not so different from the one he used to shoot Trent Priestly in the leg.

Willard Halliday looks like he's enjoying himself. Which worries the hell out of Nell; the man is smart enough to know this can't end well for him, and yet he seems to be revelling in the moment. His six-shooter is now trained on Ivan; Ollie has his rifle pointed at Nell. Ivan is holding his hands up and she's done the same, almost without thinking. The language of the Western movie, transferred to Saltwood. She feels the weight of her service pistol on her hip, knowing she cannot possibly reach it and live.

'I have never shot anyone and I'd prefer not to start now,' says Willard. 'So this is how it's going to work.' He speaks to Ollie. 'Come round here, mate. Keep your gun on the constable, while I cover Sergeant Lucic.'

The young assistant does as he's instructed, not smiling like his employer, but not seeming in the least bit bothered. Nell remembers how calm he'd been when he shot Priestly, despite having been severely beaten. She wonders how much the young man knows, how deeply implicated he is in Willard's schemes. She wonders if she's underestimated him.

'Okay, this is the tricky bit,' says Willard, addressing Ivan and Nell. 'I need each of you to stand, one at a time, then carefully, very carefully, place your guns on my desk. You first, Constable. And Ollie, if she makes any attempt at all to raise the barrel, shoot her. And I'll do the same to Ivan here.' He smiles again, perhaps trying to be reassuring, perhaps just wanting to be intimidating, perhaps just living out his gunslinger fantasies. 'If we shoot one, we'll have to shoot the other. We won't leave witnesses. But if

I wanted to shoot you, I'd have already done it. Understand? So no false moves and you'll survive.' He turns to Ollie. 'Ready?'

'Ready.' And Ollie smiles his understanding. Smiles. With his cuts and stitches and bruising, he looks like Frankenstein's monster on a first date.

Nell does as she's told, standing slowly, keeping her left hand high while gradually moving her right hand to her holster, turning ever so slightly to give the two gunmen a clear line of sight. She unclips the holster and then, using just her thumb and middle finger, lifts the gun out, holding it like something unpleasant. She takes a slow step forward, lowers it onto the desk. Next to her, Ivan watches, arms still raised. Then it's his turn, and he replicates her motions, placing his Glock on the desktop.

'Excellent,' says Willard. Nell can see the lawyer has relaxed, just a little. And his breathing seems under control. Maybe it's the adrenaline; maybe the wheezing and coughing have been an affectation all along. 'And now your phones, please.'

They repeat the actions, placing the phones on the desk.

'Smash 'em?' asks Ollie.

'No. We'll take them with us. Lay a false trail.' He again speaks to the detectives. 'What will happen now is that we will restrain you. Hogtie you and gag you. Ollie and I will sit here with you just as long as it takes me to transfer some money, make sure it has cleared. And then we will be on our way.' And the lopsided smirk returns. 'You'll be found sooner or later. Hopefully later.'

Ollie is collecting the phones when the door opens. And all hell breaks loose.

It's Claus Barker, armed with a rifle. He belts Ollie in the side of the head with his gun's stock, the assistant sinking wordlessly to the floor. Barker is turning towards Willard when the lawyer's gun goes off, a deafening roar, belching smoke, kicking back wildly, Nell seeing the muzzle flash, orange and red, like a firecracker. She doesn't wait, doesn't hesitate, she goes straight at Willard, even as she sees Barker rock backwards, shot but still upright.

'Don't fire!' yells Ivan, although it's unclear who he's addressing.

Barker glances at Ivan, sees his raised arms, turns back to Willard, now on his feet, who is about to shoot the gunman for the second time. But Nell gets to the lawyer first, reaching for his arm, grasping for the gun, grabbing it, swinging her hip into him, bending her knees so she gets under his centre of gravity, wrenching the gun arm down, barrel aiming at the floor as it discharges for a second time, the reek of cordite and smoke in her nostrils. She twists and wrenches, so that Willard can no longer maintain his grip. The six-shooter hits the floor with a loud clunk, echoed by Barker collapsing behind her, hitting the floor hard next to Ollie. She straightens Willard up, the man disarmed, no longer a threat.

But he is. He's pulled a knife from his cowboy boot, lunges it at her chest. Nell manages to parry the thrust, belt him in the face, kick him in the shins, lift her knee into his scrotum. And then, as he gasps for breath, she takes his knife arm, gets herself underneath him again and lifts with all her might, the lawyer rendered paper-light, so that she flings him clear, out through the ornate window and onto the footpath, where he lies twitching, like the town drunk evicted from a Tombstone saloon. Nell kicks some shards from the edge of the window and climbs out after him. She wants to make sure he stays down.

chapter forty-two

1994

THE FOLLOWING WEEKS, I PRETTY MUCH HIT ROCK BOTTOM. THIS WAS AFTER Max Fuller had told me that Mike and the Sarge had been on Terrence Earl's payroll as part of the forest scam, and after I discovered Lucas had been one of the thugs beating up protesters, and after I realised Eliza was having an affair. I'd never been so low, so utterly gutted. I steered clear of Lucas and Mike and went nowhere near the pub. I didn't want anything to do with Eliza, but I wasn't going to walk out, leave Wolf with her. So we lived under the same roof, but hardly spoke. If it bothered her, she showed no sign of it. Going to work helped get me out of the house, but I dreaded a confrontation with the Sarge. I'd slink in the back entrance, looking for ways to wangle off-site duties: helping with highway patrol or doing welfare checks or assisting at the court-house. But one morning the Sarge sought me out, pulling me aside and asking me how I was doing.

'Been better,' I said, no longer trying to pretend.

He smiled at that, a sardonic grin, like we were sharing a joke. 'Listen, I've some news for you.' The smile faded and he became serious. 'The magistrate will issue the death certificate for Francis Hardcastle later today.'

'That's good,' I said. 'Who identified the body?'

'I did,' said the Sarge. He added, 'Dental records came through.'

'Right.'

'Means that the company can be unfrozen. His shares will pass to Teramina and then on to Amber Jones. She'll own a majority interest. You can tell her, as executor.'

'What's the point?' I asked. 'All the money is long gone.'

'Willard Halliday tell you that?'

'He and I gained access to the accounts; Wallington plundered them,' I replied.

'Yeah, Halliday told me,' he said, brow creased with concentration. 'Nevertheless, if she controls the company, she controls the mine. No contest.'

'That's something, I guess.'

The Sarge was running his eyes over me as he spoke, giving the impression he was judging me. 'Willard said there's evidence, before Wallington stuck his nose in the trough, that Francis stole money from the company.'

'Maybe. There's his signature, looks genuine. A week or so before he died. A lot of money.'

'Good motive for her to shoot him,' he observed.

I knew what he wanted me to say, but I couldn't bring myself to agree with him. 'That doesn't make sense. You're saying she could find out about money missing from the company accounts, but she couldn't find out Wallington was stealing from her personal accounts until after he'd died? According to her, she only found out when she got a new accountant.'

'So she claimed.'

'So the accounts demonstrate.'

The Sarge regarded me coldly. 'Let me guess. Juanita Malakova. Goulburn.'

'You knew?'

'I guessed.'

'Guessed? How?'

'Her practice burnt to the ground two nights ago. Nobody was hurt, but all the records were destroyed.'

That was when the anger kicked in, washing away my despondency. It was all so blatant, done with such impunity. Willard Halliday was the company secretary: why hadn't *his* office been burnt to the ground?

'Listen, there's something else you should know,' the Sarge continued. 'Willard says there's a chance that the company didn't just gather money from shareholders. It seems to have borrowed money, with Teramina going guarantor.'

'I thought she'd already mortgaged Ellensby? Paid off the debt when she sold it.'

'Yes. That was an injection of equity. This is different. She put up Watershine as collateral.'

'What?' I struggled to accept what he was saying. 'She never mentioned that. She told me she'd mortgaged Ellensby; why wouldn't she tell me that?'

'I don't know, son. I'm just the messenger.'

'You're saying that not only will Amber not inherit any money from the company, she'll inherit debt?'

The Sarge shook his head. 'No, mate. It's not me saying it. It's Cowboy Bill and the mortgage holder.'

'What mortgage holder?'

'Terrence Earl.'

I couldn't believe it. Terrence Earl, the former police minister, as corrupt as the bum of a fly-blown sheep. Exposed by Max Fuller, but totally unrepentant. 'Earl? And he has paperwork?'

'Apparently.'

'And Juanita Malakova's records have been destroyed? How fucking convenient is that?' I didn't often get angry, but in that moment I was furious. 'What does Earl want?'

'If I had to guess, I'd say his money back. Or the land.'

I thought of Watershine. That beautiful old house—he wouldn't want that. He already had Ellensby. And then I remembered Giles Duneven, what he'd told me four years earlier: how Earl had helped save the mill. And Amber telling me that Lucas had suggested logging the land. The same Lucas who had been doing Earl's dirty work at the forest protest four years earlier. 'Earl doesn't have a financial interest in Cathcarts, by any chance?' I asked.

The Sarge seemed unsure of himself, just for a moment. 'The sawmill in The Valley? I know he helped save it. A government grant.'

'I reckon he wants access to the escarpment. The state forest up there. And the timber on Amber's land.' I shook my head in disbelief. 'So while he was building an eco-resort and expanding the national park when it suited him, he's also keen to log more native forest.'

The Sarge studied me through narrowed eyes, as if ascertaining my loyalty, and hitched up his trousers. 'Slow down, son. You're getting ahead of yourself.'

But I was on a roll. Furious, indignant. Emboldened. 'We've got to push back,' I said. 'We can't just let him steamroll Amber. Steamroll us.'

The Sarge didn't reply, not for a long moment. I felt he was still reassessing me. And then, with a kind of weariness in his voice, 'We've been through this. We took money, we're compromised.' And for emphasis: 'Fucked three ways to Friday.'

I was so incensed, I was careless of what I said. 'That's not all, is it?' I demanded. 'That protest at Fowlers Gap. The thugs, arresting those protesters—you were in on it.'

'Who said that?'

'Max Fuller. From a source in Special Branch.'

Now it was the Sarge's turn to appear harried and defensive. He hoicked up his trousers again; now it appeared more like a nervous tic than a considered gesture. Then he looked around, making sure we were alone. 'It goes deeper than that.'

'What do you mean?'

'Earl and Teramina,' he said.

'What? What about them?'

'The two richest, most powerful families in the district. The Cloverton old money down in The Valley, Earl's flash new money up above.'

'Dirty money,' I said.

'Don't be too fast to judge, son. Earl saved the mill. Kept jobs in The Valley. People like Roddie Game. He'd have been out on his arse. Not like Francis Hardcastle and Teramina Cloverton, scamming people out of our money.'

But I couldn't let it go. 'So what should I tell Amber?'

'I'd tell her to sell her land to Terrence Earl and move on.'

'How can I do that?'

'Do I have to spell it out?' He lowered his voice. 'Think of what happened to Francis. And to Teramina. These people play for keeps. Think of Amber. Think of Eliza and Wolfgang. Think of them.'

And he left me standing there, slack-jawed, out of words. *Think of what happened to Francis. And to Teramina.* And I did think of Francis and Teramina. And I did think of Amber. And of Eliza. But most of all I thought of Wolf, and what sort of father I should be, what sort of example I should set, and what sort of world I wanted him growing up in.

At the end of my shift, I went to the armoury, where we checked our guns of an evening, and took an extra box of ammunition. I didn't sign for it. And that night I took my service pistol home with me.

chapter forty-three

AMBER DIDN'T WAKE UNTIL LATE. SHE'D SLEPT WELL DESPITE HER EARLY-HOURS discoveries in the journals of the original mining company. It should have been making her feel anxious; instead, some things at least were starting to make sense. Like why Lucas couldn't find any gold, and why Teramina had been so distressed by the disappearance of her husband. And why someone had murdered Francis Hardcastle. The old records had brought comfort rather than anxiety; they gave her a guide to her future. If there was no gold, then there could be no mine. Yet she had the house, and she had the land. That was enough. More than enough. If she stayed in The Valley, she could find a job, enough to pay the rates and her bills, give her time to work out what to do next. And if she didn't need money to develop the Gryphon, then she could easily refuse the loggers access to her road.

She'd just made a pot of tea and some toast when she heard a car approaching. She thought it must be Lucas, or maybe Mike. She'd be able to talk it over with them, finalise her decision to cut her losses and seal the mine once and for all. Move on. But it was

Simmons Burnside who climbed the stairs and knocked at her door. She was glad to see him; he'd been a loyal friend to Teramina and to her. He would be a good sounding board. But he was wearing his uniform, had a gun in his holster. She hoped he wasn't on official duty, that this wasn't due to some complication involving Francis Hardcastle's death.

Amber invited him in, offered him tea, apologised that she had no coffee or milk.

'Tea will be fine,' he said and followed her into the kitchen. 'How's the mining going?' he asked. His tone was one of small talk, making conversation.

'Not good,' she said. 'I think it's over.'

'Really? What's happened?'

'There is no gold. Lucas and Mike have been searching. Even exploratory blasting. They can only find trace amounts. Uneconomical.'

Simmons looked at her, his features motionless, apparently deep in thought. 'That doesn't make sense,' he said, but she could hear in the way he framed the sentence that it was starting to.

She described her search through the old records. 'I think Francis Hardcastle was a con man. The gold wasn't real. He was salting the mine with fake nuggets. The whole project was a ruse to steal Teramina's money.'

'I think you might be right. But I think that might only be half the story.'

She poured his tea, passed it to him. 'What's the other half?'

'I think it's true. He probably was a con man. He seduced her and he defrauded her, persuading her to mortgage Ellensby and invest in the Gryphon Number Two company. More than a million dollars.'

'A million dollars? How do you know that?'

'I told you before, remember? Willard Halliday and I got access to the records. The money was withdrawn from the company the week before Francis was murdered. His signature appears to be genuine.'

'He took it?' asked Amber.

'Yes. But only a million. Fred Wallington siphoned off a lot more after Francis was dead.'

'I don't understand,' said Amber. 'Whose money was that?'

'I'm not sure. I think whoever it was, they were using the company to launder money, pretending they were finding gold.'

'So why didn't Francis take that as well?'

'I'm guessing he was scared. A million dollars was what Teramina had invested, maybe a little less. I think he was taking it back out but leaving the rest of the money there, the money that didn't belong to her.' Simmons paused, perhaps deciding on what to say next. 'I know it sounds silly, but I think Francis fell in love with her. Or felt guilty. Wanted to get her money back. So he only withdrew her money from the account, left the rest, and hoped those behind the scheme would let them go.' He took a sip of tea, watching her closely. 'I saw the two of them together at the pub, the night before Francis died. They were so happy together. So in love.'

Amber felt a little flutter in her heart. Her friend and benefactor, so close to the happiness, the relationship she had sought for so long. 'Those behind the scheme? You don't think Francis was the instigator?'

'No. I suspect he was just a front man, hired to play a role.'

Amber found herself studying the teapot, an antique inherited from Teramina. 'So who was behind it? And where did the money come from?'

'I suspect a man called Terrence Earl. Member of state parliament. Local member. Former police minister in the last government.'

'The man involved in this logging scandal?'

'The same.'

'So where did the other money come from?'

'I honestly don't know. Some from local investors, but I think that's small change. More a smokescreen than anything, a veneer of plausibility. The bulk of the money, I have no idea.'

'But why gold? Why the mine? It seems very elaborate.'

'I don't know that either. But what better way to launder money than a fake goldmine? Maybe that's why they flooded it. Not just to hide the body, but to hide the fact that there is no longer any gold there.'

'Well, it's all over now. I'm going to close the company.' And as she said the words, she realised it was true, she had already made the decision—or, rather, the decision had come to her. It was the right thing to do. She poured more tea from Teramina's antique pot; it tasted good.

'I'm afraid it's not that easy,' he said, and she could hear the foreboding in his tone.

'Why not? Aren't I the major shareholder?'

'You are. But apparently there are records showing that Terrence Earl lent money to the company, and that Teramina went guarantor on the loan. That she put up Watershine and the land here as collateral.'

'Why would she do that?'

'I have no idea. Maybe she acted under duress. It's even possible the documents are forgeries.'

'Can we prove that?'

'I doubt it.' And he told her about Juanita Malakova, the fire at her office, the destruction of the records. 'I spoke to her this morning. She's scared, says the fire was deliberately lit.'

Amber put her cup on the kitchen bench, suddenly angered at the injustice. Who were these people; why were they so intent on erasing any remnant of Teramina's legacy? 'So they might seize all of this? You're saying we can't fight them?'

And she saw a grimness in Simmons's eyes, this strong man, this policeman. 'I'm not sure it would be wise to try.' And he hung his head. 'It might not be safe.'

Her eyes widened. 'You're saying I could be in danger?'

'Yes. That's exactly what I'm afraid of.' His distress was evident. 'Someone killed them. Francis for sure, maybe Teramina as well.'

Amber looked about her, feeling herself floundering, before turning back to Simmons. 'What should I do then?'

'Honestly? I think you should leave. For your own safety. At least for a while.'

She stared at him then, and it occurred to her that maybe she shouldn't trust him. Where was his evidence? What was to say he wasn't the one with the hidden agenda?

'I want to talk it over with Lucas,' she said.

Simmons regarded her with something resembling regret. 'No,' he said. 'Not Lucas.'

She wanted to sound defiant, but when she spoke, the words were more of a whisper. 'Why not?'

He reached into his bag, withdrew a copy of the *Sydney Morning Herald*, Max Fuller's big exposé, and opened it to the photo spread. He pointed to one image in particular. Her eyes were drawn to the face of Mike Norfolk, cowering, as a man in a black ski mask was about to hit him. She looked up to Simmons, and he pointed back to the photo, to the assailant's wrist. And she saw it, the tattoo. The trident. She gasped.

'Lucas works for Terrence Earl,' said Simmons. 'At least, he has done so in the past.'

'No,' whispered Amber. 'No.' And she thought of her lover's excitement about the road, for getting the loggers to pay for its upgrade, advocating that she sell some of her timber. The cedar grove.

She felt like she was about to collapse, that the world was about to give way, that it could no longer support her. And then Simmons had his arms around her, holding her. And she fell into him and grasped him tight, as though he were a lifebuoy in a rough sea.

They stood there for a long moment, just holding each other, afloat in their own private ocean.

'We should talk to that journalist,' Amber said at last, pulling away. 'Max Fuller.'

'If we do that, there's no going back. There is no running away. You understand that? The danger?'

Before she could answer, they heard the sound of a car arriving.

She hoped it might be Fuller, miraculously arrived from Sydney. Or even Mike and Suzie. But when they rushed to the lounge, peered out the window, she saw a police car pulling up next to Simmons's vehicle. The Sarge. And with him, Lucas Trescothic.

'Go,' said Simmons. 'Run.'

And she did, fleeing out the back door.

chapter forty-four

THE SARGE DIDN'T BOTHER KNOCKING. HE FLUNG OPEN THE DOOR AND BARGED straight in, Lucas trailing him like a dog behind his master.

'Where is she?' asked the Sarge, not bothering with pleasantries.

'Don't know,' I said, straining to sound calm. 'I'm waiting for her myself.' I figured the longer I stalled, the more time Amber would have to get away.

The Sarge sneered at me. 'Lucas, go check if her bike is here.'

'Really? Me?' Lucas said.

'Really. You. I want to talk to the constable. In private.' And then, to make himself clear: 'I don't require a witness.'

Lucas seemed a bit scared by that and beat a hasty retreat back out the front door.

'You've spoken to Juanita Malakova,' he said.

'I have,' I said. There wasn't much point in denying it.

He smiled; I thought he was pleased by my candour. Then he added, 'And placed a call to Dereck Packenham in Sydney.'

That shocked me. How could he possibly know that? I hadn't even left a message. Was my phone at Saltwood police station being monitored?

His smile had vanished when he spoke again. 'So you appreciate the lie of the land.'

'Getting there,' I said.

'So why come here?'

'I'm the executor of Teramina Hardcastle's will. Amber Jones is the beneficiary. I have a legal obligation.'

'What did you tell her?'

'She's not here.'

The Sarge sighed, hoisted his pants. 'She's a nice girl. Very young. Innocent. It would be a shame if anything happened to her.'

'It would be,' I said. 'For all concerned.' It probably wasn't the smartest thing to say, but I was sick of being bullied by him.

I'm not sure how he interpreted my response, but what he said next chilled me, even if I was already most of the way there. I guess it was how he made it sound almost matter-of-fact. 'We need her to sell her land. She'll get some money, a fair amount, under the circumstances. Then she can just walk away. No one gets hurt.'

'Who's we?' I asked.

'Not your concern. You just need to persuade her.'

'Why not Lucas? They're close.'

'She's stopped listening to him.'

'She might be young, Sarge, but she's got a mind of her own. What if she refuses?'

'She risks ending up like Teramina. And you end up being a liability.' He left the threat hanging in the air.

But I wasn't intimidated, not by him, not anymore. 'So how did Teramina end up, Sarge?'

Obswith just shook his head, as if despairing of me. 'You were the one crying poor, Simmons. The one who lapped up the extra pay, and the police TA, and living in this place rent-free. Well, now's your opportunity to make some real money. She sells the land, you get a split.'

'No,' I said. 'We can do without your money.'

'Fuck you,' he said. 'You always were a dumb cunt.' And he pulled out his service revolver and shot me in the chest. Just like that. Once, then again. I remember the muzzle flash; it was quite impressive. And the noise: so loud. And the look on his face, and the way his mouth opened. Aghast.

'Blanks,' I said. 'I visited the armoury last night.' And I pulled my own gun. 'Maybe not such a dumb cunt after all.'

Then two things happened. No, three. First, the front door burst open, revealing Lucas. I had my gun on him straight away. I'd anticipated that. 'Join us,' I said.

He stepped inside, hands up.

The second thing was Amber striding into the room from the kitchen, holding something, right behind me. I hadn't anticipated that. I half turned, and then the third thing: the Sarge rushed me. So maybe I really was a dumb cunt. He shoulder-charged me and I hit the floor, desperately trying to hold on to my gun instead of cushioning my fall. I landed hard, the weapon went flying, and he was all over me, a crazed animal, clawing at me, trying to get at the gun I no longer held.

From the corner of my eye, like a film that's been edited too quickly, I saw Lucas scrambling for it, only to be collected by

Amber wielding a frypan. It rang like a temple gong when she belted him in the head. He went down and stayed down.

The Sarge was still attacking me, clawing at my arms. Amber darted past us, seized my gun.

'Get off him,' she said, and when the Sarge didn't seem to hear, she said it louder. 'Off him. Now!'

The Sarge saw the gun and stopped. He was breathing hard, like a heart attack in progress. He leant back. 'You little slut,' he said. 'You wouldn't dare.'

'You think I'm going to let you do to me what you did to Teramina?' she said. 'I heard what you said.' There was steel in her voice. 'Get up.'

The Sarge did. Stood up slowly. I was still on the floor, gathering myself, just starting to rise. I looked at Amber, the gun pointed at Obswith, determination on her face. I recall how large the revolver was compared to the size of her hands.

He hoisted his pants one last time. 'You wouldn't fucking dare,' he said again. And charged her.

So she shot him. Just the once. But it was enough.

'Wouldn't I?' she whispered.

But the Sarge could no longer hear her.

chapter forty-five

2024

IT'S MID-AFTERNOON AND THE SALTWOOD POLICE STATION IS UNDER SIEGE BY media, helicopters swooping overhead, journalists salivating at the front gate. A second shootout in two days is almost too good to be true. Saltwood is growing more and more like Deadwood by the minute. Ivan and Nell are inside the station, in the squad room, the television on the wall beaming in pictures of a Doug Thunkleton report from just outside.

'What a fucking mess,' says Ivan

'Hear from Plodder?' asks Nell.

'Strangely silent,' says Ivan.

Willard is in the local hospital, complaining of chest pains, under guard, the room next to Trent Priestly. Claus Barker has been airlifted to Canberra and is still in surgery, touch and go whether he'll survive. Ollie, full name Oliver Halliday, is in the cells refusing to talk, insisting on a lawyer, insisting that his uncle Willard be that lawyer.

There's a knock at the door, and Alice Wheelright enters, wearing a substantial grin.

'Glad you've got something to smile about,' says Ivan.

'Good news. Barker should pull through. And Willard's fine.'

'That's something, at least,' says Nell.

'Also, there's a couple of people here to see you. Promising information. Trent Priestly. With his lawyer.'

Nell and Ivan exchange a look.

'Well, please show them in,' says Ivan. And then adds: 'To an interview room.'

When Ivan and Nell enter, they are met with a stony glare from Priestly. He wears every one of his sixty-seven years, tempered and tough, skin like leather, eyes hooded and unflinching, his hospital crutches leaning against the table.

The solicitor is a young woman, dressed in a messily assembled suit, her dark hair a bob gone feral, streaked with purple and a seemingly random splotch of green. One arm of her glasses is patched with sticky tape. But when she speaks, introducing herself as Georgie Flores, her voice is clear and her accent refined; she sounds authoritative. 'My client has come here voluntarily. Wants to speak, wants to help.'

'Wants immunity,' says Ivan.

'Indeed,' says Flores.

Ivan shakes his head. 'Big ask. He's up to his neck in it.'

Nell adds for emphasis, 'Kidnapping. Abduction. Assault. Unlicensed firearm. Discharging a gun in a public place. Vehicle theft. Conspiracy. Resisting arrest. Quite the list. Not to mention graverobbing.'

'The way I hear it, his colleague saved your arse, lady. And took a bullet for his trouble,' says the lawyer, sounding unimpressed.

Nell bristles, but holds her tongue.

'What do you want?' asks Ivan.

'We've come with information. Off the record. Then it's up to you. If my client's knowledge is useful, maybe we can cut a deal and he can go on the record.'

Ivan looks to Nell, raises an eyebrow. She shrugs. 'Okay. Let's hear it,' he tells Priestly's solicitor. 'Off the record.'

'First thing,' says Flores. 'My client was convicted for participating in the Botany Warehouse Heist. That's in the past; he's served his time. We aren't revisiting those events or those charges.'

'That's not an issue we're investigating,' Ivan tells her. 'Not directly.' He turns to Priestly. 'What have you got for us?'

'I've spent enough time in prison. So has Claus. We don't want to go back.'

'I'm listening.'

'We didn't kill Wolfgang Burnside.'

'Glad to hear it.'

'We were in contact with him. Arranged to come to The Valley, to meet him, but he was dead by the time we got here.'

'Can you prove that?'

The lawyer interjects. 'We are willing to make the telephone handsets of Mr Priestly and possibly of Mr Barker available to you. You will be able to see encrypted messages between my client and Mr Burnside. Also tracking information that will show you my clients were still in Sydney on the night Mr Burnside was murdered.'

Nell can see Ivan rock back in his chair, understanding that the offer is unusual, a sign of good faith. And possibly of innocence.

'Why were you in contact with Wolfgang Burnside?' Ivan asks.

'He'd found gold. Nuggets. He sent one to be appraised by a goldsmith. An expert in such matters. This expert, he contacted us. The nugget wasn't real. It was fabricated. From our gold.'

Nell smiles.

So does Ivan. 'Your gold? The Botany Warehouse bullion?'

'The goldsmith knew his stuff; he contacted us.'

'Interesting goldsmith,' says Ivan.

'Let's leave him out of it,' says Flores.

'Let's,' Ivan agrees. 'My partner and I are chasing killers, not fences and upmarket pawnbrokers.' He nods at Trent Priestly. 'Go on.'

'We don't know if this Wolfgang bloke knew what he'd found. I doubt it. But he agreed to meet with us. We were on our way south, when we heard he'd been killed.'

'Right,' says Ivan. 'So what did you do next?'

'Well, we started snooping around. Heard the story about the old goldmine up on the hill. About Francis Hardcastle being found shot dead in the bottom of it. We figured someone was using the mine to rebirth our gold.'

'Fair assumption. Is that why you dug him up?'

'This is in no way a confession,' stipulates the lawyer. 'We are off the record.'

Priestly doesn't wait for Ivan's agreement. 'Yeah, we dug him up. We figured we could run DNA, check him out.'

'And did you?'

'Still waiting on the results.'

'So you suspect the man in the grave is not the real Francis Hardcastle, but the one member of the gang who hasn't been accounted for.'

'Possibly,' says Priestly.

'We'll need to recover the body,' says Ivan.

'Sure. It's not going anywhere.'

'Why did you try to kidnap Willard Halliday?' asks Nell.

'Straightforward. We did some research on the mine, on the company. Saw the principals were dead, saw the accountant was dead, but the company secretary was still alive. So we arranged a visit. Just a chat, you understand? He wasn't interested at first, not until we mentioned the gold. Then he agreed to meet us, just outside of town, near Halfchurch. But when we turned up at the rendezvous spot, that halfwit who shot Claus in the leg was there with this other thug. They told us it was time to get out of Dodge, said there was nothing here for us, that we should fuck off before we ended up like Wolfgang Burnside.'

'They threatened to kill you?'

'That's how we understood it, yes.'

'Did they know who you were?' asks Nell. 'About your past, your involvement with the warehouse job?'

Priestly shakes his head. 'If they did, they didn't say anything. And if they knew who we were, they were pretty stupid thinking we'd leave just because they told us to.' The old crim laughs at the thought, a mocking little cackle. 'That's when we thought we might pay this Willard character a visit and put the wind up him. And give that insolent young bastard a bit of a touch-up at the same time. I guess we underestimated him.'

Ivan looks at Priestly, then Flores, then back again. 'Don't suppose you have any proof of this rendezvous, do you? The one where they tried to scare you off?'

'Thought you might ask that.' Priestly pulls out his phone, taps away at the screen, opens the photo app. There's an image, askew and a little out of focus, of the back of a large man, presumably Barker, face to face with Oliver Halliday and another man, standing in front of a van.

'Whoa,' says Ivan. 'May I?'

'I guess,' says Priestly, handing the phone over. 'Just that image, though. Don't go scrolling.'

Ivan takes the phone, studies the image closely, then passes it to Nell. She feels her heart rate pick up a notch.

'They were driving this van?' asks Ivan.

'Yeah. What of it?'

'A lemon-coloured van? That was theirs?'

'I said yes.'

'And do you know who this other man is? The one standing next to Willard Halliday's assistant?'

'Nup,' says Priestly.

Ivan addresses the lawyer. 'This is important. You mind if I ask one of the local officers to come in just for a moment, to see if she can identify this second man?'

'We getting close to a deal?' asks Flores.

'This stacks up, you've got it.'

'Okay?' the lawyer asks Priestly.

'Sure,' says Priestly, sounding both resigned and hopeful.

Nell does the honours, heading out to find Alice Wheelright, inviting her in.

The senior sergeant enters; Ivan shows her the photo.

'That's the van Vicary was searching for,' she says without prompting.

'And Oliver Halliday. Do you know who the other man is? Looks young.'

'Ellory Earl,' says Alice. 'Entitled dickhead.'

'Earl?' asks Nell. 'Not related to Terrence Earl, disgraced former police minister? Or to Hannibal Earl, member of state parliament?'

'Yeah, Hannibal's nephew,' says Alice, her distaste obvious.

Nell sees in Ivan's eyes what she feels in her guts: breakthrough.

They thank Alice and wait for her to leave before Ivan addresses the lawyer. 'You've got yourself a deal.' He reaches over and shakes Priestly's hand. 'You've done the right thing. A good thing.'

'First time for everything,' says Priestly, before adding, 'But I want Claus off the hook. Protected. And no jail time.'

Ivan leans in. 'Your evidence may prove pivotal. In the conviction of Wolfgang Burnside's murderer, but maybe much more. I'll do whatever I can to see you and Barker are kept out of prison.'

The lawyer turns to Priestly. Their eyes meet, Flores nods, Priestly turns back to Ivan. 'Glad to be of service.'

'Before you go, something in return,' says Nell. 'Your DNA test. We don't think Hardcastle was the missing member of the Nautilus Gang. We suspect he was some sort of front man. An actor, or an experienced con artist. Possibly American. We'll run our own DNA when we recover the body; it might help us identify him.'

Priestly grunts. 'Yeah. We weren't sure. The photos of Hardcastle didn't match our recollections of our fellow.'

'I thought we weren't revisiting the robbery,' says the lawyer.

'We don't intend to,' says Nell. 'But it's clear that one or two gang members survived the shootout at the warehouse and the fire at the woolshed. One would be Radovan Burke, known as Raz. Died of his wounds about a week after the fire. Do you know who the survivor was, Trent? The one who must have brought the gold and the money to The Valley?'

'Not his name. Most of us hadn't met each other before. The survivor was a young bloke, called himself Guy, but I reckon that was just a cover name. But I can tell you how you might identify him. A physical trait.'

'What is it?'

'Let's sign that immunity agreement first.'

chapter forty-six

1994

IT WAS WINTER IN THE GREAT EXPANSE OF BARMAH-MILLEWA, THE LARGEST river red gum forest in the world. Amber stayed in her shack on its hidden island, distancing herself from humanity, restoring the small house, not much more than a hut, patching the roof, fixing a leak that had developed in her absence. If her mother had returned during Amber's time in The Valley, she could find no sign of her. She wished her mother were with her; after months of company, the solitude felt disconcerting.

Suzie had driven her out through the row of leafless poplars, up the pass to Saltwood, intending to take her to Goulburn for the train. And then, taking pity on her, driving her all the way to Albury, by which time Amber had recovered enough to go the rest of the way alone. But still she found herself revisiting that awful moment, recoiling from herself. She had shot a man, killed him. She'd always been a good shot; her grandfather had taught her at a young age. But that was different: a rifle, at distance, a considered action, the trigger gently squeezed. And only rabbits to eat or wild dogs to cull; never a kangaroo or a possum or a bird. And later, after her grandfather had died, she'd put the gun away, relying on snares and fishing. And now she'd put a bullet in another human being.

At the time, she hadn't hesitated. It was necessary; it was self-defence. In that moment, she had been her grandfather's grand-daughter: steely with resolve. Only afterwards, as Suzie whisked her away, did the enormity of her actions catch up with her: chasing her up the pass and along the highway to overwhelm her. It took several days in her own place, finding solace in her forest, for her to start coming to terms with what she had done, to slowly rebuild herself. To heal.

Simmons sought her out some weeks later, found her secure in her redoubt. She was glad to see him, no longer wanting to run and hide. She wanted to thank him, thank him for all that he had done, for her and for the memory of Teramina. That awful day, she hadn't run from the house; she had stayed, hidden in the kitchen, overhearing the conversation, Cornell Obswith attempting to persuade Simmons, to entice him. She'd heard Obswith's pitch and she'd heard Simmons resist the temptation, standing firm, putting his own life on the line to protect her. It was something to cling to: the knowledge that there were good men in the world.

The day he arrived, the mist had gathered low on the water, and pelicans floated like an armada on her lagoon. The sun was weak and the air was winter-cold when he made his way to her, having found her directions waiting for him at the Tulong store, leaving his car, walking over her suspension bridge and entering her woods. She'd tidied the modest hut, lit the pot-belly stove, baked bread, prepared a stew.

She wasn't sure how she would react when he arrived; even when she saw him approaching over the bridge, she didn't know. She simply stood and watched in wonder that he had made the journey, and found tears emerging unbidden.

'Hello, Amber,' he said.

'You've come,' she said.

'Of course.'

And without thinking, she hugged him, and it felt proper and it felt good to feel him hug her back.

Later, as they sat looking out over the lagoon, drinking tea, rugged up against the cold, watching the pelicans drift on the sunset waters, she asked after Eliza and Wolfgang.

'We've split up,' he said. 'It's run its course.'

'I'm sorry,' she said.

'Don't be. It was never going to last. I told her I wanted to quit the police, to live and work in The Valley, to be a real family. She said she didn't want that. Didn't want me.'

She heard no self-pity in his voice and was impressed by his stoicism. 'So you're no longer a policeman? Nor married?'

'Neither for much longer.'

'Where will you go?'

'Not far. Not with Wolf there. I won't abandon him. He'll need me more than ever.'

'Stay in Watershine then. Care for it.'

'I'd love that so much, but I can't. Nobody can know we've been cooperating, that we're linked.' He reached out, held her hand.

'Don't write. Don't get in contact. Nobody can learn where you are, nobody can learn we have colluded in this matter.'

'Never?'

'Not for a long time.'

Later, as they ate together, she asked what was happening with Lucas. 'He's been charged. It's out of my hands now. The detectives have carriage of the case.'

'It's not right,' she said. 'Lucas didn't shoot Obswith; I did.'

'It is right,' he assured her.

'We were so close, Lucas and me. I can't believe he was helping the sergeant.'

'You should know the truth,' said Simmons. 'It's important.'

'Tell me. I'm ready for it now.'

'I can prove none of this, and it would be dangerous for me to try. But I believe Lucas Trescothic was the agent of Terrence Earl. Right from the very beginning, Earl recruited Lucas. Had him do his dirty work, like beating up environmentalists at the forestry protest.'

'Did he kill Francis?' asked Amber, unsure if she wanted to hear the answer. She had fallen hard for Lucas, his handsome face and lithe body, his laconic manner and hedonistic good humour. She'd slept with him and enjoyed it. Revelled in it. That was just weeks ago; now the memory repulsed her.

'I don't think so. He was just a pawn, kept ignorant. That was why he was keen to reopen the mine, why he was shocked to find Francis murdered, why he thought he could find gold. Earl was manipulating him, feeding him some information, withholding some.'

'Why did they want to reopen the mine?'

'I'm not sure. I think they believed Francis had hidden gold down there. But Lucas couldn't find it.'

'So why did he remain loyal to Earl?'

'I don't know. But at the end, he made his choice: he came with Obswith to Watershine. I found papers they'd brought with them: they were going to force you to sign over Watershine. That's all we really need to know.'

'Will you try and expose them? Tell Max Fuller?'

Simmons shook his head, a heaviness to his expression. 'No. We can't risk them finding you. Or discovering who really shot the Sarge.'

— —

Simmons stayed another day, then another, and then a week, and she was so glad to have him there. They grew closer and closer in that small space, huddled together, supporting each other as they came to terms with the recent past and started once again to look towards the future. Sorrow passed through friendship and into hope, so that by the end of the week they were laughing together. Sleeping together, in the shack's one bed, sheltering from the cold as the easterlies brought the touch of snow from the alps and the southerlies from Antarctica. They started to make plans, trying to find a way for him to be close to both her and his son. But eventually, he needed to leave, needed to see Wolfgang, needed to put distance between himself and Amber lest someone suspected a conspiracy and placed her in danger once more.

The winter rains arrived the day he left, and she hunkered down in the shack, reading and cooking and venturing out for long forest walks. Some weeks later she discovered she was pregnant. It frightened her; she thought the child must be Simmons's, hoped it was, but there was always the possibility that Lucas was the father. She wrote to Simmons, an anonymous letter, posted from Echuca, couched in terms only he would understand, but she never heard back. She wondered if Eliza had intercepted it, kept it from him. A tension grew within her, between wanting him to know and understanding his request that they remain incommunicado.

She ventured to Boonlea, eager for books. And one day in the library there, she saw a newspaper article by the journalist Max Fuller: MURDER IN THE VALLEY. She read it. Lucas pleading guilty, the court accepting the written statements from herself and Simmons. Their lies.

Finally, a letter arrived from Simmons, the postmark from Canberra, with no return address. Willard Halliday was still seeking her; Simmons advised her not to write, to await his instructions.

So she stayed in her shack, full of anticipation. The baby was coming. That was her immediate priority, that and nothing else, but afterwards there was a whole world waiting for her. The Valley beckoned: she could reclaim Watershine, eventually she could build a new life for herself and her child.

PART FOUR

PART FOUR

chapter forty-seven

2024

NELL AND IVAN FLY INTO COOLANGATTA, COLLECT THEIR HIRE CAR AND SET OFF across the Border Ranges back into New South Wales, to Murwillumbah and the luminous green of the cane fields, past the grandeur of Wollumbin Mount Warning, and up the winding road to Nimbin, hippie capital of Australia.

Nell's grandmother has told her of this town, its alternative lifestyle, its communal ethos. They park the car, walk up the hill to the main street and into the Aquarius Café. And there, waiting for them, are Mike Norfolk and his partner Suzie Cocheef. Mike is looking fit, decked out in hippie chic: a hemp shirt, drawstring trousers and Jesus sandals, his auburn hair turning white with age, worn in a ponytail. He's wearing an Apple watch; Suzie's time-piece is more traditionally upmarket, and her silk caftan shimmers as she moves. 'Our youngest,' she says proudly, indicating one of the waitresses.

'I can see you in her,' says Nell.

'Thanks for meeting us,' Ivan says. 'We appreciate it.'

'Glad we can help. He's a real hermit these days. Keeps to himself.'

'You're sure you know where to find him?' asks Nell.

'Absolutely,' says Mike. 'He lives on our land. We let him stay for a bit when he got out of prison, and he's never left. Whatever he's done in the past, he's a gentle soul now. I hope you haven't come to upset him.'

'I don't intend to,' says Nell. 'But it's important that I meet him.'

'You want to come in our car? There's plenty of room and it's just five minutes. Otherwise follow us.'

'We'll drive ourselves, thanks,' says Ivan.

—◦—

They follow Mike and Suzie's car, a top-of-the-range Audi. They don't go far out of town, delayed only by some roadworks, half the road flood-damaged, before turning into a tree-lined drive, across a cattle grate, following the German SUV around an impressive ornamental lake and up to a log cabin-style house, with large feature windows overlooking the valley.

'Quite something,' says Nell when the four of them regroup on the driveway.

'We're very lucky; got in before the boom,' says Mike. 'We'll walk the rest of the way. It's not far.'

They leave Suzie at the house and Mike leads the way across a patch of lawn behind it, up a path through a dense thicket of bamboo, stems as thick as telegraph poles, then over a nascent creek, and into the rainforest. And there, nestled into the bush, is a modest mudbrick house with a small deck above a fenced-off vegetable garden, bougainvillea in bloom, like a postcard from Tahiti.

'He knows you're coming,' says Mike. 'I'm curious to know what you want with him after all these years.'

'You're welcome to stay,' says Nell. 'He may feel more comfortable with a friend to support him.'

A man steps out onto the deck. His long hair is still a rich brown, though his bushranger beard is streaked with grey.

'Lucas Trescothic?' asks Ivan.

'That's me.'

'I'm Detective Sergeant Ivan Lucic. This is Detective Senior Constable Nell Buchanan.'

The man regards them, and Nell feels a sort of melancholy lingering about him, like he has soaked in resignation so long it's become part of him. 'Come up, then.'

Inside the house there is just enough room for the four of them in the sitting room. It has a subdued comfort to it, handcrafted from recycled material, every item simultaneously second-hand and original.

'You understand why we're here?' asks Ivan gently.

'Not really,' says Lucas. 'Mike said you were investigating the death of Simmons Burnside's son Wolfgang, but I can't see how I could possibly help you with that. It's thirty years since I set foot in The Valley.'

Ivan goes to answer, and then defers to Nell.

She gives her partner a quick smile, appreciating his discretion, then turns her attention to Lucas Trescothic. 'My apologies for intruding, but there are some matters we need to clear up. As part of the investigation, but also because it affects me personally.' She can see the man's puzzlement, and she swallows hard before continuing. 'You were charged with the murder of police sergeant Cornell Obswith in May 1994. You pleaded guilty. That's correct, isn't it?'

Lucas seems troubled, staring at his hands. Nell can see the distinctive tattoo on his wrist. A trident, the edges blurred with the years. He sighs, as though he's reluctant to revisit the past. 'Yes. That's right.'

'We had cause to review the evidence at your trial. You were represented by a local lawyer, Willard Halliday.'

'Didn't do me much good,' says Lucas. 'Spent most of the time posturing in front of the judge instead of advocating for leniency.'

'You pleaded guilty despite claiming you had no memory of the crime. I assume that's still the case, the memory hasn't returned?'

Lucas frowns. 'No. I still have no recollection of what happened.'

Nell can see that Mike Norfolk also looks perplexed.

Lucas continues. 'I was laid out cold by Simmons Burnside, defending himself after I shot Obswith. I was unconscious for a good fifteen minutes, and when I came to, I'd lost my short-term memory. I don't even recall arriving at the house. Watershine. So no, I can't remember shooting Sergeant Obswith.'

'Can you remember why you shot him?'

'No.'

'So why plead guilty?'

'There were witnesses. Amber and Simmons. They were there when it happened. And DNA. Willard said pleading guilty would expedite matters and the judge might be more lenient in sentencing.'

'I understand,' says Nell. 'So neither Amber nor Simmons had to give sworn evidence before the court? Their statements were enough?'

'I think that's right, yes. I remember that Amber wasn't there for the trial. I never saw her again.'

'But she had been your girlfriend, correct?'

'That's right. For a month or two. I loved her very much; I just didn't realise it at the time. I became obsessed with the mine and finding gold, instead of understanding she was the real treasure.' Lucas hangs his head, stares at the floor. 'When I was a child, I became obsessed with Greek myths. I thought I had outgrown them. But now I look back and see the mine as a Pandora's box. We should never have opened it, been content with what we had. What I had. That was on me, I was the one who pushed it. Now I live here, full of regrets.'

Next to him, Mike Norfolk leans across, rests a hand on his shoulder momentarily.

'If you were her boyfriend, I assume you were sleeping together?'

'What?' Lucas looks half confused, half insulted. 'Why would you ask that?'

'I'm sorry. Trust me, I know this isn't easy. One more question, though, before I tell you the other reason we've come.'

Lucas says nothing, brows knitted in concentration and concern.

Nell pushes on, deciding to get it over with. 'Is it true that, well before you met Amber Jones, you also slept with Eliza Tomsett, who lived at the general store in The Valley?'

Now Lucas really does appear lost. He's rubbing at his wrist, the one with the tattoo, with his other hand. 'Yes. I did. I'm not sure . . .' And he stops mid-sentence.

'You're not sure you were the only one. Is that what you were about to say?'

Lucas closes his eyes. 'Yes.'

'What's this about?' asks Mike.

Nell takes a deep breath. 'When Wolfgang Burnside was murdered, a DNA test revealed that he was my half-brother. Same father, different mothers. His mother was Eliza Tomsett; my mother was Amber Jones.'

There is a moment of silence, of absolute stillness; both Mike and Lucas are staring at her, eyes scouring her face, searching for signs of the familiar, for echoes of Amber.

'You're my daughter?' manages Lucas at last.

'According to your DNA, as provided in evidence at the trial.'

'My God,' says Lucas.

'I was born in 1995,' says Nell. 'The fourteenth of March.' From nowhere, she can feel tears coming, pushes them down.

'But . . .' says Lucas. 'No.' And then: 'That can't be. Nine months before that, I was already in custody.'

'You couldn't have slept with my mother in June 1994?'

Lucas shakes his head. 'No.'

'I'm sorry,' says Nell gently. 'In that case, I'm not your daughter.' A shudder runs through her, imposing its own punctuation before she can finish. 'But I am your alibi.'

— —

Later, when they've had time to recover, they swab Lucas for DNA, just to make sure. Nell gives him a hug, wishes him well, and she and Ivan take their leave. Mike Norfolk leads them back to the main house, to their waiting car.

'That's extraordinary,' says Mike. 'Who is your father, then? Simmons?'

'We'll need to find out,' says Nell.

Mike shakes his head. 'Well, you can be assured of my discretion, until you sort it.'

'Thank you,' says Ivan. 'But you won't be talking to anyone anyway.'

'I'm sorry?'

'The surviving member of the Nautilus Gang. Went by the name of Guy Forrest. The one who made off with all the gold and all the money. Took it to The Valley. According to the surviving gang members, he was young, about twenty. And he had one very distinct physical characteristic. Bright red hair.'

chapter forty-eight

NELL WANTS TO DRIVE, KEEP HERSELF DISTRACTED, SO IVAN AGREES TO TAKE the passenger seat. This is her journey, but she's grateful he's there with her. For her. Again.

At Surf Beach, the house is the same, everything neat, everything uniform.

Simmons Burnside answers the door. 'You. You've come.'

Inside, the collie bounds up, licking at her enthusiastically, perhaps hoping she's there to take it for a walk. Simmons quietens the dog. Outside the feature window, the day is blue and gold, the sea shimmering in the distance. Inside, there's tennis on the widescreen. Simmons turns it off, maintaining his discipline, maintaining the facade. He offers tea or coffee or something stronger. He's so self-contained, so polite. She studies him, trying to discern what is happening in that interior, but it is too well concealed.

'Made any progress on the investigation?' he asks Ivan.

'Yes,' Ivan replies. 'We've established a working theory. Suspects helping with inquiries. Hoping to lay charges sooner rather than later.'

'Thank you,' says Simmons, but there is no sign of relief. No sign of anything really; Nell realises he's wound tight. 'Who is it? Can you tell me?'

Ivan considers the request, but answers cautiously. 'All in good time.'

Simmons says nothing. Nell can see he is good at that, staying silent.

Nell speaks. 'We believe your son was murdered because he found evidence of an old crime: a remnant, a gold nugget. Maybe more than one.'

Simmons looks at her, searching her eyes, as if he might pry out the answer. 'The Gryphon Mine?'

'Yes. The gold. It's still there.'

'No. There was no gold. They—' He stops, the former policeman counselling himself to stay mute.

'The Botany Warehouse Heist, the Nautilus Gang. You would remember that, I imagine—being on the force at the time.'

Bewilderment crosses the man's face like a winter squall. 'I remember reading about it. That's all.'

'Sergeant Cornell Obswith would remember it well, if he were still alive,' says Ivan. 'He was transferred to Saltwood from Sydney in the weeks after the robbery. Did he ever mention why?'

Simmons doesn't reply. To Nell's eye, it appears this is news to him, as if he is trying to determine its significance.

'There was evidence he was leaking to one of the gang leaders,' Ivan continues. 'Hec Curtin. Professional Standards wanted him investigated, possibly charged, but the police minister at the time, Terrence Earl, intervened, got Obswith transferred out to the bush instead. To Saltwood. Earl's electorate; his power base. Obswith was in his debt. Beholden to him. His minion.'

Simmons shakes his head. 'Long time ago.'

'The surviving gang member brought the loot to The Valley, knowing he would be protected. By Earl. By Obswith. By Willard Halliday. They set up a scheme to rebirth the gold.'

Simmons is still shaking his head. 'Nothing to do with me,' he says, but Nell can see he's troubled. Ivan is telling him things he hasn't known.

'You were ignorant of all that?' asks Nell. 'Despite working for Francis Hardcastle? And later for his widow?'

Simmons gestures around him, at his modest house. 'Does it look like I have millions of dollars? I wouldn't even have this if Wolf hadn't paid for half.'

Nell takes a deep breath. This isn't getting any easier. 'Your son. You know how he got his start in business? Who provided him with seed capital?'

Simmons just stares at her. 'Lucas?' he asks.

'Mike Norfolk,' says Nell.

'Mike?'

And she can tell by his answer that he really doesn't know, never knew. It comes as a small relief to her.

'Mike was in on it?'

'He was the surviving member of the Nautilus Gang. We have him in custody.'

Simmons has lost his calmness, is starting to tremble, ever so slightly. 'He killed Wolf?'

'No,' says Nell. 'Far from it. That was a man called Oliver

Halliday and his accomplice Ellory Earl. Nephew of Hannibal Earl, MP, grandson of Terrence Earl.'

She realises she has said too much, surrendered too much too quickly, that Ivan has only just declined to offer up the names. She steals a glance at him, but her partner gives her a slight smile, encouraging if anything. So she turns back to Simmons.

'Your son was a threat to Earl and his empire. Wolfgang was funding an independent candidate for Hannibal's state seat. He was on the brink of discovering what had happened. He could have destroyed the Earls once and for all. Brought down the whole house of cards. The whole dynasty.'

'I see,' says the man, head bowed, grieving his son. 'Thank you for telling me.'

'That's not why we're here,' says Nell, steeling herself for what is to come. 'We're also investigating a number of historic crimes. Murders. Francis Hardcastle. Teramina Hardcastle. Sergeant Cornell Obswith.'

'Teramina? You have evidence she was murdered?'

'We're investigating.'

Once again, the look of confusion. 'I'm sorry. I don't know who killed Francis Hardcastle. I can believe Teramina was murdered, but I have no evidence. As for Obswith, Lucas Trescothic shot him. He pleaded guilty.'

'So he did. You witnessed the shooting. Arrested him. Made a sworn statement.'

Simmons Burnside returns to silence. Nell can sense his trepidation. Perhaps he's starting to apprehend what is coming next.

'The DNA testing,' says Nell. 'It shows that Lucas was my father. My father and Wolfgang's father. That's according to the DNA sample on the police database, the sample taken at the time of his arrest, the DNA matching flesh extracted from under the fingernails of Cornell Obswith when he was fighting for his life.'

Simmons looks away, staring out the window. A single bead of sweat has appeared on his forehead.

'But that's not possible, is it?' says Nell.

Simmons turns back, intensity in his eyes, face still blank, still hiding his inner thoughts.

'You see, I was born on the fourteenth of March 1995. Ten months after the death of Obswith. Conceived a month after you had taken Lucas Trescothic into custody.'

Simmons doesn't speak, just starts shaking his head, a slow, disbelieving gesture.

'You swapped the DNA,' says Nell. 'After you killed Obswith and arrested Lucas, you realised Obswith had scratched at you, tried to fight you off, had your DNA under his fingernails. It was pure luck, wasn't it? The investigating detective asked you to sample Lucas Trescothic's DNA for comparison. Pretty new back then, DNA, not used much in the bush. Seen as infallible, a smoking gun. So you took his DNA, took a sample of your own, and swapped them over. Pretty desperate, a last-minute improvisation; you must have been panicking, not believing it would work. But Lucas had amnesia, had no idea what he had or hadn't done. The detectives accepted the sample. They never should have delegated to you.'

'I want a lawyer,' says Simmons.

'Bit late for that, don't you think?' says Ivan.

Simmons looks at him, at her, then away out the window once more. He stands, walks across to the glass, surveys the world, the ocean stretching to the horizon, his back to them.

'You're my father,' says Nell. 'And Wolfgang's. I have a warrant to collect your DNA.'

And now Simmons turns, looks her in the eye, as if seeing her for the first time. 'Yes. Of course. You deserve to know.'

Nell's eyes bore into him. 'Why did my mother lie? Why did my mother protect you?'

Simmons Burnside starts to weep, standing in his lonely lounge room, a man deflated, a man defeated. 'Forget the lawyer,' he says. 'I'll tell you everything. If you're my daughter, you deserve the truth. Amber deserves the truth. Wolfgang deserves the truth.'

Ivan reaches out, puts his phone on the table, starts recording. States the place and the time and those present.

And Simmons Burnside sits down and recounts the story he's kept to himself for thirty years.

'*By the time we arrived from Saltwood and reached the forest at the far end of The Valley, we knew it was going to be bad.*'

chapter forty-nine

WILLARD HALLIDAY NEVER MAKES IT OUT OF HOSPITAL. IT'S NOT JUST HIS fatty liver, clogged arteries and encroaching emphysema, or even the three vertebrae Nell cracked when she threw him out his office window. It's cancer.

'Riddled with it,' he wheezes from his hospital bed, apparently taking morbid delight in the prospect. 'Completely fucked.' There are tubes in his arm, a cannula inserted in his chest, oxygen tubes beneath his nostrils. He's unshaven, whiskers contrasting white and grey against his jaundiced skin. And yet the man is smiling, a wicked intelligence in his eyes. 'Not dying with my boots on after all.'

Ivan is unimpressed. 'You shot a man in the chest. Point blank. You don't get to walk away from that.'

'I ain't walking anywhere. You and I both know that. And the Crown prosecutor won't waste taxpayers' dollars taking me to court. I'll be dead before it can go to trial.'

'So what do you want?' asks Nell.

'Revenge,' he wheezes. 'Feel like spreading the joy.' And his phlegmy laugh threatens to evolve into a full-blown cough. 'Don't have any whisky on you, I suppose? Cut the mucus?'

Ivan and Nell have been standing, but now Ivan pulls up a seat. 'We're interested in what you can tell us.'

'I don't want anything for myself. Too late for that. Just go easy on the boy. Ollie. He was only following instructions.'

'Not much of a defence, that one,' says Ivan. 'Just tell us what you want to say. I'll make sure your nephew gets due process. I can't promise any more than that.' And the detective holds up his phone so the lawyer can see it. Willard nods his approval and Ivan starts the app recording.

The dying lawyer grows serious, a poker player making the most of a losing hand. 'For the record, that cunt Terrence Earl is the one who fucked it for everyone. Without him, it would have worked. No one would be dead—not Francis not Teramina not Wolfgang. No one would have been hurt; we'd all be in clover.' Willard shudders, taking his time to catch his breath.

'You want to unpack that?' says Ivan.

'Curtains and I, we set it up. The Botany Warehouse Heist. Together with Bert Glossop. Mates since navy days. Would have taken six months, a year at most: rebirth the gold, launder the money, flood the mine to bury the evidence. I went to see Earl. Wanted his patronage, needed his protection. He agreed. I thought we were sweet.'

Willard closes his eyes momentarily, forehead creased, perhaps seeking energy or fighting pain, before continuing.

'Twenty-five million dollars. You'd reckon that would be enough, wouldn't you? But Earl was obsessed with Teramina

Cloverton, wanted to ruin her. He hated her and everything about her, grew incensed when he learnt that Francis was making her happy. So Earl ordered him to scam her, persuade her to mort-gage Ellensby, invest in the mine. Rip her off blind. Only trouble was the poor sap fell in love with her. Married her. Tried to take her money back, planned to escape with her.'

'So Earl had him killed,' states Ivan.

'Obswith took him down the mine and shot him. Ruthless prick. Never liked him. Did whatever Earl told him to do, a rottweiler in a uniform. But seriously, who cared if Teramina and Francis got it together? We would have finished the operation, all gone our own way, smooth as a baby's bum. Francis would have his split, Teramina would still have Ellensby, they could have been happy. But Earl couldn't stand the thought of that, the narcissistic arsehole.'

'Who flooded the mine?' asks Nell.

Willard considers his answer before replying. 'Not sure. In those situations, best not to get too curious. I suspect Lucas Trescothic. Another of Earl's lackies. But I doubt he would have known anything about the body, wouldn't have known much at all. Nothing about the warehouse heist or the rebirthing or any of that.' The dying lawyer winces, and stabs at a button, calling for a nurse. 'That morphine, it's the real deal,' he says, smiling, his teeth that brutal contrast in colour: bottom row yellow and stained, top row glowing white veneers.

'Why did Earl hate Teramina so much?' Nell asks.

'Because she spurned his advances. Back in the day, back before the robbery, decades before, when they were kids. As simple and as stupid as that. Fucking pathetic. Either he was seriously keen on her, or saw her as a fast track to wealth and respectability, or a bit of both. Either way, he grew more and more obsessed. She came to me one time, seeking my help in getting a restraining order. I talked her out of it; the local coppers were never going to go against him and his influence.' The lawyer fights off another bout of coughing. 'After that, she funded a preselection challenger. That cemented the animosity for all time.'

Ivan looks across at her, and Nell nods, understanding the parallel with Wolfgang and Earl's son, Hannibal.

'You believe Teramina suicided?' asks Ivan, his voice not much more than a whisper.

The amusement drains from Willard; he seems genuinely miserable. 'I think that was Obswith as well. Threw her off the cliff. But I didn't have any proof and I wasn't about to go searching for it.' The lawyer leans over to the side of the bed, away from them, and hawks up a gob of something unspeakable into a paper towel, regarding it admiringly before scrunching it up and dropping it in a bedside bin. 'I could kill a durrie,' he says, grinning once more. 'I was glad when Lucas shot the bastard. Pity he didn't go after Earl while he was at it.'

'The logging on my mother's land,' says Nell. 'That wasn't you?'

'Me? 'Course not. That was Earl, feeding his mill in The Valley.'

It's Ivan's turn. 'Do you have any knowledge of who killed Wolfgang Burnside?'

Willard shakes his head. 'No. Suspicions aplenty, but no evidence.'

'We heard Wolfgang was funding a challenge to Hannibal.'

'Well, that would do it.' And he laughs, then subsides into a mighty coughing fit.

The nurse rushes in, inserts a hypodermic into the chest cannula. 'You nearly finished?' she asks the detectives. 'He might want a little sleep after this.'

'What was Francis Hardcastle's real name?' Nell asks the lawyer, who now has a contented smile spreading across his face.

'John Smith,' wheezes Willard. 'Can you believe that? John fucking Smith. Best actor I ever saw. Should have been in the movies.' And the lawyer beams beatifically and falls into a slumber, oblivious to his own snoring or anything else.

— —

The raids that follow Willard Halliday's testimony are quick and decisive: Terrence Earl and members of his immediate family —including his son Hannibal, the sitting member in Earl's old Saltwood-based seat of North Monaro—are all swept up. Vicary Hearst regains consciousness; he has no memory of what happened to him in Halfchurch, but he tells Ivan why he wanted to meet the homicide detectives there: he'd been told of a lemon-coloured van sighted on a property belonging to Terrence Earl, but he was concerned his phone and movements were being monitored. The *Sydney Morning Herald*'s Martin Scarsden, one time protégé of Max Fuller, writes a remarkably well-sourced series of articles detailing the whole story, starting with the Botany Warehouse Heist. Yet another true-crime potboiler is in the works.

Scarsden is there in person, two weeks after the raids, when they excavate the cisterns, the journalist standing off to one side talking with Dereck Packenham and Morris Montifore. Nell and Ivan keep their distance, watching the excavation. A misting rain is falling, blending with spray from Watershine Falls. Police divers have given the all clear, and a local man, Arnie Cocheef, has been hired, him and his front-end loader. He runs it back and forth, scooping out the mud and sand and rocks, piling them up beside the concrete pool. A second man is operating a bobcat, working away at the pile built by Arnie, consolidating it and making room for more of the debris. It's a time-consuming task: the accumulated muck has half-filled the cisterns, and to get it out the flow of water from the escarpment has been diverted away from Watershine Creek and siphoned down the home creek instead. The weather has been kind; weeks without rain and the flow from the lake above them has become tame and docile. It's only today the drizzle has returned.

'You think this is where he died? Wolfgang?' Nell asks Ivan.

'Possibly. It's almost certainly where the cyanide is from, how it got into his body. Blake reckons swimming or diving alone wouldn't have done it; there's too much flow. He must have dug into the tailings. Checking if this place could support pumped hydro.'

'So this is where he found the nugget?'

'Most likely.'

'Not from Simmons?' asks Nell.

'Never got the chance to ask him about it.'

Nell looks across at the three men on the other side of the cistern, them and Suzie Cocheef, standing watching her brother in his digger. The old schoolfriends, united once more, have come for closure. They're not talking, just observing. Lucas is on the left, stooped and slight, awaiting formal acquittal, set for a multimillion-dollar compensation. If he's happy, he's not showing it. Simmons is in the middle, under investigation, expecting to be charged with perverting the course of justice. He's staring into the pool.

He could be weeping, or it could be the rain. And Mike, off to the right-hand side with Suzie, out on bail, facing charges of robbery and likely much more, looking sprightly and unbowed. Nell finds it enthralling: that they can stand together, apparently without acrimony, considering what they've been through. What they've done to each other.

And just for a moment, as the wind mixes mist from the falls with the rain, she imagines Amber standing there with them, her mother happy to be here at her other home, relaxed in the company of her friends, the way she might have been if fate had written her story only slightly differently. Tears come to Nell's own eyes, and she feels Ivan's arm around her shoulders.

The cistern is almost empty and Arnie withdraws, the man in the bobcat taking over, clearing the last of the muck from the deepest part of the pool, the last remnants of the slag heaps that were swept into the processing pools in 1990, the day of the flash flooding, the day that Simmons Burnside almost died and Mike Norfolk saved him, the day that Sergeant Cornell Obswith shot Francis Hardcastle at the Gryphon Mine, the day Lucas Trescothic flooded the mine, as initially requested by Francis Hardcastle, as subsequently approved by Terrence Earl. He'd siphoned water from the pond behind the dam into the ventilation shaft, unaware Hardcastle had been murdered, unaware his body rested at the bottom of the Gryphon.

The bobcat operator reverses back a final time and cuts the engine. 'Here we go,' Ivan says, breaking her reverie, taking his arm from her shoulder.

They move down into the cistern, down the muddy ramp formed by Arnie Cocheef. The pool is deep, a good five metres at its lowest point. Too deep to dive without air tanks. Not too deep for a navy clearance diver. Or Wolfgang Burnside in his scuba gear. His widow Tyffany has confirmed he had dived here, and up at the lake, trying to ascertain their suitability for pumped hydro. She's standing alone above the emptied pool, not venturing down, her face unreadable. There is no sign of Wolfgang's first wife, Janine.

The cache must have once been disguised, but decades of submersion have created a telltale circle of rust. It takes some time, but the engineers work it out soon enough. A cover is prised away, a mallet and cold chisel deployed, a cordless drill. Revealing a stainless-steel handle. They twist it, and the concealed hatch bursts open, water surging out.

Ivan and Nell approach as the engineers peer in with a torch. And there it is: the hoard from the Botany Warehouse Heist, gold bars shimmering in the torchlight, untarnished.

Later, they stand by the lip of the cistern as it's carried up onto dry land. The gold bars are as perfect as the day they were smelted, still bearing their identifying marks. There are nuggets as well, convincing replicas, fakes made with real gold. And bags of money, cash, sealed against the water, some not sealed well enough. A diver withdraws a handful of mouldy paper, falling to pieces in his gloved hand.

'Pity it was 1988,' says Ivan. 'Just a couple of years later and they shifted to polymer notes.'

'Really?' says Nell. 'It's money?'

'What's left of it.'

'Wow.'

Later, they have a chance to talk with Mike Norfolk before he's taken back into custody. They sit with him in the Miners' Institute, gleaning some last details.

Mike seems happy, almost ebullient, perhaps relieved he no longer has anything to hide.

'I was only brought in at the last minute. Recruited by Bert Glossop. Willard Halliday made the approach, made it sound like easy money. He and Bert were the only ones who knew my real name. I was in a three-person team, led by Glossop and teamed with a bloke I only knew as Raz. Glossop was shot dead inside the warehouse, Raz and I got away with a case of bullion and some bags of cash. Made it to the rendezvous. But the gang leader, Curtains Curtin, he'd received a tip-off, reckoned someone on our crew was ratting us out to the police.'

'That's correct,' says Ivan. 'After the shootout, the police concocted a cover story, told the media that the heist had been overheard by a group of amateur cavers exploring the sewer system. Patent bullshit. It was an informer, part of your team.'

'I guess that explains it,' says Mike.

'And then Cornell Obswith, working at police headquarters, got wind of it, and informed Curtains in return,' says Ivan. 'Professional Standards had their suspicions, but Earl intervened, protected Obswith, got him transferred to Saltwood.'

'Obswith? I suppose that makes sense.' Mike Norfolk continues. 'Curtains thought one of us was wearing a wire. Started making us strip, one by one. Then someone started shooting, and then everyone was shooting. Except me; I was half-naked and unarmed. Off to one side.'

'The only survivor?' asks Nell.

'Raz and me. But he was wounded, refused to go to hospital.'

'Died about a week later,' says Ivan. 'You tried to save him.'

'Yes,' says Mike, taking a deep breath. 'I stayed with him.'

'You took the money and the gold from the woolshed before setting it on fire,' says Nell.

'As much as I could fit in the car. All of the money, most of the gold. Fifty-kilo cases.' Mike stares into the distance, shrugs. 'Wished I'd left it all there. I could have escaped, gone clean. I didn't realise it at the time, but it was like a millstone around my neck. I could have gone anywhere, done anything.'

'So why didn't you? Why return to The Valley?' asks Nell.

'Where else could I go with all that loot? I was twenty years old. I had no idea how to launder money, sell gold. So I came back.'

'And sought help from Earl?'

'No. From Willard Halliday. I didn't know Earl was involved, not back then. Willard was the one person who knew I was part of it, the one person I thought I could trust.'

'So you came back to The Valley, handed over the gold and money, waited for your share of the spoils.'

'More or less. Willard set me up to work in the mine—to keep an eye on Francis. They also got me to infiltrate the greenies, to find out about any potential opposition to the mine.'

'Willard Halliday has testified that Francis Hardcastle tried to retrieve Teramina's investment and was killed as a result. Did Francis ever confide in you?'

'No. He didn't know that I'd been part of the heist. Willard was smart that way, limiting knowledge. But I was the one who knew where the gold was, who delivered the nuggets to Francis, so he would have known I was more than just a paid worker.' Mike smiles. 'He was very good, you know. Francis. Very persuasive, incredibly charismatic. He convinced me I wasn't getting a fair cut. He talked me into moving the gold to the cisterns. We did it together. He said it would be our guarantee. They couldn't hurt us while we knew its location. So we moved it there. Down where we recovered it today.'

'So where did they think the gold was?'

'They thought it was in the mine. That when they flooded it, they were covering the body and protecting the gold. That they could pump the water out and recover it at some future date.'

'When Teramina was out of the way?' asks Ivan, voice solemn.

'That's my guess. I tried to warn her, but she was already losing it. She never knew if Francis was dead, or whether he had double-crossed her. She disappeared for a long while, and I thought she was safe.'

'She was with Amber Jones, down by the Murray,' says Nell.

'Most likely.'

'What about the money?'

'They had most of it. That was a bit of change you found today. So they were happy enough, laundering the cash through the mining company, or whatever.'

'And you didn't try to recover the gold?'

'How? A few days after we hid it, the flood hit. I was there with a front-end loader, trying to stop it being buried under tonnes of tailings. Fat chance. It was covered in tonnes of dirt and gravel and silt, under metres of water. Then Obswith and Simmons hiked in overland and found the mine was flooded, and I figured either Francis was gone, or he was dead. So I kept it to myself. Didn't tell anyone. And when Teramina didn't hear from Francis, I figured they'd killed him. And if they'd killed him, they wouldn't hesitate to kill me. I let them believe the gold was in the mine. That was when I started to think about what I was doing.'

'How so?' asks Nell.

'Simmons almost died in the flood. Did he tell you that?'

'He did.'

'It made me think. You know: was it all worth it? I suspected they'd murdered Francis. And the gold was irretrievable; they thought it was in the mine. So Earl and Willard and Fred Wallington got on with laundering the millions, and I was still getting my cut. In the meantime, I'd met Suzie. And instead of infiltrating the greenies, they kind of infiltrated me. I found I really did want to protect the environment. I started donating some of my split. Anonymously, of course.'

'So what happened then?'

'More than three years passed. Teramina died. Willard and Earl had laundered all the cash, so they returned to the gold, thinking it was somewhere in the mine. We went up to the lake one day, Lucas and Amber, Suzie and me. I told Amber the cover story, the one about the cave-in, the lake collapsing into the mine. And as I told it, I saw Lucas thinking: thinking that he could pump the water out of the mine and recover the gold. I don't think he knew the mine was played out; Willard and Earl used him, but they never told him the whole thing was a ruse, didn't tell him about the heist and the rebirthing.'

'You didn't warn him? Warn my mother?' asks Nell.

Mike shakes his head. 'No. To my eternal shame.'

'Why not?' asks Nell.

'The gold, of course. I thought if they reactivated the mine, I could volunteer to clear out the cisterns. Perfect cover. Get the gold, give it to them, minus a gold bar or two. Then it really would be over; I'd be free. I could leave The Valley. Suzie and me.

'But then we found Francis. And then Lucas realised there was no gold. Willard sent me down, trying to find where Francis had stashed the bullion. And I saw history repeating: Lucas and Amber, just like Francis and Teramina, the same tragedy unfolding. The murder of Francis made me realise Willard and Earl would stop at nothing. That I was expendable. Everyone was. And the clock was ticking: they'd thought the gold was in the mine but were quickly realising it wasn't. I decided to abandon any attempt at recovering the gold, started making plans for me and Suzie to bail. Then Amber shot Obswith and I knew it was time to get out.'

Nell interjects. 'Amber? Why do you say that? Is that what Simmons told you?'

'No. Amber told Suzie, when Suzie drove her out of The Valley. And that was it. Suzie and I took what money we had and left. Disappeared. I tried to warn Simmons, get him to go as well. He moved to the coast, but he wouldn't leave the area altogether, because of Wolf.'

'What about Lucas?' asks Nell. 'You knew he hadn't shot Obswith.'

'I thought he had killed Francis. He and Obswith. That he was in on it. So I figured he deserved to be convicted, even if it was for a different murder.'

'Convenient,' says Ivan. 'And then?'

'Suzie and I made ourselves scarce. A couple of years later, we used the money I'd saved to buy into Nimbin, before the boom.'

'And gave some money to Wolfgang when he started out in business?'

'We did. And warned him to steer clear of Terrence Earl, as did Simmons. Pity he didn't listen.'

'We're building a case against Earl,' says Nell. 'Him and Hannibal Earl and his nephew Ellory, as well as Willard Halliday and his nephew Oliver. Murder charges. They're facing a lot more than that, as you know, but murder is our responsibility. We're pretty sure they killed Wolfgang when he found some nuggets in the cistern and was investigating their provenance.'

Mike nods. 'And don't forget: he was going to run a candidate for parliament. Challenge Earl's son. If Wolfgang had spoken to his father, to Simmons, they could have worked it all out. Or found me, asked me. Political dynamite. It would have destroyed Earl, his whole empire. So Earl ordered him dead.'

Nell doesn't know what to make of Mike, whether to praise him or condemn him.

'We're grateful for your assistance,' says Ivan. 'We'll be putting a good word in for you.'

Mike smiles at that. 'Thanks, but I know I'm going to prison. Deserve to go. But I'm grateful for what I've had. Suzie and the kids, the life we made. Walking away from the gold, walking away from the money, was the best thing I could have done. If only I'd realised that earlier.'

'Didn't help Simmons, though. Or Lucas,' says Ivan.

'That's why I deserve prison. Time to pay my debts.'

— • —

The following week, Nell makes the drive down to Batemans Bay, to Surf Beach. Her father is there, waiting for her. She finds her attitude towards him has softened; hearing his story, his efforts to protect her mother, has made him seem more likeable.

They walk along the beach together, and she finds it easier, talking side by side rather than looking each other in the eye.

'You didn't know?' she asks at last. 'About me?'

'Never even suspected,' he replies. 'I'd asked her not to write, for her own protection. Maybe she did. Maybe it came through the general store and Eliza intercepted it. Maybe. But I can't believe Eliza would hide that from me.'

'Did you know that Amber had died?'

'Not immediately. I went back to the forest, maybe two years later, back down to the Murray, when I thought it was safe. I ventured to the shack, but it was abandoned. I thought perhaps she had left it, gone back into the world, gone travelling.' Nell can hear the emotion in his voice now, melding with the waves breaking gently on the shore. 'I went to the little store there, in Tulong, asked if there was a forwarding address. They told me then that she had died. I was terribly shocked. Devastated. I had dared to dream of a future together, and all the time she was already gone.'

'And they didn't mention me? That she'd given birth?'

'No. And I didn't think to ask. I never knew. Not until you arrived here with your colleague and claimed that you were Wolfgang's sister.'

'You guessed, didn't you? Knew that if we did a DNA test, it would match what was on the database filed under Lucas Trescothic, the skin under Obswith's fingernail.'

'Yes. That's why I denied paternity, why I refused the test.' He stops walking, turns to her. 'I'm so sorry. I was grieving Wolfgang. You can't imagine how much I loved him. It seemed in that moment that you were a usurper, come to claim his place.'

'I guess I can understand that.'

'I loved your mother, Nell—in a way that I never fully loved Eliza. And I'll come to love you, I'm sure of that now. Amber and I, we only had that week together, in that little hut in the woods. One week.'

She reaches out, takes his hand. He looks surprised.

'It's still there, you know,' she says. 'The shack on the island. Not derelict. Amber's mum lives there. We could visit sometime.'

'You're sure?'

'Yes, I think I'd like that. And I'm sure she'd want to meet you.'

'I'd like it too,' he says. 'When this is all finished.'

And a month later, on the day Simmons Burnside faces court, Nell walks in with him. Not as a police officer, but as his daughter, holding his hand and holding her head high.

acknowledgements

THIS HAS BEEN QUITE THE YEAR AND, AS ALWAYS, THERE ARE LEGIONS TO thank, all of whom have played some role, large or small, in the production, promotion and reception of my books. The readers, of course. And the critics and the bloggers and the book clubs and the libraries and the booksellers and the festivals, with their dedicated volunteers and over-worked directors. What good fortune to be a writer supported by such a community!

A huge thanks to all at my Australian publisher Allen & Unwin: Jane Palfreyman and Cate Paterson, as well as Christa Munns, Ali Lavau and Kate Goldsworthy. The books would be nothing without them. Immense gratitude to publicist Bella Breden for her tireless work and to marketing genius Sarah Barrett.

Thanks to Wavesound, who produce the audio books for Australia and New Zealand, and their amazing narrator Dorje Swallow, and to his UK counterpart, Lockie Chapman, and Wildfire Books.

Speaking of Wildfire, I'm hugely indebted to all at my UK publisher, including Jack Butler, Alex Clarke and Caitlin Raynor. They do such a wonderful job, producing and promoting books of an author who lives half a world away.

And thanks to all the translators and foreign language publishers for all of your work and support.

No writer has a better team of agents: Grace Heifetz in Sydney, Felicity Blunt in London and Peter Steinberg in New York, plus page-to-screen agent Mary Pender at UTA, translation agent Nerrilee Weir at Bold Type, and the enthusiastic team at speaker's agency Booked Out.

Thanks to Ian and Rob and the crew at Easy Tiger and Martha Coleman at Third Act Stories for bringing the earlier books to the screen. A special shoutout to Felicity Packard, writer and producer extraordinaire.

Luke Causby at Blue Cork has produced yet another stunning cover for *The Valley*, Aleksander Potočnik has created yet another stunning map, and my dear mate Mike Bowers has captured yet another author's portrait and portfolio of publicity photographs that make me appear more intelligent than in real life. Visual masters one and all—thank you so much!

Thanks to my fellow crime writers—what a glorious and talented and fun and supportive bunch.

And finally, the family. Wife Tomoko, kids Cameron and Elena, my mum Glenys, my brother and sister and their wider families.